THE STEEL BOX

THE STEEL BOX

A Western Duo

Max Brand

Skyhorse Publishing

First Skyhorse Publishing edition published 2015 by arrangement with Golden West Literary Agency.

Skyhorse Publishing books may be purchased in bulk at special discounts for sales promotion, corporate gifts, fund-raising, or educational purposes. Special editions can also be created to specifications. For details, contact the Special Sales Department, Skyhorse Publishing, 307 West 36th Street, 11th Floor, New York, NY 10018 or info@skyhorsepublishing.com.

The name Max Brand® is a registered trademark with the United States Patent and Trademark Office and cannot be used for any purpose without express written permission.

Skyhorse® and Skyhorse Publishing® are registered trademarks of Skyhorse Publishing, Inc.®, a Delaware corporation.
Visit our website at www.skyhorsepublishing.com.

10 9 8 7 6 5 4 3 2 1

Library of Congress Cataloging-in-Publication Data is available on file.

Cover design by Brian Peterson

Print ISBN: 978-1-63220-465-3
Ebook ISBN: 978-1-63220-918-4

Printed in United States of America

Prairie Pawn

The four-part saga of Paul Torridon, a character known as White Thunder among the Cheyennes, was originally published in 1928 under Frederick Faust's Peter Henry Morland byline in Street & Smith's *Western Story Magazine*. The "Prairie Pawn" is the third install-ment in the saga. The first part, "Torridon," can be found in *Gunman's Rendezvous* (Skyhorse Publishing, 2015), and the second, "The Man from the Sky," in *Peyton* (Skyhorse Publishing, 2015). The final story will appear in *Red Fire*.

I

In great good-humor was High Wolf and with reason. No fewer than twenty of his young men were on the warpath under the leadership of the young chiefs, Rising Hawk and Standing Bull, but still the man power of his camp was so great that he had been able to send out young and old to a great hunt, and a vastly suc-cessful one, so that now the whole camp was red with hanging buffalo meat and white with the great strips of back fat. It was not strange that the old warrior chose to wrap himself in his robe and walk slowly through the camp. Everywhere the women were at work, for now that the meat had been hung to dry, there was the labor of fleshing the many hides—cowhides for robes and lodge skins, bull hides for parfleche, shields, and everything that needed stiff and powerful leather. Three days like this, in a year's hunting, would keep the entire camp in affluence.

So, therefore, smiles and flashing teeth turned toward the chief as he went on his solitary way through the crowd, apparently oblivious of everything, but with his old eyes missing not the least of details, until he had completed the round of the teepees and returned to the center of the camp where, near his own big lodge there stood a still more brilliant teepee, a nineteen-skin beauty, of snowy hide, with just enough gaudy paint to show off its white texture.

Without envy, but with a critical eye, he regarded this lodge, moving from one side to another, as though anxious to make sure that all was well with it. Then he struck with his walking staff at the flap of the tent. He was asked to enter, and, stepping inside, he found there an old woman, busily beading moccasins. She rose to greet him. It was one of his squaws, Young Willow, though there was nothing young about her except her name. Time had shrunk and bowed her a little, but her arms were still long and powerful, and she was known through the whole tribe for the work of her strong hands.

High Wolf tapped the hard floor of the lodge impatiently with his staff.

"Why are you not fleshing hides?" he asked. "It is not always summer. When winter comes, White Thunder will have to sit close to the fire, and even then his back will be cold. He will not have anything to wrap himself in."

In spite of the awe in which she held her husband and master, Young Willow allowed herself the luxury of a faint smile, and she waved to the furnishings of the tent. There was only one bed, but there were six backrests made of the slenderest willow shoots, strung on sinew, and covered with the softest robes, and between the backrests were great sacks of dried meat, corn, and fruit. There were huge, square bundles, too, encased in dry rawhide, almost as stiff and strong as wood. One of these she opened. It was filled with folded robes, and, lifting the uppermost one, she displayed to her husband the inner surface, elaborately painted.

2

"And there are many more," said Young Willow. "There are so many more than he can use that I have to keep them in these bundles. He has enough to wear, enough to wrap his friends in in cold weather, enough to give away to the poor and the old warriors, and besides there are plenty to use for trade. He is rich, and there is no one else among the Cheyennes who is as rich as he. Look!"

She took up a bag, and, jerking open its mouth, she allowed the chief to look down into a great mass of beads of all colors, all sizes. There were crystal beads that flashed like diamonds, there were beads of crimson, purple, yellow, black, gold, and brown. There were big and small beads, dull and bright beads.

Even the calm of the chief was broken a little and he grunted: "This is well. This is well. Who gave him all these beads?"

"Whistling Elk brought them yesterday," said the squaw. "When he came in from the traders, you know that he brought many things. But most of his robes he had traded for these beads and he came to the teepee here and told White Thunder that he wanted him to have the beads. White Thunder did not want to take them."

The chief grunted.

"Why not?" he asked sharply. "Does a treasure like this fall down every day like dew on the ground?"

"White Thunder said that he had more than he required. But Whistling Elk reminded him that his son would have died, if White Thunder had not cured him with a strong medicine."

"I remember," said the old man. "That is very true. The son of Whistling Elk became very sick."

"He was as hot as fire," said the squaw. "The medicine men could not help him. Then White Thunder had him carried to this lodge. Listen to me. For three days he gave that boy nothing to eat except water in which meat had been boiled. He wrapped him in cold clothes, too. On the fourth day the boy began to sweat terribly. His mother was sitting beside him and she began to cry and mourn. She said that her son was melting away. But White Thunder smiled. He said that the sickness was melting away and not the body. He was right. The boy slept, and, when he opened his eyes, they were clear and bright. In half a moon he could walk with the other boys."

"I remember it." The chief nodded. "Heammawihio has clothed White Thunder with power as he clothes a tree with green leaves. If he is rich now, still he is not rich enough."

"He has sixty horses in the herd," said the woman.

"Still he is not rich enough," said High Wolf. "I have given you to this teepee to take care of him and cook for him. It would be better for you to displease me than to displease him. It would be better for you to displease underwater spirits than to displease him, Young Willow!"

He spoke so sternly that she shrank from him a little, and immediately explained: "Wind Woman and three young girls are all working to flesh hides for White Thunder. They can do more than I can do alone. Besides, I am working here at this beading to make him happy."

She showed the moccasin and the chief deigned to examine it with some care. He handed it back with a grunt and a nod.

"He did not go to the hunt," he said. "Why did he not go? Was he sick?"

"His heart is sick, not his body," said the squaw sullenly. "He has all that any warrior could want, and yet he is not a warrior. Look. There is always meat steaming in the pot. It is the best meat. There is always fat in it. The flesh of old bulls is never given to him. The dried meat of young, tender cows and calves fills those sacks. He lives like a great chief. But he is not a chief. He has never made a scalp shirt. He has never taken a scalp or killed an enemy or counted a coup!"

"So," said the chief, "you work for him with your hands, but in your heart you despise him."

4

She answered sullenly: "Why should I not? He is not like us. There is no young man in the camp who is not stronger and taller."

The chief made a little pause in which his anger seemed to rise. "What young man," he said, "has come to us from among the Sky People?"

She was silent, shrugging her shoulders.

"What young man," he said, "could drive off the water spirits when they were tearing down the banks of a great river?"

At this she blinked a little, as though remembering something important, but half forgotten.

"What young man among us . . . or what old man, either . . . what great doctor or medicine man," went on High Wolf with rising sternness, "was able to bring the rain? The corn withered. Dust covered the prairie. In the winter we should have starved. But White Thunder went out and called once, and immediately the clouds jumped up in the south. He called again and the clouds covered the sky. The third time he cried out, the rain washed our faces and ran down to the roots of the dying corn . . . but these things you forget!"

"No," she muttered, "I never shall forget that day. No Cheyenne ever has seen such strong medicine working."

"But you," went on the chief sternly, "are not contented with such things. What are scalps and scalp-takers compared to the strength of a man who can call down the Sky People to help him? Since Standing Bull brought him to us, everything we do is lucky. There is no drought. The young men and the children do not die of sickness. The buffalo come up and stand at the edge of our camp and wait for us to surround and shoot them down. Our war parties have struck the Crows and the Pawnee wolves and brought back horses and scalps, and counted many coups. But this man is not great enough for you to serve! You despise him in your heart while you work with your hands. Do you think that he does not know? I tell you, Young Willow, that he sees the

5

thoughts in your heart as clearly as he sees the paintings on his teepee."

This speech he delivered in a stern and gloomy voice, and the squaw began to bite her lips nervously.

"I am willing to work for him," she whined. "All day my hands never stop."

"There are other women who would work for him," said the chief. "There are other women who would be glad to live in the presence of such good medicine all day long."

"All day he never speaks," she answered in feeble self-defense. "There are many backrests in this lodge. It is a lodge for a great and noble chief to fill with feasting and friends. But he never calls in friends, except Standing Bull or Rising Hawk. He would rather sit on his bed of rye grass and rushes, wrapped in an unpainted robe. Then he takes a flute of juniper wood and makes sad music, like a young man in love. Or he goes down to the river and sits on the banks. The three young warriors who have to be with him to guard him, they stand and yawn and wish to be hunting or on the warpath, but he sits and plays the flute. Or else he takes his pistol from his breast and shoots little birds that fly overhead near him. Even a child would be ashamed of such a life."

"Can a child take a pistol and shoot little birds out of the air?" asked the chief sharply. "Can any of the warriors do that?"

"No man could do it," she replied. "It is medicine that kills them with the flash of his pistol. But when does he take the war rifle and go on the warpath?"

"You speak," said the chief slowly, "like a fool and the daughter of a fool. But you have given me a thought. If he makes sad music on the flute, it is because he has seen some beautiful girl among the Cheyennes. He is in love. Now, Young Willow, learn the name of the girl he has seen, and he shall have her, and you . . . you shall come into my lodge and name the thing you want as a reward. Only learn the name of the girl he wants."

II

Under a spreading willow on the bank of the river lay White Thunder, his hands beneath his head, his sad eyes looking up through the thin branches, noting how they changed their pattern against the sky as the wind stirred them. He looked neither to the right nor to the left, because, in so doing, he would be forced to see the three who guarded him. Every moon three chosen and proved young warriors were told to watch him day and night. In the day they never left his side except when he entered his teepee. And in the night they slept or watched outside his lodge. The vigilance of the Cheyennes netted Paul Torridon about in the dark and in the daylight, so that he had given up all hope of escape from them. If there were any hope left to him, it was something that he could not visualize, something that would scatter the tribe and by a merciful accident leave him free to return to his kind. Particularly he wished to avoid the attention of these three, because he knew their hearts were burning with anger against him. They had yearned to go off with the hunt, but, since he refused, they were forced to remain idly in camp watching him, instead of flying their horses among the wild buffalo—a sport for a king.

The three were talking, softly. For though they despised him, they held him in awe, also. As a man, he was to them less than nothing. As a communer with the spirits, he was a dreadful power. Now they mentioned a familiar name. Torridon half closed his eyes.

"What do you say of my horse?" he asked.

"I say," answered a voice, "that the horse would come to you even through a running river."

Another answered sharply: "And I say that no horse will swim unless it is forced. It would be a strong medicine, for instance, that would make a horse go into that stream. A horse has no hands to push himself away from sharp rocks."

Torridon thrust himself up on one arm, and shook back the hair from his face. It was quite true that the river beneath them was not a pleasant ford for horses. Men could manage it easily enough, but it was thickly strewn with rocks, and among the rocks the current drove down strongly.

Torridon whistled, and up to him came a black stallion at a sharp trot and, standing before him, actually lowered his fine head and sniffed at the hand of his master as though to inquire his meaning.

The three young braves looked on with hearts that swelled with awe.

"Do you fear the water, Ashur?" asked Torridon in Cheyenne.

He flung out his hand in a little gesture, and that gesture made the horse turn his head toward the river. But so seemingly did Ashur understand the question, so human was that turning of the head to look at the water that the young braves murmured softly to one another.

"You see," said Torridon, who was not above a little charlatanry from time to time, "that he has no fear of the water. He asks me for what purpose he should go into it, however."

The young Cheyennes were filled with amazement. "But in what manner did he speak?" asked the eldest, who had taken his scalp in regular battle and therefore was the accepted leader of the little party. "For I did not hear a sound."

"Tell me," said the untruthful Torridon, "do you have a sign language?"

"Yes, with which every Indian can speak."

"Well, then, a horse has signs, also."

"But a horse has no fingers with which to make signs."

"He has a tail, however," said Torridon smoothly, "and also two ears, and a head to nod or shake, and four hoofs to stamp."

There was a general exclamation of wonder.

"However," said the scalp-taker a little sullenly, "I still think that no horse would cross that water, except under a whip."

Torridon pretended to frown. "Do you think," he asked, "that when I put a spell on a horse it is less than a whip on his back?"

"Even a child," replied the young warrior truthfully, "may speak about great things."

"Very well," said Torridon, "this is a knife that you have admired."

He took from his belt a really beautiful weapon, the point curving only slightly from the straight, the steel of the finest quality, with the glimmer of a summer blue sky close to the sun. The haft was ornamented with inset beadwork, to roughen the grip. It was a treasure that Torridon had received from a grateful brave to whom he had given good fortune on the warpath, the fortune immediately being proved by the counting of a coup and the capture of five good horses.

"It is true," said the young Cheyenne, his eyes blazing in his head. "But," he added, "what have I to offer against it?"

"You have a new rifle," said Torridon carelessly.

The other sighed. The rifle was a very good one. It was the pride of his young life. However, the knife was a gaudy trinket that inflamed his very heart with lust to own it, and he reassured himself by looking down at the dangerous water.

Besides, a horse was to be persuaded through the midst of that water without the use of a whip or a spur, and with no man on its back to direct it. He nodded as he turned again to Torridon. "Look!" he exclaimed suddenly. And he laid the rifle at the feet of a companion.

"And there is the knife," said Torridon. He took it again from his belt, and, with a little flick of the wrist that he had learned from Rising Hawk, he drove it half the length of its blade into the ground before their companion.

Then he rose to attempt the venture. On the edge of the bank he took off his clothes. White as polished marble he flashed beneath that strong sun. The wind blew his hair aside, and he laughed with pleasure at the cool touch of the air and the angry hand of the sun.

The Indians looked significantly at one another, partly admiring and partly in contempt. The Cheyennes were huge specimens of manhood. He was of small account who stood under six feet in height, and they had shoulders and limbs to match, but Torridon was made slenderly, tapering and graceful. He was fast of foot, the Indian youth knew. How would he appear in the water?

He did not leave them long in doubt. He merely paused to adjust a headband that would bind his unbarbered hair. Then he dived from the bank.

There was only a slight sound as he took the water. Then, through the black shadow of the pool under the bank, they saw him rise glimmering. He struck out through the current. It was true that he had not the might of arm that many of them possessed. But neither did he have their bulk to drag through the water, and he used the stroke that Roger Lincoln, that flawless hero of the plain, had taught him.

"It's only in the brain that you can beat an Indian," Roger Lincoln had been fond of saying. And he had taught Torridon many things as they voyaged over the plains together. A most unreceptive mind had dreamy Paul Torridon for woodcraft or for the arts of hunting, but at least he could learn the craft of swimming from a perfect master.

He glided rapidly through the water, now, lying face down, rolling a little from side to side to breathe, and the long strokes of the arms and the thrashing feet carried him rapidly through the stream.

He could hear them on the bank behind him calling: "*Hai!* He is being pulled by a string!"

He swerved past a reaching rock, stepped on another, and leaped onto the farther bank. There he wrung the water from his long hair and waved a flashing arm.

"Ashur!" he called.

The black stallion was already at the brink of the stream, looking wistfully after his master. At this call, he advanced his forehoofs into the water and sniffed at it, but immediately he withdrew and bounded away, throwing his heels into the air.

The wagerer shouted with triumph: "The knife is mine, White Thunder!"

Torridon made no reply. He sat down, dripping on the bank, and seemed more interested in the flight of a hawk that was swinging lower and lower through the sky above them.

"Come back, White Thunder!" cried the brave. "You see he never will take the water!"

Now for an answer, Torridon raised an arm and pointed. He was more than half ashamed of himself to resort to such trickery and sham. But, after all, these people had forced the role of medicine man upon him quite against his will. They had dressed him up in fake garments of mystery; they had stolen him away from the girl he loved and from his best of friends. It was hardly more than fair that they should be called upon to take something for which they were even asking. So he pointed at the descending hawk, as though it were a symbol sent down to him from the Sky People, who were so eternally on the tongues of the Cheyennes.

It made a great sensation among the three braves. Torridon saw them pointing and whispering together, and he with whom Torridon had made the wager hastily caught up a handful of pebbles and sand and began to shift them from hand to hand, blowing strongly on them—making medicine against the medicine maker.

Torridon laughed. They would take that laughter for invincible scorn of them. As a matter of fact, it was pure amusement and good nature. Of Ashur he had had no doubt from the first.

Now, indeed, the black horse returned to the edge of the water. He sent one whinny of complaint across to his master, and straightway he plunged in. Torridon was very confident. Out here on the plains the rivers were few and far between. They were apt to be comparatively still, also. But where Ashur was raised, two stormy creeks had cut the grazing lands, and the horse that aspired to the richer, farther pastures had to cross them both. From colthood Ashur had been a master of the difficult craft.

He came swiftly, snorting the froth and water from his nostrils, so low did he carry his head, stretching it forth over the surface. A smooth, strong glide of water seized him and dropped him through a narrow passage between reaching rocks. That instant the heart of Torridon stood still and he regretted the bet. But now Ashur came again, more strongly than ever, pricking his little ears in recognition of the master who waited for him. A moment more and his forehoofs grounded. He climbed out, shook himself, and then, leaping to the side of Torridon, he turned and cast back at the young warriors a ringing neigh of almost human defiance.

III

A shout of mingled wonder and applause came across the water to Torridon, but he had turned his head toward the plains that stretched off to the north. Naked as he was, weaponless, for an instant he was on the verge of throwing himself on the back of Ashur and flying away into the wilderness. But when he looked back to the farther shore, he saw that three rifles were gripped in three ready pairs of hands. It was their business to watch him, and watch him they would—aye, and scalp him gladly if the worst came to the worst!

He abandoned his thought with a sigh, and then swam back to the waiting three. Ashur followed him obediently, his nose in the little smother of water raised by the kicking heels of his master. The rocks reached for the fine horse again, and in vain, and Torridon stood again with his guards, whipping the water from his body with the edge of his hand, laughing and panting.

"Look!" cried the youngest of the three warriors suddenly, but in a voice muffled with awe. "He has brought down the power from the clouds, and now he is going back again!"

He pointed, and Torridon, turning his head, saw that the hawk was rising even more swiftly than it had descended. He laughed again to himself. No doubt this tale, liberally reinforced by the imaginations of the three, would soon be circling the village and adding to the great stock of folly and lies that already circulated about him among the Cheyennes.

The eldest of the trio took up his rifle and laid it at Torridon's feet.

"When I made the bet," he said, "I forgot that you could command the air spirits out of their places. Of course they made the horse light and showed him where to swim through the rocks."

"I saw a ripple go before him," said the youngest of the three gravely. "Of course something invisible was stopping the current to let the horse through. This is a great wonder. I, who did not see the making of the rain, at last have seen this."

Torridon dressed quickly. There was not much dressing to do, for he was equipped like any other young Cheyenne in breechclout, leggings, and a shirt. There were distinctions, for the leather was the softest of deerskin, white as snow, and worked over in delicate designs with beads and porcupine quills, while the outer fringe of the leggings was enriched with glittering beads and even some spurious hoofs of buffalo, polished highly. He put on his moccasins first, and stepped into the rest of his apparel, after wriggling into the tightly fitted shirt. Then he sat down and began to dry his hair, by spreading it to the sun and the wind.

The three regarded him with profoundest silence. They had seen such things that it was well to be quiet for a time, and rehearse the affairs in their own minds. Afterward, even the elders would be glad to invite them to feasts and let them talk of the prodigies that White Thunder on this day had performed. One of them had turned the hawk into an eagle, already, in his mind's eye. And another had made out the form of the water spirit that drew the stallion through the river.

At last, Torridon took up the rifle that was his prize. He examined it with care.

"Rushing Wind," he said to the young man who had given up the gun, "how many times have you fired this?"

"Three times."

"And what did it do?"

"It killed three buffalo," said Rushing Wind, his breast heaving just once with mingled pride in the weapon and grief because of its loss.

Torridon handed it back to its first owner. "Take it again," he said. "It is good medicine in your hands. I already have many guns in my lodge. I do not want to empty yours. Besides," he added shamelessly, "as you have seen, I have other things than guns with which to do what I wish."

The latter part of this speech was accepted by the young men with nodding heads. But Rushing Wind hesitated about the return.

"My brother is rich," he said. "Nevertheless, even a rich man wants something with which to remember a great day."

"That is true," agreed Torridon. He reached out and took the knife from the belt of Rushing Wind. He replaced it with his own rich knife and waved his hand. "By that exchange," he said, "we can remember one another."

Rushing Wind returned no answer. He had seen himself, a moment before, compelled to fall back upon the war bow and arrow. Now, not only was the rifle his once more, but, in addition, he wore at his belt such a jewel as would make even the great war chiefs look on him with envious eyes. His heart was too full for utterance, so that he was forced to scowl bitterly.

Torridon, understanding perfectly, arose to cover the confusion of the warrior and led the way back to the camp. At the door of the lodge he invited them to enter; they perfunctorily

perfunctorily refused, so as to remain lounging outside, while he entered the cool shadow of the teepee. He was still amused, still inclined to laugh to himself so that Young Willow, at her beading, glanced keenly at him.

She was a little afraid of this youth, though as the daughter of one great war chief and the wife of another, she despised this counter of no coups, this taker of no scalps. He was an outlander. The joys and the sorrows of the tribe did not affect him; he pretended no interest. Their victories were things at which he shrugged his shoulders; their dances and celebrations left him cold and unstirred. Therefore, she both hated and despised him, but also she was afraid. She, with her own eyes, while all the tribe was witness, had seen him call up the rain clouds. At his bidding, the lightning had flashed and the thunder had roared. He had disappeared in the middle of the confusion. Some said that he simply had ridden off through the darkness of the storm, but it was whispered everywhere that no mortal could have ridden through the assembled Cheyennes at that time. Had he not been wrapped in a storm cloud and snatched away?

For her own part, she knew that she was honored to have been selected as the keeper of this lodge, and, as such, all that she said was now listened to, and the chief men of the nation stopped her when she was abroad and asked after the latest doing of White Thunder. If there were little to tell of interest, fortunately Young Willow had a sufficient imagination; no audience that asked wonders of her should go away with empty ears.

Now the youth sat smiling to himself. "White Thunder," she said, "where is the knife that you wore at your belt?"

"I have given it to Rushing Wind."

She raised her head. "Do you know that that is a medicine knife, worth five horses if it is worth a handful of dried meat?"

"So I was told."

She muttered angrily: "One spendthrift makes a naked lodge. You gave away the white saddle yesterday?"

"The young man had nothing but a buffalo robe to ride on."

"It is not the seat that makes the horseman," said this quoter of proverbs, "neither is the horse judged by the saddle."

"Saddle and mane make a horse sell," he retorted, having picked up some of the same sort of language from this ancient gossip.

Fairly stopped by this, she returned to her beading. It was true that the goods in this teepee were not hers, and it was also true that the generosity of the Cheyennes was flooding the lodge constantly with more than the master of it could use. Nevertheless, she was old enough to be parsimonious. The aged ask for a full house and larder.

Torridon lounged against a supple backrest and raised his eyes to the top of the teepee with a great sigh. Time, time, time! How slowly it goes.

"Aye," said Young Willow, spiteful after her last silencing, "you may well sigh. For in a hundred winters we shall all be bald."

"That is true," he answered, "and it is also true that even a little time will hatch a great mischief."

She looked askance at him, rather suspecting that there was a sting in this speech, but not quite confident of the point. So she pursed her withered lips and consulted her profound heart to find something more to say.

He, in the meantime, began to finger some of the articles that hung beside the backrest, taking down a great war bow of the horn of mountain sheep, tough and elastic, able to send an arrow four hundred yards in battle, or, in the hunt, drive a shaft to the three feathers into the tough side of a buffalo bull.

"A strong bow for a strong hand . . . for the weak hand it is a walking staff," said the venomous old woman.

"Yes," said Torridon, "or it would do as a whip."

She caught her breath and mumbled, but the reply was too apt not to silence her again.

He laid aside the bow and picked up the favorite solace of his quiet hours. It was a flute of the juniper wood, from which one could draw plaintive sounds, and by much practice upon it, he was able to perform with a good deal of skill. He tried it now, very softly. And he half closed his eyes in sad enjoyment of the harmony he made, for the sorrowful love sorrow.

As for Young Willow, she would have admitted at another time that it was excellent music, and she would tomorrow attribute the skill of the youth with the instrument to the direct intervention and assistance of the Sky People. Now, however, she was looking for trouble.

"Sorrow, sorrow, sorrow," she muttered. "A sorrowing child is never fat."

He lowered the flute from his lips and looked vaguely upon her, as though he had only half heard what she said.

So she, glad of a quiet audience, went on sharply: "And sorrow and love are brother and sister. They go hand in hand. Who is the girl that you make music for, White Thunder?"

At this, he actually dropped the flute and sat bolt upright, staring at her, and very wide awake indeed.

Young Willow pretended to go on with her beading, but her grin was very broad, so that it exposed her toothless, dark gums. She had stung him at last.

IV

Busy at her work, or apparently busy, Young Willow said: "There are many beautiful maidens among the Cheyennes. Even the Sky People draw down from the clouds, and wonder at them."

"That is true," he agreed absently.

He had been too amazed by her remark to pay much heed to what followed.

"So," said Young Willow, "it is no wonder that you, White Thunder, should have come down to us. Tell me, therefore, the name of the girl."

"Of what use would it be if I should tell you?" he asked.

"Of what use? I would myself go to High Wolf, and he would go to the father of the girl. Presently all would be arranged with the father."

"And she would be brought home to this lodge?"

"Yes."

Torridon smiled faintly, and the squaw frowned, unable to read his mind, no matter how she tried. She was angry with herself, when she found that she was baffled so early and so often by this youth. His white skin was a barrier that stopped her probing eyes, as it were.

"What should I do with a woman?" said Torridon.

"A wife is better than many horses," said the squaw sententiously.

Torridon fell amiably into that mode of maintaining the discourse. In a way, he feared to be left to his own thoughts, for since Young Willow had turned the conversation into this channel the picture of Nancy Brett stood like life before him, in all her beauty, her gentleness, her grace. He tried to turn from that hopeless dream into the present. So he answered the squaw: "A bag of fleas is easier to keep watch over than a woman."

"Ha?" cried the squaw. "I think you are talking about the Arapahoes, or the Dakotas. You do not know our Cheyenne girls. After the sun has gone down, they still have firelight to work by."

"People who work forever," quoted Torridon, "are dull companions. You cannot dig up wisdom like a root."

Young Willow grunted. Her eyes had a touch of red fire in them as she glared across the teepee at her young companion.

"You cannot judge a woman by her tongue," she replied.

"No," said Torridon, "but with a small tongue, a woman can kill a tall man."

"Very well," grumbled Young Willow, "but you know the saying . . . a woman's counsel may be no great thing, but he is a fool who does not take it. I am giving you good advice, White Thunder."

"No doubt you are." Torridon yawned rather impolitely.

"Aye," she answered, "but only a pretty woman is always right."

"No," he replied, "a pretty woman is either silly or proud."

"For a proud woman," she said, "take a heavy hand."

He raised his slender hand with a sigh. "My hand is not heavy, Young Willow. Even if I had a lovely wife, how could I keep her?"

"With a whip, perhaps."

"A Cheyenne girl," he said more seriously, "wants a strong husband. She wants to see scalps drying in the lodge and hear her man counting his coups."

"You are young," said Young Willow tactfully, for she had been pleased to the core of her heart by the remark dispraising beauty in a woman. "You are young, and a man is not grown in a summer."

"I never shall take scalps," said Torridon, sighing again. "I never shall count coups, or steal horses. How could I be honored among the Cheyennes or by a woman in my own lodge?"

This plain statement of fact took Young Willow a good deal aback. It was, in short, what she had said at greater length to High Wolf. But at last she replied: "Take a wife, and I shall teach her how to behave. She will not be able to draw a breath that I shall not count. Afterward, you will have sons. You will be a great chief."

She painted the rosy picture with a good deal of warmth. And suddenly Torridon said gravely: "Let us talk no more about it, Young Willow. Are you tired of doing the work in this lodge?"

"I? No, no!" cried the squaw.

"Then stay with me, and I shall not ask for a Cheyenne girl as a wife. There is only one woman in the world who I could marry, Young Willow."

"And she is not in this camp?"

"She is far away."

"She is a Blackfoot," said Young Willow instantly. "They are tall, and a short man wants a tall wife. They have big eyes, and the white men love only big eyes." Her own small eyes became mere glints of light.

"No," said Torridon. "Big eyes are good to look at, but not to look. It is not a Blackfoot girl. I never have seen a Blackfoot."

"Then you have seen a Sioux girl smiling. They always are smiling, and they always are untrue."

"In short," said Torridon impatiently, "it is no Indian girl at all."

"A white woman?" asked Young Willow.

"Yes."

"She is tall and proud and rich," said Young Willow.

"No, she is small," mused Torridon. "Or rather, she is no size at all, but she fits into my mind and heart . . . "

"As the saddle fits the back of a horse," suggested Young Willow.

Torridon merely sighed.

"When you were carried away in the storm," said the squaw, "and disappeared over the prairie, then you went to Fort Kendry to find her there?"

But, at this direct question, Torridon recovered from his dream, and shrugged his shoulders. "I am going to sleep," he said abruptly.

He settled against the backrest and closed his eyes. Young Willow was too well trained in the lodge of her husband to utter a word when one of the lords of creation was resting. Therefore, Torridon heard nothing except the light, faint click of beads in the rapid fingers of the squaw from time to time.

And he passed into another of the weary, sad vigils that he had kept so many times before. At last he actually slept and dreamed of great woe and misery, a dream so vivid that dreary, wailing voices thrummed in his ears loudly. He wakened to find that the sounds were no dream at all, but that from hundreds of throats, apparently, a paean of grief was rising through the village. The noise came slowly toward the teepee. He heard the screaming of women, who seemed maddened with woe.

Young Willow dashed into the lodge, her hair flying in long strings, her breast heaving.

"Why do so many people cry out, Young Willow?" he asked her, bewildered.

"You!" shrieked the squaw, shaking her bony fist at him. "You that make medicine when you wish, but let our men go out to die! It would have been better for us if you had been left in the sky!"

"But what has happened? Has someone died?"

"Has someone died?" exclaimed the squaw. "Eleven men are dead and Rising Hawk has brought home the rest, and all of the eight are wounded."

"Rising Hawk has brought them home?" exclaimed Torridon. "Then tell me what has become of Standing Bull?"

"He was lost! He was lost! He was captured in the battle and carried away by the Dakotas, and by this time they are eating his heart! He was your friend! He was your friend! Could you make no medicine for him?"

She ran out of the lodge again, raising her voice in a shrill keen as she burst through the entrance.

Torridon, amazed and shocked, followed. It was to Standing Bull that he owed his first captivity in the tribe. It was to Standing Bull, also, that he owed his recapture after the first escape. And yet he had been so much with the Cheyenne giant that he was shocked to hear of his capture. There was little chance that such a warrior as Standing Bull would be spared except for the sake of tormenting him slowly to death when the Dakotas had reached their homes after the war raid.

Torridon wrapped himself hastily in a robe and stepped into the entrance of the teepee in time to see the mass of the crowd of mourners move past. Every relative of a dead or wounded man was called upon by invincible custom to mourn, and with a dozen deaths to account for, it seemed that half the tribe was officially interested.

At that moment Owl Woman went by. She was the young squaw of Standing Bull, the mother of his son, and as handsome a woman as could be found in the tribe. She had disfigured herself for life. Her hair was shaved from her head, and the scalp gashed across and across, so that blood had poured down and blackened over her face and shoulders. She went with bare legs, and along the calves she had ripped up the flesh again. As a crowning token of her affliction, she had actually cut off a finger of her left hand, and what with loss of blood and the shock of her grief and the torment of her exhaustion, she staggered rather than walked, her head rolled on her shoulders, and Torridon could hear her sobbing. It was not the noise of weeping, but the heavy gasp of exhaustion and hysteria.

The other mourners made way for her, partly because no victim had been of so high a rank as her husband, and partly because she had honored herself and the whole nation by this perfect expression of her grief. A dreadful picture of despair and madness, she staggered on past Torridon and he closed his eyes, feeling very sick indeed at the sight.

He did not need to ask questions. From the babble of the crowd and the exclamations of the mourners he learned the details sufficiently. Standing Bull and Rising Hawk actually had pushed so far into the land of the Dakotas that they had entered the deep and narrow ravine leading toward the village over which Spotted Antelope was the great chief. But while they were passing through, that formidable warrior had fallen upon them, taken them in the rear with a mighty attack, and crushed them.

Standing Bull indeed had played the hero. He had allowed the remnant to get away, assisted as they were by the savage fighting of Rising Hawk, who had actually found time to count four coups and take a scalp in the short encounter.

The sound of the mourning rolled farther away, though the very heart of Torridon still was stabbed from time to time by the sudden shriek of a woman. He opened his eyes and saw before him the silent form of High Wolf, robed to the eyes, and those eyes were fixed on the face of Torridon with a terrible malignity.

V

It was plain to Torridon that the anger of the war chief was less because of the loss that had fallen upon the young braves of his tribe than because of some passion that he held against the white man himself.

"*Hau*," said Torridon in quiet greeting.

The chief, uninvited, strode past him to the interior of the lodge, and Torridon followed him, seeing that some tiding of grave importance was about to be communicated to him. When he faced High Wolf, the latter said harshly: "It is true that White Thunder does not love Standing Bull. Standing Bull brought him to the Cheyennes. On account of that, White Thunder has given over the whole war party to the Dakotas. Twelve men are dead. Twelve men are dead and scalped, or else they are in the hands of the enemy. Why have you done this thing, White Thunder? If you did not love Standing Bull . . . well, you have the thunder in your hand and you can throw the lightning. Why did you not kill him and let the rest go?"

The first impulse of Torridon was open and frank disavowal, but suddenly he saw that merely to protest was of no avail whatever. To these red children of the prairie, he was the possessor of the most wonderful and potent medicine, and, if he wished, he could extend the aegis of his might over all their war parties, even the most distant. To deny that he possessed that power would, in the eyes of High Wolf, make him appear the merest hypocrite. It might mean, at once, a knife in the throat, or slow burning over a fire. He thought of this as he looked the old chief in the eye and answered slowly: "Even good medicine may be used wrongly."

High Wolf blinked and then frowned. "Then what did they do? Did you make medicine for them, after all? No man heard you so much as sing a song when they left the camp."

"Why should I sing songs or shake rattles like the other medicine men?" asked Torridon scornfully. "When the corn was dying and the dust was deep and white on the plains, did I sing a song to make the rain come?"

"You called to it," said High Wolf, "and the heavens were covered with clouds. Why did you not call again, and send strength to Standing Bull?"

"If they had gone slowly and laid in wait," said Torridon on the spur of the moment, "they would have had no harm. But they ran in like wild buffalo, and like buffalo they were killed."

High Wolf apparently checked an angry exclamation. Then he replied: "Before the night comes, we send out fifty braves to go north. Tell me, White Thunder. What will be their fortune?"

Torridon was taken well aback. He had had to make medicine for these strange people before, but he had not been called upon to make prophecies.

As Torridon paused, the chief continued: "Now Spotted Antelope rides far south from his village. He waits for us. How shall we pass him, or how shall we fight against him? He has two or threescore fighting men. Their hearts are big. They laugh at the Cheyennes. What medicine have you for that, White Thunder?"

Like one who has his back against the wall, Torridon replied: "What is the use in sending the Sky People to help the Cheyennes, when the Cheyennes will not know how to use them?"

The return of the chief fairly took his breath. "You have been one who speaks with a single tongue in the camp of the Cheyennes. Tell me now, White Thunder . . . will you give me your promise to ride with a war party against the Dakotas and never try to escape from them? Will you go with them, and make the Sky People fight on our side?"

There was no possibility of refusal. The passion of the chief swept Torridon before it, like a cork on a flood. He dared not resist.

"I can give you my word," he said gloomily.

High Wolf paused, his eyes still glittering. "I go to the young men," he said. "Rising Hawk burns like a fire. He shall ride out again in spite of his wound. You, then, will ride with them and give them fortune?"

Torridon, dumb with amazement and woe, merely nodded, and the old man was gone, leaving the boy regarding earnestly a most terrible fate. He had but the slenderest doubt as to what would come of this. Pawnee or Crow or Blackfoot, all were dangerous enough, but the Dakotas, each as able a warrior as ever bestrode a horse, were distinguished above all for their swarming numbers. They could redden the plains with their men, if they so chose. He who invaded their country was like a fly walking into a spider's web.

Young Willow came back into the lodge and, in silence, set about cleaning the rifle, though it needed no cleaning, and then laying out a pack that consisted of dried meat and ammunition, together with a few other necessaries. Plainly she had been told to do these things by High Wolf. And when Torridon glanced at her, he thought that he spied a settled malice in her expression.

Ashur was brought, the saddle put on him. Still the sounds of mourning filled the camp, but other noises were blended with them. Wild yells and whoops cut the air, somewhere a battle song was being chanted, and, going to the entrance of the lodge, Torridon saw half a dozen braves in front of their teepees dancing about in the fantastic step of stiff-legged roosters. All were painted for war; several were wearing war bonnets of eagle feathers. Nearby their horses were being prepared by industrious squaws, just as Ashur was being fitted.

The preparation was speedy. Torridon had known war parties to make medicine and go through formalities for a fortnight. Now everything was rushed through; the Cheyennes were red hot for vengeance, and old customs had to give way before the pressure.

For his own part, he wondered that, on an expedition of such importance, every man worthy of carrying arms was not enlisted, leaving the defense of the camp to the very old and the very young. But Indian measures were rarely so whole-hearted as this. They loved war and they loved scalps, but they hated to commit all their forces to a single action. They believed in skirmishes rather than in pitched battles.

So at last Rising Hawk was seen, mounted on a spirited pony, a dressing on his left forearm, which had been cut across by a bullet in the late action. Before him went two medicine men, complete in masks and medicine bags, and all the weird implements of their profession. As they came closer, they halted and held back, and one who had a mask like a wolf's head over his shoulders pointed at Torridon, and then turned away.

Of course they were jealous of him and of his reputation. Their income for healings and for soothsaying had fallen away sharply since the coming of the white man to their camp, with his marvels of rain-making, and all the rest. No doubt, in their heart of hearts they were wishing the worst of ill fortune upon the expedition that he was to accompany.

Rising Hawk, however, greeted the white man courteously. Torridon mounted. They rode on from the camp. The warriors fell in behind them. Children and young braves rushed out to see them pass, and so the procession grew.

At the edge of the camp, they broke into a gallop. Young boys, yelling like demons, rushed bareback before and behind them, and whirled around them like leaves in a wind. And so they were escorted as far as the verge of the river. Up its bank they passed until they came to the ford, crossed this, and at last they were committed to the width of the prairies.

Torridon turned in the saddle, on the farther bank, and looked across the stream and back to the distant village. He felt almost a touch of homesickness in seeing it thus. Anything was preferable to that grim expedition against so dangerous a foe as the Sioux. But the dice had been cast and he was committed. Even so, he could not help considering a sudden break away from the Cheyennes, and then trusting to the speed of the black stallion to take him safely out of range of the pursuing bullets.

His honor held him, albeit by a single thread, and he remained trailing at the rear of the party, full of his thoughts.

A horseman dropped back beside him. It was Rushing Wind, his late guard, who was pointing an excited hand at the sky.

"Look, White Thunder, already your thoughts are answered by the Sky People. They have sent down their messenger to give you good fortune again!"

Torridon followed the direction of the pointing arm and saw that a hawk was circling slowly above them, keeping pace with the progress of the party. He forced back a melancholy smile from his lips.

But in the meantime, every brave in the party had taken note of that hanging hawk against the sky, and the same thought seemed to fill every breast. Their eyes flashed. Rising Hawk could not keep from raising his long lance and shaking it victoriously against the sky, and the braves went onward with a great gaiety of demeanor. Already they had forgotten the recent crushing defeat that the Sioux had inflicted upon their nation. They were as full of confidence as a body of children at play.

VI

As though the sting of the wound in his arm was a constant spur, they went north like the wind, with Rising Hawk constantly urging them to greater efforts. A dozen horses dropped dead under the fierce riding. That was in the early days, and the rest grew thin, but wonderfully hard and fit, and the boys were easily able to keep the horse herd within striking distance of the riders. Torridon spared Ashur every other day. But even those alternate journeys on random ponies hardly were necessary, for Ashur was laughing at the miles. All his running under Torridon or with the herd barely had sufficed to thumb a little of the flesh off his ribs and cut the line of his belly a little harder and higher. But on the days when he ranged with the herd, the Indian boys were happy. There were four of them, like four young winged imps, ever flying here and there, merciless to the steeds, slaves to the braves on the warpath. But when Ashur ran with the herd, their work was nothing. He ranged back and forth at the rear of the trotting ponies. He guarded and guided them like sheep, and they feared him and respected him. He was a king among them.

His size, his grandeur, his lofty air and matchless speed made Torridon feel every day more keenly his own lack of force of hand. He was as no one in the party. Surely, in battle, the least of all the warriors would do far more than he.

In the day he was little regarded, but in the evening, after food, Rising Hawk and the chief men of the party were sure to draw close to him and discuss plans and futures. He was very reticent. He had been forced to promise them good fortune. If that good fortune did not develop, he would get his throat cut as a reward for his false prophecy. In the meantime, he would not speak more, except enigmatic sentences.

And so they came, at last, among the big, bleak, northern hills. They had seen nothing of the famous Spotted Antelope, whose party was rumored to be south by the river, waiting to intercept their passage. But the river was many days behind them. They had plunged for four days through the very heart of the Dakota lands, unspied. But on the fifth day they rode over a ridge and came swooping down on four horses and two men at the edge of a creek. So infinitely distant were these Sioux from any thought of danger that they could not believe their eyes until this mysterious Cheyenne charge had scooped them up and made them safe prisoners.

The coups were duly counted, the scalps were promised, but then Rising Hawk determined to extract what information he could from the prisoners.

The first was a stalwart brave of forty-five, hard as iron. He did not stir an eye or abate his contemptuous smile while splinters were driven under his nails and then set on fire. Torridon, transfixed with horror and fear, saw the Cheyennes prepared to take sterner measures and could not stand it. He snatched his pistol out and sent a bullet through the poor fellow's brain.

He half expected that the Cheyennes, their cruel taste once sharpened, would rush on him in a body. To his amazement, they took not the slightest heed of his action. They merely ripped the scalp away from the dead man and turned to the second prisoner. He had borne up as calmly as the other until this moment, but it appeared that the slaughtered warrior was his father. Now his nerves gave way. He was only a lad of fourteen or fifteen, early on the warpath. In another moment he was groaning forth answers to the questions of Rising Hawk.

It was true that Spotted Antelope was far away to the south and not expected for many days. In the meantime, the Sioux village for which the march was aimed had been shifted from its old site to one a little more southerly, among the lower hills, between two shallow streams of water. It was a scant half-day's march distant. There was no dream of danger threatening among the villagers. They felt that Spotted Antelope was an ample shield between them and the Cheyennes. In conclusion, the youth begged a knife thrust that would end his wretched life, since he had proved a coward and betrayed his people.

Even that mercy was denied him. Rising Hawk felt that something more could be gained, perhaps, from this glib talker.

For now, all was as he wished. There were some sixty or seventy braves within the village. One rush should carry it, and, after that, there would be the scalps of women and children—cheaply taken, and just as valuable as the scalps of matured warriors.

They pushed on until the evening. Rising Hawk himself, riding in advance, spied on the enemy from the crest of a hill and came back with the report that the Sioux were in their hands. All the village was preparing for the night; the horses were being driven in in the most leisurely fashion. Should they not attack now and overwhelm that town with a single rush?

They turned to Torridon for an answer. He answered with simply an instinct to delay the horror that seemed sure to come. Let them rest throughout the night. They were weary, now, from the long march. In the morning they would be fresh, and the Sioux would be cold with sleep. In the gray dawn the blow should be struck. Rising Hawk submitted to this advice with some grumbling, but he did not make any appeals. It was felt that the mighty medicine of Torridon alone was worthy of credit for having brought them undetected into the heart of the enemy's country, and he was looked upon with great respect.

They pitched their camp at the throat of a blind cañon. It ran straight in toward the heart of the higher hills, and, around the first bend, they camped for the night. The cañon was a pocket that would conceal them from the foe. In the morning they would break out and slaughter!

Wrapped in his blanket, Torridon lay long awake, staring at the distant, cold shining of the stars. He felt weak and small. It was not the cold of the night that made him tremble. And he wished, with closed, aching eyes, for the end of tomorrow, whatever it might bring.

He slept and dreamed that the attack took place and that he himself rode in the forefront, shouting, and that in the village he was slaughtering more than all the rest—slaughtering women and children, until the iron hand of a Dakota warrior fell on his throat. He wakened, half choking. There was a touch on his shoulder.

It was Rising Hawk. All around him stood the shadowy forms of the warriors. The horses had been brought in, soundlessly.

"What has happened?" asked Rising Hawk.

"There is danger," panted Torridon.

"Aye, White Thunder," said the chief. "There is danger. Last night you would not let us strike. Now the time has passed. The Dakota boy has escaped and gone to warn his people. What medicine have you now to give us a victory, White Thunder? Or rather, after all our work, what medicine have you that will take us safely home?"

Torridon staggered to his feet. Across the sky was stretched a thin, high-riding mist. Behind it rode a young moon. Everything could be half seen—the tall, ragged rocks at the sides of the ravine, the tall gloomy forms of the Cheyennes.

He thought he could see, too, the arrival of the Dakota boy at the village, the mustering of the warriors, and then what? According to the plan that had been made and that the boy could not have failed to know, the Cheyennes were to wait until morning to attack. What band of Dakotas could hear this plan without determining on a counterstroke? No, they were already out and coming, moving swiftly and softly across the plain—on foot, perhaps, to make sure of greater noiselessness. And then the Sioux would come to the mouth of the ravine—perhaps they were here already, and creeping up, rifles ready, murder in their savage hearts!

Torridon looked wildly around him. How should they escape? The walls went up like perfect cliffs. No horse could mount them. And if the men saved themselves, they would be saved only for the moment. On foot, this vast distance from home, they would be hunted down and speared, like starved wolves.

"What are we to do?" asked Rising Hawk more harshly. "Do you tremble, maker of medicine?"

Bitterness and mockery was in his voice, and Torridon said in husky answer: "Leave the horses here . . . go down the ravine . . . every man softly . . . every man softly. Do you hear me, Rising Hawk?"

"I hear," said the war chief. "Are we to leave our horses and have them caught . . . while we . . . ?"

That was not the thought in the mind of Torridon, but suppose that they tried to move from the valley on horseback, and gave to the Sioux the huge targets of man and horse together? So he thought and he insisted almost angrily: "Leave the horses here with the boys. Move out with the rifles. Quickly, quickly, Rising Hawk!"

"It was at dawn that we were to take scalps," the chief reminded him with a voice like a snarl. "Now we shall be lucky if we save our own."

Nevertheless, he gave the order, and they moved down the cañon slowly, softly. The warriors were both angry and nervous—angry because after all their march they now appeared to be turned back with but a single scalp, nervous because they dreaded any move, no matter how short, without their horses under them.

They passed down the ravine—Torridon in the rear, stumbling, making more noise than all the rest of that shadowy party, for his knees were very loose and wobbly beneath him. Yet they gained the mouth of the ravine unhindered. Not a shot had been fired against them, and the way home across the prairie was open.

He could have shouted for joy, but he was withheld by the fierce rush of another thought upon him. Somewhere across the dimness of the moonshine, surely the Sioux were advancing with all their warriors—their boys left at home with the old men and the women to keep guard against the chance of any counter-stroke. So they were coming, or else they were unworthy of the name that they gained in generations of fierce campaigning until all their kind upon the plains trembled at the dreadful name of the Dakotas. Tribe after tribe they had thinned to the verge of extinction; tribe after tribe they had thrust west and south. Their pride and their courage and their self-belief were all equally great.

So they would surely come, to rush the Cheyennes in the throat of the valley. They would come hastily, though silently. Once they closed the mouth of that ravine, the Cheyennes to the last man were theirs, and they would make even the late crushing victory of the great Spotted Antelope seem like child's play compared with the slaughter that they would make among the rocks.

So thought Torridon, and then he saw the great opportunity. No rushing of a village. No butchery of women and children. But a stroke of war!

It lay before him so clearly that already he seemed to see the dark figures trooping. He found Rising Hawk.

"Half on each side of the ravine, among the rocks . . . scatter the men, Rising Hawk," he advised. "Then wait and wait. The Dakotas are sure to come. They come to trap us, and they will be trapped like fish in a net. Every Cheyenne will be drenched with blood, and there will be scalps in every teepee."

Rising Hawk hesitated, not from doubt, but because the incoming of that thought numbed him with pleasure. He gave the orders instantly, and the idea spread like fire through the ranks. Despite all discipline and the necessity of silence, a grim murmur ran among the braves. They split into two sections. One rolled to the eastern side of the valley, the other rolled to the western side, and in a trice all sight and sound of them had disappeared among the shrubs, among the splintered rocks.

Even Torridon could hardly believe that the ground was alive with such a dreadful little host of trained fighters. But up the valley, from the place where the boys still kept the horses, there was occasionally the sound of a hoof striking against a rock, or the distinct noise of a snort or a cough, as one of the grazing animals sniffed dust up his nostrils.

And now only time could ripen the tragedy and bring it to perfection. But as he lay, he heard a whisper of one warrior to another: "We cannot fail. How can we fail? The Sky People fight for us. They will lead our bullets into the hearts of the Sioux. *Hai!* We have strong medicine with us this night."

Torridon found his lips stretching into a stiff and painful smile, and his heart was hot and glad. He had hunted beasts before this day. Now he was a hunter of humans, and his veins were running with hot wine.

VII

The moon was westering fast. The light it cast seemed to grow dimmer, but this was only in seeming and not in fact, for the sky was mottled with a patterning of broken clouds, and in the distance the curve of the river was beginning to be visible, like a streak of smoke across the lower ground.

Torridon began to take sights with his rifle, aiming at rocks on the farther side of the valley, shifting to shadowy bushes, and promising himself that it would be difficult work to strike a target by such a light as this. A light that constantly changed. Yes, when he looked now down toward the river, he saw that it was no longer a strip of smoke, but a width of dull, tarnished silver. Then he understood, the dawn was coming.

He was cold and stiff with lying in one place. Dew clogged his hair and moistened the tips of his ears. But wild excitement made him forget such minor evils. The dawn was coming, the light slowly, slowly, was freshening—and then suddenly out of the lowlands came a troop of figures!

They were like black, striding giants through the ground mist. And, he could see, faintly, the shimmer of light on their rifles. They had taken long, long to come, but now they were coming swiftly.

He turned his rifle toward them—then remembered that their keen eyes might detect the shining of the steel of the barrel. Hastily he muffled the gun under his robe.

Surely fifty other men among the rocks were making similar movements, but there was not so much as a whisper of sound. Very well that this was so, for there was no wind. The morning was deathly still, and the sky was turning milk-white with the coming of the day.

Straight on came the Dakotas. With a wildly beating heart Torridon counted them. Forty—sixty—seventy-two striding forms, black as jet through the land mist. Coming rapidly and yet without a whisper of sound.

They gained the throat of the ravine. Let not a Cheyenne move. Another ten strides, and the foe would be in the mouth of the trap.

But in the mouth of the ravine, as though suspicious of the greatness of their luck, the Sioux made a considerable halt, until, up the valley, came the sound of stamping and snorting horses. Then with one accord, no signal or order given, they moved forward, drawn by their lust for horseflesh and their burning hunger for Cheyenne blood. They went with their straight bodies now bent well forward, their rifles swinging, and presently they were well within the gap . . .

At that instant, a single rifle clanged from the opposite side of the ravine. In the middle of the Sioux band a warrior bounded into the air with a cry that seemed to Torridon the hugest sound that ever left human lips.

Before the dead body reached the ground, fifty rifles had spat fire and the Dakotas went down like toppling grass. They were all in a close body. If a bullet missed one it was almost sure to strike another. A great shout of woe and terror rose from them, and, as it fell, the shrill yell of dying men still hung high in the air. They wavered—then they broke back for the mouth of the ravine. Too late! Loading as they moved, the Cheyennes were slipping from among the rocks. That instant of wavering was costly. Against freshly charged weapons the Dakotas made their rush, and the blast of the second volley withered and curled them up and sent them scampering in plain panic down the valley.

After them went the Cheyennes, for they remembered, now, the horses and the boys with whom their trap had been baited. They rounded the turn of the ravine. The ground was littered with fallen guns, which the enemy had dropped in their flight, and in the growing light the Dakotas could be seen clambering hastily up the sheer walls of the rocks.

There were few loaded weapons to fire after them. But there was enough work to secure those who had not managed to gain the rocks. The fleetest of the Cheyennes had overtaken them, and, in the largeness of their hearts, a few prisoners were taken.

Madness took the Cheyennes by the throat. Up and down that ravine men danced and yelled in the fury of their joy. The scalps had been torn from the dead or the dying. The weapons had been gathered, the fallen stripped of clothing.

Before full day showed the real horror of the cañon, Torridon took Ashur and rode him down the valley, the stallion snorting with disgust. At the mouth, facing the brightening lowlands, he waited for the Cheyennes to come after him and begin the southward march. And then it was that temptation swelled big in the heart of Torridon. There was no one near him. Once away, no horse among their numbers could overtake Ashur.

But his promise held him—that and the knowledge that he was deep in hostile country where, in a day or two, scores of manhunters would be on the trail.

So he hesitated, and at last the torrent of warriors poured out around him. Their work was finished. Twenty-six dead men lay in the cañon. Five captives, their feet tied beneath the bellies of ponies, were carried along, and among them—strange chance— the boy who had escaped from them and given that warning by which the Sioux had been drawn into this dreadful man trap.

As every man went by Torridon he cast a present or a promise to the white man. Beaded moccasins, hunting knives, a deer-skin shirt, even one or two rifles were donated. A spare pony was loaded with these gifts, and well burdened by them.

But this was not all. Rising Hawk was hot to go at once against the Dakota village and strike it while its defenders were away and before those stragglers across the hills could regain the town.

He was dissuaded with difficulty. The way across the high hills was very short. It was certain that the stragglers from the battle already had carried themselves and their tale of woe to the town, and at that very moment the Dakotas were able to throw into the field a greater manpower than that of the invaders.

But though dissuaded from an attack, upon one point Rising Hawk had made up his mind. Among his prisoners was a tall youth, wounded through the left calf and bleeding freely in spite of what bandaging they could do. He never could live through a single day of riding. But he was the son of Spotted Antelope, and in the camp of the Sioux, still living and reserved for the return of Spotted Antelope, was Standing Bull. Why not exchange the son of the chief for the big Cheyenne?

They journeyed rapidly around the hills toward the town. Before they saw it, they heard a sound like the noise of a rising wind. It was the many-throated wail from the village. And as they came in view and drew nearer, they heard the noise increasing, a sound that took from the heart of Torridon all the hot pride of victory.

Such a victory never had been before—twenty-six Sioux fallen and five taken, and not a single Cheyenne had been lost!

Yet all the manhood of those stern Dakotas was not broken. Re-armed with every chance weapon they could pick up, the survivors of the late battle, reinforced by old men and young boys, sat their horses in a long line. They were drawn up close to the outer line of the lodges, to be sure, but nevertheless it was plain that they intended to fight their defensive fight, in case of need, in the open field and not from behind shelter. Up and down their ranks rode an old chief, no doubt exhorting them to be of good heart in spite of the disaster.

Rising Hawk sent in the boy who had been captured before. It was only a few minutes that they had to wait. Evidently the son of Spotted Antelope was highly prized in the Dakota camp, and presently the great form of Standing Bull was seen riding out from the village, with an escort of two warriors.

The son of the Sioux chief was sent forward to meet them, likewise accompanied by two Cheyenne warriors. So the parties met. The Cheyennes took their comrade and turned away. The Sioux returned to the village.

And so it was that Torridon clasped hands with Standing Bull again.

The giant Indian made no secret of his joy at finding himself among his friends again, but he declared that he never had had a doubt that his good friend, White Thunder, would devise some means for his delivery. He had been assured in a dream, he vowed, that White Thunder was coming to his aid, with the Sky People. Now it was accomplished.

The happiness of Standing Bull, indeed, was complete. For, having brought Torridon into the tribe and recaptured him after his escape, he felt that everything that was done by the medicine of the white man redounded largely to his credit. In this belief he was not crossed by the remainder of the Cheyennes.

Of the entire party of fifty, there was not a single man who had not at least counted a second or a third coup. And twenty-six scalps hung dripping at their saddlebows. They were enriched with honor, and they had avenged a recent defeat so thoroughly that the whole Cheyenne nation and all the most distant tribes of it would rejoice with them.

Rising Hawk was now a man of note. On the strength of this brilliant action, performed while he was yet wounded from the other battle, he stood fair to succeed High Wolf when that old man at last died or resigned his leadership of the tribe.

As for Torridon, he did not receive so much honor for his suggestion of the trap at the mouth of the ravine. It was rather because he had predicted the time at which they would take scalps. And even for that the regard he received was of a peculiar nature. To be sure he had done well. He had fought with the foremost. But still there was little honor paid to his person. It was to his magic powers that honors were accorded in the most liberal sense. They looked upon him not so much as a brave or wise man but as a peculiar instrument to which the spirits had confided an overwhelming power. He was hardly thought of as an individual at all.

Trusting in that power, straight south rode the war party. If they met with Spotted Antelope, they were wildly confident that victory again would be theirs. So Torridon spent anxious days until the river was crossed and at last they entered the comparatively friendly prairie where the power of the Cheyennes ruled.

VIII

A treble dignity invested Standing Bull when the war party returned to the village, so that even he could dispute with Rising Hawk the honors and the dignities of the expedition, though all that he had done was to be delivered from the hands of the Dakotas.

But, in the first place, he it was who had brought Torridon to the Cheyennes, and at second-hand, as it were, all the wonders that Torridon had worked since his arrival. Again, Standing Bull had taken prominent part in the first unfortunate expedition against the Sioux and duly counted his two coups before capture. Thirdly, the big man had the credit that comes of entering the jaws of death and escaping.

When the multitudes poured out from the Cheyenne camp, they yelled the name of Standing Bull louder than all the rest, except for a continual roar that lasted from the time the party was first met by fast-riding young men until the whole band had conducted the warriors to the center of the camp, and the burden of that roaring noise was the name of White Thunder. They called upon him, however, as they would have called upon a spirit. But they called upon Standing Bull as upon a man.

When that warrior returned, therefore, he found all in order with his reputation, but all out of order in his lodge. His favorite wife was a wracked and helpless woman, lying stretched on her bed, too weakened by a debauch of grief that had followed the tidings of the loss of her lord to do more than raise her head and smile weakly in greeting. Her shaven head glistened repulsively under the eye of her husband; her body was slashed and torn; her scalp was crossed with many knife slashes, and, beyond this, she had given away practically everything in the lodge and the entire horse herd of her husband in the midst of her grief in order to propitiate the Sky People and to give more lasting rest to the spirit of Standing Bull. In all this, she had acted a most pious part, but it left Standing Bull a beggared man.

For that, he cared not at all. There were many gifts from his friends. White Thunder alone gave ten horses to make a handsome beginning of a horse herd for his old friend, and High Wolf donated a store of provisions. In a day, the lodge was well supplied with all the necessaries. So fluid was prosperity in an Indian tribe. It ebbed and flowed like the sea.

The entire stage was left to be monopolized by Rising Hawk and Standing Bull. White Thunder had withdrawn to his teepee, where he lay on his bed and slept longer than any warrior should, and the whoopings and the yellings only made him turn from time to time and exclaim impatiently.

Young Willow, grown suddenly tender beyond her wont, watched over him. With a new-cut branch she waved the flies away from him, and with ambidextrous skill saw to it that he slept and that food was ready when at last he wakened.

He lolled at ease against the most comfortable of his back-rests and ate of the meat that was placed before him—not simply dried flesh of the buffalo, but stewed venison, freshly killed, and roasted venison, turned at the fire on a dozen small spits and handed to him bit by bit by the squaw.

With burning eyes of pleasure she regarded the man of the lodge. "So," said Young Willow, "you rode out groaning, and you have come back famous!"

"Fame is noise," said Torridon sententiously—and wearily, also, for he was still tired from the long ride.

"Noise?" cried Young Willow, growing angry at once. "Fame is all that men live for and all that the dead are remembered by!"

"The people shout today, they yawn tomorrow," sighed Torridon.

"Good fame is better than a handsome face," said the squaw.

"It is a breath," said the man.

"It is to men what their breath is to the flowers," said the squaw.

"The flowers soon wither," said Torridon, "and so what becomes of them?"

"The sweetness they have left on earth is remembered," replied Young Willow.

He felt himself fairly beaten, and, acknowledging it by his silence, he smiled almost fondly on that grotesque face, and she smiled back at him, gently.

"From the time we left until the time we returned," said Torridon, "I fired my rifle only twice."

"And then?" she asked him hungrily.

"Then," he admitted, with a lift of the head, "I saw a Sioux jump his height into the air each time." He added, chuckling: "They must live on springs, because they die in the air."

Young Willow laughed, like the cawing of a crow. "That is a good thing to remember," she said. "How many spirits, White Thunder, came down at your call?"

An honest man would have shrugged his shoulders and declared that there was not a spirit in the air on that day of bloodshed. But Torridon had discovered that honesty availed him nothing. If he put all on a common-sense plane, it was simply believed that he was deceiving the people and hiding the truth, and veiling his powers.

He said as gravely as possible: "There was a spirit in front of every man. There were eighty Sioux, and yet all their bullets could not find a single Cheyenne. I shall tell you why . . . I had placed a spirit in front of every warrior. The ghosts turned the bullets away. Some of those bullets went back and killed the men who had fired them."

At this prodigy, Young Willow opened her eyes and her mouth. She drank, as it were, of the mystery. Doubt was far from her. This was a story that would thrill the very hearts of the men, the women, and the children, and she could be fairly sure that White Thunder would not tell the story himself. It was in her hands. Beads and shells would be showered upon her for the telling of such a miracle. In fact her housekeeping for the white man was turning out a sinecure of great value, in her eyes.

"You saw them, White Thunder?" she breathed.

"I alone," he said. "There is a veil before the eyes of other men. A spirit like a great bat flew before Rising Hawk. Bullets glanced from its wings and made sparks of bright red light."

There was a little more of this fantastic conversation. Then, when Torridon went to sleep again, the squaw slipped from the lodge, fairly bursting with her tale. She went back to the teepee of her husband to find that High Wolf was in serious conversation with Standing Bull.

The old chief turned on the squaw with a harsh voice. "What of White Thunder?" he asked.

She concealed the miracle that had just been confided to her. She preferred to retell it herself to small gatherings. "He still sleeps."

High Wolf made a gesture of impatience. "The Sky People have sent us a pig in the form of a man," he declared scornfully. "Has he done no boasting?"

"Only that two Dakotas fell under his rifle"

High Wolf and Standing Bull exchanged glances.

"That is nothing to him?"

"He sleeps again." Young Willow smiled.

"He neither has danced nor sung?"

Young Willow shrugged her shoulders. "He has had a few Dakotas killed, and taken a few scalps to make the Cheyennes proud. But what is that to him? If he wished, he would wash the Dakotas into the rivers so thickly that the Father of Waters would be choked on his way to the sea. The Cheyennes come home and sing like children over a few beads. White Thunder sleeps so that he may dream of happier things."

The two warriors listened to this speech with the deepest attention.

"He is not happy, then?" asked High Wolf.

"He is as always. I spoke to him about fame. He turned my words into the thinnest air."

High Wolf gestured toward the door, and the squaw departed. After she had gone, High Wolf said: "From the time you first brought him to us, I knew that he was a gift from the heavens. But I never knew until now what his powers could be."

"Use him now, while he is with us," said Standing Bull. "Use him like a magic rifle that will soon be gone. For he is unhappy among us. I cannot tell why, but he is unhappy."

"I, however, know the reason," returned the chief. "It is because of a woman."

"Ha?" cried Standing Bull. "If it is a Crow, a Blackfoot, if it is even a Sioux, there are enough horses in the tribe to buy ten girls for him."

"Tell me," said the old man, "how often do the whites sell their women?"

Standing Bull made a face of disgust. "A woman to a white man," he admitted, "is like a child to a mother." He added: "Is it a white girl?"

High Wolf nodded. "It is a white girl," he said.

At that, the big man threw out his arms. "It is she who lives at Fort Kendry, I saw her. She is no bigger than a child. In twenty days she could not flesh a robe. She has no more force in her hands than there is in the claw of a sparrow. Why should a man want her?"

"This is not a man. It is a spirit," said High Wolf.

The warrior made no answer.

"Heammawihio," went on the chief gravely, "has given power to you in this matter. It was you who brought us White Thunder. It was you, also, who followed him to Fort Kendry and brought him to us a second time. Therefore, it is plain that the Great Spirit wishes to work through you in all of these things. Perhaps it was to free you that we were given this last great victory over the Sioux. At any rate, it is clear that you must do what is necessary to keep White Thunder happy . . . that is, to keep him with us. You must bring to him the white girl that he wants."

Standing Bull groaned. "Twice in the trap makes a captured wolf," he said.

"Look over the tribe," said High Wolf. "Take the finest horses and the strongest braves, but fix this in your mind . . . that you must ride to Fort Kendry and bring the girl here."

IX

For a whole week, Standing Bull purified himself every day. It became known throughout the village that he was about to attempt some great and secret thing. For every day he went to the sweat house and there he had water poured over red-hot, crumbling stones until the lodge was filled with choking, blinding fumes. In these he remained for a long time, and then came out, staggering and reeling like a drunkard. He would run down the hillside naked, the steam flying up from his body, and plunge into the cold river. In this manner he was driving out evil and preparing himself for a great deed.

He fasted, also, eating sparingly only once every second day, and he never smoked, except ceremonially. With his hands he touched no weapons. He was much alone, and used to sit on a hill overlooking the camp and the river for hours and hours at a time. Sometimes he was seen there in the midday. Again, the growing dawn light discovered Standing Bull on the hill. Perhaps he was wrapped in a buffalo robe. Perhaps he was half naked, as though unaware of heat or of cold.

His poor wife, Owl Woman, cured by the return of her husband, was up and about the camp, frightfully worried by the procedures of her spouse. She had harried herself until she was a mere caricature of a woman, but she was honored throughout the village because of the extremity of her devotion. Even that harsh and incredulous critic, Young Willow, was heard to say: "She was just a young woman before . . . now she is beautiful."

"Beautiful?" echoed Torridon, always willing to argue with the squaw.

"No good woman can be ugly," said Young Willow.

Owl Woman, therefore, was seen about the camp anxiously inquiring what could be in the mind of her husband, and then rather naturally she told herself that it was because she had deformed herself so greatly by mourning. She even came to Torridon and brought him a gift of carved bone to ornament a backrest. She wanted to know how she could win back her husband.

He accepted the gift, gave her a simple salve to hasten the healing of the wounds that covered her body, and then told her to go home and cover her shaven head with a mantle, and to be seen singing around the lodge. As for her husband, he assured her that the heart of Standing Bull was not estranged. He simply was having a struggle with spirits.

Common sense, of course, would have dictated all these sayings to any man, but she received them with devout thankfulness. She took the mantle that he gave her and went off with a step so light and swift that the cloth—it was a bright Mexican silk gained from the Comanches—streamed out behind her as she went.

Torridon watched her going until Young Willow broke in on his thoughts with her harsh voice: "Why do you sneer and smile to yourself after you have given advice to people and shown them the truth? He that scorns others must sit on a cloud."

On the evening of the seventh day, Standing Bull himself came to Torridon. He looked thin. His eyes were sunken, and his lips were compressed.

"I am going to try to do a great thing," he said. "Give me a charm to help me, White Thunder."

"There are all sorts of charms," said the young man. "If I gave you a charm at random, it might be the worst thing in the world for you. Tell me what you want to try."

"I cannot tell you that," grumbled Standing Bull. "Only . . . it is something to make you happy."

"Shall I tell you the quickest way to make me happy?" said Torridon. "Send away the young men who watch me day and night. Let me have Ashur and one minute to get away from the camp. Then I shall be happy, Standing Bull, but nothing else matters to me."

"Do you ask me to give away my right hand, White Thunder?" asked the chief gloomily. "Then I must go away and carry no luck from you." He departed slowly in a sort of despair.

Then he began to make the round of the camp. His reputation was now so big that he was able to call on six of the best warriors in the village and enlist them to follow him wheresoever he chose to lead them. The desperate nature of the work that he had in mind kept him from revealing the secret. Chiefly because, if it were rumored about the camp and came to the ear of Torridon, he was afraid that great magician would blast all their plans.

At last he had his party together. There were three horses for every man; the braves were painted for the warpath, and Standing Bull rode with them three times around the village. As he came opposite each of the cardinal points of the compass in making this circuit, he blew smoke offerings, but, after the third circle, he bore away to the northwest. They crossed the shallow river, and disappeared over the plains, while Torridon, together with most of the gathered tribe, watched their going.

"Standing Bull is like a buzzard," said Young Willow. "He is always hungry and therefore he is always on the wing."

But Standing Bull was not thinking of fame; he was facing forward to the dreadful difficulty of his task and wishing that, in all the world, some other duty could have been assigned to him. Sometimes he wished that the entire Cheyenne nation could be behind him for the work. But again, he realized that such numbers could do nothing secretly, and at the first approach of an armed tribe all the people who lived outside the fort would retire within its walls—Samuel Brett with his niece among the rest. He realized, also, that he never had seen the face of the girl. He had seen her only in the dusk, and, if there were more than one girl in the house, he would be shrewdly put to it to select the right one.

It was no wonder that with these thoughts in his mind he went on the journey with a depressed heart. All the way his words were few, but the warriors followed without a sign of discontent until they came over the lower hills and at last looked down on Fort Kendry.

Then they assembled together and Red Shirt, chief of the followers of the big leader, spoke for the rest. "Have you come for white scalps, Standing Bull?" he asked with much gravity.

"You, perhaps, never have taken one?" said Standing Bull pleasantly. For the entire tribe knew about the long-tressed scalp that hung in the lodge of Red Shirt.

"Because of that scalp I took," said Red Shirt frankly, "I cannot ride into a trading post without fear. For the white men never forget. Because of that scalp, many Cheyennes have died, and now I know that it is better to fight with the Crows or the Blackfeet or the Dakotas, even, than to fight with the white men."

The rest of the men listened in silence that agreed totally with their spokesman, and Standing Bull saw that he would have a good deal of explaining to do.

He said cheerfully: "I, too, my brothers, know that the white men are dangerous. I have not brought you here to take scalps, but to do something still more important. I shall tell you simply, now that you have come to the place where the thing must be done."

He made a pause and swept his hand toward the fort. The rambling group of unpainted walls, some stone built, all rough and carelessly made, the ramshackle roofs, the twisting fence lines, made a very study in confusion. But at the tops of the walls of the fort itself they could see the little round mouths of the cannons that made such miraculous noise and killed at such a miraculous distance.

With equal awe and hate the band looked down upon this stronghold of the white skins.

"We do not love these people," said Standing Bull, "but one man with a white skin has done much for the Cheyennes. I speak of White Thunder."

A unanimous grunt of agreement greeted this remark.

"Now, my brothers," said Standing Bull, "we wish to keep White Thunder among us, I am sure. We never have known hunger since he came. He can bring the rain from heaven, and he can turn the bullets of the enemy in battle. He can bring ghosts to protect us and to send our bullets straight into the hearts of our foes. To keep him, we have our young braves guard him. That is hard work. Besides, someday he may find a way to trick our cleverest young men and to escape."

"That is true," said the youngest of the party, a keen stripling of twenty years. "When I guarded him, I trembled with fear. I would as soon try to hold the naked lightning in my hand as to keep White Thunder from doing what he wanted to do."

"But," said Standing Bull, "if once we can make him happy among us, all will be well. And that can be managed, I think. Here in Fort Kendry is the thing that he wants. It is not horses or money or buffalo robes. It is a squaw. There is a girl here who he loves. Because she is not with him, his heart is sick. Now I, my brothers, hope to catch that girl and take her back to him. You see that our business is not so dangerous as the taking of white scalps."

Red Shirt exclaimed impatiently: "I, Standing Bull, know the white men, and I know that they put more value on their women than they do on their scalps!"

Standing Bull scowled at this opposition. He said at length, bitterly: "I shall take the chief risk. I cannot make you help me. But if you stay here, I shall go down alone and bring the girl away, or die in that work. I am trying to do something for all the people of the Cheyennes. Who will help me? Let us bring the girl to White Thunder, and he will stay with us as contentedly as a bird in a nest."

They stared at him, hardly able to believe. Red Shirt suggested that there were pretty maidens among the Cheyennes. But Standing Bull waved him to scorn.

"White Thunder," he explained, "does not think like a man, but like a foolish boy that is sick. We, like parents, must try to please him. Because the boy has been given power."

This simple reasoning appeared conclusive. One and all agreed that they would do their best. If they succeeded, even though they returned without scalps or horses, certainly they would be gloriously received by the Cheyennes. So they loosed their reins and went on toward the fort.

X

Once before, Standing Bull had gone to Fort Kendry. But though he had come there in the daylight, he had done his work in the night and escaped again under cover of the dark. He had no fear that he would be recognized now, or suspected of any evil intention. To mask the real purpose of his journey, he had seen to it that some of the extra horses were loaded with buffalo robes of good quality. To all intents, they would appear like a small band of warriors who had come in to trade and get what they could. In the meantime, they would look around them for the girl.

They hardly had come into the village before they were welcomed. The more important traders had their quarters within the fort itself, where they worked for the fur company. But in the village were independents that picked up a little business here and there from just such small parties as these. As the Cheyennes entered, wrapped to the eyes in their robes, their long rifles balanced across the pommels of their saddles, first one and then another agent greeted them fluently in their own tongue and tempted them with bottles of whiskey. Both of these, Standing Bull passed by, but a third man he followed into his booth and looked at the display of goods. There were beads of all kinds, together with hatchets, knives, tobacco, tea, sugar, coffee, flour, calico, clothes, and ribbons of many colors, blankets, and a hundred little foolish trinkets. Standing Bull himself was enchanted by the appearance of some little bells that, as the agent pointed out, could be tied in the mane of the horse, or in the hair of the warrior.

"So," said Standing Bull to Red Shirt, "a brave would be known before he was seen. His friends would be glad. He would walk with music." And he jangled the bells.

But Red Shirt was entirely absorbed in the contemplation of a jug of whiskey; the pungent fragrance of it already was in his nostrils.

However, nothing would be done, no matter what the temptation, until Standing Bull gave the signal, and certainly he would not give such a signal on this day. The number of the robes was small, barely large enough to excuse their offering in trade, after so long a journey to present them. On the first day there should be no trafficking. Indeed, if possible, Standing Bull intended to get his party away from the fort before the warriors had tasted the unnerving fire of the whiskey. One bottle of that would be enough to start a debauch that would ruin all plans.

In the midst of all this confusion, while the trader and his boy were panting with eagerness for plunder, another form appeared, a tall and magnificently made frontiersman, garbed in the finest of deerskin, heavily beaded, with his long, blond hair flowing down about his shoulders. A pistol in one side of his belt balanced a heavy knife that was in front, and in his hands he carried a long, heavy rifle, using it as lightly as though it were a walking staff. He went straight to Standing Bull and raised a hand in greeting.

"*Hau!*" grunted the Cheyenne in response.

"*Hau!*" said the other cheerfully, and speaking the Indian tongue well enough. "Men tell me that you are Standing Bull, the chief of the Cheyennes?"

Standing Bull wanted nothing so little as to be recognized. He maintained a grim silence and looked the other in the eye.

The white man continued: "We have heard of you. The Dakotas have been here. They had something to say of you and your big medicine."

Here the boy interrupted: "Hey, you! Are you gonna try to swipe these half-wits out of our booth? Back up, will you, and let us finish our trade with them, or else we'll . . . "

51

His employer silenced him with a back-handed cuff that sent the youngster staggering. "It's Roger Lincoln, you little fool," he said, and added: "Glad to see you, Mister Lincoln."

Now at that name there was a little stir among the Cheyennes. In fact, it was known from the Dakotas to the Kiowas and Comanches, over the length and breadth of the plains. They moved back a little, partly as though they did not know what to expect, and partly as if they wanted a better chance to examine and admire the white man. They found him perfect in his appointments, from his hat to his beaded moccasins. Except for the whiteness of his skin—and that was weather-browned enough—he might have stepped into the ranks of any Indian tribe of the plains, a chief, or the favored son of some rich brave.

"I have a house close by," said Roger Lincoln. "I do not wish to make a trade with a friend. I wish to talk to you about better things than buffalo robes. Will you come?"

He added to the trader a brief sentence, promising that he would not barter for a single one of the robes or any other possession of the Cheyennes. The trader, biting his lip, nodded, and watched in silence while the troop filed off at the heels of Lincoln.

The latter took the Indians to his own trading booth a short distance away, and there he seated them in a circle in his room and offered them tea, sweetened with heaps of sugar. With loud smackings, the red men tasted it, rolled their eyes, and poured down the scalding hot tea. They held out their cups for another service, and again the cups were filled brimming. A pipe was passed. Good humor began to possess Standing Bull, greater than the doubt and suspicion in which he had stood when the white man first greeted them. He waited for the meaning of this to be expounded, and presently the meaning was made clear.

"Now, my friend," said Roger Lincoln, "look around you at everything. You see rifles here and pistols there. Here are some barrels of powder. There is lead for making bullets. There are some bullet molds. Here are some knives. See them. Take this one for a present and feel its edge. Also, there are saddles and bridles. Here you see the clothes. There is enough red cloth to put a headband around the head of every Cheyenne . . . man, and woman, and child. There are beads in these boxes. And here is a little chest stored with all sorts of wonderful things. Back in this corner you can see the hatchets and the axes."

The nostrils of Standing Bull fanned out and quickly contracted as he drew in an envious breath. "The white men," he said, "are rich. The Indians are very poor."

"Nevertheless," said Roger Lincoln quickly, "they are men, and a man is worth more than you can put on his back or into his hands."

Standing Bull smiled, touched with pleasure almost in spite of himself. "Perhaps it is true," he agreed.

"Have you looked at all these things?" asked Lincoln.

"I have seen them very well."

"But look at them again. Examine them. Feel them with your hands. Try the weight of this axe. You see that it has a tooth that will never grow dull, and that hatchet was made to sink into the brainpan of a Dakota."

Standing Bull sighed with a great delight.

"Here, also, are buttons brighter than silver to put along the edges of your trousers. Here are some coils of rope, and look at these iron tent pegs. You know how they are used? And here is an iron-headed hammer that never will break."

The Indians followed every word with intense pleasure and interest.

"Come back with me," went on Roger Lincoln. He led the way out of the shack and in the rear a large corral opened. In it were fifty or sixty horses to which an attendant was forking out well-cured hay. "You have the eye which sees horses," said Roger Lincoln. "When you look at these, you will see that they are not like the other horses of the plains. They are taller. Their legs are longer and stronger. They are crossbred. They are not soft like other horses of white men. They are bred out of plains ponies by fine stallions. Mounted on such horses as these, Standing Bull, you would sweep away from an enemy. You could strike and fly off again out of danger like a hawk playing with a buzzard."

The Cheyennes devoured those horses with greedy looks. It was true that they understood horseflesh perfectly, and now they proved it by the red-eyed silence in which they observed these animals.

After this, Roger Lincoln went on slowly and impressively: "I am not a rich man, my friends. I have worked many years, and what you have just seen is what I have saved. I have paid for these things with blood, you may be sure. I had hoped that with them I could trade and make more money. At last I could go back among my people and sit quietly in a pleasant lodge by the side of a stream, with trees around me, and take a squaw, and raise many children.

"But dearer than peace and happiness are the life and the happiness of a friend. Do you hear me, Standing Bull? You have in your lodges a man with a white skin, and you call him White Thunder. Is it true?" He said the words as one who puts a statement in question form for the sake of politeness. The Cheyenne leader stiffened a little. His keen eyes turned gravely upon the other, and he said nothing.

"For that man," said Roger Lincoln, "if you will bring him in safety to Fort Kendry, I will pay you everything that your eyes have seen. If you find anything more, you are welcome. I will give you also even the house in which you find all these things and everything down to the ground on which it stands. I have promised. No man has heard me say the thing that is not so."

This speech made a vast impression upon the Cheyennes. They drew back a little, murmuring, and among the companions of Standing Bull there was only one opinion. Such a princely offer of dazzling wealth should be accepted at once. Never had they seen such riches heaped together. The whole tribe would be rejoiced.

Standing Bull simply replied: "He is not ours to sell. The Sky People sent him to us, and, if we let him go, they will send us bad luck. Besides, High Wolf never would sell him. And who but a fool, after all, would give up a power that can turn the bullets of the Dakotas as if they were pebbles thrown by children? Do not talk foolishness any more. Besides, Roger Lincoln is a wise man. Would he pay such things except for a man who is worth twice as much? If White Thunder is worth so much to the whites, he is worth ten times more to us!"

He turned to the big, white man and shook his head solemnly. "Our eyes have not seen White Thunder," he said. "We do not know about what you are speaking."

XI

Those men who early went to the Western frontier were, almost without exception, children. Great-shouldered, hard-handed, often hard-hearted children, but, nevertheless, children they were. Nothing but childish reasoning could have induced them to leave the cities and the comfortable lands east of the Mississippi for all the chances, the labor, the dangers of the prairie, except that in their heart of hearts they loved a game more than they loved anything else.

So it was with Roger Lincoln. Well-born, well-educated, calm-minded, brave as steel and as keen, he could have had the world at his feet, if he had chosen to live among the civilized. But rather than his knowledge of books he preferred to use his knowledge of the wilderness. Rather than his knowledge of civilized society he preferred to use his knowledge of the barbarians. A fine horse was more to him than a learned companion, and a good rifle better than a rich inheritance.

Stately, gentle, soft of voice, beautiful of face, and mighty of hand, he looked the type of some Homeric hero. There was no cloud of trouble on his brow. His eye was as clear as the clearest heavens.

Yet beneath all this there was the heart of a child. It began to work in him now that he heard the lying reply of Standing Bull. His lips trembled and then compressed. His breast swelled. An almost uncontrollable passion enthralled Roger Lincoln, and the Cheyennes drew a little closer together, overawed and frightened.

"I have been to the Cheyennes a good friend," said Roger Lincoln. "There are many in your tribe who know that I never have harmed them. Your own chief, High Wolf, remembers a day on the waters of the Little Bender when the Crows were closing around him and there was no hope of help. On that day he was glad that Roger Lincoln was his friend and a friend to the Cheyennes. I split the Crows as a child splits a twig. They ran away, and the Cheyennes followed them and took a great many scalps. There were other days of which I could speak. I have kept the Cheyennes from trouble whenever I was near them. I respected them and thought that they were men and truth speakers. When they came to a trading post where I was, I saw that the traders did not cheat them. I used to stand up in the councils of the white men and say that no matter what they thought of the other red men of the plains, the Cheyennes were real men and brave men and that they spoke the truth.

"Because I thought all these things, today I was willing to do more than is just. My dearest friend is among your lodges. You keep him there. His heart is breaking. What wrong had he done you or any other Indian? He was young and had harmed no one. He was my friend. I have no other friend half so dear to me as this White Thunder. But you stole him and kept him, after he had done good to one of you. I do not want to name the warrior whose life he saved on the island at the forking of the river. I would not like to say that any man would be so base as to betray the friend who saved him. And yet this is what happened.

"I did not want to talk of these things. Instead, I offered to make a bargain with you. I offered you a ransom. What do you do when a most hated enemy is taken in battle? If his friends offer you horses and guns, you take them and set him free. But you did not take White Thunder in battle. You tricked him into coming to your camp and, after that, you surrounded him with guards. You threatened to kill him if he did not work great medicine for you. And all that I say is true. Now you will not take such a ransom as never was offered to Cheyennes before.

"You forgot the wrong you have done to White Thunder. Instead of keeping him, you should cover him with presents. You should give him whole herds of horses, and then you should set him free.

"Or when Roger Lincoln asks, because of the good I have done for you, you should set White Thunder free even if he had killed one of your chiefs. But he has killed no one and he has done you no harm. Only out of the wickedness of your hearts you are keeping him to be a slave to you, to bring rain to your crops and make medicine against the other Indians.

"Now, I tell you that you will come to a day when you will groan at the thought of White Thunder. You will tremble when his name is mentioned. You will wish that you had starved of hunger without corn rather than that he should have been kept in the tribe like a prisoner.

"I tell you this, and, when I speak, it is not the whistling of the wind. I have been your friend. Now I am your friend no longer. From the moment that you leave Fort Kendry I am your enemy, and you shall pay for the evil that is in you. This is my token of what I will do and of how much I hate you!"

There was a big chopping block nearby and in it was stuck a splitting axe—an old and rusted blade with a wide bevel, useless for felling trees but acting like a wedge to tear open sections for firewood. This axe the frontiersman caught up. His childish fury had reached its climax, and with fury in his eye he swung the axe and cast it from him. With one hand he had wielded its heavy mass and it spun lightly away and drove its blade into a post of the corral. So heavy was the shock that the whole fence trembled. And the bright eyes of the Cheyennes flashed at one another.

That blow would have driven the axe head well nigh through the body of a warrior.

"Go!" said Roger Lincoln, and before the wave of his hand the Indians drew back.

They filed through the store. They reached the street and turned down it, still walking one behind the other, their muffling robes high about their faces. They took their horses with them to the edge of the town and there they sat down in a clearing in a circle.

Standing Bull took out a pipe bowl of red catlinite. This he filled with tobacco, mixed with dried, powdered bark to make it burn freely and give pungency to the taste. He fitted in the long stem and lighted the mixture. He blew a puff to the earth spirits. He blew a puff to the cardinal points. Then he held up the pipe to the Great Spirit and chanted slowly a sacred song that, rudely translated, ran somewhat as follows:

Heammawihio, lord of the air,
We are not even master of the ground.
But we are your children, and we are in trouble.

In this last line the entire band joined, singing like a chorus, singing heavily.

Heammawihio, your way is the way of the eagle.
Our way is the way of the prairie dog, creeping in holes.
But we are your children, and we are in trouble.

Heammawihio, your eye sees all things and all thoughts.
But even in the sunlight our eyes are darkened.
But we are your children, and we are in trouble.

Heammawihio, for your enemies you keep
the polished spears of the lightning.
And we have nothing but our weak hands
with which to strike.
But we are your children, and we are in trouble.

Give us good council, open our minds, be pitiful.
We have no words or thoughts, except to pray to you.
But we are your children, and we are in trouble.

Between the verses of this solemn song, Standing Bull had smoked a few pulls from his pipe. Now it was handed around the circle. Each man smoked. Each man was silent. When the pipe was empty, the ashes were knocked from the bowl, and then the council began. Standing Bull invited all to speak who had an idea that might be of service in their present difficulty.

Red Shirt was eloquent at once. His thought was of immediate and complete surrender. From White Thunder, as he said, the Cheyennes had received many services. They could make no repayment for the rain he had brought to them, the Dakota scalps that he had placed in their lodges, or the members of the tribe who he had saved from sickness. It was fitting, therefore, that they should set the white man free. The additional argument was that of Roger Lincoln's enmity. Certainly they should set White Thunder free at any rate. In addition, they had great treasures offered to them by Roger Lincoln. And, beyond this, there was now thrown into the scale the terrible hostility of this famous warrior. It would be far better at once to return to Roger Lincoln and propose amity. He, Red Shirt, had hardly been able to keep his tongue quiet when he had heard the magnificent proposals of the white hunter refused.

After him spoke Rushing Wind, the same who had made the wager with Torridon about the crossing of the river. He was equally hot on the other side. What treasures, he asked, could be offered by any man to offset the magic powers of White Thunder? He, Rushing Wind, had seen the great enchanter at work. He had seen spirits called down from the air in the form of hawks. He had seen the work those spirits could accomplish. White Thunder knew the language of bird and beast. He could draw the buffalo out of the plains and bring them close to the village. Everything was possible to him. He was a treasure in himself beyond price. As for Roger Lincoln, he was one man. What could one man perform against the entire Cheyenne nation?

If only, then, they could get what they came for and win the squaw who would keep the enchanter happy, they could wish for nothing else. The medicine of White Thunder would be turned against Roger Lincoln himself and soon that famous scalp would dry in the lodge of a Cheyenne. He, Rushing Wind, hoped that he would be the lucky man. At least, he was not afraid.

This speech of a headlong youth was received in silence. Only the eyes of the older warriors turned gravely to one another, exchanging a thought.

Finally Standing Bull said, though gently: "No white man ever is alone. Roger Lincoln is a name that can gather a tribe of white warriors. Because I am leading this party, now I must think deeply and pray to Heammawihio for guidance. For myself I wish nothing. I am doing all this for the sake of our people. I shall pray with a pure heart. May I receive guidance."

He filled his pipe. The others withdrew softly from about him.

XII

When night came down upon the camp of the Cheyennes, where they had improvised some comfort in the woods, they found that the clement weather had changed much for the worse. The moon for which they hoped did not appear. Instead, the sky was covered with deep gray clouds in the evening, and, as the darkness began, the rain commenced, also, falling small and soft, but gradually penetrating their clothes with wet and cold. The trees gradually were drenched with moisture. A heavy pattering began in the woods that sounded like the fearless striding to and fro of wild beasts. The fire burned small, with much smoke and little heat, as all the fuel was soaked that they threw into the heap. There was small comfort for them. They were in a far land. They were close to the power of the white men. And their hearts were heavy with the knowledge that they had done wrong, and were contemplating a greater evil.

For, as the darkness came thick, and the rain began to descend, Standing Bull had advanced from among the woods and announced that, after consulting the Great Spirit with all his heart, he could not understand any message, and therefore he took it for granted that they should continue with the work on which they had come.

That evening he would look over the situation. As for the rest of the warriors, he recommended to them that they earnestly pray that a dream might be sent to one of them suggesting the proper course for the war party.

With that, Standing Bull left them and slipped away among the woods and among the scattering houses until he came close to the square-built log cabin of Samuel Brett.

Here he began to prowl with the greatest caution. The cold of the rain, driven to the bone by occasional flurries of wind, he quite disregarded. He moved in the darkness as though he had been moving in the open light of day, and trying to make his approach unnoticeable under the battery of a hundred suspicious eyes. From rock to rock, from bush to bush, he worked softly, until he came close to the house.

After that, he worked back and forth under the wall. By the kitchen door he paused and smelled cookery. He was hungry, and the odors tempted him. There were such fragrances as he never before had connected with food. However, he banished this passing weakness at once. Completing his tour of investigation, he found two windows, but both were closed and darkened against the night and the rising storm.

He came back to the kitchen door, and pressed close to it. It was a work of some danger. There were considerable cracks in this home-made door, and through the cracks ran long fingers of light that traveled far into the night and showed the rain sifting down steadily. In addition, those fingers of light must be touching his person, and, if anyone were abroad to watch him, he surely would be revealed.

However, it was necessary for him to learn something of what was inside the house. So he put his eye to crack after crack until through one of the apertures he was able to see the corner that included the stove and the sink.

Two women were there washing tins and dishes. One washed. One dried. He could see the face of her who dried. She was young, slender, dark of eye and skin. She was pretty enough to have caused the heart of a young brave to leap. Doubtless it was she who White Thunder wanted.

As for she who washed, her back was turned. She was doubtless the squaw of the house. Yet her back was not flat and broad. The nape of her neck was delicately rounded. However, the squaws among the whites were not like the squaws among the Indians.

He waited, listening. Their voices were like the sounds of two brooks running through a still woodland, bubbling, and often running together with laughter. Those sounds were pleasant to the ear of Standing Bull. But he thought of the strong-handed squaws in his teepee. He thought of Owl Woman, who nearly had slain herself in the intensity of mourning for her lost lord.

Then his mind grew more contented. To each people, their own women. But his own women were the best in the world, he was sure. Besides, one of them had given him a male child so that the memory of Standing Bull should be kept strong and his spirit alive among men.

At last, she who washed turned from the sink. The heart of Standing Bull sank. She was as young as the other. She was younger. Her hair was not dark, but light. The radiance from the lamp shone through it, making it glisten at the outer edges. Her cheek and throat were as sleek as the cheek and throat of a baby. She had large, dim eyes. They did not dance and sparkle like the eyes of the darker girl. There was not much life in this paler creature. And, therefore, doubtless White Thunder could not have chosen her.

However, he who is wise reserves his judgment. Standing Bull reserved his. Who, after all, can step inside the mind of the white man and be sure of his thoughts? He lives by contraries. The creature will fight, but he cares nothing for the glory of the counted coup, or the symbol of the scalp. He fights to destroy bodies. The red man understands that there is no true death except to the spirit. And so in all things, the white man, in spite of his medicine and his wisdom, lives by contraries, doing foolish things. Therefore, it might be that White Thunder would prefer this paler girl, this dim-eyed, sad-faced creature.

But why, after all, should she be sad?

Something stirred at the edge of the woods. Instantly Standing Bull was close down at the foot of the wall of the house, where the darkness covered him. Footsteps came up to the door, a big man was seen there, striped by the light that shone through the cracks. He thrust the door open.

As the door closed upon him, gay voices broke out. There was laughter. Standing Bull understood not a word, but very well he recognized the sound of rejoicing. Then he crept back to his place of espial and stared through again. The big man had placed on the floor the body of a young deer that he had carried upon his shoulders. Now he sat at a table near the stove—a powerful fellow with huge shoulders and a stern face. His clothes were beginning to steam. A white squaw, older than the two girls, came hurrying in to him. They exchanged words. Her hands were full of cloth, and with it she returned to the other room. The dark-eyed beauty went with her and left the paler girl behind.

She, as was right, tended the hunter. The fragrance of coffee made the air sweet and pungent. There was the scent of frying venison, and the meat hissed and snapped as the heat seared it. Bread was brought forth. It glistened white as snow as the knife of the girl divided it. She laid the food before the hunter. The mouth of Standing Bull watered and he swallowed hard.

Swiftly the hunter ate, and hugely. Like a starved brave returned from the arduous warpath he devoured his food. Then he leaned back in his chair and lit a pipe.

Oh, white man, are there no spirits in your world? Without ceremony, brutally, crudely, he filled and lit the pipe. He leaned back in his chair, chewing the short stem, shifting it from side to side in his white, strong teeth. As he smoked, he talked. The girl was washing dishes again. Tobacco smoke filled the air. A heavy, thick, sweet odor, unlike that of Indian tobacco.

The hunter drew the smoke into his lungs. It poured forth at his mouth and his nose as he talked. His words became living images in smoke. They rose and melted slowly and flattened against the ceiling.

Standing Bull watched, fascinated. He felt the muscles tightening along his spine. He bristled as a dog bristles, when a strange animal comes near. And Standing Bull, out of instinct, fumbled the haft of his big hunting knife. That rough blond scalp would look very good in the lodge.

The man inside now spoke and beckoned, and the girl stood before him. Was she his daughter? Was she his youngest squaw?

No, the white man kept only one squaw, for in all things his ways were the ways of ignorance. It was even said—a wonder not to be believed—that sometimes he helped the women in their work around the lodge.

Now the girl stood before the big man. He put out his hand and laid it on her head, and her head bowed a little, as though under a weight.

He spoke to her. His rough voice was softened. His gesture indicated that he talked of some far thing. He shook his head and denied that far thing. Then he appeared to argue. He talked with gestures of both hands. He was eager. Almost he was appealing.

To all of this talk the girl replied with short answers. A brief word. A syllable. Presently tears began to run down from her eyes. They fell on her round, bare arms. They fell on her hands, which were folded together. She was not talking at all, and indeed she did not seem even to be hearing what the big hunter said. Her eyes looked off at that distant thing of which they had been speaking before. They were sad eyes. They were like blue smoke. Looking at them, Standing Bull sighed a little.

Suddenly the white hunter jumped up from the table and threw his hands above his head. Standing Bull grinned, for he expected the blow to fall on the girl, but, instead, the white man struck his own head and then rushed from the room.

But still the young squaw paid no attention. She was still looking into the distance, still weeping. She sank into a chair. Her head fell against the wall. Her eyes closed. She wept no longer. She was as one who grief has sickened past tears.

Then by revelation Standing Bull knew what he should have known before. This was the girl.

Dim of eye she was now, but it is happiness that lights a woman, as fire lights a branch and the branch lights the forest. She wept, and she was in sorrow for the sake of a man who was far away, and that man was White Thunder. It was all clear, clearer than any story told in pictures, as though an old sage were at hand to explain their meaning.

Standing Bull slipped away through the woods and rejoined his anxious companions. He came among them with a glistening eye, but he said not a word. Much that was done on distant trails was better left untold until one returned to the village. For what was described on the trail, that was remembered, but what was unnamed at the time, afterward could be expanded.

He closed his eyes. He was regardless of the smoke from the fire that was pouring into his face. Somehow, he would be able to turn this night's adventure and the real peril he had endured into a story of some worth. He was sure of that, if only he could have patience. He would invent; it needs time to search the spirit.

Then, by dim degrees, his thoughts turned back to the white girls. He tried to think of the one of the dancing eyes. But instead, all that he had in mind was the eyes of the other, like blue smoke, covered with sorrow.

He wondered greatly how she would appear if she saw White Thunder. Was not White Thunder just as the girl? There was a veil over his eyes, also. Partly of thought and magic, partly of grief.

Standing Bull no longer wondered that his friend the white magician sorrowed for this girl. He was himself beginning to understand that there is other beauty than that found in red skins. The taste of it, like the taste of a strange and delightful food, entered the soul of Standing Bull.

He stood up. Rather, he leaped to his feet with a grunt that startled his companions out of slumber.

"What is wrong?" asked Red Shirt.

"Nothing," said the leader. "But the fire is all smoke, and the evil ghosts are throwing it into my face."

XIII

Big Samuel Brett hardly had settled to his second pipe and the narration of the day's hunting when a hand struck at the door. He went to open it, cautiously, one hand ready to thrust it home again and the other hand occupied with his rifle.

"It's Roger Lincoln," said a voice from the rain.

The door twitched wide, instantly, and Roger Lincoln came in, glistening with the wet, his deerskins soaked through and blackened.

"You been swimming in it, it looks like," said Samuel Brett. "Come in and dry yourself out at the stove."

Roger Lincoln waved his hand. "I've been stalking," he said.

"Deer?"

"Indians."

Brett whistled. His eyes widened, and then drew into the shadows of his brows. "Where?"

"The trail came here."

"To Fort Kendry?"

"To your house."

"It's that darned drunk Crow with the crooked nose," suggested Samuel Brett.

"It's a tall Cheyenne by the name of Standing Bull. He was watching through your door."

"I got nothing to do with the Cheyennes. Never traded with them, worse luck," said Brett.

"They want something to do with you, however. That fellow was very curious."

"Every Indian is half wolf," said Brett easily. "They gotta go snoopin' and sniffin' around. Why didn't you collar him?"

"My hands are off that gang until they leave the fort. I've told them so. After they start, the knife is out."

"With the Cheyennes? You could've picked an easier job. Ah, then I understand. It's young Torridon?"

"It is."

The face of Samuel Brett darkened. "You're wrong again, Lincoln. There never was a Torridon that wasn't a snake and deserved to be treated the same as a snake. And if . . . "

The hand of Lincoln was raised again, and Brett shrugged his shoulders.

"I shouldn't talk that way. I've tried to argue you out of it before, Roger. But if the kid showed a white face to you, he'll show a black face before you're through with him. I know the breed."

"Perhaps you do," said Roger Lincoln a little coldly. "But I've not stopped in to talk about Torridon. I've come to tell you that a hard-headed, hard-handed Cheyenne brave is watching you. Why, I don't know, but I don't think he's going to do you much good. Man, watch your house!"

He said it with gravity, and the other nodded assent.

"I'll get Murphy's dog, tomorrow, and keep it around. He's a man-eater, that brute. And Pat offered him to me."

"Take the dog by all means . . . and sleep light. Good bye."

He was gone, in spite of the hospitable protests of Brett. The door closed. Roger Lincoln went back toward his house with a mind filled with misgivings.

Samuel Brett, however, was not alarmed. He had lived all his days in the midst of danger. That which is too well known is apt to be taken too lightly.

To be sure, when he went to bed that night he saw that the door was well secured, and that his rifle and two pistols were at hand nearby him. But after that he slept profoundly, and the rumble of his snoring filled the house.

The night grew wilder and wilder.

Before morning, the Cheyennes in their clearing had been forced up from their blankets, and they huddled around a newly built fire, removing to the shelter of the trees. It was only a mock shelter. The heavy rain, driven far in through the foliage by the whip of the wind, came sluicing down upon them in quantities. Over their heads the storm yelled and roared, and the day came slowly upon them.

They prepared a meal of a few mouthfuls. When it was eaten, they smoked a pipe with some difficulties. And then Standing Bull asked for dreams.

Yellow Man was the only one who could oblige. He declared he had dreamed that he was back in the Cheyenne village, and that, in the middle of the night, he had stepped outside his lodge. Suddenly the night had become terribly dark. All was blackness. A wind hooted in his ears like an owl. And when he stumbled back toward the lodge, it was gone. He ran here and there. He could find nothing, though his teepee stood in the center of the camp.

At last a star began to shine. He found that he was alone in the midst of a great plain. Nothing was near him. There was no village in sight. It was as though the wind had blown him to a great distance. He dropped to the ground, thereby hoping to see something against the horizon. Something he did see. It was a tree standing on a hill. The star was right behind it, and, indeed, the star was in the middle of it. From the distant heavens, straight through that tree or ghost of a tree, the star was shining.

This was the dream of Yellow Man. Let anyone who could interpret it.

This strange story was received in silence. But when Yellow Man left the circle, a little later, Red Shirt remarked with a grunt: "My blood is cold, brothers, and I think that when we come to the lodge of Yellow Man, we will find the women and the children wailing in it."

There was no further comment, but all the braves had the same gloomy thought. Red Shirt insisted that this was a token that they should give up the attempt that they had in mind. Even if peace was not made with Roger Lincoln, it would be best to try nothing more, but to make the best and quickest way back to the village on the prairie.

Standing Bull answered, logically enough, that a dream in which a village disappeared and a star shone through the ghost of a tree might mean a great deal to Yellow Man, but it hardly had significance for the rest of the party or their work. He had made up his mind. They would attempt what they had come for.

That day, the storm still held, growing momently more violent. They could hear the roaring of the river, swollen with a great voice. And during the day, they went down to trade off their buffalo robes. Under the keen eye of Standing Bull and against his express admonition, they did not dare to take whiskey in exchange. And in the evening they went back to their camping grounds with a load of ammunition, a few knives, many trinkets and beads.

When the darkness came on, Standing Bull made his further preparations. Two of the men were to keep the bulk of the horses at the edge of the woods, prepared to rush them into the prairie on a moment's notice. The remaining four, and Standing Bull himself, were to go back with chosen ponies—and one extra mount—to the vicinity of the house of Samuel Brett.

There, a pair of the warriors would keep the animals at the edge of the trees, taking what care they could that the ponies should not neigh or make any noise of tramping or fighting. Then, accompanied by Red Shirt and Rushing Wind—especially chosen for this purpose by Standing Bull as being the keenest of the band that accompanied him—the leader would go toward the house and try to take the girl from it, in silence if he could, by force and slaughter of the rest of the household if necessary.

The others listened to the plan in silence. They saw that it was desperately bold. The explosion of a gun and a single shot would be enough to bring out the rest of the settlers, gun in hand. But not one of the braves would draw back from his leader in such a time of need. Certainly Rushing Wind and Red Shirt did not know fear.

All was done as had been planned, the horses were established under the trees that stood nearest to the house, and then Standing Bull began to approach, taking the lead, as was his right and his duty.

He went forward, crouching, shifting from bush to rock, and rock to bush, and gradually working his way closer. He had covered most of the distance when there was a snarl and then a furious barking just before him.

He heard the rush of a dog through the darkness!

XIV

There was no better watchdog in the world than that borrowed man-killer that now was lunging at the Indian. His was a crossed breed. He was mastiff, boar hound, and wolf, mixed discreetly. He had the cutting power of a wolf, the wind of a hound, and the grip of a mastiff, together with the heart of the latter dog. He was as good as half a dozen armed guards to keep off strollers and the overcurious, because men do not like to face the danger of a dog bite. The bite may only break the skin, but the broken skin is apt to lead to hydrophobia. Who can tell?

Standing Bull never had seen that dog before. He did not need to see him clearly, however, to realize what was coming. The monster charged through the whipping rain. Straight at him came the dog, with a savage, brutal intaken breath of satisfaction.

At the last instant the Cheyenne twisted on his side. A snake could not have moved more quickly. The dog shot past, trying in vain to check its impetus, and, as it went on, Standing Bull drove his hunting knife through the heart of the creature.

There was no sound. The dog fell limply, and Standing Bull wiped off the blade of the knife, listening intently as he did so.

Nothing stirred in the house. He could only trust that the sudden cessation of the growling of the big animal would not rouse suspicions in the house. And so far nothing indicated that they were on their watch. They had consigned their safety into the keeping of one power. That power now was removed, and Standing Bull felt that perhaps swift success would crown his work.

His two attending shadows drew close to him. They did not congratulate him on the deed he had just performed, but congratulation did not need to be spoken. Standing Bull felt that the very air was electric with the admiration of his friends.

Therefore he went on swiftly to the door. It was the one weak point of the house, being thin and, as already noted, full of cracks. It was the hope of Standing Bull that a little work with a sharp knife might so enlarge one of the cracks that he could reach the latch bar and open the door without more ado.

He worked rapidly, but with the greatest care. Even the squeak of a heavily pressed knife in wet wood might be enough to catch the ear of a sleeper and undo all that had been accomplished up to this point.

Presently, when the soft wood had yielded sufficiently, he thrust the point of the blade through the crack and worked it upward. It clicked on iron, the iron stirred, and with a slight creak of the hinges, the door sagged inward.

Big Standing Bull crouched on the threshold, his heart thundering in his breast like a charge of wild buffalo. But still nothing stirred in the interior. Neither the breath of fresh air entering, full of the dampness of the rain, nor the sound of the door turning on the hinges had been enough to disturb the slumberers—or were they waiting among the shadows all this while, smiling to themselves, their guns ready as soon as the door, like the mouth of a trap, had admitted sufficient victims?

Even on the verge of entering, Standing Bull thought of all these things, and hesitated. But something had to be done. The rain beat like hammers on the surface of the ground. It rattled on his own broad shoulders so loudly that he could have sworn that a whole tribe would have been alarmed by such a noise.

In through the door he went, and moved hastily to one side. The other two followed him. He could hear them breathing, and the faint creaking of a leather jacket as its wet folds were drawn tight at each inhalation.

He got to his feet, but, when he made a step, the water squelched and hissed in his moccasins. He had to pause again, listening with the rigidity of a statue, and then he sat down and dragged off the moccasins. In his naked feet he proceeded with greater ease.

First he went to the stove and from this took out a half-burned stick of wood. There was a glowing coal at one end, while the other end was cool enough to hold. The coal made a dim point of light that tarnished quickly in the open air, and then freshened to an amazing degree when blown upon.

Standing Bull was satisfied. It would have been very well if he could have guessed in what room the girl was sleeping, but, since he did not know, he would have to look.

All the doors stood open upon the big kitchen, in order that the fire might send its heat through all the chambers. This was partly an advantage and partly a great disaster. For though it meant that he would have no difficulty in opening the doors, every move that he made was now likely to strike upon the ears of all the sleepers.

The two helpers went behind him. He had told them beforehand what he wanted them to do. He dared not entrust the actual kidnapping to them. He felt that the body of this slender white girl was so fragile that it would have to be touched with the greatest care.

He stepped through the first doorway. It was like walking into the throat of a cannon. Then, blowing softly on the dying coal, he got from it the faintest of glows, yet enough to enable his straining eyes to distinguish the vast shoulders of the white hunter in the bed.

Instantly he veiled the coal with his hand, and, as he stepped back toward the door, he was startled to hear a woman's voice exclaim: "Sam! Oh, Sam!"

"Aye?" growled big Samuel Brett.

"There's something wrong!"

"What could be wrong?"

"I . . . don't know . . . I just have a feeling. Sam, do get up and see if everything's all right."

"Now, what's ailin' you?" asked Samuel Brett. "What could be wrong?"

73

The Indian, in the darkness by the door, kept his hand on the haft of his knife. What the words meant, he could not understand. But his very blood was frozen with fear.

"I don't know . . . "

"I *do* know. Nobody could get past that dog. It's got eight legs and two heads. It can look both ways at once. I never seen such a dog. And if it found a man, it'd eat him."

"Suppose that he was knocked senseless . . . "

"Supposin' that the sky wasn't blue, well, it might be green!"

"You can bully all you please. I tell you, I got a feelin' that there's somebody in this house."

"Hey? What?" asked Samuel Brett in changed tones. "Well, I'll get up and look around."

The bed squeaked as he sat up. But then the cool of the night air made him shiver. "I'm darned if I get up and catch a cold for the sake of pleasin' the whim of a silly old woman. You go to sleep and leave me be." He settled back with a groan of comfort into the warmness of the bed.

Freed from the direct danger, Standing Bull drew once more into the kitchen. There were two other doorways. Into which one should he go next?

He chose the middle one. A gesture in the dark placed both the Cheyennes on guard at the door of the white man's room. Then Standing Bull proceeded into the next chamber. At the first flare of the coal beneath his breath he found himself looking into the same face that he had seen in the kitchen of the house—the same pale face, the same pale hair. But the eyes were not dim. They were sparkling and wide with incalculable terror as the girl sat up in the bed and supported herself with both shaking arms.

How long had she been there, awake, listening, thinking that she heard a sound, denying that it could be so?

Standing Bull went straight toward her and she shrank back against the wall. Her lips parted and her throat worked, but no scream would come. Time was short with Standing Bull and every instant in that house was of infinite danger to him; yet he dared not take her out into such a night clad only in a thin night-gown of cheap cotton.

He pointed to the clothes that lay upon a chair and made a commanding gesture. She obeyed, her enchanted eyes of terror fixed on him, and her movements slow, like those of one whose body is numbed with deadly cold.

He had drawn a knife that the fear of it might stimulate her and keep her from screaming for help. Under the dull glow of the coal, the blade of that knife seemed to run again with blood, and he could see her like a shadow among shadows dressing with stumbling hands and numb fingers from which the clothes slipped away.

At last, at a sound in the next room, he could wait no longer. He caught up a heavy buffalo robe that covered the foot of the bed, and, throwing it around Nancy Brett, took her in his arms. Hers was like the weight of a child, thought Standing Bull. He strode to the door of the chamber.

Inside the next room, Samuel Brett was rumbling: "Darn me if I can go to sleep. Where did you leave the candle? Eh?" There was a noise of fumbling. The man of the house began to mutter beneath his breath, impatiently.

But Standing Bull with his burden went on toward the rear door, and, with Rushing Wind carefully opening it, he passed through and out into the night.

There had been only one sound from his captive, and that, as they reached the open air, was a faint sigh. She became limp in his arms and he knew that she had fainted. So much the better.

He began to run. Inside the house there was a sudden shout. The rear door was slammed shut with a great crash, as Red Shirt leaped through and swung the door to behind him. In another moment the whole settlement would be up.

XV

The shout of Samuel Brett was enough to have alarmed whole legions. And the ears to which that shout did not reach certainly were touched by the sound of rifle shots, as Brett ran from his house toward his horses. From every house men began to turn out, but for a time they were a little uncertain as to whether they should fly to the fort for protection, stand firm on the defense, or else act as aggressors.

By now Standing Bull had reached his horses. He mounted. It was unfortunate that the girl had to be carried. But perhaps it was better to have her senseless than that with her screams she should guide the whites as with a flaming torch.

The five galloped back to the main body of the horses at the edge of the wood—the whole body then rushed out across the plain beyond, and the thick curtain of the rain drew together instantly behind them.

The care with which Standing Bull had distributed his forces from the start now began to tell, for there was no sign of sudden pursuit. He did not follow the river, but cut back across the hill, hoping that the enemy would hunt for the Cheyennes along the riverbanks, for that was the easiest course. In that direction the greatest number of miles could be made.

Now, when the first rush of the flight was over, Nancy Brett recovered her senses with a groan. She was given no sympathy. They made the briefest of halts, during which she was clapped into a saddle and tied securely to it. A whip cracked on the haunches of the half-wild Indian pony. It pitched high into the air, and came down running, with the Indians rushing their own mounts beside it. So they dashed on into the night, and the cold whip of the rain in her face began to rouse Nancy Brett.

It was so strange, so utterly incomprehensible, that her mind was in a whirl. She knew something about Indians and their ways. They might capture the daughter of a great and rich man and hold her for ransom. Or an Indian might even kidnap a woman with whom he was in love. But she was certain that neither of these motives appeared here.

She was sure that she never had seen this monster of an Indian before. And as they tore on through the night and the dawn began to come nearer, she looked more curiously at her captor. No, she never had seen that homely profile before.

When day came, they pitched camp—or rather made a short halt—at the bank of a stream. There the saddles were changed, the used horses turned into the herd, and the next best mounts requisitioned. In this way, they would shift the saddles half a dozen times in twenty-four hours of work, reusing the horses in turn. Standing Bull, regarding his captive, was amazed to find that she seemed to be bearing up against fatigue and fear very well indeed. There was more color in her face than there had been when she wept in the kitchen of the house of Samuel Brett.

He wished that he possessed sufficient English to pronounce the name of the great white medicine man to whom he was bringing her. But he did not even know that name in the first place.

She made no trouble, however. Her grave, blue eyes never stared at them. She seemed only watchful to do what was wanted of her. And Standing Bull wondered greatly. She acted, in fact, almost as an Indian girl would have acted at such a time as this.

All the day they rode on under a gray sky. There were only the halts for the changing of saddles, and to eat a little dried meat at the same time. The girl was no longer tied to her horse, but the pony she rode was tethered to the saddle of Standing Bull. He watched her begin to droop as the afternoon wore away. When they at last halted on the edge of night, she almost fell from the saddle.

"She must sleep," said Red Shirt uneasily, and looked toward the northwestern horizon.

"She must sleep," answered Standing Bull. "But first she must eat."

She would have refused food. He commanded with a savage growl, and she choked down a few morsels in fear. Then, wrapped in a robe, she slept. The Indians already were sleeping, except Standing Bull. He needed no sleep. His heart was full of glory for the thing that he had done. He began to frame in his mind the song he would sing when he reappeared in the Cheyenne village. The notes of the chant ached in his throat and the sweetness of fame among his fellows made the head of Standing Bull sway a little from side to side.

The sky cleared during the night. When the clouds had blown down to the horizon, he roused his sleepy command. He touched the girl, and she sprang to her feet with a faint cry. In two minutes they were on their way again.

So they pressed on until they were three days from Fort Kendry, and trouble for the first time overtook them. Had it not been for Nancy Brett, they could have made somewhat better time, and yet the horses hardly could have stood up to more work. They were growing very thin. Sometimes at a halt many of them were too weary to begin to graze.

And while the party was in this condition, on the pale verge of morning, saddling for the day's ride, Yellow Man was seen to throw up his hands, whirl, and fall without sound, while the sharp, small clang of a rifle struck at their ears. Glancing wildly about them, they could see a wisp of smoke rising above a small cluster of shrubs and trees nearby.

"Take two men," said Standing Bull to Red Shirt. "Take three if you will, and go back. If there is one man, bring us his scalp. If there are more, skirmish and delay them."

Red Shirt went instantly to execute the order. With Standing Bull and the girl remained only that capable young brave, Rushing Wind. And the three of them, with the larger body of the horses, struck away across the prairie. As they did so, they saw

Red Shirt's party approach the trees in a wide circle, and out from the trees rode a man on a fine, gray horse.

Roger Lincoln!

They knew well that it was he the instant the gray began to run. It was not likely that two gray horses on that prairie had the long and flowing gallop of the mare, Comanche. She drifted easily away toward the north, with the party of Red Shirt and his three braves hopelessly laboring in the rear.

Glancing keenly at the girl, Standing Bull made sure by the light in her eye that she, too, had recognized the rescuer and that hope had come to her. So strong was that hope that it enabled her to endure a whole day of savage riding, and as the evening drew near they knew that the Cheyenne village was not far away. So great had their speed been that the party sent back to block Roger Lincoln had not been sighted again since first they disappeared. Perhaps the gray mare had failed, after all, and the four warriors now were blockading Roger Lincoln in some nest of rocks.

So hoped Standing Bull, and smiled at the thought. He talked with Rushing Wind as they changed saddles for the last time. Yellow Man had fulfilled his weird dream of the night before. He was dead, but his body, lashed to a pony's back, was being brought back to his family. Not two hours of steady riding lay before them. And if the girl collapsed, they could tie her to her saddle and finish the ride at any rate, like a whirlwind covering the plains.

So, as they made the change of saddles, they helped her to her new mount. She was a dead weight in their hands. With sunken head and lips compressed she sat the saddle, both hands clinging feebly to the pommel.

"Tie her now in her place," suggested Rushing Wind. "She is very weak."

It was done at once, and, while Standing Bull made sure that the fastenings were secure, he heard an excited call from Rushing Wind.

On the northern horizon, clearly seen against the red of the sunset sky, there was a flash as of silver, and, when Standing Bull looked more closely, he made out a horseman coming steadily toward them.

Roger Lincoln! Or was it one of the Cheyennes who, having killed Lincoln, had sent back one of their number on the captured horse to give the news to the village and bring out food and a medicine man to the wounded of the party?

So muttered Standing Bull, but Rushing Wind cried excitedly: "I tell you I can see that it is the white man! I can see the paleness of his long hair about his shoulders even at this distance. But what has become of the others?"

"He has dodged them," said Standing Bull gloomily. "Or else . . ."

"Or else he has killed them!" exclaimed Rushing Wind. "He has killed them, Standing Bull. I feel that they are dead men and that we never shall look on them again. Shall we go back to face him?"

"He has great medicine in his rifle," said Standing Bull in grave thought, "but I would not run away from any single warrior. Nevertheless, it is not for us to think of ourselves. We are working to bring happiness to White Thunder, and through him to the entire tribe. Is it true?"

"That is true," admitted Rushing Wind, still staring at the far distant rider.

"Let us finish that work," said Standing Bull. "Afterward we may be able to ride out and find Roger Lincoln on the war trail. I hope so. In his death there would be enough fame to make ten braves happy. Now let us ride. Pray to the wind to help on our horses, or the white man will send our souls where he has sent all five of our companions before us. Ride, Rushing Wind, and call on the ghosts of our fathers to make the legs of our horses strong."

By the time they were in the saddle, the form of Roger Lincoln was beginning to grow more and more distinct until, even in that half light, they were sure of the blond hair about his shoulders.

Nancy Brett cast one last, desperate look over her shoulder, and then set her teeth to endure the last stage of the journey as well as she could. If she was not strong, she was not brittle stuff that breaks. Only by degrees her power had failed her in this long forced march.

Making no effort to keep the horse herd running before them now, Standing Bull drove the last three ponies straight across the prairie and toward the Cheyenne village.

XVI

How earnestly Standing Bull prayed for the night, then. And night was coming down upon them fast. In a few moments, there would not be sufficient illumination to enable the white man to use the great magic of his rifle on the Cheyennes, and without that gun Standing Bull feared Lincoln not at all.

But the gray mare, Comanche, drew closer and closer. She seemed supported on wings, so rapidly did she overtake the straining Indian ponies. She had been matching her wonderful speed that day against half a dozen animals, and yet she had the strength to make such a final burst as this.

Standing Bull, throwing glances over his shoulder from moment to moment, suddenly exclaimed: "Rushing Wind, my brother! Look and tell me if what I think is true! That the gray gains on us no longer!"

Back came the joyous cry of the younger brave: "She has lost her wings! She is flying no longer!"

"Ride hard, ride hard!" urged Standing Bull. "Now that he cannot gain, he will no longer try to push the mare. He will take to the ground and fire on us."

He had rightly interpreted the intention of the white scout. Now that the last strength had gone from beautiful Comanche, Roger Lincoln pulled her up short and dropped to his full length on the prairie. It was wonderfully long range, and the light was very bad indeed—far less than a half light. Yet at the explosion of the gun, Rushing Wind ducked his head and lurched forward with a stifled cry.

"Brother, brother!" called Standing Bull anxiously. "Did the bullet strike you?"

"No, no!" answered the boy. "But I heard it singing past me more loudly than a hornet. I am not hurt. Heammawihio, to you I vow a fine buffalo hide, well painted. I shall make your heart glad because you have saved me today."

There was no second report. In another moment they were out of sight of Roger Lincoln in the thickening dusk. And now the stars began to come out, pale and winking. Other lights like stars, like red stars, appeared on the southern horizon.

"That is our city," said Standing Bull. "We are free from pursuit."

He drew up his horse. So weak was the girl that, as her horse stopped, she lurched forward and almost sprawled to the ground. But she recovered at once, and sat with stiffened lip.

"Look," said Standing Bull to his fellow warrior. "I have never seen such a woman before. I saw her in the house in Fort Kendry, crying as a baby cries. I smiled and thought she was worthless. But you see, my friend. Out of such metal a man could make arrowheads and knives. White Thunder . . . you will see . . . he will be mad with joy."

"I shall stand by and watch," said Rushing Wind, laughing. "He pretends that nothing matters to him. He yawns when warriors make great gifts to him. But now we will see him cry out and shout and dance. But, for me, I prefer the girls of the Cheyennes. It needs a strong back to dig roots and a big hand to hold an axe."

Standing Bull, however, made no answer. Once or twice he turned and stared earnestly into the darkness behind him, but there was no sound or trace of Roger Lincoln. It was as though he had permitted the night to swallow him after that single shot into which he had thrown all his skill.

Now the Indian leader rode close to the girl. With a strong hand beneath her arm, he supported her greatly. She let her head fall straight back, sometimes, so utterly weakened was she.

"She is tired. She is like a dead reed. It may break in the wind, Standing Bull," cautioned the younger man.

Again Standing Bull made no reply, but looked earnestly on the face of the girl. There was no moon. There were no stars. Yet he could see her. It was as though he beheld her by the light of her own whiteness.

They came to the edge of the village before they were discovered. They entered, of course, in the midst of pandemonium. And straight they went to the lodge of White Thunder. It was as white as his name, made of the skins of nineteen buffalo cows, all of an age, all killed at the perfect season, or cured in exactly the same fashion.

Fires glimmered dimly through open lodge entrances. In the center of White Thunder's lodge there was a fire, also. Standing Bull took the girl from her horse. She lay in his arms with closed eyes. Then he stalked into the lodge.

Paul Torridon lolled against a backrest, by the firelight, carefully sharpening a knife. Young Willow was at work cleaning the great iron cooking pot that simmered over the central fire all the day.

"Brother," said Standing Bull, "I have come back from a far land and a far people to bring you a present."

At the sound of his voice, all the noise outside the lodge was hushed. Only a child cried out, and the slap of a rebuking hand sounded like the popping of a whiplash. All that Standing Bull said clearly could be heard.

"When I brought you alone," said Standing Bull simply, "I saw that you were unhappy. I decided that I would bring you a present that would fill your lodge with content."

Here Torridon stood up and waved a hand in acknowledgment. Then, taking closer heed of the burden that the big Indian carried in his arms, Torridon stepped closer.

"She should be worth much to you," said Standing Bull in conclusion, "because five good men and brave warriors have died that she might be brought to you." Suddenly he stretched out his arms and the burden in them.

Torridon peered at it curiously, the white face, the closed eyes—and then with a great cry he caught Nancy Brett to his breast. Young Willow, her eyes glittering like polished steel, threw a robe beside the fire, and on it Torridon kneeled, and then laid down the girl, crying out her name in a voice half of joy and half of sorrow.

Standing Bull strode from the teepee, herding Rushing Wind before him into the outer darkness. He raised his great arm and stilled the clamor that began to break out from the crowd that surrounded him.

"Be still," he said. "In that lodge there is a woman who is worth five men. Heammawihio demanded their lives before we could bring her here. And he knows the worth of human beings. It is her spirit that is great. Her body is not strong. Now all go away. Your shouting would kill her. Go away. The village should be silent."

Out of respect for him, the throng was still. He walked through them to his teepee, and there was Owl Woman, the perfect wife, waiting to greet him. The firelight turned her to golden copper; her smile was beautiful. But to Standing Bull she suddenly seemed like a hideous cartoon of a woman, with a vast, stretching mouth, and a great nose, and high cheek bones. He made himself take her in his arms. She had been boiling fat meat in the pot. The odor of cookery clung to her garments. And Standing Bull remembered how he had ridden grandly from Fort Kendry, and the slender body that had lain in his arms, and the fragrance as of spring wildflowers that had blown from her hair against his face.

The Steel Box

"The Steel Box" first appeared as a five-part serial, "The Stranger," in Street & Smith's *Western Story Magazine* beginning in the January 12, 1929 issue. It was one of eleven serials to be published that year by Frederick Faust. It is an unusual Western story in which two cowpunchers, Tiny Lew Sherry and Pete Lang, find themselves in the midst of a mystery involving suicide, murder, family intrigue, a hilltop fortress, a ship lost at sea, revenge, and romance. This is the first time it appears in its entirety since its original publication.

I

They were holding beef out of Clayrock, for the UX outfit. Eighteen hundred steers, strong with good feeding and apt to want their own way, were quite enough for two cowpunchers to handle, even two like Pete Lang and Lew Sherry, whose range name was Tiny Lew. But the beef had had their fill of good grass on this day, and had been drifted enough miles to make them at once contented and sleepy. They began to lie down, slumping heavily to their knees, and so gradually down—unlike the grace of a mustang dropping for the night.

"Trouble and beef . . . that's all you get out of a bunch like this," said Tiny Lew Sherry as he circled his horse quietly around the herd. "And *we* don't get the beef," he concluded.

"Shut up and start singing," said Pete Lang. "Which if you was an orator, these shorthorns wouldn't vote for you, anyway. Sing, darn you," said Pete Lang.

"You start it, then. I got no singing in my throat tonight."

THE STEEL BOX

Lang began, to the tune of "My Bonnie Lies over the Ocean."

Last night as I lay on the prairie,
And looked at the stars in the sky,
I wondered if ever a cowboy
Would drift to that sweet by and by.

Roll on, roll on,
Roll on, little doggies, roll on, roll on,
Roll on, roll on,
Roll on, little doggies, roll on!

"Will you quit it?" asked Tiny Lew plaintively. "It makes me ache to hear such mournful lingo."

"You've got too much education," said Lang. "I always told you so. If there was any nacheral sense born into you, it was read out in books. But there's that speckled steer got up again. Will you sing him down, sucker, or are you gonna start wrangling until the whole herd begins to mill?"

Tiny Lew tipped back his head and his bass voice flowed in a thick, rich current, carefully subdued.

There's old 'Aunt' Jess, that hard old cuss,
Who never would repent;
He never missed a single meal
Nor never paid a cent.
But old 'Aunt' Jess like all the rest
To death he did resign
And in his bloom went up the flume
In the days of Forty-Nine.

The speckled steer lay down again with a grunt and a puff.

"A fine, soothing song is that," sneered Pete Lang. "Let 'em have some more. You oughta be singing in a hall, Tiny."

Tiny Lew, unabashed, continued his song with another stanza.

There is 'Ragshag' Jim, the roaring man,
Who could outroar a buffalo, you bet;
He roared all day and he roared all night,
And I guess he is roaring yet.
One night Jim fell in a prospect hole—
It was a roaring bad design—
And in that hole Jim roared out his soul,
In the days of Forty-Nine.

"I've had enough," said Pete Lang. "Whistle to 'em, son."

Slowly the two cowpunchers walked or jogged their horses around the night herd, sometimes with low, soft whistles; sometimes they sang a word or two of a song and hummed the rest of it, and the great, fat steers, plump for shipping on the next day, quieted under the soothing of the familiar sounds, and with that human reassurance about them—like a wall to shut away danger of wolf or mountain lion, danger of the very stars and winds—they went to sleep.

Then the two cowpunchers drew their horses together and let the mustangs touch noses.

"It's quite a town, Clayrock, by the look of the lights," said Tiny Lew.

"I've had my share of talking juice in yonder, under them lights," remarked Pete Lang. "It's got one trouble. The kind of red-eye they peddle there over the bar ain't made for boys, but for growed-up men. You'd better keep away from that joint, Tiny."

Tiny Lew stretched forth a hand and took his companion firmly by the back of his coat collar. Then he heaved Pete Lang a yard out of the saddle and held him dangling against the stars.

"Do I let you drop, you little, sawed-off son-of-a-gun?" asked Tiny Lew pleasantly.

"I'll have your gizzard out for this," declared Pete Lang, keeping his voice equally low, for fear of disturbing the steers.

Tiny deposited him back in the saddle. "It's so long since I've had a drink," he said, "that I'm all rusty inside. I'm lined with red rust, two inches deep. I'm more full of sand than a desert. A couple of buckets full of red-eye would hardly be heard to splash inside of me, Pete."

At this, Pete Lang chuckled. "Look here," he said. "You go in and tip over a couple. These here doggies are plumb sleepy, and I can hold 'em till morning. Go in and tip over a couple, and then come back and I'll make a visit for myself, before morning."

The big man glanced over the herd. Every steer was down. Now and again, the sound of a horn clicked faintly against a horn, or a tail swished could be heard distinctly, so still was the night.

"I'd better stay," said Tiny Lew with indecision.

"You drift, son," replied his companion. "Besides, you're only a nuisance, tonight. The thoughts that you got in your head, they'd disturb the peace of a whole town, let alone a night herd like this. Get out of here, Tiny. You've near strangled me already." He touched his throat, where the strain of his collar had chafed the skin when Sherry had lifted him from the saddle. The big fellow slapped Lang on the shoulder.

"So long, Pete. Wish me luck, and no fights, and a safe return."

"All right," said Lang, "but I warn you that a mule makes a safer ride than a horse into Clayrock . . . there's so much quicksand and so many holes in the ground. Don't find no friends, and don't stay to make none, but just tip down a couple and come on back."

"Right as can be," said Tiny Lew, and turned his pony's nose toward the lights of the town.

He rode a pinto, only fifteen hands high, but made to carry weight, even weight such as that of Tiny, and tough as a mountain goat. They split straight across country, jumping two fences that barred the way, and so entered at last the first street of Clayrock. It was a big, rambling town, with comfortable yards around the houses, and, as Tiny Lew rode in, he could hear the soft rushing sound made by sprinklers on the lawns; he could smell the fragrance of the gardens, too, and the umbrella trees stood in shapely files on either side of the way.

"Civilized," said Tiny to himself. "Pete was stringing me along a little."

He came to a bridge over a little river, and, in spite of his hurry, he reined in his horse to watch the flash and swing of the current as it dipped around a bend of the stream. There was sufficient distance from the arched center of the bridge to the nearest houses to enable him to look about him, over the head of Clayrock, as it were, and he saw that the town was snuggled down among the hills—easy hills for riding, he judged, by the round outlines of the heads of the hills. Only to the south there was a streak of darkness against the higher sky, and the glimmer of a number of lights that he thought, at first, must be great stars.

But then he realized that stars cannot shine through such a dark cloud, and finally he was aware that it was a flat-faced cliff that rose over Clayrock—the very feature that gave the town its name, of course. The select center of the town, no doubt.

Tiny Lew went on. He had no desire to see select centers, but presently, on the farther side of the river, he found the houses closer together. The gardens ended. People were in the streets. He passed a moving-picture house where the sign was illuminated with crimson lights. And so he reached the Parker Place.

There were two larger hotels in Clayrock, but they were not like the Parker Place. It stood off a bit by itself, on a hummock, so that it was able to surround itself with a narrow wedge of lawn or garden, and it had a beaming look of hospitality. Tiny Lew Sherry did not wait for a second thought, but turned in the head of his mount toward the stable. There he saw his horse placed at a well-filled rack, and went into the hostelry.

No sooner did he push open the door than he heard a chorus sung in loud, cheerful voices—the chorus of a range song, which made him feel at home at once. He went into the bar. A dozen cowpunchers reached out hands for him, but Sherry broke their grips and went on into the gaming room. He knew that he was too sober to drink with fellows such as these.

In the rear room there was not a great deal of light except for three bright pools of it over the three tables that were occupied, but there was comparative quiet. That is to say, the roar from the bar was like the noise of a sea breaking on a hollow beach. It was so loud that the bartender had to ask twice what he would have.

Sherry had no chance to answer for himself. From the next table rose a slender form—a tall and graceful man who tapped the bartender's shoulder. "Not the regular poison, but some of mine," he said. "I can see that you've made a voyage and have just come to port, partner. And a good thirst like that shouldn't be thrown away on the filth they have behind the bar, out yonder."

Sherry was willing to agree. He thanked the stranger and asked him to sit down; as a matter of fact, he already was seating himself, uninvited.

The drinks were brought. The stranger raised his glass, and Sherry saw that the lean, brown hand of the other shook a little.

"Drink deep," he said.

And Sherry drank, but his mind was troubled.

II

He was troubled for several reasons, any of which would have been good enough, but the main one was a sort of savage keenness in the eye of the other. He was a lank man, with a yellowish skin, and a proud, restless way of turning his head from side to side, and in this head there was the most active and blazing pair of eyes that Sherry ever had seen.

"You hail from where, stranger?" asked this fellow.

"I've been punching cows for the UX outfit," said Sherry. "What's your line?"

"You punch cows?" said the other, dwelling on this answer before he made his own reply. "I've seen my storms, but I've never had to duck into such a rotten port as that to weather them. Cowpunching!"

He laughed shortly, and the gorge of Sherry rose. But, like most big men, it took a long time to warm him thoroughly with anger. He was willing to waive the peculiarities of a stranger, particularly since he was drinking this man's liquor.

"You've never been a sailor?" the host asked.

"No," said Sherry.

"You've never lived, then," said the other.

"What's your name?" said Sherry.

"My name is Harry Capper. What's yours?"

"Sherry is my name. I'll let you into the know. Some of the boys around here would take it pretty hard if they heard you at work slamming punching as a trade."

"Would they? Would they?" snapped Capper, his buried eyes blazing more brightly than ever.

"You have to do the thing you find to do," said Sherry with good humor. "Besides, you couldn't sail a ship through this sort of dry land."

He laughed a little at his own remark, but Capper refused to be softened.

"I thought that you looked like a man who would be doing a man's work. There's no work off the sea. There's no life off the sea . . . except on an island."

He laughed in turn, with a sort of drawling sneer. Sherry made up his mind that the wits of Harry Capper were more than a little unsettled.

"I'll tell you what I'll do," said Capper. "I'll spot any landsman ten years, and show him more life in half the time at sea. Rough and smooth. Into the wind and with it. What does a landsman ever get a chance to do? But suppose you have four thousand tons of steel under you, and the steel loaded with a cargo, and the engines crashing and smashing, and a rotten crew to work the craft, and leagues between you and your port, and a fortune if you get to it . . . well, that's living!"

"You've commanded a ship?"

"I never sailed in command, but I've been first officer to bring more than one ship home. You don't always finish where you start. That's one thing about the sea, too."

Again he laughed, and more than ever Sherry was convinced that this man's brain was addled. He would have liked, too, to hear something about the steps by which the other had risen to the command of vessels when he sailed in subordinate roles. He had no opportunity, for suddenly Capper started to his feet.

He sat down again, almost at once. His nostrils quivered, and his eyes flared more villainously than ever; he was staring at Sherry with an almost murderous intensity as he said: "I'll show you some of the things that you learn at sea. Look at the fellow just coming into the room. He looks like a swell, don't he?"

Sherry saw a man of middle age come into the room and stand for a moment near the door, drawing off his gloves slowly. He had a fine, thoughtful face, a most magnificent forehead, and the whole bearing of a quiet gentleman who lives more inside himself than in the world.

"You'd say that a fine gentleman like that wouldn't talk to a bird like Harry Capper, beachcomber and what-not?"

"And will he?" asked Sherry, beginning to feel a good deal of disgust.

"I think he will . . . if I ask him," said Capper. "You'll see, now." He turned suddenly in his chair. "Hello," he said. "Come over and have a drink with me."

The newcomer started a little at the sound of this voice, but now he replied courteously: "I'm not drinking, Capper. Thank you."

The sailor laughed in his unusually disagreeable manner. "You'd better think again," he said with a great deal of ugliness.

The other hesitated for a moment, then he came to the table and sat down.

"This here is by name of Sherry," said Capper. "And this is Oliver Wilton, an old messmate of mine. Ain't you, Oliver?"

The other made a little gesture that might have expressed assent, or simple irritation.

"Sure, he's a messmate of mine," said Capper. "We've sailed around the world together. We got a lot of the same charts in our heads. We've seen places. We've seen Bougainville Island, and Choiseul. And Treasury Island, and Ronongo, and Buena Vista, and San Cristobal. Have we seen them, mate?"

He reached across and slapped the shoulder of Oliver Wilton, and the latter winced from the touch of the sailor. He had refused whiskey and was merely making a pretense of sipping his beer, while he watched Capper with an extraordinary expression that, Sherry thought, contained elements of disgust, fear, and keen anger.

And the surprise of Sherry grew. It was beyond words amazing that a gentleman should submit to such familiarity from such a fellow as Capper.

"But Oliver left the sea," said Capper. "You don't mind if I call you Oliver, do you, Oliver?"

"I suppose not," said the other.

Capper grinned with delight at the torment he was inflicting. "Of course, you don't mind," he said. "Not a good fellow and a rare sport like you . . . why, the things that we got to remember together would fill a book, and a good fat book, at that! Am I right, old man?"

Oliver Wilton bit his lip.

"Close-mouthed old boy he is," said Capper, "but always willing to stand his round of drinks. Slow in the talk, but fast in the drinking was always his way."

At this broad hint, Wilton presently ordered a round of drinks, and Sherry could not help noticing the curious glance that the waiter cast at the sailor and at Wilton who would sit at such a table.

"You're not taking more than you can hold?" said Wilton to the sailor.

"Me?" chuckled Capper. "I always got room in my hold for the right kind of goods to be stowed away in an extra corner. Always! So bring on the new shipment."

The drinks were duly ordered, and then Wilton said suddenly: "I'll see that they fill out of the right bottle. They have a way of substituting in this place." He got up and hurried from the table.

Capper leaned back in his chair, his face filled with malicious satisfaction. "He's a rum old boy, eh?" he said. "But he's on the hook. Oh, he can wriggle if he wants to, but he can't get off the hook. It's stuck into his gills. I suppose," he went on, his face flushing with a sort of angry triumph, "that there's nothing that he wouldn't give me, if I asked for it. I start with asking for a drink, but I might ask more. Oh, I might ask a whole cargo from him. But he's got that good a heart that he never could turn down an old shipmate."

He laughed again in that peculiarly disagreeable manner of his, and Sherry stirred in his chair. He had had enough of this company and he determined to leave after the present round. Moreover, Pete Lang would be expecting his return before long.

Wilton came back, himself carrying the tray.

"There you are," said Capper. "I told you he was a rare old sport. Pay for the drinks and play waiter to bring 'em, too. That's his way. Big-hearted and an open hand for all. That's him, always."

Wilton set down the drinks.

He seemed much more cheerful, now, although Sherry could not help suspecting that there was something assumed in the present good nature. But he sat down and offered the glasses with a smile.

"Good luck and good health to you, Capper," he said, "and to you."

"Why," said Capper, leaning a little over the table, "that's a kind thing, sir. A mighty kind way of putting things. And here's to you, with all my heart."

It seemed that Capper was genuinely moved by the cheerful manner of the man he had been tormenting, and he showed his emotion in his voice.

Sherry, in the meantime, with a nod to the others, picked up a glass, in haste to be done and away.

Half the contents were down his throat before he heard the exclamation of Wilton: "Hello! That's not your glass!"

At that, he lowered the glass. It had had rather a bitter taste, he thought. Already Capper had finished the glass he had taken up, and, hearing the alarmed exclamation of Wilton, he now snatched the one from the hand of Sherry and swallowed off the contents, saying, with his brutal laugh: "I've got to have my own, of course."

Sherry, half disgusted, stared at Capper. His temper had been frayed thin by the repeated insolence of the other, and now the striking muscles up and down his arm began to tighten.

"I ain't had enough drinks," said Capper suddenly, "to make me feel so dizzy. I . . . " He half rose from his chair and slumped heavily back into it, his head canting over upon one shoulder.

"Gents," said Sherry, "I've gotta leave you. I'll pay for a round, but then I have to start back . . . "

He rose in turn, and then a stunning darkness struck him back into his chair and he heard a voice, apparently from a great distance, saying: "Here is a pair of helpless drunks. What will you do with them?"

III

Flashes of sense returned to Sherry, thereafter. He knew that he was being dragged, half carried, to another place. He knew that he was allowed to slump heavily to the floor. And after that, he had a sense of cold and darkness. When he was able to get to his knees, his eyes were still half open, half shut, and it was at this time that he heard the crash of a revolver, inhaled the pungent fumes of burned powder, and was dimly aware of the red spitting of fire.

That roused him fully and quickly to his senses, and, starting to his feet, he stumbled upon a revolver that lay upon the floor before him. He picked up the gun and found the barrel warm to his touch, and a wisp of smoke floated in the deep, narrow gullet of the weapon. It was his own revolver! He knew it by four significant notches that he had filed into the handles of it for certain reasons best known to himself.

Startled by this, he look around, and then he saw the stranger, Capper, lying on his side against the wall, with a crimson trickle of blood down his face, and an ugly, purple-rimmed blotch on his forehead. He was dead, and Sherry knew it at a glance. He did not go near the dead body, but he looked wildly about him. There was only one means of escape, but that appeared a simple one—a large window at the farther side of the room. To this he ran. It was locked!

But what was that to Sherry? Outside, he saw the ground; by fortune he had been placed upon the lowest floor of the hotel, and he was a mere stride from freedom.

A hand struck at the door.

"What the dickens is up in there?" asked a rough voice.

For an answer Sherry took his Colt by the barrel and with the heavy butt of the gun he smashed out a panel of the window. A second stroke brought out three more, and a third opened a gap through which he could easily make his exit, but at this moment the door was sent open with a crash.

Sherry whirled against the wall, his Colt ready. It was not the first time that he had had to fight his way out from a tight corner, but apparently the hotelkeepers at Clayrock were more thoroughly prepared for trouble than the hotelkeepers of other communities. No fewer than five men charged through the doorway, and Sherry, in his first glance, saw a sawed-off shotgun—most convincing of all persuaders—a rifle, and three leveled revolvers.

Courage is admirable, and fighting skill is delightful in its full employment, but even a disposition such as that of Sherry could see that this was not the time to strike back. It was better to be armed with a conscious innocence than to use his gun.

"Stick up your hands!" came the grim order.

And he obeyed quietly.

They found the dead body at once. There was an outbreak of exclamations. They herded Sherry into a corner of the room and took his gun away from him; an armed guard stood upon either side, while the other three lifted the dead man and placed him on the bed.

"He'll never be deader in a thousand years than he is now," pronounced one who Sherry recognized as the waiter who just had served him.

"And what'll we do with this bird?" asked another.

"Stick him in the jail."

"Why in the jail? Here's his gun warm in his hand. Judge Rope is about good enough for this bum."

"Bill is right," said another. Then: "What you gotta say about this, stranger?"

Before Sherry could speak, a quiet voice said through the shattered window: "If you boys will listen to me, I think I can explain this."

"It's Mister Wilton," said the bartender, attempting to convey an air of much respect.

They wrenched open the rest of the broken window, and Wilton climbed easily into the room. "I was half afraid that something like this would happen," he said. "That man is entirely innocent . . . unless you want to hang a man for self-defense. I knew that dead man. His name was Capper. He sailed before the mast on a ship that I commanded. And when he sent up word to me today that he was in town, I came down to see him. He was always a wild, reckless fellow. A little wrong in the head, as a matter of fact. I was afraid that he might get into mischief, and so I came down to take what care of him I could. I even had a drink with him . . . and it was the drink that polished off the pair of them. When they were carried in here, I wanted to follow, but the door was locked. So I walked around into the garden to look through the window. A very lucky thing that I did. I saw Capper, like a mad creature, as he was, throw himself at this fellow while he was still half conscious. He barely had sense enough to defend himself. You can see the bruise on his forehead, where Capper struck him. Capper was a madman. Mad with drink, no doubt. He managed to tear the gun out of the holster of Sherry, here. But that brought Sherry out of his whiskey sleep. He grabbed the gun back and knocked Capper away, and when Capper started to rush in again . . . he shot him dead."

He made a pause here. Silence and then a murmur of surprise followed this statement.

"Funny, I didn't hear no racket in here," said one.

"They weren't shouting," said Wilton. "Their brains were too filled with whiskey fumes for that. And, after all, the finish came in about two seconds . . . before I could get in through the window, in fact. Sherry seemed to come to his senses. He saw the dead body and made for the window, and started smashing it open. He saw, of course, that the case looked black for him, and he didn't know that he'd had a witness who could clear him."

There was a general murmur again; it was of pure assent except for one bearded man, wearing a heavy plaid raincoat. He was a rough customer, with a growth of beard of several days' ripeness upon his chin, and overhanging brows, from beneath which he peered earnestly out at the others. Now he advanced upon big Lew Sherry and stood before him with his legs well braced, and his hands upon his hips.

"Boys," he said, "before you let this gent loose, I want to tell you a few things about him."

"Go on," said the bartender, who seemed to be in charge of the crowd.

But others were gathering, and the room was full of pushing people.

"If a dog bites once," said the man in the raincoat, "you call it bad luck and let him go. If he bites twice, you shoot him, I take it?"

"Go on," said the bartender. "What are you driving at?"

"I'll show you in a minute." He turned back upon Sherry. "You know me, Tiny?" he asked.

Sherry had worn a dark scowl from the moment he first eyed the other. He hesitated now, but at length he said: "I know you, Jack."

"And how did you come to know me?" asked the other.

"By breaking your jaw for you," said Sherry. "I see you wear a lump on the side of your ugly face still."

The man of the raincoat grinned in a lopsided fashion. "And how did you come to bust my jaw?" he asked, while all grew hushed with interest, listening to this strange conversation.

"Because you jumped me," said Sherry, "and you well know that you did, Jack."

"I jumped you," admitted the other. "And why did I jump you?"

"Ah . . . that's what you're driving at, is it?" asked Sherry.

"It is. Why did I jump you?"

"Because . . ." began Sherry.

"Listen to this!" exclaimed the other.

"Because," said Sherry in repetition, "I killed one of your cousins, and shot up another pair of them."

An exclamation greeted this statement.

"You hear him?" asked Jack.

"It was fair fight," protested Sherry.

"Mind you, gents," said Jack, "the four of them was in one shack. They'd been felling some timber above the rest of the gang. In that there shack they had the fight. He claims that he killed one of the three and laid out the other two. They wasn't babies, any of those three. I ask you, does it seem nacherel and to reason that he could do it by fighting fair . . . this gent, mind you, that's just plugged a drunk through the head?"

Sherry looked swiftly around the encircling faces, and all that he saw appeared grim reading indeed to him.

"I got no grouch against this here bird," said the bartender, "but it looks like sense in what Jack says. When a dog bites twice . . . it shows a habit."

Sherry searched his mind for an answer, but he found none.

Then the quiet voice of Wilton broke in: "It seems to me, men, that you might ask what happened *after* this shooting scrape at the lumber camp. Did this man bolt?"

"There's a question," said Sherry. "You can answer that, Jack. Did I run for it?"

"You come into camp and bragged about what you'd done," said Jack. "You come in with a cock-and-bull yarn."

"Did I take care of the two boys that were laid out but not dead?" asked Sherry. "Or did I leave 'em to bleed to death, as I might've done?"

"You come in an' bragged!" repeated Jack, furious at the memory. "I ask you boys to use your common sense. And here you got this gent red-handed. It ain't the first killing. And the one I tell you wasn't the first, either. Here's his gun." He snatched Sherry's gun and held it high. "There's four notches filed in this here. Tell me, was they filed for fun, Sherry?" He waited, then he answered himself with: "And there'll be five notches in there tomorrow."

At this, a decidedly stern rumble of anger ran through the listeners. It was after the palmy days of outlawry when gunmen were rather more admired than condemned. Law had entered the West, and the gunman was an unpopular character.

At last Sherry said loudly: "Gents, you're on the wrong trail. This Jack, here, is trying to run me up a tree. I'll tell you the honest truth. There's not a notch there that isn't for the finish of a white man in a fair fight. And that's straight, so help me."

This speech made an obvious impression, and Sherry could see the effect as he looked about over the faces of the listeners. He noted that Wilton stood a little apart from the others—or rather, out of an apparent respect for him, the rest would not rub elbows too closely with their superior. As for Wilton himself, he seemed to be watching this scene as he would have watched something on a stage, in which he had very little concern. There was even a faint smile on his lips, from time to time, as he followed the different arguments.

Jack was not to be downed. "White men?" he exclaimed. "And what else have you accounted for?"

Sherry saw that he had led himself into a corner, but he added quietly, in reply: "I've been in Mexico, boys. And I've had to live in Louisiana among some unpeaceable gents. That's all that I got to say about that."

"It looks sort of black for you, Sherry," said the bartender. "Though I've got nothing against you."

"It's gonna look blacker for him," insisted Jack. "It's gonna look black as choking for him, before we get through with him. This ain't a jay town that's to be buffaloed and talked down by a slicker like this Sherry. He's an educated gent, too. Reads a lot. Knows a lot. How did he ever have to leave home, I'd like to ask? I tell you, if you knew the inside of this one, you'd find it hotter'n cayenne pepper."

Jack had piled up his points with some adroitness and there was no mistaking the hostile air of the crowd when Wilton interrupted the proceedings again to ask: "If he came into camp, how did he happen to get off, up there, without trouble?"

"There *was* trouble," said Jack. "But he was the pet of the boss of the show. And that got him off. There was a lot of trouble, but this Sherry is one of those sneaks that always aims to play in with the straw boss, damn him and all his kind."

This stroke produced another thunder, more thunderous than the rest.

"But suppose," said Wilton, "we find out just what story was told by both sides when they came into the camp that day?"

"The kids told a straight yarn," said Jack. "They told how they'd been sitting around having a little poker game in the evening. Sherry lost. Like the yaller quitter that he is, he grouched. They shut him up. He scooped for the money with one hand and begun shooting with the other before any of them could reach for their guns."

"Well," said Wilton, "but isn't it odd that a straight story like that could be disbelieved?"

"Because the boss ran the show and ran it crooked, to help Sherry," declared Jack. "There ain't much difference between the speed of anybody's draw . . . hardly a fraction of a second. How could one man do that work against three, and come off hardly scratched?"

The patience of Sherry, which had been fairly well maintained up to this point, now was ended, and he flared forth: "Jack, if you think there's very little difference in the speed of a draw, I invite you . . . and any friend of yours . . . to stand up to me inside of ten paces, and we'll start the draw with an even break."

Jack was so staggered by this proposal that he actually took a backward step.

"One of the three did no shooting at all," said Sherry grimly. "He died while he was lugging out his gun. The second feller got in one shot as he dropped, and the third got in two. And here's the proof of it. Here's the first one." He touched a white scar that clipped the side of his cheek. "Here's the second one." He pulled up his left sleeve and exposed a forearm white as the skin of a baby. He doubled his hand, and beneath the skin appeared enormous, ropy muscles, bulging so that they threatened to leap through the skin. Against that setting, turned still whiter by the contraction of the great muscles that stopped the flow of the blood, appeared a large purple patch. "That was the second shot that plugged me," said Sherry. "And as for the third, it's along the ribs of my left side, and it left a mark you all can see."

Silence followed. Eyes turned slowly to Jack, who protested eagerly: "He could have picked up those marks in any fight. He admits that he had plenty of them, all over the world."

The voice of Sherry was low and bitter: "You yellow dog," he said. "You know that I was dripping blood when I got to camp. And that was why you jumped me. You never would have dared, otherwise. You forgot that my right hand was still ready for you."

Jack bit his lip, and his keen eyes flashed from side to side, seeking for a new idea, but, before he could find it, the big man continued quietly: "I told the true story, when I came into camp. We were playing poker. I'd had my share of the luck. It's a lie that says I hadn't. Matter of fact, I was the winner, and a big winner, as things went in that camp. So big a winner that straight poker wasn't good enough for the rest of them. I'd discarded an ace of clubs before the draw. And after the draw I called a hand of four aces. I wanted to argue the point. But the winner went for a gun. I had to beat him to it. And I did. You've heard this mangy coyote yelping at my heels. But I've told you the absolute truth."

Again silence weighed upon the room, and again Jack took a backward step. He had changed color, now.

"He'd be glad enough to see me hanged," said Sherry. "That sort never drops malice. That sort of man hunts in packs, getting others to take the risks that he hasn't the nerve to take for himself. As for this job here, it's a bad one. I'm sorry for it. I'll tell you straight that I had nothing against Capper. I never saw him before today. I don't know exactly what happened. My brain was slugged. I woke up when the gun went off. Then I saw my own gat at my feet, still smoking. And yonder by the wall where you found him lay Capper. Well . . . it looked black for me, and that was why I tried to run. I've put my cards on the table, boys. There's truth and nothing else in every word that I've spoken. Now, make up your minds."

It was not certain how the crowd would decide, until the bartender stepped forward and confronted Jack. He was not a big man, that bartender, but he was a fighter by nature.

"You," he said. "This town is kind of cramped and small for your style, I reckon. You'd better blow."

And Jack blew.

IV

The strain of that impromptu trial had been so great that everyone sighed with relief as the tension relaxed. And now, after having accused Sherry so bitterly, the crowd milled around him in unfeigned good will.

One big fellow slapped him heartily on the back. "Sherry," he said, "if that's your name, I've got to say that I weigh within a few pounds of you, and yet I've got a chestnut mare at the hitching rack outside that can carry me. If you need that horse to help you on your way, don't let me stop you from trying to catch up with Jack . . . the poison skunk . . . the hydrophobic rat!"

But Sherry waved his big hand. "That's finished," he said. "I never hunted trouble in my life, and I never will. I never went half a mile after another man with a gun in my hand. And I never will."

A cheerful current of humanity curled closer about him to sweep him down toward the barroom, but he pushed them away with a good-natured might. Then he strode through them, and, at the outer door of the hotel, he caught up with Wilton. Him he touched upon the shoulder.

"I want ten seconds," he said, "to tell you something. I want to tell you that if it hadn't been for you singing out, I might have hung today."

Wilton smiled and nodded. "I actually believe that you might," he said. "Our fellows in Clayrock are a rough set. They act first and think afterward."

"That's why I thank you," went on Sherry in his quiet bass voice that, however, no matter how softly it was controlled, had a rumble in it like the echo of a far-off peal of thunder. "A few words are just as good as a thousand, I suppose. But you saved my hide. And there's a lot of that hide to be grateful for."

"By the way," said Wilton, "what was your college?"

Ever so slightly, Sherry started. "What?" he said. And then he paused, and deliberately looked Wilton in the eye. "I don't know what you mean," he said.

Wilton chuckled. "Of course you don't," he said. "I should have known beforehand that you wouldn't understand what I meant."

"And now that I've thanked you," went on Sherry, "will you let me ask you what you put in that glass?"

Wilton started in turn. "What I put in the glass?" he echoed.

"Mister Wilton," said Sherry, "the point is this. I'm no hero at whiskey. But I can hold my share of it. And tonight I seem to have passed out cold in two drinks. That's why I ask you what you put in that whiskey!"

Wilton sighed. His eyes half closed. "Suppose," he said suddenly, "that you walk up to my house with me?"

"I'd like it fine," said Sherry. "But I can't. For the reason that my bunkie is riding herd for two, just now, and he expects me back."

Wilton answered, with much quiet point: "Nevertheless, I think you should come along with me and I think that you will.

Between you and me, Sherry, I confess that you appear to me a fairly reasonable and honest fellow . . . and, if you are, you'll agree that you owe me something."

"I owe you," said Sherry carefully, "for some very opportune remarks during that impromptu trial of me a few moments ago."

"Impromptu?" said the other. "Is that your word for what I said?"

Sherry turned full upon his companion. It was a very bright night of stars, and the lights of the town were now few and dim, for most people had gone to bed, and altogether there was not nearly enough illumination to enable him to see the face of his companion.

"I don't know what you're driving at," Sherry said with a good deal of bluntness.

"You don't?" Wilton hesitated for an instant, as though many answers were rushing to the tip of his tongue, though he said finally, in a controlled voice: "That surprises me. But I go back to the doped drink. Of course, it was drugged. But what on earth, my dear young friend, could make you think that I would drug the liquor?"

"Because," said Sherry with his usual openness, "you seemed upset because I had taken the glass that you intended for Capper . . . poor wretch."

"The glass that I intended for Capper, and that he intended for me."

"What?"

"That's it, exactly. As I put down the drinks, I saw Capper's hand flash over the top of one of them and I thought . . . I couldn't be sure . . . that his hand dropped a film of something white into the liquor. What I did definitely see was that Capper deftly exchanged glasses with me. Naturally I couldn't stand for that. The fellow was half mad, and capable of anything. Between you and me, I should not have been very sorry if he had poisoned

himself with his own hand . . . while intending it for another."
The voice of Wilton turned hard and grim.

"It sounds a mixed-up business," commented Sherry. "I got
the wrong glass as you were slipping it back to him?"

"Exactly."

"It seems odd," said Sherry. "I don't see what point there was
in his poisoning you. He acted to me more like a fellow who
would be apt to blackmail you . . . who was holding his knowledge, say, over your head."

"Knowledge?" cried Wilton with a sudden burst of extreme
fury. "That gutter rat . . . that sneaking, paltry, vicious little
cur . . . knowledge of me!"

Sherry was amazed. It was actually the first time that Wilton
had so much as raised his voice, during all these singular scenes
in which Sherry had watched him, but once the flood broke
through, it raged in a torrent.

It was over at once.

"I don't know whether he had anything on you or not," said
Sherry. His tone implied that he did not care, either. "I saw him
rubbing your nose in the dirt . . . I watched you taking water
from him. Maybe he had nothing on you . . . anyway, it was
damned queer to my way of thinking."

"Yes, yes," answered Wilton rather hurriedly. "I suppose it
was. It was almost as queer an action, say, as that of a man who
draws a gun on a drugged and helpless companion and shoots
out his brains."

V

To this startling retort, Sherry listened with wonder and horror.

"We'd better walk up the hill to my house," repeated Wilton.

And Sherry went with him, his brain suddenly benumbed,
almost as it had been when he was completely under the authority
of the drug that had been dropped into his whiskey. What hand

had dropped it there? The hand of Wilton or Capper? And for what purpose? And now he himself was accused by the very man who had saved his neck from a mob execution.

"You say that I deliberately pulled my gun and shot down a helpless fellow?"

"I tell you what I saw with my own eyes," said the other. "Capper was shot exactly where he lay. He hardly stirred a muscle."

"Great Scott!" gasped Sherry. "Could I have done that, I ask you? What had I against Capper? What had I to gain by his death?"

"A man under the influence of a drug doesn't think along very straight lines," replied the other. "You were in a haze. You still suffer from some of the effects."

"Shot him where he lay . . . helpless?" groaned Sherry.

"Exactly. There was blood on the wall behind his head, when they picked him up."

"The blood was splashed against the wall in his fall," urged Sherry.

"In the midst of that blood there is a bullet hole," said Wilton. "I think that's fairly conclusive."

He had led the way up a steep incline from the heart of Clayrock, and now as they came before an open iron gate that gave upon a winding driveway, Sherry halted and laid his great hand upon one of the iron pillars that supported the weight of the gate panels.

"I murdered that man while he was lying there?" muttered Sherry.

Wilton did not answer this. Apparently he thought that he had made the case conclusive enough beforehand.

"I don't understand it," said Sherry. "Great Scott, I don't understand it. Man, man, all my life what I've avoided, as other people avoid death, is any accusation of bullying another person. I've never taken an advantage. I've never fired when a man's head was turned. Heaven knows that I've been low . . . I've been in the muck . . . but one thing at least I've always done . . . I've fought fair."

At this, Wilton laid a hand upon the shoulders of the other and patted it kindly. "I believe every word you say," he said. "But a drugged man is an insane man. Particularly people put under by some of those tricky Oriental poisons. And those are exactly what Capper would have used, as a matter of course. And, driven out of his head for a moment, what a man does then is exactly what he would never dream of doing when he is normal."

"That's clear enough," said Sherry huskily. "That's clear enough and that's bad enough."

"It is, isn't it?" murmured the other. "I'm sorry for you, Sherry. I hated to tell you the truth about this, as a matter of fact. But I had to, and for very selfish reasons."

"Will you tell me what those reasons are?" asked Sherry.

"I've never told a soul in this world," said Wilton. "But the fact is that I'm going to tell you the whole story." He began to walk up the long driveway.

"Why not tell me here?" asked Sherry.

"Tell you the story here?" cried the other. He laughed with the sudden harshness that, now and again, came into his voice. "Why in the name of caution should I tell you a story where the whole world might listen to me? No, no! Wait till we get to my house. I have one room there that really is private." He laughed again, the same jarring laugh, as he repeated this.

And Sherry, amazed, unnerved, sick at heart, went unwillingly up the path beside his companion. The drive doubled twice, cutting along the face of that bluff that he had noticed before rising above the town, and finally it came to the front of the house on the hill that had showed lights that had seemed as much stars as lamps.

It was not an imposing house. It was built all in one story, and it followed the natural conformation of the ground slavishly.

There had apparently been no attempt to level a sufficient space, for the foundations were laid according to the natural contour of the land. The result was an indescribable living line to the upper contour of the building, which pitched up and down heedlessly, like a boat upon the waters, bringing up with a high head upon the northeastern end of the ridge.

"She lies here like a snake, doesn't she?" murmured Wilton.

"Yes," said Sherry in full agreement. "Like a snake ready to strike."

He saw the other twist sharply about and glance at him, but now they passed under the face of the dwelling and went directly to that highest spot where the house came to an end. They passed around to the very extreme point, and Sherry exclaimed with real wonder: "Why, it's like the bow of a ship!"

It did, in fact, contract toward that point, so that it gave the whole edifice a strange likeness to a misshapen vessel struggling through the sea. Yes, and in another instant the clay rock seemed a vast wave, which was upholding the ship toward the sky, ready the next instant to dash it to destruction. These strange images jumped full-grown into the brain of Sherry, and he dismissed them again with a shrug of his powerful shoulders.

"D'you like the place?" asked Wilton in a strangely eager voice.

"You have a view from up here," replied Sherry noncommittally.

All the plain about them was dotted with the lights of single houses, or streaked with the lights of whole streets. For Clayrock was not a town standing by itself. There were many other smaller villages scattered around it, so that, to carry out the first metaphor that occurred to Sherry, if this house of Wilton's were a ship at sea, it was steering by the lights of a most dangerous and twisting channel.

"And now," said Wilton, "we'll go into my room."

He stepped up to the door and turned a switch, which caused a flood of light to spring up within. Into the interior, Wilton peered through a small hole that he uncovered and then covered again. After this, he unlocked the door and waved Sherry ahead of him.

"Go first," he said, "and let me tell you that I never go across this threshold without expecting to be met with a bullet through the head or a knife in the throat."

With this odd introduction, he closed the door behind him, and waved Sherry up a second short flight of stairs that rose from the little entrance hall.

"This is my own private way of coming in and going out," explained Wilton, and unlocked the door at the head of the stairs.

VI

He again waved Sherry in before him. "And here is my room," he said.

The illusion of a ship's cabin was almost perfect. The very windows were rounded at the tops, small, and where the chamber narrowed at the front end of the house, there was actually a round light. The ceiling, too, was manifestly curved, as though following the lines of an upper deck. To make the resemblance perfect, a narrow flight of steps, hardly more than a ladder with wooden rungs, lifted to a trap door out of one corner. Up this went Wilton while Sherry followed him, wondering.

The manner of his host was as matter of fact as that of any man he ever had met in his life, but his words and his ways were odd, indeed. They passed from the ladder-like stairway to the roof of the house. Or, more properly speaking, it was the roof of the room beneath, with little relation to the rest of the building. The sense that he was in a ship persisted still with Sherry, although now, to be sure, it was more like voyaging through the stars than over any terrestrial ocean.

"I want you to take note of a few of the features here," said Wilton. And he called attention to the fact that on three sides the room gave down upon the sheer face of the clay rock, a dizzy fall. Upon the fourth side, it looked down at least twenty feet upon the nearest portion of the roof of the remainder of the odd building.

"A little fort, you see?" remarked Wilton. "Now, step closer to the edge. Anywhere closer to the edge."

Sherry obeyed, but with caution. He had a giddy feeling that this singular fellow might thrust him over the side into oblivion. The roof on which he stepped yielded, as he thought, the slightest particle beneath the pressure of his weight, and he heard the faint ringing of a bell from the room beneath. He stepped back in haste.

"What's that?" asked Sherry.

"An alarm, of course. Come down with me again."

They returned to the room below, and Wilton carried on his methodical demonstration of his house. Sherry listened carefully, knowing that something lay behind all this, but unable to guess what.

"Have you tried the weight of the door?" asked Wilton.

He set it ajar, and Sherry moved it back and forth. It seemed the weight of lead.

Wilton explained with his usual calm: "There is a half-inch sheet of bulletproof steel of the finest quality sunk in that door, and, in fact, every wall of this room is secured in the same fashion . . . the ceiling and the floor, too. Those solid shutters that close over the windows are lined with half-inch steel, as well, and the trap door leading to the roof. This room, you will see, is such a strong box that, if a bomb were exploded under it, it might be knocked off its base, but it would hardly be more than dented by the explosion."

Sherry nodded. He could not help wondering if Wilton were a little mad.

"Now, then," said Wilton, "you will see that it would be very hard for anyone to get into this room, but, still, there are drills that would eat through half an inch of steel as though it were soft pine. I can't depend upon steel alone. I need something more, and here it is." He set wide a door and revealed a shallow closet where Sherry, with experienced eye, noted at once a formidable little armory.

He saw half a dozen repeating rifles, revolvers, and automatic pistols, pump guns, double-barreled shotguns, and two with sawed-off barrels, terrible at such close range as fighting within the limits of a room. Sherry examined them with care, and he saw, also, ranged boxes of ammunition for all the different types of weapons.

"You might stand a siege," he said.

"I might." Wilton nodded. He opened a second door, and pointed at several tiers of boxes. "Canned food and distilled water," he explained. "Yes, I could stand a siege." He turned and faced Sherry. "You want to know why I expect such a thing to happen?"

"Of course," agreed Sherry.

"I'll tell you why. No . . . it would take a great deal of time. I can't tell you this moment all the details. But after the . . . "

A bell rang. The ring was twice repeated with a pressing haste.

"That's my niece, Beatrice," said Wilton. He went to the door and laid his hand upon the knob of it. Then he turned and looked earnestly at Sherry: "She's an unusual sort of girl, you'll see."

He opened the door, stepping straight back behind the panel, as it swung slowly inward, delayed by its own weight, and Sherry found himself staring into a white, sad face, the eyes surrounded by deep shadows.

A girl came into the room with a graceful step which yet had little lightness in it.

"I've brought you a note, Uncle Oliver," she said.

"Beatrice," Wilton said, "this is Lewis Sherry. Sherry, this is my niece, Beatrice Wilton."

She came up to Sherry and shook hands, with one of those casual and forced smiles that Sherry had always hated. Then she turned back to her uncle. "This is the thing, Uncle Oliver." She handed him an envelope.

He frowned down at it—then suddenly crumpled it in his nervous grasp. "Where did you get this?" he asked.

"I'll tell you another time," she answered.

"And why not now? I don't mind talking before Sherry."

"Ah?" she said, and, half turning, she looked with a keenly searching glance at the big man. It was as much as to say: *Have you been enlisted?* It was to be inferred from her voice and her manner that she was not altogether on the side of her uncle. There was a definite gap between them. "If you don't mind, then, I'll tell you exactly. I was taking the short cut up the hill . . . "

"When?"

"Half an hour ago."

"What were you doing out as late as that?"

Instead of answering, she paused, and deliberately looked straight into the face of her uncle. Then she went on: "I was as far up the path as the place where the old root sticks its elbow out of the ground, and there a hand touched my arm."

"By Jove," breathed Wilton.

"It wasn't very pleasant. I turned around, and the other arm was caught. There were two men, one held me on each side."

"What sort of men?" asked Wilton, who had turned gray and now sat down.

"I couldn't see. It was pitch black there among the trees. I strained my eyes at them, because of course I wanted to try to recognize them. I think, in addition, that they hadn't trusted the darkness. They had either blacked or masked their faces. So I could make out nothing, except that one of them was about middle height, and the other was a great deal taller. About as tall, I should say, as Mister Sherry." She regarded Sherry again, but only for the sake of more accurately estimating his height.

"You tell a story well," said Oliver Wilton ironically. "You never are in a hurry to get to the point, my dear."

"Thank you," she replied, her eyes as dull and dark as ever while they watched her uncle. "I have to take it by degrees. That forestalls questions afterward, you know . . . if you'll pay attention the first time. I say that I couldn't make them out. I was frightened and . . . "

"*Bah!*" broke in Oliver Wilton.

She repeated sternly: "I was frightened." It was as though she insisted upon the possibility of fear, and her uncle would not allow it in her. "They gave me this letter," she went on, "and they said to me . . . 'Tell him that we're straight as a string. With him, too. Only . . . we want turkey talked.' After that, they let me go. Those were the only words they spoke to me."

"Then how did you know that they were referring to me?" He asked this sharply, suspiciously.

"I guessed. I don't know how." She was sneering openly.

It was more than dislike that existed between these two. It was actual hatred, as Sherry was beginning to understand. And he considered the girl more keenly than before. She might have been beautiful if her air had been more happy, her eyes not quite so dull, with only flashes of emotion passing through them, from time to time. But a settled melancholy seemed to possess her, and she was faintly frowning all the time.

She had brown eyes; her hair was a very dark auburn. And sometimes, as she turned her head, the red highlights upon her hair seemed to be repeated in the color of her eyes, making a weird effect. Her skin was very white, her eyes unusually large, and the upper lids, when she looked downward, were distinctly marked with purple. Some women make up in this manner to give a touch of thoughtful distinction to their faces, but Sherry did not need to be told that all was natural with her.

He never had seen man or woman at all like her. He put her into a new category and reserved judgment. He was only ready to say one thing: that she possessed as much force—as much danger, say—as any man. And he had known dangerous men.

Another of those unpleasant little pauses had come between her and her uncle. Then she said good night to them and left.

Wilton closed and locked the door behind her, and turned back to Sherry.

"That's one reason I live in a steel box," he declared.

VII

It was an odd thing, indeed, to learn that a man's reason for fortifying his room as though it were a blockhouse is the existence of a young girl. But there was something so extraordinary in the manner of Beatrice Wilton that it appeared to Sherry that there was some justification of the attitude of his host.

At this point, Wilton asked the cowpuncher to sit down. He said in his quiet way: "You've seen and heard a good many strange things since you came to this house with me, Sherry."

"I have," admitted Sherry.

"I wanted to show you the face of the situation first. Now, I must tell you why I've been so frank. But first of all, I will give you another bit of testimony."

They went to a clothes closet that was, in fact, large enough to serve as a dressing room, with a small window, like a porthole, opening to the south. From this he came back carrying a gray felt hat, which he held up, and Sherry saw a half-inch hole punched neatly through the crown.

"Air hole, for hot weather," said Wilton. "Put there by some kind friend . . . I don't know who. I was walking up the hill one evening and this hat was shot off my head by some man in the brush. I went after him . . . found nothing. The trees and the bushes make a thick tangle, you know."

"I know," said Sherry.

Wilton, with a sigh as though of relief, tossed the hat back through the door, where it rolled, unregarded, upon the floor of the dressing room.

"What do you think of this affair, Sherry?" asked the other.

"What you mean," answered Sherry, "is that you're in danger of your life. And I gather that you think Beatrice Wilton may have something to do with your danger. Is that it?"

"That's it." Wilton nodded. "It doesn't seem possible to you?"

"Miss Wilton, you mean?" inquired Sherry.

"Yes."

"I don't know," said Sherry. "I've been living on the range a long time. You don't suspect women of murder . . . not on the range. Besides, what has she to gain by finishing you?"

"I am her guardian," said Wilton. "She has a half million or so of property."

"And what of that?" asked Sherry sharply.

"You think I'm a fairly callous fellow?" Wilton smiled. "Well, Sherry, that property goes to her the moment that she marries, or, on my death."

Sherry thought this over with a frown. "You think she's hiring killers to go after you?" he said.

"I don't know," answered Wilton. "My life is endangered. I know that. I know that Beatrice has plenty of reason for wanting to get rid of me. I know that she's not fond of me"

"You're letting me into this pretty deep," said Sherry.

"You want to know how you're interested," said Wilton, "and I'll tell you. I have an idea that during the next ten days there will be special efforts to get at me. During that time I'm going to live under a guard." He narrowed his eyes at Sherry again. "You're a fighting man, Sherry," he continued, "and I gamble that you're an honest man. Will you take the job of trying to keep me alive for ten days?"

"I had an idea that something like that was coming," said Sherry. "But before I give you an answer, I want to know what there is in the job?"

"I don't think," said Wilton, "that one man would be enough. I'd leave it to you to pick out some other good fighting man, some reliable fellow. You can pay him whatever you like. And I'll pay you . . . a thousand dollars a day."

Sherry frowned.

"You don't like that?" asked Wilton curiously.

"A fee like that," said Sherry, "is almost too big to be paid for honest work. However, I'll think it over. Tell me, Wilton, if you suspect any other person besides your niece?"

"I suspect every living soul around me," said Wilton in his calm way, which he retained even when saying the most startling things. "I suspect even you. You may have been planted some-where at the hotel so that I could fall in your way. Yes, I suspect everyone."

"Why should other people want to get at you?"

Wilton considered, his glance fixed upon the ceiling. "I don't think I'll answer that," he said.

He looked straight at Sherry, and suddenly the big fellow realized that his host was a man capable of anything—certainly capable of banishing all shame.

"You want me to watch over you," answered Sherry, "but at the same time you want to blind one of my eyes. Is that very logical?"

"I can tell you this," said Wilton. "If ever sailors come near this house, be on your guard against them. Outside of Beatrice, the next danger that I know of has to do with the sea. Someone from the sea, Sherry, is going to take a try at me."

"Someone like Capper?" suggested Sherry.

"Like Capper," agreed the other. "But a great deal more for-midable. Capper was a good deal of a fool. Bloodthirsty. Exactly that. I mean to say . . . he was so interested in making trouble that he hardly cared if he ruined himself in making the other fellow suffer. However, I expect that we may have a visit from a more dangerous sailor than Capper."

"And that's all that you can tell me?"

"I can tell you a little more than that. There are several sets of people that want me to die."

"Within ten days?"

"Yes, within ten days."

"Your niece is one of them?"

"When her father died," said Wilton, "he left her money in trust for a year. At the end of that time, the control of her money was to pass into my hands, if I cared to undertake the work of guardian. That work meant giving up my own affairs entirely. But I decided to make that sacrifice."

He looked straight at Sherry, and the latter looked straight back at his host. There had been a little ironical intonation on the last word.

"And the sailors? You can't tell me why they're after you?"

"No, not a word about that."

"You don't know how these people might try to come at you? Guns, you say?"

"I don't know," replied Wilton. "I'll tell you some of the things that I'm half suspecting . . . poison administered in food, with a blow arrow, or perhaps through the bite of a snake. Or again, there's something to be feared from the thrust of a Malay knife. And, of course, I've already had a bullet through my hat."

Sherry shrugged his shoulders. "Why shouldn't you close yourself up in your steel box, here, and pretend that you're being besieged for ten days. You have everything you need."

"I have this place," said Wilton, "because I can sleep here with a slightly greater sense of security. But no place is completely safe. Suppose a bomb loaded with poison gas were thrown through a port into this cabin, one night?"

"They'll do anything to get at you?"

"They'll do absolutely anything," Wilton assured the cow-puncher. Suddenly he rose to his feet. For the first time he betrayed a real emotion. "There are people that I know of," he explained, "who would sell their souls for the sake of shooting me through the head. Do you understand?"

Sherry nodded. Under those last words there had been an electric thrill of hysteria, and Sherry understood, in a startling burst of insight, that the calm of Wilton was totally affected and unreal. It was a calm surface with a storm beneath.

"Well," said Wilton, "you've heard as much as I can tell you. What do you say to this proposal, Sherry?"

"A thousand dollars a day," repeated Sherry. "And for the sake of that, I'll have to get a partner, and then the pair of us will have to go on guard . . . and the moment we start work, we'll both be targets for the same hands that are aiming principally at you?"

"You will, of course."

"Well," said Sherry, "the money . . . and the fun . . . interest me."

"You'll take the place?"

"Yes."

Wilton sat down at a table and scratched a letter. Then he rose and passed it to Sherry, who read:

Riverside National Bank
Mr. H.A. Copley

Dear Mr. Copley:
If I am alive ten days from this date, please pay $10,000 to Lewis Sherry. If I am dead, destroy this letter.

Yours very truly,
Oliver Wilton

"Will that do?" asked Wilton.

"Of course," replied Sherry. "When do I come up here?"

"At once!"

"We're driving in a bunch of beef tomorrow morning at dawn. By nine o'clock I'll be here, and I'll have a man with me."

"That leaves me another night," muttered Wilton, "with only my own pair of eyes to keep watch. But I suppose that I'll have to."

"I'm going back to camp, then."

"At nine tomorrow?"

"I'll be back."

"Good night," said Wilton. "And if this talk keeps you awake tonight, don't waste your time . . . spend it cleaning your guns, because you'll need them before you finish working for me."

VIII

Eighteen hundred steers dismayed by the sight of many houses, the snorting of a locomotive on the railroad, and the intricate, strong fences of the cattle corrals near the station, filled the air over Clayrock with booming and bellowing. As Pete Lang and Tiny Lew Sherry looked at the lashing tails, and listened to the clashing of the horns, Lane said: "Now, Tiny, we've done our job, and, if you ain't particular hostile to the idea, I'm gonna let the watches run down while I lubricate my innards. The thirst that you were talking about the other night is a dog-gone lake of sparklin' spring water compared with the charred wood and the white ashes inside of me. Just gimme a steer to the layout you found, and . . . "

"Drop it," said Sherry with a grin, "you're just getting ready to work."

Pete Lang, recoiling his rope, stopped his hands to look at his friend. "Have you been exposed to the sun, partner?" he asked. "You ain't scrambled your brains like a plate of eggs, I hope?"

"For ten days," said Sherry, "you're not going to so much as look sideways at liquor . . . you're going to keep to a desert trail and thank heaven for water when you can find it."

Pete Lang finished the coiling of his rope and tied it in place. "You got a terrible saddening influence over me, Tiny," he said. "Now what do you want?"

"You," said Sherry, and told him the complete story of his exploits in Clayrock—the strange death of Capper having already been described, as a matter of course. But now he went on to the details of his talk with Wilton, and the odd proposal that Wilton had made to him.

"Now, how do you size it up, partner?" asked Lang.

"I don't know," said Sherry. "Except that I know you and me are going to go up there and take that job."

"Do you know that?" murmured Lang. "You know a brain full, then, and you got a long start on me. But what sort is Wilton?"

"I don't know," said Sherry.

"Is he a crook?"

"There's a large chance of that. Otherwise, he would have told me why the sailors are after him, no doubt."

"Is that your only reason? Why, Tiny, this gent is a hard-boiled skunk, most likely. He's probably so mean that he could live on jerked coyote with cactus thorns for dessert. You're still young, Tiny, and now you just foller along with papa and leave Clayrock when I leave."

Sherry shook his head.

"Why, Tiny," exclaimed the cowpuncher impatiently, "it's a crooked frame! This Wilton is probably going to be bumped off, and you want to be in on the digestion of the bullets. Is that the way that you figure it?"

"Five thousand apiece for us, and ten days to wait," said Sherry. "Doesn't that sound to you?"

"Like funeral music, it sounds to me, Tiny." He pushed his horse closer and tapped Sherry on the shoulder. "It ain't the coin that pulls you in," he said.

"What is it, then? The trouble?" Sherry grinned. "Am I being drawn in by the chance to chew lead, old fellow?"

Pete Lang reined his horse back again. "I never seen a 'puncher made high, wide, and handsome like you, Tiny," he remarked, "that wasn't a hit with the ladies. The bigger they come, the harder the girlies steps up and slams them. A little man like me," said Pete Lang, looking down regretfully on a wiry body not more than a shade under six feet in height, "a little man like me," he repeated, "has always got a streak of meanness in him that saves him from tons of trouble. By the look of the bait, the wise wolf knows the trap. That's me, big boy. But a poor bison like you comes along and steps in and breaks off both legs at the knees."

"Are you accusing me of being drawn into this by the girl, Pete?"

"Nothing but!"

"A girl actually likely to do a murder, old boy? Do you think that my tastes run in that line?"

"There's only two things necessary for a girl to have . . . youngness and a pretty face."

"I said nothing about her face. I only told you that she seemed tired, with circles around her eyes."

"If she hadn't been a beauty, you never would have noticed the shadows," declared Lang. "Kid, keep away from that Wilton and all his crowd. He's a bad actor."

"You've never laid eyes on him," said Tiny with some anger. "Why do you talk so much about a man you've never seen?"

"I can see him in the corner of your own eye," answered Lang. "You've already been thinking the same things that I've been saying. Isn't that true?"

"Let me alone, will you?" cried Sherry. "Confound it, are you afraid to tackle this job with me?"

"Scared as a rabbit," replied Lang with the heartiest earnestness. "I don't want any part of that bet. You come on with me and chuck the girl. Besides, she's got too much money to be good."

"What do you mean by that?" demanded Sherry.

"Never give a starved dog too much raw meat," said Lang.

Sherry laughed. "You've got to come along with me," he said.

"Not on this trail, kid. My way leads toward moisture."

"Well, so long, then."

"Are you dead set?"

"Yes."

"So long, Tiny. We've rode a good many trails together. I hate to see you barging off. But bullets and poison and knives make too big a shadow for me to see the girl that's under it all."

They shook hands, and presently Sherry had jogged his horse back up the street and swung it gloomily around the corner, in order to head toward the house on the cliff. It had been a great disappointment for him to part with Pete. Of all the men he had met in the West, no one had been revealed to Sherry as so keen a fighter, so true a friend, so keen an eye upon the trail—all qualities that in the house on the cliff seemed likely to be tested.

He had reached the first bend of the road leading up the cliff when hoofs clattered behind him, and Pete Lang drew rein at his side.

"You'd've let me go," said Pete. "You cold-blooded fish, you! You'd've let me slide, an' heaven forgive you for it. But I was made with a heart inside of me, and so I've got to foller along after you."

"Old boy," answered Sherry, "I was never gladder to see any man's face."

"But," cautioned Lang, "I told you before and I tell you now. This is a bum steer that you're following. You're drifting in a blizzard, kid, and I only hope that you don't hang us both up on barbed wire."

To this, wisely, Sherry made no answer. They approached the gate of the Wilton place.

Before it, Lang drew rein again. "We gotta go in here?" he asked.

"Yes," said Sherry. "This is the place."

Lang sighed. "Well," he said, "there's no writing over the gate to tell us what kind of trouble we're going into. Make a noise, cayuse, and scatter up that gravel." With that, he whacked his pony with his quirt, and the mustang, with a snort, fled through the gate and up the winding way, the gravel and dust flying like smoke beneath the hoof beats.

Sherry followed at a more leisurely pace, so that he found his friend already dismounted, and tethering his horse to the hitching rack before the house. He followed that example, and heard Lang muttering: "I never seen a house in my life that looked like more trouble."

Beatrice Wilton came out of the house in a wide-brimmed straw hat, with a gardener's trowel in her hand. She paused near Sherry, and he looked at her with a fresh interest, for the strong, bright sun, seeping through the thin brim of the hat, tinted her skin with rosy gold.

"You've come to stay, I take it?" she said.

"I think I have," said Sherry, and he introduced Pete Lang.

"And you, too?" asked the girl, looking straight at the cowpuncher.

"I foller along with Tiny," answered Lang. "If he rolls down his blankets here, I suppose I stay along with him."

She swung her glance back to Sherry. "I think that you'll make Uncle Oliver feel quite safe," she said, and, with a nod to them, she went off down the first walk of the garden.

Lang looked after her, and then grinned at his friend. "And that's your girl with the shadows under her eyes, is it?" he commented.

Sherry sighed. "I didn't remember that she looked like this," he said.

"You're a young liar, son," said Lang. "But I'm here to make a statement. You got no chance with her. She's a thinker, me boy, and none of her thoughts are gonna be about you, unless she finds you in the way. Now, let's go in and see the gent in the trap."

IX

They found Oliver Wilton fairly quivering with excitement in spite of the strict control that kept his voice steady. He could speak evenly enough, but he could not keep his hand from shaking. He made a brief examination of Peter Lang.

"You're a friend of Sherry's?" he inquired.

"We've daubed ropes in the same outfit for a spell," was Lang's characteristically oblique answer.

"You shoot straight, Lang?"

"I can hit a mark if it ain't too small," said Lang.

Wilton did not smile. He turned sharply upon Sherry. "Is this a first-class fighting man?" he asked.

"First-class," said Sherry, emphasizing both the words.

"You know him?"

"I'll tell you how I met him . . ." began Sherry.

"Never mind," said Wilton with a sigh. "If you trust him, I can. And you haven't come too soon, Sherry. Have you talked to Lang?"

"I've told him every word that you told me."

"Before I'd agreed to him!" exclaimed Wilton, flushing with anger.

"If he hadn't stayed, I wouldn't have stayed," answered Sherry. "And as for repeating what we hear, we don't talk for our living."

"No," said Wilton, his teeth clicking together. "You're going to fight for it, and you can begin fighting now. I've had word from the hotel that there's another ruffian down there talking about me. His name is Fennel. Joe Fennel, he calls himself. He tells people in the hotel that he doesn't have to work for a living. He declares that he knows enough about me to make me keep him in luxury for the rest of his life." He raised his clenched fist shoulder-high and his face contorted with rage for an instant. Then the hand fell as he controlled himself again. "I want you to find out about that man," he snapped.

"I won't be very popular around that hotel," said Sherry.

"On the contrary, I gather that the crowd is all for you. I think I arranged that little matter for you, Sherry."

Sherry nodded.

"Find Fennel and talk to him. Don't let him know that you come from me. Try to see if the fellow is real or a sham. Here's the doctor now. He's been telling me about Fennel."

A tall man came into the room. He was partly bald—a premature baldness that, in fact, accentuated his youth, for he could not have been much past thirty years of age. The baldness, too, made his brows appear the more lofty; it was the commanding feature of his face—a great and swelling forehead that made him look to be an intellectual giant. He was introduced as Dr. Eustace Layman, and he shook hands with a firm, crisp grip.

"I was repeating what you told me about Fennel," said Wilton.

"He's a drunken old scoundrel who spends most of his time in his room, soaking up whiskey behind locked doors," said Layman. "He's a sailor and he's certainly a bad actor."

"I'll persuade the hotel to throw him out as an undesirable," suggested Wilton angrily.

"I wouldn't," replied the doctor. "I don't think they'd do it. He seems to have plenty of cash and doesn't care how he spends it. Besides, if you pay too much attention to him, people may think that there's something in what he talks about. I mean . . . that he knows something black about you."

"How do you happen to know so much about him?" asked Wilton. "You seem to have him by heart."

"Because I've been called in to see him. He almost had a fit the other day."

"Fit? I wish he'd strangled in the course of it."

"Too much alcohol . . . that was his trouble. Depressed heart action and subnormal temperature . . . that sort of thing."

"How far gone is he?" asked Wilton with an eagerness that quite broke through his usual easy manner.

"He'll last indefinitely," said the doctor. "He's a tough fellow. A real old sailor, and bad weather seems to line them with leather, inside and out."

"Will you go down to the hotel today?" asked Wilton of Sherry. "Will you try to see the old rascal and find out about him? I'll show you your quarters first. After you've made yourself at home, perhaps you'll go down and look things over."

Sherry agreed, and, with Pete Lang, he was shown to their quarters. They could not have been more confined if they had been in the steerage of a ship, and in fact, nothing could have been more like a cramped cabin than their room, which was lighted by round ports that, and which had a built-in bunk on either side of a narrow passage. It lay just underneath the room of their employer, and, as they stowed their luggage, Sherry asked his friend what he thought of the lay of the land.

Lang paused in the smoothing down of his blankets. "We're riding herd on a new range, kid," he said. "We gotta take time to find out the natures of these steers. All I know is that there's gonna be trouble."

When they were fairly settled, they went down together to the hotel and almost the first person they found in the card room was their man. He looked the perfect part of a hardy sailor. His skin was like mahogany; around the cheek bones it had a polished, ruddy look, while the lower part of his face was clouded with unshaven brush. At the very moment of their entrance, Fennel was heard calling for a drink in a husky voice, as one whose vocal cords have been strained and frayed by constant shouting against the scream of the westerlies.

Lang said aside to his companion: "I'll start talking with this fellow. You get a chance to slide up to his room. Get into it if you can."

"If the door's locked?"

"If the door's locked, that may block us for today. Make a try."

It was not hard to find the room of Fennel on the hotel register, and Sherry went up to it at once. It lay at the end of the southern corridor on the second floor of the hotel, and luckily the hall was empty as Sherry passed into it. He tried the door—it gave at once to his hand, but he paused, with a chill working through the muscles of his back. He had been in many an unpleasant situation; he had had to fight his way through many a tight corner, but never before had he gone unlawfully into the room of a stranger.

So, half guilty and half determined, he waited for an instant until he remembered the seamed face of Fennel, and then he pushed on into the chamber.

It was a little corner room that had two windows, but both of these were closed and the air was foul with the stale fumes of bad tobacco smoked in some ancient pipe. The chambermaid had not yet made up the bed, and Sherry told himself, with a sneer of disgust, that the sailor must have slept all the night in such an atmosphere.

On the wall facing the bed, in such a manner that the sailor could see it the last thing at night and the first in the morning, was a picture of a clipper ship. It was apparently an enlarged photograph of old standing; the edges were splintered or furled by much wearing, and there was a visible crease across the center of the picture. Still it was a stirring thing, for it showed the clipper driven before a gale, leaning dangerously in the wind, and yet holding onto a main skysail with a dogged persistence. Such a picture must have been taken from the poop of an ocean liner as it crossed the bows of the sailer, and it showed Sherry the very leap of the waves, the very straining of the cordage.

He admired that picture for a moment only, and saw the inscription under it: *TITANIA*, OUTWARD BOUND!

Somewhere he had heard of her—a queen of the tea fleet, and afterward a sturdy veteran, lugging merchandise from England to the western coast of America, and always a flyer.

However, he had other things to think of. Perhaps Fennel had sailed on the *Titania*, but that was only a small bit of information.

He pushed up a window softly and opened the shutter a crack. It was not a great distance to the ground, and for a good athlete there was a drainage pipe running down from the gutter of the roof above, straight past the window to the earth.

So, having established that in case of need the sailor could be reached from the outside of the hotel, Sherry closed the window and shutter and turned back to the room itself.

Everything was in disorder. On the bureau lay a belt containing a large sheath knife, several blackened, cracked pipes that looked as they had been smoked in many a gale at sea, so eaten was the wood by the fire; there was a blue-and-yellow handkerchief, a pocket knife with a roughened horn handle, a tattered newspaper, and several boxes of matches. On the corner table stood two whiskey bottles, one nearly empty and the other quite gone. Beside them was a tumbler. The top of it had been broken off, and the fragments glittered on the floor. All a miserable confusion, but doubtless order enough to please a man who might have spent most of his nights in the forecastle of a ship.

Last of all, Sherry saw a sailor's chest of strong three-quarter-inch pine, all dovetailed, painted black, with brass drop handles, and a two-inch rising board beneath. It was not locked. He lifted its watertight top and looked in.

Most of the things, he was surprised to see, were new, and of cheap, heavy, coarse stuff, such as a sailor might be expected to take to sea with him. Fumbling through it, Sherry noted a feather pillow, cot blankets, canvas shoes, a pair of knee-boots with pegged soles, plate, basin, quart and pint pots of block tin, a housewife containing needles and thread—heavy and coarse and strong—mending wool, scissors, and tweezers. And all these things were new! However, there was a pair of very battered working boots without any nails in the soles or heels, and these were indeed so extremely battered that Sherry wondered at finding them with the rest of these comparatively new goods. The soles, for instance, had been worn completely through.

There was nothing else to see in the chamber. He left it in haste, and returned to Lang, below.

X

Although it was not late in the morning, Fennel already appeared to have an excellent lead, and, as Sherry entered, he was singing, or attempting to sing, an old chantey of the sea. But fog filled his throat, and his breath came with a wheeze and a sputter. Nevertheless, some rhythm remained.

There's a saucy wild packet—a packet of fame—
She belongs to New York, and the Dreadnought's *her name,*
She is bound to the westward where the strong winds do blow—
Bound away in the Dreadnought *to the westward we'll go.*

Now the Dreadnought's *a-sailin' down the wild Irish Sea,*
Her passengers merry, with hearts full of glee;
Her sailors, like lions, walk the decks to and fro—
She's the Liverpool packet—Oh, Lord, let her go!

Then a health to the Dreadnought *and to her brave crew,*
To bold Captain Samuels and her officers, too.
Talk about your flash packets, Swallow Tail, *and* Black Ball,
The Dreadnought's *the flyer that can lick them all.*

If the voice of Joe Fennel was almost totally inadequate for the singing of this ballad, still he rendered it with such life, and at the end smashed his hand so heavily upon the table that even the bartender, a sour man, could not help smiling.

"Another shot all around," said Joe Fennel to the barman, "and smart's the word. There's your mate. Come here, kid, and sit down!"

Sherry joined them at the table. The whiskey was brought.

"This round is mine," said Sherry.

"I say no!" coughed Fennel, spilling a handful of silver on the table. "Take the price out of this, and keep the change. Free and easy is my life, lads. I got no call to go aloft again, like a fly into a spider's web. Some works by their hands, and some by their heads . . . and some," he added with a sinister joy, "by the pickin' up of information. And that's the ballast that I sail with now. Information, hearties! You couldn't see my Plimsoll line, I'm so deep with it. Talk has been paid for before now, and silence'll be paid a long sight better. And if you doubt me, ask the squire that's got the house on the hill!"

He paused to drink, and then cough and laugh.

"I'm sendin' up a boy with a message for that skipper that I'm gonna come and call on him. I'm gonna tell him to have his wallet all shipshape and Bristol fashion because I'm gonna review it. He's been law and lord on blue water. But I'm gonna be law and lord to him on dry land, as sure as ever a ship wore the name of the *Princess Marie!* Another shot all around! When I speak, run, steward. This ain't a sailor's home."

Sherry stood up. "I've had enough," he said.

Lang rose beside him.

"Are you takin' in sail at the first squall?" demanded Fennel. "Never take in sail for a squall that you can look through. Ain't you men enough to see light through a shot of grog?"

They waved their *adieux* to Fennel in spite of this urgent plea, and, as they left, they heard him ordering two bottles of whiskey that he went off carrying under his arm.

The face of Lang was contorted with disgust and contempt as they got into the open. "It's enough to turn a longhorn like me into a temperance preacher, kid," he said. "The low-down skunk! Drinking by himself, paralyzing himself slow and gradual in his room. Think of it, kid. Think of it, Tiny. It's gonna make me give up red-eye."

Sherry thought of the broken glass and the bottles he had seen in the sailor's room, and he nodded his assent. Then Lang asked him what he had found in the room of Fennel. He listened with the keenest attention.

"New clothes, did you say, Tiny?"

"New, cheap stuff."

"And old boots?"

"The soles were as thin as paper. The leather of them was rotten, if ever I saw rotten leather. They were so old, Pete, that the folds of the leather were hard and brittle. I scarcely can see how a man could put on boots like that"

Lang was so struck by this that he paused and laid a hand on the shoulder of his friend. "As old as that!" he said in wonder.

"As old as that." Sherry nodded. "What do you make of it, Pete? After all, there's nothing so very strange about a pair of old boots. I've had them myself."

"In a sea chest. In a sea chest," insisted Lang. "I tell you, that's the point, old boy. You never been to sea."

"Have you?"

"Well," said Lang, deliberately giving that question his shoulder, "I'll tell you what . . . it's a dashed funny thing. Old boots and new clothes to rig up a sea chest." He shook his head and walked on, so deep in thought that he looked like a man in pain.

At this, Sherry no longer bothered his companion with questions, for he knew that Lang, absorbed in thought, was like a python struggling to assimilate some gigantic meal. A strange fellow was Pete Lang. No one ever had come to the bottom of his nature, but a more useful man upon the trail to handle the problems thereof, Sherry never could have found. He began to look to Lang already, as to a man capable of working a miracle.

Lang said at length: "I'll see. I'll see."

He spoke rather like an impatient father, teased by questions, although as a matter of fact, Sherry had not said a word. And so they returned up the hill to the house of Wilton and found him in the garden with his niece. From a distance they heard his voice in a hard tone of irritation, speaking rapidly. Only in brief pauses could she have answered. They could not hear her voice, until they came out of the brush, and then they heard Wilton come to the fiery end of a sentence and heard the girl say distinctly, quietly: "No."

It was a sort of key to all that had gone before. He had been storming at her about something, and she had been holding the fort of discussion with that single word: *No.*

"You won't reason!" exclaimed Wilton. "You won't listen to reason at all. You don't want to hear me!"

"No," she said. "I don't."

It amazed Sherry. He slowed and would have halted, but Lang took his arm and forced him on. They heard Wilton exclaim with greater emphasis than ever: "And what, under the name of heaven, could I possibly have had to do with it?"

To this she returned no answer at all, but pointed toward the two who were approaching. Wilton faced about on them with a start. And Sherry saw the girl watching them with the keenest curiosity. Then she turned and went off in haste. Looked at in full face she appeared a worn and weary woman, indeed, but, as she went off, with the turn of her neck and the lightness of her step, she looked more child than woman—a happy, careless child.

This thought of her made a great impression upon Sherry, for he was one of those men who do not reason very closely, who cannot go with mathematical precision from premise to premise, but with bursts of intuition his mind leaped ahead, as though a light had been cast on the future. So he saw Beatrice Wilton with new eyes, and wondered at her—and at himself.

Wilton was vexed, plainly.

"How long have you two been standing there?" he asked.

"We ain't been standing," said Lang.

Wilton waved a hand, as though he would have said that he doubted this, but the point was not worth further discussion. "You fellows have learned to walk silently, while riding the range," he said. "Now, what do you want?" He corrected himself with a faint smile. "I forgot that you've been doing my errands. You found the man, did you? You found Fennel, as he calls himself?"

"We found him. We had a drink with him," said Sherry.

"You drank with him!" cried Wilton. "But I wouldn't do that, if I were you."

"He's not exactly the poisoning kind," said Lang.

"How does he look?" asked Wilton.

"I'll show you," answered Lang. He took out a pad of paper and a stub of soft pencil, and with that he rapidly worked up a sketch, as Sherry had seen him do a thousand times upon the range when his swift hand would jot down things big and small—the line of mountain against the sky—a bunch-backed cow with her tail to the blizzard—a coyote, lolling a thin tongue and laughing at the ranch dogs. Or perhaps it would only be a Spanish bayonet, distinguished for peculiar uprightness—or a close-up, as it were, of the dreadful thorns with which the cactus is armed. With half a dozen sweeping lines Pete Lang could show you a mustang bucking, a rider just lurching up from the saddle, out of balance. And so he now worked on the face of Fennel, the forehead covered close to the eyes with matted hair, the odd bulge of the forward part of the head, and the lower features masked with the scrub of beard. In that half minute of work he even was able to impart to this sketch the evil sneer of Fennel, the peculiar and working malice.

"By Jove, I know him!" exclaimed Wilton under his breath as he peered at the paper. Then he shook his head. "He's a liar. He never was one of us," said Wilton.

"One of who?" asked Sherry innocently.

His reward was a keen, stabbing glance.

"What did he talk about?" asked Wilton.

"About the value of silence," answered Sherry, "which he said you would certainly pay for . . . as surely as ever a ship wore the name of the *Princess Marie*."

The hand of Wilton froze in mid-gesture. Then slowly he raised it to his face. He looked like a man who had been struck by a mortal bullet. And so, without another word, he turned and went slowly toward the house.

XI

Now that they were left alone, Sherry stared after Wilton for only a moment, when he turned to Lang and said quietly: "Guilty, your honor."

"Guilty as sin," said Lang. "Guilty of what, I wonder? What's this dirty rat, Fennel, got on Wilton? What's Wilton done in the South Seas that you read about? I tell you what, kid, I'm beginning to get red-hot about this. I'm beginning to get red-hot all over. And I'll never leave the trail until we've run it into some sort of a corner. Wilton guilty, the girl looking like she had fire in the hollow of her hand . . . the dickens is to pay up here, Sherry, what with the steel-lined room, and the rest."

"Let's take a walk and think this thing over," said Sherry. "I never think so well as I do when my legs are moving."

"It keeps the blood stirred up." Lang grinned. "You think like a wolf, kid . . . with your teeth."

However, he strode off at the side of Sherry, and they pushed back through the woods that grew close behind the house of Wilton where big spruce and pine were commingled.

"How do they ever get rain enough to keep them going?" asked Sherry.

"Where does the water come from to make this run?" countered Lang, and he pointed to a trickle of water so small that it made a mere silver gleam, winding along upon the ground.

"Where from?" murmured Sherry.

"You got no eyes," answered the cowpuncher. "You can have a whole spring jumping out of the top of a hill, if there's other higher ground anywhere around to send down the rain water.

Look at them mountains over yonder . . . ain't they catching the rain and filtering it down through the strata? And one of them strata turns up here like a leaky pipe and lets out some water. Hey, kid, this is real country."

The clay rock, so narrow and slender that it rose above the town like a raised hand, now spread right and left and grew into a considerable plateau; the surface was very broken; the trees did not always stand straight, but jutted at considerable angles, at times, from the irregular surface of the land.

"This would make a first-class hole-in-the-wall country," remarked Lang. "You could hide twenty men, out here, and they could thumb their noses at everybody that tried to find them. Look around, kid. Was there ever in all the world a better country for a murder?"

Sherry agreed with a nod, for they had come out from among the trees, at this moment, and found themselves at the edge of a bluff at least two hundred feet high. Just at its base the river curved close in. Sherry kicked a stone clear of the edge and they saw its dizzy drop, its disappearance, and the sparkling leap of the water around its fall, like the spring of a fish.

"Tap a gent on the head here," said Lang, "and drop him where that stone dropped, and you'd never hear much report about him. Look where that water gets white."

Racing along the base of the cliff, the water hardly showed the speed of the current, except that it was dark instead of limpid, but at a little distance farther from the town, the current struck rocks that jutted above the surface like the prows of swift ships, each spurning a bow wave, and covered with spray.

"That machine would eat a man pretty small," suggested Lang, and Sherry agreed with a grunt.

They walked on. The surface of the ground grew more and more broken. It was chopped across the face by many small ravines, deep as a man, and sharp-sided.

"What's the good of carrying on here?" asked Sherry. "Walking is one thing, but climbing is another. Why you can't talk at this work, let alone think."

"You'd make a general," said Lang ironically. "You'd fight in the dark."

"Fight?" queried the big man.

"Tiny," exclaimed the other, "you make me tired! You make me ache! Ain't we here fighting for our lives?"

"I don't follow that exactly," said Sherry. "We fight to save the life of Wilton, as I make it out . . . and instead of keeping an eye on him, here we are, rambling away through the woods."

"If we didn't live under the nose of a tiger," said Lang, "d'you think that he would pay a thousand a day? Ask yourself that, old son."

It made Sherry glance briskly about at the trees.

"And if that's the way of it," went on Lang, "we ought to know the lay of the land out here."

They went on in silence; in fact, it was such hard work that there was little opportunity for talk until at length something crackled through the branches over their heads. Lang stiffened, attentive.

"What the deuce was that?" asked Sherry.

"You shut up," cautioned his companion. He had delivered that advice in a whisper, and now he commenced to stalk forward with a cat-like agility, pausing from time to time.

In one of those pauses, distinctly though faintly, Sherry heard a soft thud, such as might be made by an axe with a sharp edge, shearing through a tough, green branch.

Presently, peering around the corner of a large pine trunk, Lang beckoned Sherry to his side, and the big man looked around at a very odd sight.

In the center of a small clearing stood Beatrice Wilton, with a revolver in her hand, and, even as Sherry looked, she took quick aim, swinging the gun smartly up from the hip, and firing. The dim spurt of smoke was the only sound to tell that a bullet had been discharged—that and the same dull, quiet thud that he had heard before. He understood it now. It was the impact of a small-caliber bullet entering the trunk of a tree. A silencer appeared on the muzzle of the revolver.

To Sherry there was something wonderfully grim in the appearance of this girl, her mouth set firmly, determination in her eyes—the very poise of her body showed that she was practicing for more than mere game.

Twice more he saw her fire, and each time the bullet struck home in a small sapling not more than six inches in diameter.

Then Lang waved Sherry back, and they stole away through the woods and back toward the house, with a painful slowness.

When they were on the edge of the trees, again, with the house partly outlined beyond them, Sherry asked: "What do you make of it, Pete?"

"You talk sad and you talk small," said Pete. "It sort of riles you, kid?"

"Why should it?" protested Sherry.

"Why shouldn't it?" snapped Pete Lang. "You get yourself all heated up about a girl . . . and then you see her practicing with a silencer on a gun . . . and hitting the mark . . . and looking as though the mark was a man. A silent gun's a murderer's gun, Tiny."

Sherry groaned. "I've nothing to say," he admitted. "But I want to ask you what . . . "

"Don't bother me," said the cowpuncher. "I gotta think, don't I? For myself, and Wilton . . . and you, you poor snowblind cayuse, you."

They went on toward the house, and, coming out into the garden, they saw, on her knees in a bed of flowers, busily at work with a trowel, a big garden hat shading her face, no other person than Beatrice Wilton herself.

She looked up to them with a cheerful smile. "Have you been wandering around in the woods?" she asked.

"To see what the lay of the land was like," answered Lang, for Sherry was dumb with amazement.

"They're grand old trees," she replied. "And Uncle Oliver won't sell them."

They went on past her.

"Nice gent, that Wilton," said Lang. "She's sure gotta be grateful because he ain't sold the old trees off of the place."

"What does it mean?" asked Sherry. "How the dickens could she have come back here before us, old-timer?"

"She knows the woods. There may be level ways, if you know the angles and the corners. That's not what bothers me."

"What in heaven's name does, then?"

"The cool way of that girl. Cool as ice, Tiny. But no coolness under the skin. She looked after us all the way until we got around the corner of the house."

"How did you tell that? I didn't see you look back."

"I felt her look. She's got that kind of eyes," said Lang.

* * * * *

They went to their small room, and they hardly had settled down in it before their employer tapped at the door. He invited Lang to go up with him to the office, while Sherry stretched out on his bunk to piece together what they had learned.

Presently both Lang and Wilton came back; Wilton was pale with anger and excitement.

"Sherry," he said, "I think that I'm paying you boys well. I've offered to double that pay if one of you will get rid of Fennel for me. You understand? I'll double the money. It'll be twenty thousand dollars on the nail. Lang, here, refuses."

"I don't follow that . . . entirely," said Sherry slowly. "One of us bumps off Fennel. Is that it?"

"That wouldn't stop us," broke in Lang with an odd glance at his companion. "It ain't the first man that Sherry, here, has slipped a slug into. But you gotta hold your horses, Wilton."

"I tell you on my honor," said Wilton gravely, "that that man may ruin me."

"If he's the real article?"

"Real article?"

"Not a fake, I mean."

"How could he be a fake? He knows already . . . "

"He's a danged actor," said Lang with conviction. "Did you ever hear of a sailor with a whole new outfit . . . and one old pair of sea boots . . . with holes in the bottom of 'em? A fine comforting thing a pair of boots like that would be, going around the Horn."

"By heaven!" exclaimed Wilton, and quickly struck his hands sharply together.

"And how long ago," said Lang, "did sailors stop calling whiskey and rum grog? He's a fake."

XII

The reaction of Wilton to this strange remark was odd, to say the least. He glared hard at Lang and asked sharply: "Have you been at sea?"

"I ain't spent all my days on the range," admitted Lang.

Wilton continued to regard him with distinct disfavor. "You haven't spent all of your days on the range, eh? How did you sail?"

"Before the mast."

"Where?"

"And what's that got to do with the job here?" asked Lang bluntly.

The fist of Wilton balled suddenly. Then he controlled himself. "You're sure that Fennel is a faker?"

"As sure as I'm standing here."

"Lang, there's a good deal depends on this!"

"By the way you carry on, I suppose there is," replied the cowpuncher.

Before Wilton could make further remark, there was a loud rap at the outer door.

"Will you open and see who's there?" Wilton asked Sherry.

So Sherry went to the front door and opened it for Dr. Eustace Layman, whose usually pale face was now flushed from walking up the hill. He came in upon them with a wave of his hand in greeting.

"I've been called in to see this fellow, Fennel," he said. "The rascal is drinking himself into an early grave."

"I wish he were under the sod already," commented Wilton. "Is he seriously ill?"

"Typical alcoholic. Subnormal temperature, jerky hands, dull eyes, and a sinking in the pit of the stomach."

"What did you do for him?"

"Told him to stop all liquor at once. The rascal simply cursed the world of doctors, and poured himself another drink under my eyes. After that, he gave me a letter to carry to you."

"A letter for me?"

"Here it is."

Wilton received it. "It seems the scoundrel is a sham," he said to the doctor. "Lang saw through him. Lang has been at sea."

"A sham?" murmured Layman, and looked askance at Lang. "Are you sure of that? He appears like the real article, to me. He's low enough to be really in the part."

"He ain't so low as all that," said Lang. "He's got a brain in his head."

"Did you guess that by his talk?" asked the doctor.

"By his eye," answered Lang. "You can change a good many things, but you can't keep thought out of a gent's eye."

"Ha?" said the doctor. "You're a clever fellow, Lang. I can see that."

Wilton, in the meantime, was tearing open the envelope. "He's printed the letters," said Wilton. "He wouldn't trust his handwriting, it seems." Then he gasped, and, suddenly crumpling the letter, he thrust it into his pocket as though he feared that some hand might snatch it from him.

"What's upset you, Oliver?" asked Layman. "If the fellow's a fake, how can he trouble you like this?"

Wilton slowly drew out a handkerchief, and dragged it across his forehead. He looked white and sick; in fact, he had to lean one hand against the side of the doorjamb. "He's coming here," said Wilton. "He's coming here sometime this afternoon, and he invites me to meet him in my garden, Eustace."

"Nonsense," replied the doctor. "Make him meet you in your room, of course. Or rather, don't see him at all . . . if Lang is right about him. What's to be gained from talking to a mere sham and . . . ?"

"You talk like a fool!" exclaimed Wilton. "I've got to meet him. This afternoon . . . I'm going up to rest, now. Will you go up with me, Eustace?"

They went together out of the little chamber and climbed the stairs. On the way, Sherry could hear Layman making some suggestion, and to it Wilton answered in a loud and angry voice: "I tell you, I won't have any more of the stuff. Either I'll have a good, normal sleep, or else I'll get on without it altogether."

The door of the steel room closed behind them, and Sherry sat down heavily on the bunk nearest him. "My head's spinning," he confessed. "If this rat, Fennel, is a sham, how can he upset Wilton like this? Why should Wilton plan to see him at all?" Lang did not answer, and Sherry continued: "Why didn't you tell me that Fennel was a sham?"

"What good would it do to tell you? What good? The thing you tell is the thing that you've lost. I gotta few ideas already in my head about these people. But if I tell you, then they'll die. Telling a secret is killing it at the root. You can throw the reins and dismount, old-timer. I'm gonna drift this herd if I can, and you can't help me much."

Even this bluntness did not disturb Sherry, who stretched himself on the bunk and folded his hands under his head. "I'm not a clever one like you," he said. "You can do the thinking for the party . . . call me when I'm wanted." And instantly he closed his eyes and pretended to sleep.

"You ain't a man, you're an ox," said Lang. "You were made up of nerve and muscle and bone, and the brains left out. I would rather . . . "

Sherry heard no more, but slept in fact until he was wakened by a dimly heard tap on the door, and then by the squeak of the hinges as it was opened.

Eustace Layman came in to them, saying: "You boys may find Wilton a little trying for the next few days. The truth is that he's upset and his nerves are frayed very thin, indeed. I want you to bear with him, if you can."

"We're paid for that," replied Sherry.

"You're well paid," replied the doctor, "and, for my part, I think that you're paid for nothing."

"You think that?"

"Wilton's imagination is running away with him. I never knew an old sailor who wasn't apt to have more daydreams than were good for him, and I believe that's the trouble with my friend, Wilton."

"Is he an old sailor?"

"He was on the sea for years. Became a skipper, in fact."

"Did you ever hear of a ship called the *Princess Marie?*" asked Lang.

"Great Scott, yes," said the doctor, "and so has everyone else who knows anything about the Wiltons."

"How come that, Doctor?"

"Why, that was Everett Wilton's ship, of course," said Eustace Layman. "The one that foundered in the typhoon."

"Foundered?"

"Sprang a leak in a heavy wind and went down."

"I don't recall hearing of any such a thing," said Lang. "Not while I follered the sea, and I used to hear a good deal about the China Seas, and that part of the world."

"You know that bit, eh?"

"Pretty fair."

"She was only two thousand tons, but she was a new, strong boat. She was such a good one that Everett put his brother in command of her, because he didn't want to trust any other person with such a large part of the Wilton fortune. Well, she struck this typhoon of which I was speaking, sprang a leak, and went down. Twelve of the crew in two boats made Hevavo. You know that port?"

"Yes, in San Cristobal."

"The ship was a clean loss, and she wasn't insured for half her value, and the cargo wasn't insured at all, I believe. It was a hard blow for the Wilton fortune. It cut the Wilton money in half, I should say."

"And that was the *Princess Marie*," murmured Lang.

"That was the ship. She was only six months old. Everett had great hopes of her. I've always thought that it was the loss of the ship that made him so despondent."

"Made him sort of low, did it?" queried Lang.

"Low? Why, man, you know that he committed suicide?"

"Suicide!" cried Sherry, springing up.

Dr. Layman drew back a step.

"Suicide, of course," he said with a slight frown. "He made sure of himself by jumping off the bluff into the river. The rocks nearly cut him to bits . . . but there was enough left for the purposes of identification."

"Suicide," muttered Sherry. "How long ago?"

"Nearly a year."

"No wonder his daughter is half a wreck," said Sherry grimly. "I'm glad that I've heard this."

"One runs into these melancholy temperaments," said Layman. "It's in the Wilton blood, of course. Strong-tempered people . . . never can quite tell what they'll do." He turned toward the door. "You'll bear with Wilton, boys, for a few days?"

"Of course," said Sherry.

The doctor nodded cheerfully to them and went out. They could hear him whistling blithely as he walked away from the house into the garden.

"Cool fellow, eh?" commented Sherry.

"Cool?" said Lang. "He's too cool. I don't like him worth a cent, I can tell you." Then he added: "It's a fine job that we've got into. I'd rather ride herd on five thousand mavericks than try to handle this job."

"Suicide . . . shipwreck . . . it's a fine job . . . you're right. But you won't chuck it, Pete?"

"Have you still got hopes of her?" asked Lang with brutal suddenness.

To which Sherry replied calmly: "Of course I have, old son. She's walked into the middle of my brain and I'll never be able to get rid of the thought of her."

XIII

The afternoon came on chilly and dark. The wind lay in the northwest, with the sting of the higher snows in it, and carrying black clouds that looked as though they were about to drop a cargo of rain over Clayrock in passing. But as they spread southward, the darkness departed, and they sank over the south horizon in droves of milk-white fleeces. Under this sky, Wilton sent forth his two guards, saying briefly: "Look over the garden. Print the paths in your brains. Come back here in an hour. I'm going out to meet Fennel."

He said it with a desperate quiet, like a man full of his fate. And Sherry and Lang went out and leaned against the wind, which, leaping straight across the valley, smote the great clay rock with a constant volleying.

Three paths opened from the house. Sherry took one, and Lang another, and they strode off on their exploration. Pausing at every juncture of paths, Sherry tried to make careful note of them all, but he found that he was having very little luck. There seemed to be two systems employed in the layout of the paths through the Wilton garden. On the one hand, there were two winding paths that worked up the hillside with gradual curves to make the ascent easier. On the other hand, there was a much briefer way of ascent or descent, and that was a path that dropped in sharply angling zigzags to the foot of the slope. All these paths intersected here and there in the most random fashion, for the garden had not been laid out in any methodical pattern, but the paths had been made for the sake of convenience to get up and down the hill. Sometimes the two curving ways crossed one another and recrossed; sometimes the path of descent cut sheer across the others, turned abruptly, and dropped again toward the foot of the rock. Sherry, work as he might, could not untangle this confusion and bring the scheme to any order in his mind. He even lost the main ways two or three times, and found himself in some little clearing among the trees, where the Wiltons had laid out bright scraps of flower garden in their random way.

The second time he entered one of these, Beatrice Wilton sprang up from a rustic bench on which she had been seated, her head resting in both hands, and out of her lap something dropped with the bright glitter of steel to the ground.

She stepped hastily forward—as though she hoped that with her feet she could hide the thing. But Sherry shook his head.

"I saw it," he said.

She waited for an instant, as though about to reply, but then she apparently changed her mind and stooped and picked up the revolver. She slipped it inside her jacket and faced Sherry again with a defiance as distinct as it was silent.

It roused a little impatience in his mind; he pointed toward the hidden weapon. "Why do you carry that?" he asked.

"We have rabbits here," she answered. "One gets a whack at them, now and again."

"And you have a silencer on it, too."

"Of course. That's to keep from scaring the other rabbits."

"Let me see the gun," he demanded.

She paused. "Well . . ." she consented. And she held out the revolver unwillingly.

It was of a very small caliber, but specially made in every respect, with a long, delicate barrel, on which the silencer looked oddly out of place. When Sherry broke the gun open, he found that it was loaded with long .22s. He shut it again with a snap. Then he handed it back to her.

"You don't like it," she said.

"No," he answered. "I don't go in for murder." Even as he spoke, he felt that he was being foolishly blunt and rude, but he was hardly sorry as he watched her eyes widen at him.

"That's a great deal to say," she observed. But he saw that she was not angry. She was rather frightened, and her face was full of suspicion. "But I know," she went on pleasantly, "that you fellows from the range don't stop to pick your words. At any rate, you know well that one has to learn to take care of oneself in this part of the world."

"No woman does," he told her.

"And why not?" she asked.

"Because the men look out for them, of course. You're a Westerner. You know that better than I do."

"I understand you now," she replied. "Western chivalry! But I know the truth."

"Look here," said Sherry. "Why don't you come out in the open? Maybe I could help."

She turned her head away a little, and he knew that she did so to cover a faint smile of derision, or of doubt, but that hardly mattered so much as the new view he had of her in profile. For from that angle, he saw no longer the shadows of trouble about her eyes, nor the pain, which stiffened her lips; at a stroke she seemed five years younger, delicately and purely lovely.

He, rather breathless, went blundering on: "I see what you think. You've heard yarns about me in the town. About the killing of Capper. I'll tell you straight. There was something in the whiskey . . . and it drugged me. Whatever I did, I don't remember it . . . any more than that bench remembers anything. Do you believe that?"

She looked back at him, as cool as any man. "You're here as a fighting man," she said, "and Uncle Oliver doesn't make mistakes."

"I've done my share of fighting," he admitted. "But I don't apologize for that. I never hunted trouble in my life."

"You simply stood where it was sure to come, you stood and welcomed it?" she said.

He raised his head and looked at the clouds shooting in close-mustered ranks out of the north. "Well," he replied thoughtfully, "perhaps you're right about that. I haven't thought about it in that way. However, you'll admit that I know something about guns."

"Yes. Of course."

"Then take my advice. Throw that gun away. Give it to me, now. No good will ever come to you from that sort of a revolver. It'll never kill a rabbit, though it would easily kill a man." He watched her with dread as he said this, and his heart sickened when he saw her flinch. "Will you do that?" he persisted. "Will you give the thing to me? And if it's merely protection of some kind that you want . . . protection against what I can't tell . . . why not let me take on the job?"

She, for an answer, held both her hands away from her, palms up. "You'd never understand," she said. "And heaven knows it's something that I can't explain. I daren't explain it even to myself."

Sorrow and doubt of her so filled the heart of Sherry that he scowled upon her for a moment, and then he said: "I've warned you. You'll find out that I'm right."

He turned about on his heel and went off—but slowly, for he yearned to hear her calling him back. But she said not a word, and, when he reached the circle of the trees and looked back at her, she was sitting on the bench once more, with her head in her hands.

The hour was nearly over, and, therefore, he went slowly back in the direction of the house. He would have been lost if it had not been for the occasional glimpses he had of the white façade through the trees. But by their help he was able to correct his course several times and at last he came out on the more level ground before the Wilton house. At the same moment Lang stepped from among the trees, his head down, as if he were heavy with thought. He hardly glanced aside at his friend as Sherry hurried up to him.

"Can you make out this queer place?" he asked Sherry.

"I found the girl," said Sherry hastily, "sitting among the trees with that murder gun in her lap. She talked oddly, Pete. I can't make her out. What in the world is happening in her mind?"

"The dickens is loose all around here," muttered Lang for an answer. "But I'm going to study it out . . . I am going to study it out," he declared more resolutely. "I only wish that we had a few days' more time. But we're pinched for time, Tiny. We're mighty pinched for time. They're all wrong . . . they're all crooked, and yet we gotta try to read them."

When they came to the house itself, Wilton stepped out to meet them. He had put on a heavy overcoat and muffled his neck in a scarf. Nevertheless, he trembled, and he explained his shuddering by saying curtly: "I'm too long off the sea . . . every cold snap sends a chill through me. We're going down the straight path," he added. "Fennel will be somewhere along it, I think. And now, boys, you understand what I'm facing, don't you?"

"A pile of trouble," said Lang, "and you're a fool to run yourself into such danger. There ain't any need of it."

Wilton made an impatient gesture.

"I didn't bring you here to be judges of what was best for me," he said angrily. "I brought you both here as fighting men. Do you hear? When I walk into that garden today, I'm walking into peril of my life. I expect you to be close to me . . . close behind. If so much as a leaf stirs . . . shoot, and shoot to kill." He added by way of a spur: "You get your money if I live through the ten days. You don't get a penny, otherwise. Follow on close behind. Do you hear?"

They nodded, and he walked on with a brisk but uncertain step, as though his legs had become weak at the knees and his feet had no feeling of the terrain.

Behind him went the two guards, Lang muttering to his companion: "He's never going to walk back, Tiny."

Then they turned the first angle of the path, and saw Wilton stiffly halted, and before him, half lost under the shadow of a pine and leaning against its trunk, the tall form of Fennel. He was laughing in silent content—a most gruesome grimace.

XIV

"We'd better close up on him . . . Wilton is scared pretty near to death," said Pete Lang.

So, with Tiny Lew Sherry, he advanced to the side of their employer. Still the drunken sailor—if sailor he were—leaned by the tree and laughed at them until it became hideous, impossible to watch him. For it seemed as though he were mocking all three, like some devil beyond the reach of human strength or malice. And yet here were three armed men, mature, strong, capable of hard battle—and yonder seemed only a shaken rag of humanity. It was the unreasonable laughter that made the man appear so terrible.

"Stay close to me," muttered Wilton hoarsely, as the two came up. Shame was actually driven from him. He kept his eyes fixed upon the nondescript form of Fennel, enchanted with terror. "I'm afraid to be alone near that man, Sherry. You stay close to me. You, too, Lang. If I ever get through this, I'll make you know my gratitude."

At this last moment, Lang still attempted to argue. "Look here," he said, "what's the good of this? You know that he's not a real sailor. He's lying. He's simply trying to blackmail something out of you. Why be a fool like this? Let me go and tell him to get out of this. You don't have to talk to him at all. I wouldn't, if I was you."

Then Wilton, in spite of fear—or because of it, perhaps—turned in a fury upon the other. "Look here, you," he said, "I tell you that man knows everything! I've hired your hands, not your wits. Do as I tell you!"

Sherry stared at Wilton. It was hard to think that the man was sane, yet making such richly implied admissions of guilt as this. In fact, he saw that Wilton was *not* sane. His common, saving sense was swallowed up completely by blank fear.

However, now Wilton was facing forward toward the enemy, and he went ahead with a quick, light step, which certainly belied the state of his emotions. Or perhaps it sprang from the desperation of one who wanted to have this suspense ended, no matter what the cost might be.

Fennel did not leave his tree as the trio approached him, but remained leaning against it, still laughing, so that the sound became audible—a husky wheeze, rather than normal human laughter. A beastly imitation of the human sound. He wore an ancient and faded felt hat, was wrapped to the throat in a tightly buttoned overcoat that dragged almost to the ground, and on his feet were partly visible wrinkled boots, like those which Sherry had seen in the sea chest of this seaman, or pseudo-sailor.

When they were very close to him, at last Fennel left the tree and advanced toward them a few steps, entering the path, but with a staggering step. The man appeared very drunk. Even the upper part of his face was darkly flushed.

Wilton halted as the fellow approached him.

"He never was aboard, but I know him," Sherry heard him mutter, plainly thinking aloud. "*Where* have I seen him before?"

Then Fennel, having drawn close enough, said in his thick way: "You think I'm gonna talk to you when you got your pair of bulldogs with you, eh? Damned if I am. I ain't gonna talk to you at all unless they fall back astern a half cable length, say."

Wilton hesitated. Twice he turned back toward his companions, and twice he faced again toward Fennel, but at last he snapped over his shoulder: "Fall back, boys. Fifteen or twenty steps, say. D'you want to walk on with me, Fennel?"

"You an' me side-by-side, like old friends, which we are or ought to be," said the rascal. "You and me together, skipper, like the good old days."

With that, he actually took the arm of Wilton, while Sherry looked on with disgust and wonder. The pair drew ahead; they were almost around the first bend, when Sherry and Lang started to follow, Lang saying: "Dashed if I like this. I don't like it at all."

At fifteen or twenty paces it really was rather hard to follow the two through such a labyrinth as this garden, where the paths twisted and dodged so unreasonably, but by the sound of the voices they were guided on their way—by the voice of Wilton, rather, for that of Fennel, husky and obscure, was lost in the wind.

"I don't like it," reiterated Lang.

They almost stumbled on top of the pair, at the next turning of the path, for Wilton and Fennel had halted and Wilton was expostulating in a rapid voice, with many gestures that had both fear and appeal in them. When he saw his guards behind him, he caught the arm of Fennel and drew the man rapidly ahead, as though it was even more to his interest than that of the sailor to be free from observation.

Twice again Sherry had view of the couple, and all the time his sense of the guilt of Wilton was increased; every glimpse of the man showed that he was in a blue funk—because of the presence of such an obvious reptile as Fennel.

They came next around a sharp corner into that straighter path that went down the face of the slope with only a few angles in it. They could look straight before them for a hundred yards, but now there was no sign of either Wilton or his companion.

Lang gave Sherry a significant glance, and they hurried ahead. Lang had his revolver in his hand now, but Sherry still kept his under cover. He was a more practiced warrior than his friend.

They had at least a partial explanation of the disappearance of the other two, the next instant, for they went blundering past the hidden mouth of a narrow path, adjoining. Up this they turned and went over two windings of it. Then Lang held up a hand; they both halted. Not far away there was a rustling through the brush.

"Go get it," said Lang. "I'm going to hunt around here. Go get it and bring it back."

Sherry hesitated, not as a man depressed by fear, but rather as one gathering himself for a spring. Then he leaped away into the trees. He had spotted the rustling, faintly crackling noise that he had heard, and now he made toward it with all his speed, swerving around the broad trunks of trees, dodging this way and that, and still sweeping invincibly toward the place from which the sound had been audible.

He almost overran his quarry. Had the face been turned away, he would have plunged past the bush, but that white glimmer of skin warned him just as he was springing by. He whirled in midstride, a trick learned only on the football field or in the squared circle of the boxer, and, gun in hand, lunged straight in upon— Beatrice Wilton!

As a lion takes up a cub, so he took her out, by the nape of the neck—so to speak— and held her up.

She was utterly white. She was trembling in his grasp. The revolver with the silencer on its narrow muzzle hung helplessly, almost shaking out of her hand. "I didn't do it!" she stammered at Sherry. "I swear that I didn't do it!"

"You didn't do what?" he asked her. Then he saw something on the other hand. He turned it up. The palm was smeared; the fingers were thick with crimson.

"Blood!" exclaimed Sherry.

She herself held that hand before her face, saying stupidly, in a mutter: "I didn't do it. I didn't do it."

The lips of Sherry compressed and his nostrils expanded. He took the gun away from her, none too gently, and found the barrel warm. He opened the cylinder. One bullet had been freshly discharged and the empty shell remained. A faintly pungent odor rose to him. Burned powder, of course. Then he took her firmly by the arm.

"You're coming back with me," he said.

She drew in a gasping breath. He had heard exactly that sound once before. It had been in a Mexican drinking place, and the gasp had come from a man who had received a knife thrust in his heart.

"I can't go," said Beatrice Wilton.

"Why not? What've you done? Whose blood is that?" He snapped the brief questions at her.

"I don't know . . . mine, perhaps," she said.

"Are you hurt?" he asked her, more savage with grief than with angry suspicion, even.

"I don't know," she whispered, and began to shake violently again. "Only . . . don't take me back there. I couldn't stand that . . . I . . . "

"You've got to come. Or else tell me why." He urged her forward, as he spoke, and she turned up a pale, sick face of fear and horror to him.

"Please! Please!" she begged.

Lew Sherry picked her up in his arms and she made no resistance, but her head rolled helplessly over on his shoulder. He glanced down and saw that her eyes were closed, though her fists were tightly clutched.

So he bore her back in one arm, straining with the weight of her, but with his other still-armed hand fending off the branches. He came close to the path and there he paused. He said huskily: "Listen to me. If you've done something, if you want to dodge it, tell me what you've done. Then I'll take you away. I'll take you so far that you'll never be found. I'll . . . I'll look after you. You understand?"

He thought she did not hear, at first. Then she opened her eyes at him, but not with understanding, only with sick trouble.

Sherry choked, and because he did not know what else to do except obey the original instructions of Lang, he carried her tenderly out into the narrow irregular pathway.

He saw Lang at once, kneeling in some tall grass near the verge of the path, and suddenly the girl twisted in the arm of Sherry and pressed her face hard into his shoulder. He was beside Lang, now, and, looking down among the grass, he saw a man's body lying face down. At that very moment Lang turned the body face upward and exposed the white, troubled features of Wilton himself.

He had been shot through the head. There was a very small purple spot between the eyes, and a very thin trickle of blood ran down over the right eye and onto the right cheek, where it disappeared in a blur.

XV

As Beatrice Wilton, half fainting, leaned against Sherry, he lowered her to the ground.

Pete Lang stood over her. "Miss Wilton," he said, "d'you know anything about this?"

"No! I only know that I . . . I stumbled over the body."

"Did you see the sailor? Fennel, I mean?"

"No."

"Did you stop here?"

"Here? By Uncle . . . ?"

"Yes. Did you stop here?"

"No, no!"

"You went straight on past him?"

"Yes, yes!"

"You'd better go back to the house," said Lang.

"I'll go," she agreed. She looked up to Sherry with the same appeal in her eyes that he had seen there before, then she moved away. But still, at a little distance, she turned again, and flashed back to Sherry a wild glance of appeal.

Sherry remained, staring at his friend, and Lang stared back at him.

"What became of Fennel?" he asked. "He must have done this."

"Fennel? I dunno," muttered Lang. "Look here, kid. Is there apt to be two Twenty-Two-caliber, high-power revolvers in the same town at the same time . . . both of 'em with silencers on their guns?"

"She couldn't have done it," protested Sherry, although he knew that his voice was weak with the lack of conviction. "She simply could not have done it. You know that, Pete. Tell me you realize that."

Pete Lang grunted savagely. "She lied straight off the bat," he pointed out. "How could you want me to talk soft about her, eh? She lied like a streak. She didn't stop near the dead man. You heard that?"

"Well, and what about it?" asked Sherry.

"Well, man, didn't you see the blood on her hand?"

"Brush is full of thorns," said Sherry desperately. "You take a young girl like that . . . let her see a dead man . . . and what will she do? Bolt, of course. No looking where she's going. And the result will be blood on her hand, if she scratched it on a thorn.

159

You see that, Pete? Of course you see that there's a lot of sense in that?"

Pete Lang looked upon his friend with an air of pity. "I'm kinda sorry for you, Tiny," he said. "That's all that I got to say to you. I'm just kinda sorry for you. Now, we'll leave things be. The sheriff will want to see this, without too much of the scene changed. You scatter down to town and let the sheriff know about it. And then head straight on for the hotel and take another look at Fennel's room. It ain't going to be hard when they know that he's suspected of murder."

Sherry was very glad indeed to have something active to do. He made no protest against the manner in which his friend had taken the lead in this affair, but like a good lieutenant, he marched unquestioningly to obey orders.

He got his horse at the stable behind the house and went down the steep road to the street in one furious plunge, with a rattle of flying gravel before him and a rolling of loosened stones behind.

It was easy to find the sheriff. He sat like a little wooden image in front of the hotel, staring unwinking before him and occasionally smoothing his fine white beard. Sheriff Herbert Moon never drank and never smoked. He had no nervous need of occupying his hands with trifles and his brain with a cloud of smoke. He ate little. He talked less. And he held down his office of sheriff not by dint of popular speeches or appeals to friendly voters, but by sheer brilliance in his office, wherein his record was flawless and unequaled during these past twenty-five years. Exactly half of his life he had spent in catching criminals of all kinds. The work had made him look at least fifteen years older than his actual age. But still he stuck to his task. Nothing changed. He hated change, men said, and that was why he remained in Clayrock, living in the same little shed that had served him as a youth, twenty-five years before, and propping it here and there, from year to year, as its knees grew weaker, and its pathetic back threatened to break.

He never had married. He never had so much as looked at a woman. He had no friends. He lived, in fact, encased in solitude, like a sword in a battered but strong sheath. But when there was use for the weapon—lo, the pure, bright flash of the steel when it was drawn.

So it was with Sheriff Herbert Moon, who sat at rest, all passive, resting in body, in mind, and in soul, until the summons came that brought him out upon the man trail. In twenty-five years, he had killed or captured two hundred and twelve criminals single-handed. In that list there was no account taken of the sweepings of drunkards from gutters in the early days of the mining boom. But two hundred and twelve times he faced danger for the sake of upholding the law, and he had nearly always won.

It was said that for every year of his service in Clayrock, Sheriff Moon carried a scar. Some silver dot or streak upon his body for every one of twenty-five years of labor. But his face was unmarked. Only, below the chin, there was a long, puckering slash. He was ashamed of it. He always muffled his neck with some scarf, so that he was given rather an old-fashioned appearance by this peculiarity of his dress, and, indeed, it was merely to harmonize with that necessary neck mask that he had allowed his beard to grow, and had trimmed it slender and narrow. If his neck apparel was old-fashioned, so should all his appearance be.

Time, from the moment that he made those two alterations in his appearance, made but a gradual change in the sheriff. Only, each year his attire seemed more threadbare. Men declared, mockingly, that he never had bought a new suit of clothes for twenty-five years. Some men vowed that he was a miser, and that he must have a fortune stowed away in some corner. However, not a soul was aware that the salary of the sheriff had stood still for a quarter of a century. No one thought of increasing it. The buying power of the dollar dropped to thirty percent. But the sheriff asked for no raise of pay and none was given him. Of the rewards that he earned by his courage, he took no account, but always gave the money, as it came in, to charity.

"A man cannot live on blood money, you know," said the sheriff.

To this little man—"He's so small, that's why he don't get shot up bad," said the tough citizens of Claryock—to this little sheriff, on the verandah of the hotel, appeared big Lew Sherry. He leaped from his horse. A billow of thin dust swept before him as he halted in front of Herbert Moon.

"You're Moon? You're the sheriff?"

"That's my name, sir," said the sheriff.

"Wilton's been murdered in his garden. I came along to report. He was shot through the brain. The body's lying where it fell. Pete Lang is waiting to show you everything."

The sheriff stared, for an instant, his lips parted. Against the white of the beard, those lips seemed young and smooth and strangely red.

"Dear me, dear me," said the sheriff. "Wilton is dead. Another rich Wilton, and in a single year. Dear me, dear me." He did not rise at once. He continued to look at Sherry as though the big man had told him the most remarkable thing in the world.

"I'm going to tell you one thing more. The man that did the shooting was Fennel . . . the drunken sailor that lived here in the hotel and talked so much and drank such a lot more," said Sherry.

"I'm glad to know that." The sheriff nodded. "Of course I want to know who did the murdering. Thank you, Mister Sherry."

"You know me?"

"Of course. Since the day you killed Capper. I've known you ever since that day. I have to know people who can shoot so straight," said the gentle voice of Herbert Moon.

It made Sherry feel a little uneasy. We like to read the character of a new event in its face. We don't wish to go by opposites. This fellow appeared to Sherry like the most inoffensive of men.

He looked like a learned man, tired of study, retiring from his labors. But he was a famous warrior. He was not one who had killed a great many. After his first month in office, he had not had to. Men usually surrendered when this terrible and quiet little man came upon their traces. But he almost frightened Sherry with his gentleness.

"Are you going back with me?" asked the sheriff.

"No. I'm going to stay here, just now."

It occurred to Sherry that he had better not announce his intention of searching the room of Fennel. That might interfere with the sheriff's ideas of what was best. And most desperately did Sherry want to conduct that search in person, in the hope that, in some fashion, he could be able to fasten upon the sailor the crime of that day.

For there was ever, in the back of his brain, the image of Beatrice Wilton, with the blood upon her hand. In his own pocket was her gun, the silencer attached, the empty cartridge. He felt that that was her destiny—and he carried it—he would guard it.

He went into the hotel and said bluntly that he wanted the key to Fennel's room. The clerk, impressed by this sternness, handed it over without remark, merely staring, and Sherry went up to the chamber.

It was almost exactly as it had been when he last saw it. But there were four whiskey bottles upon the table instead of two. Three of them were empty. But the fourth was still untouched.

Suddenly Sherry struck his knuckles against his forehead. He turned. The clerk was in the doorway, a little frightened, but very curious.

"Has anyone been in this room drinking with Fennel?" Sherry asked.

"Nobody," said the clerk.

Sherry stared at the whiskey bottles again. It was most odd. According to the mute testimony of those bottles, Fennel had consumed more than a quart of whiskey in his room since Sherry last examined the place. But that was not possible. What, then, had become of the liquor?

A small matter, no doubt, but when there is murder in the air, small matters loom large.

XVI

"Is there anything wrong?" asked the clerk.

"Murder, that's all," said Sherry gloomily. He enjoyed, mildly, the confusion and the astonishment of the other.

"I knew that no good ever would come out of a rat like that. I never seen such a fellow for absorbin' whiskey. A couple of quarts a day, sometimes. I never seen anything like it. He was a regular sponge," declared the clerk.

A sponge, indeed, if two quarts of whiskey could be consumed in a single day!

He brooded upon the problem and upon the room, and, as though to get more light on the subject, he opened the window nearest to the table.

"You take a man with a brain full of alcohol, that way, he'd be sure to do pretty nearly anything. Crazy with drink, day and night. Sometimes you could hear him laughin' and singin' in his choked way here in the room in the middle of the night."

Sherry listened with only half his mind. The other half was fumbling vaguely, as a man will do at a problem in geometry, when all the lines and the angles go wrong for him. And in that state, he stared at the drainage pipe that ran down the wall and noted with dim unconcern that a spot on it was of different color from the rest, fresher, as though it had rusted less. He touched that spot, and it gave on hinges to his finger. It was, in fact, a trap door let into the pipe. It brought Sherry quickly out of his haze. What was that used for? He stared more closely. He could see that the edges of the metal had been cut not long ago. It would not have been a difficult task, for the pipe was lead.

Then a thought came to Sherry, and he hurried out of the room and down to the garden to a point just below the window of Fennel's room. The clerk was leaning out the window.

"Find anything, Sherry?" he called with eagerness.

Tiny Lew stood still, his eyes half closed, his breath drawing deeply. But there was no mistaking the odor that welled up thick and rank from the ground all about the vent of the drainage pipe. Close about it, the grass was brown and dead. It had been soaked with alcohol poured down the pipe. And that was the meaning of the trap door in the drain. That was the explanation, too, of the Herculean drinking of this sham drunkard.

"Find anything?" exclaimed the clerk again.

"Not a thing," said Sherry, and went straightway to his horse and cantered away for the Wilton place.

He had a strangely powerful impulse to turn the head of the horse on the out trail and leave Clayrock and its evil crime behind him forever. Curiously enough, it was not the thought of Beatrice Wilton that stopped him now, but the knowledge that Peter Lang was yonder in the garden of the house, using his wits to solve this mystery.

So Sherry held on his way to the Wilton house, and walked his horse up the steep carriage road to the stable. The Chinese cook came out from the kitchen with a tin of scraps in his hand, stared at Sherry with fear and wonder, as at a dangerous being from a strange world. Sherry went around to the front of the house, and there he found the sheriff, Lang, and Dr. Layman all gathered in a close group discussing some clothes that lay on the ground before them.

Lang had discovered them among the trees, by closely following up the trail of Fennel, where it left the spot where Wilton had fallen. They consisted of the overcoat, the old hat, and the clumsy boots of Fennel, which he had worn when he confronted the three a little earlier on this tragic day.

"Murderers run, of course, after they've done the killing," said the doctor. "I suppose there isn't any doubt that Fennel is the man who did this thing?"

"It looks that way, of course," said the sheriff.

"Thank goodness, he can't go far," said Layman. "Not with his build and his face. He'd made himself well enough known around Clayrock, and in a few hours you'll have him, Sheriff."

Here Lang put in: "There's somebody else to be considered in this job."

Sherry glared at him. And when he failed to catch the eye of his friend, he said roughly: "What d'you mean by that, Pete?"

Pete Lang waved off the question. "I'll talk to the sheriff," he persisted. "Murder's a black thing, and, if there's any way of getting to the truth about it, I want to help."

"Aye," said Herbert Moon in his soft voice, "murder is black. But in this part of the world there are too many who don't agree with your viewpoint, I'm afraid. Murder is black. And there's always night gathered around it. Can you help us out of the dark, Mister Lang?"

"I can," said Pete Lang. "I want to tell you what I've seen Miss Wilton do."

"Pete!" cried Sherry in agony.

"Man, man!" protested the doctor. "Beatrice? Beatrice Wilton? What are you talking about?"

"I think you know your duty, Lang," was all the sheriff remarked.

"I know my duty. I'm gonna do it. I got a clear case. I'm gonna state it. Me and old Tiny, yonder, seen this here girl practicing off in the woods with a small-caliber revolver with a silencer on it, so that you didn't hear any explosion. You just heard a sort of puff. Well, a while back Tiny ran into her in the woods sitting pretty thoughtful, and that gun in her lap. And now I want to point out that Wilton was killed with a bullet out of just such a gun, and that him and me, following close on behind, didn't hear any sound of a gun."

"It was the wind!" exclaimed Sherry eagerly. "The wind was howling and roaring through the trees, just then. There was enough wind to kill the sound."

"The sound of a revolver . . . not more'n forty yards away," persisted Lang.

Sherry groaned. He saw the absurdity of such a claim as he had just made.

The doctor and the sheriff said nothing. They watched and listened intensely, their eyes never stirring from the face of Lang, who continued: "It ain't easy to say these things. I gotta explain that I hate sneaking murder. And a woman that shoots to kill is a lot more sneaking than a man, because she's got a lot more chances of getting off, if she's caught. Well, this one is caught, and I hope she hangs for it . . . and the prettier her face, the more I hope that she hangs! After we started hunting for Wilton . . . missing him on the path . . . we heard a sound in the woods. I asked Tiny to go after it. He did, and he found this here girl crouching in a bush. There was a gun in her hand.

"The barrel of that gun was still warm. There was an empty shell in the cylinder. The girl was scared to death. The first thing she said was . . . 'I didn't do it.' Sherry had to carry her back to the place of the killing. She pretty near fainted. And . . . there was blood on her hand."

So, rapidly, heaping up the important facts, one on another, Pete Lang made out the case against the girl.

The sheriff joined his small hands together and, raising his head, looked up at the dark flight of the clouds across the sky.

Then Dr. Layman exclaimed bitterly: "Moon, you're not going to take this thing seriously? You don't mean to say that you'll register all this against Beatrice Wilton?"

The sheriff did not answer.

"Great Scott, man!" cried Layman, "Don't you know Beatrice Wilton? A lady if ever one . . . "

"A Wilton," said the sheriff. "I know that she's a Wilton. And they have a strange sort of a record, Doctor Layman."

"Whose voice have you against her?" asked the doctor, who seemed in an odd state of fear and excitement. "That man's. An unknown cowpuncher. A gunfighter . . . proved by the fact that Wilton hired him for that purpose. He testifies against Beatrice Wilton. Sheriff, may he not have some reason for wanting to put the blame on other shoulders? Doesn't it stand to reason that, unless he had some such purpose, he never would have accused her? A Western man doesn't go out of his way, as he has done, to accuse a woman against whom he could not possibly have any grudge?"

The sheriff looked mildly upon the doctor and appeared to be considering this statement, while Lang raised a finger and pointed it like a gun at the speaker.

"You're talking a lot and you're talking loud," he cautioned.

"Do you think that I care a whit for your threats?" demanded the doctor, actually taking a step nearer to Lang. "I despise you and all the rest of your gunfighting crew. Sheriff, I want you to tell me right now that you're going to discount the testimony of this ruffian."

The sheriff merely said: "Mister Sherry was with Lang. You were with him at the time the shooting must have taken place, Sherry?"

"I was," said Sherry gloomily.

"Have you any reason to suspect that Lang is twisting the truth?" persisted the sheriff.

Sherry stared at the face of his friend.

"It's all right, Lew," said Lang gently. "You don't have to stick by me in this. I know just how you feel."

Sherry groaned aloud. "I can't turn a lie against Pete," he confessed. "Lord forgive me . . . but I got to say that everything he's said is correct. He hasn't exaggerated a single thing."

"I'm sorry to hear it," said the sheriff. "It makes it necessary for me to see Miss Wilton. Will you tell me where she is?"

The doctor threw up both hands to the sky, and, letting them fall again, he struck one against his forehead heavily. "She's in that room to the right. The one with the French door opening on the garden."

"Will you come with me?" asked the sheriff of Sherry.

The big man followed little Herbert Moon to the indicated door. They tapped.

"Who's there?" called the uncertain voice of the girl.

"Sheriff Moon," said the man of the law.

There was a frightened gasp inside.

And Sherry, interpreting that stifled cry with blinding suddenness, gave his shoulder to the door and burst it open, with a shivering and crashing of broken glass. He, lurching into the chamber, saw Beatrice Wilton running to the center table. Her hand had scooped up the revolver that lay there and raised it toward her own head when the reaching hand of Sherry struck at her.

The weight of the blow flung her against the wall, and the gun exploded with its ominous, soft noise and thudded a bullet into the ceiling, while Sherry, leaping on, gathered the girl safely into his arms.

XVII

Following swiftly on the choked noise of the shot, Lang and the doctor would have rushed into the room, but the sheriff turned toward them and waved them away.

"It's my duty to examine Miss Wilton," he said. "Mister Sherry is already here. He'll serve me as a witness. If you gentlemen wish to assist me, you may search the grounds again. Doctor Layman, perhaps you'll inform the coroner?"

With that, he closed the broken door in their faces and turned back to the room.

Beatrice Wilton had sunk into a chair. Leaning to one side, supporting herself with one stiffened arm, while her head hung low, she looked about to faint. Sherry stood behind her, his arms folded. He needed that stricture of his big, hard arm muscles across his breast; otherwise, he felt as though his heart would tear its way out of his breast.

The sheriff took a chair by the center table. He waved to Sherry to take another, but Sherry shook his head.

"Miss Wilton," said the sheriff, "you are under arrest for the death of Oliver Wilton. Whatever you say now may be used against you in a court of law as admissible testimony. Nothing will be forced from you. You are fully warned about the danger of talking?"

She swayed a little. So much so, that Sherry put down a hand as if prepared to steady her. But then she straightened herself and looked slowly around the room, as though she wished to gain strength and courage from familiar sights. Sherry, with an aching heart, followed that glance. It was a dainty place, thoroughly feminine. There was an Italian bed, low, with a gilt back, and before the bed a painted screen that almost obscured it, so that the chamber could serve as a living room. All was bright and cheerful, gay little landscapes on the wall, and three rugs blurring the floor with color. But the broken door seemed to Sherry to have a strange meaning; so had the security of this girl been lost, and the danger of the world been let in upon her.

Now she looked back at the sheriff and nodded slowly. "I understand," she said.

Her voice was steady, and the heart of Sherry leaped again—with admiration, this time. And he told himself, bitterly, that he cared little what she had done. She was beautiful, and she was brave. That, in itself, was enough for him.

"You know that I don't want to take advantage of you?" went on Herbert Moon. "For that matter, your friend Sherry wouldn't let me, I suppose."

She looked hastily over her shoulder at the towering form and the frowning brow of Lew.

"You didn't know he is your friend?" went on Moon.

And she, still glancing up, smiled faintly at Sherry—an incredulous smile, he thought.

"What I want you to do," said the sheriff, "is to talk freely. Times like this unlock the heart. They break down the barrier that we ordinarily erect against the eye and the ear of the world. Well, the more freely you talk now, the easier it will be to establish your innocence. We have certain facts against you. I'm not allowed to tell you what they are. I even should not tell you that a statement by a suspected person immediately after arrest usually bears with double force in the eyes of the law. In this time of excitement and confusion, truth is supposed to be nearer to the tongue of the one under arrest. You have something to say, of course. Will you say it to me now?"

Sherry broke in: "Why should she talk now? This is a case where she ought to have a lawyer. If I were she, I wouldn't say a word to anybody without the advice of a lawyer, and a good one."

"That is usually a good rule," said the sheriff. "I'm sorry to say that a great many officers of the law are only interested in securing convictions. But I have grown old in my work, Mister Sherry, and I hope you'll believe me when I say that I have only one great wish in every case . . . and that is to secure justice, not prison stripes, for the accused. Now, Miss Wilton, will you talk to me?"

Sherry suddenly left his post at the back of her chair and stood beside the sheriff, facing her. At that, her eyes no longer wandered. She spoke to the sheriff, but her eyes, all the while, were fixed upon the handsome, stern face of Sherry. And sometimes she looked down to his big hands, sun-blackened, and sometimes her glance swept across the great breadth of his shoulders—famous shoulders were they, up and down the length of the range.

She said: "I was walking in the woods. I was disturbed . . . "
She paused. "I was afraid," she murmured.

"You were afraid," said the sheriff, encouraging her gently. "Will you tell me of what you were afraid?"

She moistened her lips, tried to speak, hesitated. And then, looking earnestly upon Sherry, as though she were drawing strength and inspiration from him, she continued: "I was afraid of my uncle."

Sherry raised a warning hand.

"I wouldn't interrupt her!" exclaimed Herbert Moon with some asperity.

"Don't you see," broke in Sherry, "that if you admit you were afraid of your uncle, you furnish with your own testimony a reason why you might have wished to . . . "

"To kill him?" She spoke straight out, her voice perfectly steady. "I understand that, of course. I'm trying to tell the truth."

"You were afraid of your uncle," said the sheriff. "You said that, as my friend here interrupted. Sherry, I'm afraid that I'll have to complete this interview without you. Will you step outside?"

Beatrice Wilton stiffened suddenly in the chair. "No!" she exclaimed. "Please let him stay. He helps me . . . he really helps me to tell the truth."

"Then . . . by all means," said the sheriff, as gentle as ever. "Let us continue this conversation, like three friends. And will you remember, my dear young girl, that it is always best to tell the whole truth . . . usually even to win in the law, and always, I trust, for the sake of the God who hears us all."

Now there was not a great deal of religion on the cow range, and the stern men of the law were hardly apt to have sacred names upon their lips any more than the reckless cowpunchers and gunmen who they tried to keep in order. Therefore, Sherry heard this speech with a little shock of surprise and of awe. And the girl looked for a moment from him and toward Herbert Moon. But instantly her glance came back to the big man.

"You were afraid of your uncle," went on the sheriff. "And why were you afraid of him?"

"My father's money was left in trust for one year. At the end of that time, it passes into the hands of my guardian. Uncle Oliver is my guardian. In a few more days, my money would all have been placed in his hands. But still I would have a claim on it. Now, suppose I died. Uncle Oliver would be the next heir. You understand?"

The sheriff nodded. "Your uncle would have been the next heir. And you thought that he was capable of . . . taking your life for the sake of that money?"

"I didn't know. But I was afraid."

"What gave you such an idea?"

"There were a good many things. He had queer ways. He lived in the house like a general in a fort. He was always practicing with weapons in the woods behind the house. Besides, I once overheard . . . " She paused.

However, the sheriff did not offer to encourage her, and it was Sherry who nodded slightly.

Then she went on, speaking directly to him: "It has been a rather lonely house to live in . . . since my father's death. I don't know why. It used to seem very cheerful, before. It was like living at the top of a wave. One could look down all over the town and the plain, and the hills and the mountains beyond. But afterward, it seemed cold and dark. I was always lonely. I used to hate the house and spend a good deal of my time in the garden or walking among the trees. And one day I was out very late. I should have been home before. It was really after sunset. Yes, I remember that I could see patches of red sky in the west, between the tree trunks. I was coming in slowly, even late as it was, because I hated to reach the house, and because I went slowly, I suppose, I made little noise. Then I came on the sound of voices. I heard my uncle talking excitedly."

"And who was the other man?" asked the sheriff.

"I don't know. He spoke more softly. I hardly made out a word he said. It sounded a little like the voice of Doctor Layman, however."

"Will you go on then?"

"I heard my uncle cry out . . . 'I tell you that I haven't them. I've lost them. I haven't a single one.' Then he swore, like a man frantic with excitement, and he went on . . . 'Do you suppose that if I were able to find them, and have them, I'd waste my perfectly good time here trying to . . .'"

"How did he finish that sentence?"

"He didn't finish it. But then he said . . . 'Heaven forgive me. Heaven forgive me. People think I'm an honorable man. If they knew what I had in mind and heart . . . and then you come here to badger me. But I swear that I haven't one of them. Would I be staying here if I did have them?'

"After that I clearly heard the other man say . . . 'That's your responsibility. You have had them. They were in your charge. You ought to know that you'll have to make good for them. You ought to be able to lay your hands on enough money to make a part payment. That's not asking a great deal.'

"My uncle answered, excited as ever, but a wind began to rise, and I couldn't hear any more. I went on back to the house. And ever since that moment, I've been sick with fear of him. I've never known when I'd die in my sleep. I've feared even the food on the table before me."

"Very well. And then today?"

"I used to go out with a revolver, practicing. I thought that I should learn to take care of myself, you see. Today, I was in the garden, doing that. I'd filled my revolver and fired one shot . . . at a sapling."

"Did you hit it?"

She blinked. "No . . . I think not. I walked on through the trees and came out onto a path . . . and saw a man lying face down. I leaned over him. I saw it was Uncle Oliver. I touched his face to try to rouse him. My hand came away sticky with blood. Then I went mad with fear and ran off into the brush . . . and you found me there . . . and brought me back." She smiled, a twisted smile, at Sherry, and then closed her eyes and turned white.

XVIII

At this moment it appeared to Sherry that the poor girl had proved her case completely, and he stepped a little forward so that he could turn and look more fully into the face of the sheriff, for he wanted to see the conviction appear in the eyes of that man of the law. But he only saw the sheriff lean forward with a peculiar keenness of expression, and instead of using gentle words, or none, when the girl was so overwhelmed, Sheriff Moon said quickly: "Of course, it isn't a pleasant thing to see a dead man. It's not pleasant a bit. That unnerved you. That sent you off scampering through the brush. I suppose that your brain spun and turned dark, didn't it? Poor girl."

"Yes, yes," she muttered, without opening her eyes.

Comforting enough the words of the sheriff had been, except that they had called up the grisly picture of the dead too vividly, but in sound and manner they were not so kind—they had come out rapidly, with a sort of savage eagerness, which Sherry was at a loss to account for.

He said to himself: *There's poison in that little man. There's poison in all little men. For often it seems that the smaller the man, the more waspish the temper.* For his own part, anger advanced upon him slowly. He could endure many taunts and many insults, but only by degrees passion inflamed his brain, until at last he could not endure, and had to fight. So he felt now that the sheriff had allowed bitterness to master him and had struck at a helpless girl.

Her eyes opened again, and she was looking at him, her eyes very wide, but little seeing in them.

The sheriff stood up. "I won't bother you any longer," he said. "You've made your statement as complete as you care to have it, I suppose?"

"I don't think of anything else," she said.

"I'm going outside," said the sheriff. "But Mister Sherry will stay in here with you, in case you want anything, or if you feel faint. Mister Sherry will take care of you."

He went out with a brisk step, and all at once she roused herself out of her trance and sprang up and ran to Tiny Lew. She looked very small. She did not come up to his shoulder, and she caught with her hands at his arms, hard and stiff as the large steel cables that made a ship's crew curse when stowing them below in ample circles.

"He doesn't believe in me," said Beatrice Wilton.

"He's a fool if he doesn't!" exclaimed Sherry from his heart. "But he didn't say that he didn't believe. You take these fellows of the law and they're great on not committing themselves."

"He doesn't believe in me," she repeated, shaking her head, as though she were casting off the importance of Sherry's faint denial. "Tell me. He doesn't believe what I said?"

"They're queer . . . all these manhunters," he told her. "It don't matter what he thinks, though. He's not the judge. And he's a long way from being twelve men on the jury."

At this, the strength of her frenzy of fear relaxed a good deal; she was faint, rather than frantic, once more, and she dropped into a chair by the table, locked her hands together, and stared at him over them.

Sherry was fascinated, for it had been many years since he had lived in the land where women's hands are white and slender and soft. He almost had forgotten that there are hands that have not been thickened, and spread, and blunted by pulling at the reins, or by swinging axes—hands not reddened from work in dish-water, or in washing suds on Mondays—hands not roughened from scrubbing with sand soap, from dragging heavy brooms across splintered floors.

But she was out of the other world, delicately and softly made, and so Sherry stared at those two hands that gripped and fought at one another until they trembled. The wrists were like the hands. No bulging cords stared from them. He could have held them both easily in the grip of one hand, but the more he felt the excess of his power over her the more he was subdued by two intense emotions—a vast pity for her, and vast awe because of the delicate cunning with which Nature had made her.

When she spoke again, her voice had changed. She was hoarse, as though she had been screaming into a wind, or sobbing heavily for a long time.

"Do you think he'll bring me up for trial? Do you think that, Mister Sherry?"

"That's not for him to say," he told her. "That's for the coroner's jury to say."

She held out both her hands to him, palms up; her eyes were half closed and he had a shuddering fear that she was about to weep.

"Don't you understand?" she asked. "Everybody in this place does just as Sheriff Moon wants. He does the thinking for all Clayrock. They would think nothing of accusing me, if he so much as frowned at me. They would think nothing of . . . of . . . "

She could not say the word, but she unclasped her hands and laid one of them against her throat. He saw that a fine blue vein ran up the right side of her neck, and it seemed to Sherry that he was looking through translucent white and seeing that vein, deeply hidden.

"Great Scott," said Sherry. "What are you thinking of? Do you think that people would allow such a thing? Do you think that there are jail doors that would hold you? Do you think that there are not hands that would bring you safely out?"

He held such a hand out to her, not as one who calls attention to himself, but as a man speaking out of the heat of emotion that gathers him up as a strong draft gathers up a powerful flame.

He was a magnificent man, this Lewis Sherry, not meant to be ironed out into a common background of stiff white shirt fronts, and black dinner jackets. Out of such a background little appears except grace, and cunning, stinging words, but Sherry looked at that moment like a glorious animal with hands as strong as metal, and with the divine mind all on fire for action.

She looked at him from foot to head, and suddenly she smiled on him. "*You* would tear the doors open for me," she said in the same husky voice.

Then as though she gathered strength from him, and from the thought, she lifted herself from the chair and came to him, still smiling. She stood just under him, so that she had to bend back her head a little to look up into his face, and a sad sense of sweetness, like the fragrance of late roses in the fall of the year, possessed Sherry. He wanted to ask her not to smile, her beauty and her nearness made his heart ache so with the knowledge that she trusted him so deeply, and that she was so near perishing.

"I'll never lose all heart again," she told him. "I see that you believe in me."

"I do," said Sherry. "I believe in you."

He could manage to make the words simple, but he could not take control of his voice, which rumbled out in a great organ peal, a declaration of faith. If he had said that he loved her, that he worshiped her, that he would serve her in all possible ways, it could not have been put more clearly than by all that his voice inferred. And she glowed beneath him. The weariness and the trouble that had marked her face disappeared, and out of her shone that light that joy kindles in a beautiful girl.

She was saying: "If you want to help me, go to Doctor Layman. If anyone knows a way of doing things for me now, he is the man. Tell him that I asked you to go to him. And, oh, if you wish to help me, follow what he says. For he's wiser than all the rest. He's even wiser than the sheriff . . . and so much kinder."

He knew that he was close to some frantic declaration, and because he was ashamed to break out, and because, too, the mention of another man had somehow brought a sobering touch to him, he left her at once and stumbled out into the garden.

He was met by blinding light. During the brief time he had been in the room with the girl the wind had changed, and the dark cloud masses, no longer shooting south, were rolling toward the northeast in walls and towers between which the rich blue of the sky reached through. It was nearly sunset; the light was golden; hope suddenly filled the world—and also the heart of Lewis Sherry.

The sheriff had gone off to the town, and Sherry found the man he wanted pacing up and down through the garden, pausing now and then to kick at a stone, his head bent toward the earth.

"Beatrice Wilton told me to come to you," said Sherry. "She said that you would know what to tell me to do."

The doctor looked up at him by degrees; his hands were locked behind his back, which made his slender figure seem yet more spare, so that he looked to Sherry, at the moment, a very type of the intellectual—his physical existence was so dominated by that imposing brow.

"She sent you to me?" queried the doctor.

"Yes."

"The deuce she did," murmured Layman. He actually walked on, kicking the small stones out of his way as he went, and yet Sherry was not offended, for he told himself that it was the sheer excess of sorrow of mind that forced Layman to be rude. At length, coming to the end of the path, the doctor turned upon him and said slowly: "She sent you to me. Did she say what right you had to come to talk to me about her?"

"She said," quoted Sherry, "that you would know what I could do to help her."

"To help her? Does she need help?" asked the doctor in the same sharp way.

Sherry was a little irritated. "After her talk with the sheriff," he said, "I think that she does."

"The sheriff was stubborn, was he?" murmured Layman. "I believe he has that reputation. But she couldn't do anything with him?"

"Nothing but tell her story," said Sherry.

"And that did no good?"

"Not a bit . . . so far as I could see." Then Sherry added: "Suppose I ask just why she sent me to you for orders?"

The doctor looked at him in doubt. Then he shrugged his shoulders. "Suppose I say that we're engaged to be married. Would that make any further explanation necessary?"

XIX

The vague hopes that had been rising in the mind of Sherry were rebuffed. As a strong wind will clear away mist suddenly, so the passion of Sherry was blown to tatters in an instant. Then, slowly, he settled himself to face the new problem.

"I don't mind saying that it makes a lot of difference," he said quietly.

"I thought so," said the doctor. "It takes a well-balanced youngster to see Beatrice a few times without losing his head."

He nodded at Sherry. It was really impossible to take offense at this bluntness on his part, for it was plain that he was partly thinking out loud, partly expressing a viewpoint to another. There was no malice in his manner. It was simply the expression of a calm conviction. So Sherry made no answer.

The doctor went on in his rather irritated manner: "That may change your viewpoint altogether, as a matter of fact."

"About helping her?" asked Sherry.

"Exactly."

"No," said Sherry, "it doesn't at all."

"*Ha!* I wonder," said the doctor. He began to pace up and down again, kicking in his half-abstracted and half-venomous way at the small stones in the path. He halted, with his back turned. "No one can help her without pouring his whole heart into the job."

"I suppose not," answered Sherry.

Layman swung about on him. "You're free to go. You know that," he said. "You won't get the ten thousand that you were hired for."

Sherry did not reply to this. He wondered if the other were trying to torment him as a test of his temper and of his steadfastness.

"You're not going?" inquired Layman.

"No."

"In addition, there may be danger in staying about this place and trying to help Beatrice. Have you thought of that?"

"More sailors, do you mean?" asked Sherry.

"*Ha?*" exclaimed the doctor. Then he went on, thoughtfully: "You've looked a little way beneath the surface, at least."

"Thank you," said Sherry dryly.

"Don't be proud," said the doctor. "There will be plenty of time for you to show what you're made of before this little affair is over." He laughed suddenly, and added: "I can assure you of that. Plenty of time, and plenty of ways."

He went up to Sherry and gripped his arm with such force that the big man was surprised. "You went down to the hotel. Did you find out anything about Fennel? Did you find out anything about the murderer?"

"I found out that he's pretty deep," said Sherry.

"In what way? What did you find out?"

"He posed as a drunkard. Matter of fact, he probably never touched a drop except in public."

"Huh?" said the doctor. "How could that be? I've said that he was a victim of alcoholic poisoning. Do you think that I imagined it, my friend?"

"Good bye," said Sherry.

"What?"

Sherry walked off, but Layman followed after him and touched his arm.

"You're right," he said, when the other turned again. "I have no right to take advantage of your generous attitude toward Beatrice . . . and me. But the fact is that I'm half mad. This thing has upset me, naturally. You see that, Sherry? As a matter of fact, I value your help hugely. It might make the difference of the turning of the scale."

"I hope so."

"So go on and tell me about the sailor . . . the pretended sailor . . . whatever he was. You say that he didn't drink?"

"I don't go against a doctor's word. I suppose you know your business."

"I'm not a genius of the profession," said Layman. "But I think I know alcoholism when I see it. It's not the rarest disease in this part of the world."

"Very well. I tell you only what I know. I've been in Fennel's room twice. I saw that more than a bottle of whiskey had been used up between visits. Well, that seemed incredible. A man with more than a quart of whiskey in him doesn't walk up a path and confront another as Fennel confronted Wilton a while ago . . . even allowing that he's a freak and can carry twice as much liquor as a normal man."

"More than a quart? Of course not. That's impossible for human nature, without making a man nearly senseless, I suppose."

"Very well. The liquor was gone. I looked about to find how it had vanished. And I saw a little trap set into the lead of the drainage pipe. I went down below. The ground was reeking with whiskey fumes. There you are. It's fairly clear that, if Fennel drank enough to have alcoholic poisoning, he dodged a lot more by pouring the stuff down the pipe."

"What idiots," said Layman, "men can be. There's a fellow with murder planned, and incidentally he wanted to work up a great reputation as a drinker. And so the drainage pipe scheme. Well . . . and still there's no trace of Fennel. And the fool of a sheriff," he went on, "is trying to hang the guilt on the shoulders of Beatrice Wilton. Heaven forgive him for a blind man."

"I don't see this . . . why should Fennel have killed Wilton?"

"Is that strange? He couldn't get what he wanted. Look at his clothes. Rags and tatters. And a beggar never gets enough. He wants nothing less than a fortune laid into his hands. So with our friend Fennel. He couldn't get what he wanted. So he used a gun."

"I don't see him using a gun with a silencer," said Sherry. "He didn't impress me as that type. A common fore-the-mast sailor would hardly go in for the niceties."

"You forgot what the newspapers do for people these days," said the doctor bitterly. "They not only suggest crimes, but they also suggest safe ways of working them. If murders were never reported in the public prints, you'd find the lists cut down ten percent in no time."

"But there was Fennel," persisted Sherry, "not asking for a great deal. Apparently all that he wanted was enough to keep drunk on. Wilton would have given him that much."

"Wilton was a stubborn fellow," said the doctor. "What makes you think that he would have given it?"

"Because he was almost frightened to death," said Sherry.

"Are you sure of that?"

"I walked down the path behind him. He hardly could keep himself in hand."

"Fennel a sham . . . Wilton frightened to death by a sham . . . hands pointing at Beatrice . . . great heaven," said Layman, "who can see through this muddle?"

They were interrupted by the arrival of the sheriff, the coroner, and the coroner's jury, who had been hastily gathered. They were brought into the living room of the Wilton house, where the murdered man had been placed on a couch. He looked very pale and peaceful to Sherry, with the smile of death on his lips. And yet that death seemed more horrible than usual in such a place, for all the process of a normal life was scattered about—a newspaper here, a book, open and face down, there. The disarray of the chair, the rumpled corner of a rug, all seemed to make it impossible to believe that Oliver Wilton lay dead.

The coroner was a fat man whose wind was quite gone. He dropped into a chair and fanned himself with his hat. "Pretty neat room, ain't it?" he said. "I never been here before. You, Pat?"

Pat admitted that it was his first visit.

"That's the trouble with a lot of these rich swells," declared the coroner. "They're above the common people. They got no time for them. And then the first thing that they know, they trip up their heels, and they got to have just as much law around as the next man."

There was general agreement with this statement.

Then the coroner ordered the room to be cleared except for the clerk, the sheriff, and the first witness, who was to be Dr. Layman.

Back to the garden went Sherry and Pete Lang. And the face of Pete was serene and happy.

Sherry said to him quietly: "I suppose you're heading back for the range, Pete?"

"And why?" asked Pete.

"Because you're through here, as far as I can make out."

"And how do you make it out, son. Will you tell me that?"

"Your boss is dead, Pete. There's no more money here for you."

"Then I'll be a dog-gone philanthropist," said Lang, "and work on just for sheer patriotism, as you might call it."

"To hang a girl if you can?" asked Sherry coldly.

"That rides you, partner, don't it?" asked Pete.

Sherry was silent, and Lang looked calmly upon the stern face of his friend.

"I'm gonna work, and work," he said. "I never felt more at home than I do right now. The law can do what it wants, but I got an idea that Pete Lang is the one that's gonna prove the case."

"What makes you think that?"

"Lemme ask you . . . what become of the letter that Wilton received from Fennel?"

"I forgot about that. It must be in his coat pocket. I remember that he put it there."

"I remembered, too. And here it is." He spread it out in the hand of Sherry, and the letter read:

Dear Skipper: So that we can cut the business short, suppose that you cum along with some of the perls? I don't ask for much. Just say that you bring along a handful, and not of the smallest. That wood hold me. I don't want to rob you. I just want my shair.

Respektfuly,
Fennel

"But he didn't bring the pearls," said Sherry, "and so he was murdered."

"Didn't he bring them? What do you think of this?" asked Pete calmly.

And, scooping a hand into his pocket, he brought it out with the palm well filled with the milky luster of a heap of pearls.

XX

Over these jewels they bowed their heads. They were by no means of uniform size, shape, or quality, but some were like small pears, and others were irregular globes, and others, again, were what are called *perle boutons* by jewelers, that is to say, flat on the bottom, and formed like hemispheres. There were very small pearls, and there was one pear-shaped jewel of considerable size.

"You're going to show those to the coroner and his jury?" asked Sherry.

"Of course," said Lang. "These and the letter. They're testimony, ain't they?"

"You're not going to show them," declared Sherry firmly.

"And why not, Tiny? Is there anything else in the case that argues as much as this?"

"And what does it argue?" asked Sherry.

"That Fennel never killed Wilton."

"How do you make that out?"

"That's a simple trick. Look here. Fennel writes to Wilton. 'Bring me down a flock of pearls,' he says. Wilton does it. Still, Fennel shoots him? Why, I ask you? It ain't reasonable and it ain't likely. A gent holds up Wilton. Wilton comes through with the goods. At least, he takes down the stuff that's asked for. He wouldn't've done that if he hadn't intended to pass them over."

"And then?"

"Then what happened is easy to guess. The girl, all worked up about things, comes through the woods, sees Wilton, and takes a crack at him. He drops on his face. Fennel, scared to death, figures that his turn is coming next . . . maybe that the bullet really was meant for him. He beats it into the trees."

"Why should he chuck off hat and shoes and coat?"

"Why not? He wants to make tracks as fast as he can go. As he goes whisking through the brush his hat is knocked off. He can't make time in that long overcoat . . . you remember that it pretty near dragged the ground? . . . so he throws that off. And still his shoes are in his way. Look at the size of those shoes. Twelves, I'd say. Well, he chucks those shoes off, too, and goes on bare-footed."

"Through that rough going?"

"What's rough going to a sailor that's hardened up his feet using them bare to go aloft on iron-hard cordage?"

Sherry, stumped and disgusted with this perfect logic, still struggled. "Look at it another way," he suggested. "They walk down the path together, Fennel and Wilton. Fennel wants to see the goods, and Wilton shows him the pearls. Fennel says they're not enough. That's the point, perhaps, where they stop and argue. You remember?"

"Yes."

"Wilton insists that's all he'll give to Fennel. Fennel gets angry. Finally he pulls a gun and shoots Wilton down, in a blind rage."

"And goes on without taking the pearls that he's just seen Wilton, by your account, drop back into his coat pocket?"

"Yes, because he's too frightened by what he's done."

"Tell me straight, Sherry. Was Fennel the sort of a fellow who would be easily scared?"

Sherry bit his lip. Certainly Fennel had appeared to be a man who had plenty of nerve.

"Half a second to lean over and drag out this stuff. Was Fennel the fellow to overlook such a sure bet as that?" went on Lang, triumphant in his progress toward the truth. Then he summed up: "Fennel couldn't have been shown those pearls, if he committed the murder. And he wouldn't have shot unless he'd had a chance to see them. And once having seen them, he would have taken them along when he bolted."

"Maybe the pearls were only a dodge with him," suggested Sherry. "Perhaps he only wanted to use the pearls as a snare to trap Wilton and get him out into the garden?"

"You can fit in a perhaps to pretty near anything," said Lang, "but I tell you this, old son, when I finish telling my yarn to the coroner and his jury, I'll lay the long odds that they put the girl in jail charged with murder in the first degree."

"And that," said Sherry, "is what you're not going to do."

"Hello!" cried Lang. "And why not?"

"She's got to have a fair chance," said Sherry. "You can't stack the cards against her."

"Stack the cards? I'm not pulling any tricks against her. What have I got against the girl?"

"You hate them all . . . everything in skirts," said Sherry. "Isn't that true?"

"I see through them," answered Lang. "They've smashed my life. They've double-crossed me every turn."

"But here's one case where you're going to talk soft and be nice," said Sherry.

"Are you as hard hit as that?" asked his friend.

"I am."

"You want me to hold out this stuff?"

"I do."

Lang groaned. "Don't you see, man," he urged, "that the girl's a cold-blooded little piece? She's too pretty to be good, in the first place."

"She's got a hard enough row to hoe now," answered Sherry. "When the sheriff and I broke into her room, she tried to shoot herself. That's about enough to finish her, I suppose, when the sheriff gets through talking. I ask you again . . . will you give her a chance, man?"

At this, Pete Lang struck a hand against his forehead. "Here's my only pal," he said, "and he comes to me and says . . . 'Pete, old man, for the sake of old times, will you gimme a chance to tie a rope around my neck and hang myself from your front door?' What am I to say? Boy, boy, you'd never get nothing out of her except a big laugh when she was in the clear."

"You may be right," said Sherry.

"What do you think yourself about her?"

"Lord knows."

"Tiny, you think that she's guilty."

"I do," groaned Sherry.

"But you'd carry on?"

"I love her," Sherry said with a sad simplicity.

Lang rolled a cigarette with fumbling fingers. "You love her," he said. "You gotta chuck yourself away for her. By grab, it's always that way. The straight gents love the poison." He lighted his cigarette, and through swirling smoke his tormented eyes stared at his friend.

Sherry held out his hand and waited, and finally Lang made a convulsive gesture of last argument. "They'll jail her and try her, without this," he said. "But with this handful of stuff, they'll hang her. Without it they won't, I should say. They'll only hang a doubt on her that'll disgrace her all her life, until a poor sucker like you comes along and marries her . . . and gets his throat cut a couple of months later."

The hand of Sherry still waited in mid-air, and at last Lang clutched and shook it with vigor.

"I'm wrong," he said. "I'm turning loose another plague on the world, and all because it wears a pretty face. Lord forgive me for the damage that she's gonna do."

"We've got plenty of other things to do around here," said Sherry. "We want to run down the whole secret life of this Oliver Wilton. It may be that we'll learn enough to clear her altogether. You're fighting on my side now, Pete?"

Lang nodded mournfully. "But mind you, son," he cautioned gravely, "the best thing that we can do is to turn in our evidence straight, and then pack and ride for the range. We never have had any luck in Clayrock. We're never going to have any luck. And there you are. It's my hunch. I've given you a fair warning."

To this Sherry made no answer, for the door opened, and he was summoned in before the coroner to give his testimony.

They wore gloomy, stern faces, these twelve men. One might have thought that they had eaten something extremely bitter to the taste, so were their mouths puckered and awry.

The coroner was no stickler for form or legalities. He said directly: "Things look bad for the girl, Sherry. Now, what you gotta say about her at the murder?"

Sherry looked slowly around the room. "Nothing," he answered at last.

At this, the sheriff rose from his chair. "You've said things in my presence, Sherry. I want you to say them again. It's your duty."

"My duty?" said Sherry. "My duty to help toward the hanging of a girl I know is innocent?"

He said that in such a ringing voice that the jury started of one accord, and the fat coroner so hastily clapped his spectacles upon his nose that they dropped off at once before he could examine Sherry carefully.

"What you think," said the coroner, "ain't specially interesting just here and now, Sherry. We think that you're a straight shooter . . . both ways of using the word. Now we want to know what you seen and heard and did today, about the time that Wilton was murdered? And though I take a lot of interest in a gent that's willing to help a poor girl, still, justice has gotta have its chance in the game. I ask you, man to man, will you talk out?"

Sherry raised a finger at them. "I can tell you what I saw and heard," he said, "but I can't tell you what I felt. And that's what counts. And every man of you that has a wife, and every man of you that has a daughter, knows what I mean."

"That's not testimony," said the sheriff.

"The coroner runs this court, I believe, and not the sheriff," said Sherry icily.

"My dear lad," said the quiet voice of Moon, "we have our own way of fulfilling the law in this county, but we know testimony when we hear it. We don't want your opinions. We want your facts."

"To hound Beatrice Wilton!" exclaimed Sherry, black rage swallowing his judgment. He stepped toward the sheriff. "But if you're loading the dice against her," he said, "I want you to know that there are those who will stop your game."

"Hold on, young man!" exclaimed the coroner.

The jury gazed at the audacious Sherry with frightened eyes. For twenty-five years the sheriff had played something more than human role in that community.

"He's young," said Herbert Moon as gently as ever. "He's young and he has a heart . . . a big heart, and a hot one. I hold nothing against him, but I think you'll get nothing worthwhile out of the testimony of Sherry, coroner."

"It looks like you're right," agreed the corner. "Sherry, are you gonna talk, or do we have to bind you over for contempt . . . is that the right word, Sheriff?"

"If you think that you need more testimony . . . yes," said the sheriff. "I suppose that we can hold him until he'll talk."

"If we need more?" muttered the coroner. "Well, we'll try Pete Lang, next. Sherry, we're finished with you, for a while."

So Sherry walked from the room, and found the doctor walking up and down the hall outside. He cast a bitter eye upon Sherry as Lang was called in to play his part of witness.

"You meant well, Sherry," he said, "but do you think that holding back in this fashion will be of any real use to Beatrice? They'll all guess blacker things than you could have said about her actions."

Sherry did not answer. He felt that he had played a foolish part. This was a riddle that wits could not solve. But perhaps a force of hand could serve his purpose. So he looked darkly upon Layman and said nothing.

XXI

The testimony of Lang was as disappointing as that of Sherry. He did not refuse to talk, but he refused to say anything of importance. "I don't know," was his invariable answer when he seemed to have been crowded into a corner, and at last the coroner said to the jury: "You boys can see for yourselves. Lang won't talk . . . he's an old bunkie of Sherry's."

They dismissed Lang.

The witnesses were not allowed to be present at the pronouncing of the verdict, but through the door the voice of the foreman was plainly heard declaring that in the estimation of twelve citizens of that jury, Beatrice Wilton was guilty of murder by shooting Oliver Wilton with Exhibit A, which was the girl's own revolver, displayed upon a table in front of the coroner, together with the cast-off clothes of Fennel, and other items of interest in the case. She would be held in the Clayrock jail for trial.

But, the verdict having been given, the prisoner surrendered to the sheriff, Sherry and Lang were admitted to the room again. They found all the men in the room wearing long faces, unwilling to look at one another, with the exception of the sheriff, whose expression never varied, it seemed. A cheerful quiet always possessed his eye, and he looked as brightly and calmly upon Sherry and Lang and the girl as upon any of the jurors.

The latter were anxious to leave, but the sheriff would not let them go at once.

In the meantime, Beatrice Wilton sat by the window, utterly different from what she had been before. Sherry had dreaded facing her; he had expected that the strain would have broken down her nerve strength entirely and left her a wreck, but, instead, she appeared perfectly calm and self-possessed. She and the sheriff alone had themselves under perfect control, while Layman went up to her, with Sherry and Lang as a sort of rear guard.

Layman sat down beside her and took her hand. "Beatrice," he said, "it's going to be a long, hard fight."

She looked at him without an answering word or gesture, and her quiet manner staggered Sherry. If she had strength enough

for this, she had strength enough for anything, he told himself—
strength enough, say, for the slaying of a man. And once more
the overwhelming surety of her guilt possessed his mind.

But there were compensating facts, if only they could be
known, and he would know them, if there were strength in him,
and wit in Lang, to unravel the skein of mystery.

Layman went on: "We'll need every penny we can put our
hands on."

"You can sell some stock for me, Eustace," she replied.

"As soon as you give me power of attorney, and full rights to
act for you, of course."

"Yes, naturally."

"But in the first place, I intend to close the house and dis-
charge the servants, Beatrice."

"Of course."

"And these good fellows who have wanted so much to help
you, dear." He nodded to Sherry and Lang.

"Yes, naturally," she said again.

But here Lang put in: "We ain't hired men, ma'am, but we're
volunteers. If we could have a chance to look through that house
when we want to, it might be that we could turn up some things
that would be useful to you."

"My dear Lang," said the doctor blankly, "what on earth
could you discover in the house?"

"Enough, maybe, to save Miss Wilton," replied the
cowpuncher.

"Lang," began the doctor, "of course I know that you have
the best will in the world, but . . . "

Beatrice Wilton leaned forward a little and raised a hand to
silence Layman. "You already know something," she said. "I'm
sure that you know something that the coroner hasn't heard, Pete?"

She let that familiar name fall with such a gentle intonation
that Sherry saw his hardy friend start a little, and he smiled in
dour understanding.

But to this question Layman interposed: "My dear Beatrice, don't you see that it's going to make everything more difficult for me if I have to divide my time between the house and . . . "

"And the jail?" she finished for him, undisturbed.

Even Layman, cool as ice ordinarily, now flushed a little. "I can't very well be in two places at once," he complained.

"Of course you can't. So let Lew Sherry and Pete Lang stay in the house."

"There's every reason against it," urged Layman. "These are known men, Beatrice."

"Known?" she echoed, raising her brows a little.

"I don't want to insult them. It's no insult to say that they're known to have come here as guards to your uncle."

"But what has that to do with me?"

"Don't you see? You'd have them up on the hill like a sort of standing army, ready to rush down and smash the jail open, say, in case the trial went against you. Isn't that obvious? People know Sherry, particularly. He has a long and . . . efficient . . . record behind him. You understand, Beatrice, that from the very first, you must try to win public opinion to your side of the case. And you can't do that when you have two aces up your sleeve . . . and everybody knows about them. It's really very important. You ought to see that, dear."

"I didn't dream that it could mean so much," she said. "Of course, if that's the way of it, we'll just have to close the house."

"Naturally," said Layman. "Great Scott, what a blunder to have posted them up there like a pair of trained eagles on a crag. If you win, you win . . . if you lose the case, the pair of them come and split open the jail and take you out."

Sherry could see the point of this argument clearly enough, but Lang persisted with much solemnity. He leaned a little closer to the girl and said slowly: "I think that I might turn up something worthwhile at the house. Serious and sober, ma'am, I'd like to try."

She looked earnestly at the cowpuncher. Then: "Well, Eustace?" she asked.

The doctor hesitated. He looked at the girl rather than at Lang. "Lang is a keen fellow," he said suddenly. "If he has an idea, let him try his best, of course. We can't afford to turn down any chances, no matter how small."

"That's settled, then, and the two of you will be here?"

She looked to Sherry and he, in turn, bowed his great, heavy bulk above her chair.

"You have small chances, anyway," he said, "and never a better chance than right now."

She looked fixedly up at him, not frightened, but thoughtful, considering, and again his judgment said to him—"Guilty!"—and again his heart leaped and reveled in her beauty, and drove him on.

"What chance?" she asked him.

"Here are three of us," he replied. "I can answer for Pete. If Layman hasn't a gun, I can lend him an extra Colt. The coroner is a fossil. The jury has not more than two fighting men in the whole outfit. We're not more than six steps from the door. Get up from your chair and walk straight for the door. You'll be halfway there before anyone challenges you. Then run. We'll cover your going and pile out behind you . . . "

"The sheriff?" she said.

"If Moon draws a gun," said Sherry through his teeth, "heaven help him."

"Eustace," whispered the girl.

Layman, his face white, but his eyes very bright, listened, and said not a word. Lang dropped a hand upon the massive shoulder of his friend. It was his silent consent.

"It's your one real chance," said Sherry. "Do you understand me? For life."

"Where could we go?"

"I'll find a place to take you. Lang and the doctor and I will take care of you."

"Sherry and Lang!" called the sheriff.

"He suspects something. Now is your time," said Sherry.

"You mean it?"

"Yes, yes. But quickly."

Suddenly color leaped into her face. "Not one step," said the girl. "Why . . . it would be ruin for you, all three."

"Sherry!" said the sheriff.

Sherry turned heavily away and Herbert Moon went halfway across the room to meet him.

"I love a brave man," said the sheriff, "but, my dear young fellow, even courage shouldn't attempt to move mountains."

XXII

The town of Clayrock was filled for the trial days before it was due to be called. The town was put on the map, in a way, and the three hotels did big business. Prices for all things rose.

In the first place, there were the reporters who swarmed in. Newspapers in these days have to have their thrills to give hungry readers, and what is there better for this purpose than the case of a young and beautiful girl accused of murder? To make it better still, suppose the girl to be well raised, well educated, of good family. To cap the climax make the victim a blood relation—her father's own brother.

It was all that the newspapers could wish for, and they sent their reporters on long before the trial to work up the ground.

They found something to work. In the first place, there was the question, still wide open: "Did Fennel perform the murder, or is Beatrice Wilton guilty?"

Of course, the papers took sides. To some Beatrice Wilton was plainly guilty and the reporters almost said so. The man

Fennel was an elusive shadow. He was hardly to be called a man; certainly he had disappeared from Clayrock with as much thoroughness as though the wind had blown him through the town to be dissolved in air. So one faction seemed to doubt that Fennel ever existed. His battered shoes, his ragged overcoat—still whiskey-tainted according to some—and his old hat were in evidence, of course, but they were discounted heavily. He had no motives. His past was unknown. His relations with Oliver Wilton were yet to be established. In the meantime, here was Beatrice Wilton, young and beautiful, to be sure. But when has beauty not meant trouble? And behind her lay the dark background of the Wilton family. Into the dim past, they traced its sources. They listed down upon the account a blockade runner in the Civil War; a pair of brothers who had joined the '49ers and only one of whom had come home, well-to-do, but streaked with silver scars. They followed the Wiltons into older days still. There was a Wilton-Durham feud in the first part of the nineteenth century. Some said that three had been killed. Some said thirty. There had been duels, too—there was a story of a Wilton who had fought with an enemy across a dining room table, the muzzles of their outstretched pistols overlapping. And in the times of swords, still one found that the Wiltons had been involved in violence.

Then, what more natural than that this "proud, keen, vigorous, fearless girl" should have taken her affairs into her own hands? She wanted possession of her own fortune. She did not want it to pass into the hands of her uncle even for a moment. That was motive sufficient—for a Wilton.

So the newspapers of the hostile faction printed photographs of Beatrice that showed her unsmiling, straight-eyed, keen as any man.

To the other reporters—and theirs was the larger faction—it appeared that she would make better copy as the beautiful and tragic form involved in mysterious danger, innocent, but entangled. They loved to print pictures of Beatrice Wilton in her softer humors, to show the exquisite delicacy of her profile, to show her smile, and the large eyes looking down. They combed her past and found it fragrant. Scandal never had touched her. They hunted down her schoolfellows and interviewed them, and learned from them all that was kind and good about their old school companion. They picked up little anecdotes. They printed columns and columns. They stole from one another. They invented, refurbished, borrowed, re-dyed, trimmed, decorated, and gilded these tales of Beatrice Wilton. They loaded the telegraph lines with the tidings of her. They photographed her house, her room, her garden—particularly that dark spot where her uncle had been found dead—her horse, her dog, her saddle. Nothing was too minute to deserve attention if it had once belonged to Beatrice Wilton. If she had but looked on a thing, it became of value.

That was not all. They could not very well stop short with Beatrice, but they went on to all the other figures in the case, and made them interesting enough. There was the story of Everett Wilton, of course, rich, happy, young—as men of affairs go— and yet a suicide. Perhaps a suicide because of the blow that had fallen upon his fortune when the *Princess Marie* sank. Could it be that in the mind of Beatrice Wilton there had been some motive of sheer revenge for the same reason? At least, it helped to make one side of the case stronger.

Furthermore, they could take up Dr. Layman, the betrothed of the girl. He was a great help to her. The hostile sheets made little of him, and refused to give him much space, but the friendly journals dwelt at length upon his steadfast devotion. The hours he spent near the jail. His constant visits to the prisoner. His hours of consultation with the lawyer. And, above all, his calm, aloof, aristocratic manner. He was the soul of honor; his straight, steady eyes told what this man was. And could it be dreamed that he would cling to a murderess? Stuff and nonsense! A gentleman of breeding and of position has better taste and better fortune, let us hope. So they spread the doctor at large across their sheets. He made an excellent figure for the photographers. His lean face and pronounced, handsome features always reproduced well, and he was the more desired because he had courteously and firmly requested the reporters to take and print no more pictures of him. Of course, that made the shutters click far more busily than ever.

Then there was the quiet sheriff, he who was known to be the force behind the arrest and the prosecution of the girl. He had collected terrible, deadly facts. He was a man of flawless repute. He could not be accused of partisanship. And yet he stood indubitably against Beatrice Wilton, a vast weight upon the side of her guilt. He no longer even pretended that he was hunting the trail of Fennel—which was mute proof that he believed the girl was the criminal.

Pete Lang, also, came in for his share of notoriety. First of all, he was a rough fellow of the range, and, secondly, he had been the first at the side of the murdered man. Some newspapers even suggested that, since he had been the first at the dead body— since no one had seen the dead man fall—why might not Peter Lang be the guilty man?

Consider, for instance, that he was a marksman of skill, and that the bullet had been planted squarely, fairly between the eyes of Wilton. As for motive? Well, motives are rarely known until they are confessed, and, being employed by Wilton, it might well be that a testy word had been enough to bring the cowpuncher's revolver out of his pocket. And then he had caught the fancy of the reporters by saying bluntly: "I hope I'm nearer to guilty than she is."

But not even the fine form of Peter Lang, or the murdered man, or Layman, or the famous sheriff, or the mysterious Fennel, or even Beatrice Wilton herself, so seized upon the imagination of the public press as did another, unaccused figure. And that was Lewis Sherry.

As for photographs, they flooded the papers with pictures of him. They showed him mounting and dismounting. "He makes every horse look small." They showed him walking down the street, towering above Pete Lang. "And yet Lang is nearly six feet tall." They gave the dimensions of his shoulders, the span of his hand, and his weight. He became in a few days as physically well known as the person of the world's champion pugilist, and his handsome head was nearly always included on the same page with Beatrice Wilton. They made both a harmony and a contrast—lion and panther, as some reporter suggested.

And when they came to delving into the past of this man of the range, the reporters found enough to glut their typewriters and crowd the telegraph wires. He was the hero of many fights; he was the hero of many deaths. And every fight was set down in detail, and every wound was recounted.

He, too, they said, was a hearty advocate of the girl's. And was he not more than that? And, suppose that she were condemned, would not the giant strike in her behalf, even if it brought about his own ruin?

To big Lew Sherry they could apply all the pet terms of Western literature. He was the "desperado," the "gunfighter," the "killer," this "brave and reckless man," this "outlaw." And they went on and coined other terms of their own.

Sherry tried not to notice these things, but he could not help it. Clayrock was simply littered with copies of Eastern newspapers containing these accounts, and the home journals also began to boom the issue with all their might. The *Bugle* was on the side of Beatrice Wilton, and therefore Lew Sherry was a gentle hero. The *Morning Blast* was against the girl, and therefore to it Lew Sherry was a probable villain.

He called on the editor one day. People fled before him. Doors slammed and crashed. Many footfalls scurried up and down. But when he came to the editor's office, he found a little squint-eyed man who wore dark-cloth guards over the sleeves of his shirt, like a grocery clerk, and who peered up to him from beneath a green eye shade.

"What do you want of me, Sherry?" he asked.

"I want you to stop this nonsense," said Sherry.

"Do you?" said the editor. "And can you tell me any reason why I ought to stop it?"

"For the sake of common sense and decency, for one thing," said Sherry.

"Common sense and decency are all very well," said the editor, "but I wish you would point out a time when they were worth balancing against a growing circulation. I've trebled this paper's circulation inside of the last week. I've made it the biggest sheet in the county. And I'm going to keep it there . . . as long as Lew Sherry will furnish me with good copy, as he's doing today."

And suddenly a pair of cameras clicked in the corner of the room, and Sherry, with wild words, turned and fled more swiftly than from the mouth of a cannon.

He went to the sheriff, even, and dourly demanded that these libels should be stopped.

"I'm a peaceful man," said Sherry. "They're making me out a crook and a general all-around bad actor."

"Steady, steady," said the sheriff. "After a few more days of this, you'll know what it means to run for office, for instance."

XXIII

Let crime increase and follies spread, the press must still be free. And when Sherry had mastered that slogan and understood it might not be altered, he gritted his teeth and made no further protest. But, when a cameraman one day pointed a machine too closely at him, he picked up the heavy and expensive offender and heaved it after the artist. Man and machine rolled in the dust, and Sherry stood over them.

"The next time I'll use a quirt on you," said Sherry. "And the time after that . . . I'll use my hands."

It almost frightened the cameraman to death, but it did not prevent others from clicking pictures of him as busily as ever. It furnished much grist to the papers, moreover. I'LL USE MY HANDS! said a caption beneath an actual photograph of the big paws of Lew Sherry.

A weight of care descended upon Sherry as he saw this tide of publicity flowing in his direction, day after day.

"Trouble is going to come out of it," he assured his friend Lang. "Some young fools are going to come up here to make a reputation out of me. A short cut to headlines is what I offer to anybody who can drop me. And a bullet from behind wouldn't be wasted, either."

"Sure," agreed Lang. "When you go out, I'll go along with you every time. I'll watch your back for you. But I figure the same as you. The more that's said about a man, the nearer he is to his last picture. But hang the newspapers, say I. Did you see the last lingo that they printed about me? About me having a busted heart because of a long-lost sweetheart, and a lot of stuff that would've made you creep only to read it, old-timer." The giant grinned broadly. "I half believe that you sent 'em up that trail," growled Pete Lang. "Come on with me. We're going to finish the house today."

They had searched it from the top downward. To the room of Oliver Wilton, of course, they devoted their utmost care.

"He made it like a safe, because he had it lined with stuff that was worth getting," said Sherry. Therefore, they spent two days going over every crevice of the place and tapping every inch of the walls. But they discovered nothing.

Then they worked down through the other chambers of the house. No one disturbed them. The servants had been discharged, according to Layman's plan, and Layman himself, coming out to the place now and again for books or papers for Beatrice Wilton, was the only one they encountered. He was curious, at first, as to the reason of their stay in the house. But when they evaded his questions rather pointedly, he did not press them. Only he said to Sherry, one day: "Do you think, my friend, that you are doing any good for Beatrice Wilton by tying her name to all your old adventures?"

"Am I dragging her through the dust?" asked Sherry with some sharpness.

"Come, come," said the doctor with perfect good humor. "You understand what I mean, of course. I know that you boys want to do nothing that isn't for her good, but the fact is that you are making a whale of a lot of talk, and the more talk the worse for Beatrice. It's openly said that you're hired by me to be on hand in case we want to beat the law at the last moment. Of course, that is going to be a weight on the minds of the lawyers who will fight for her."

"You want me to hit the trail?" asked Sherry.

"Exactly," said the doctor, who was the most frank of men.

"If I could," said Sherry, "I'd do it. But the fact is that I have to stay. I can't break away. I've tried to before, and it's against my nature."

So the doctor no longer pressed upon that point. To Pete Lang he was rather an offensive personality. But Sherry liked him for the very coldness of mind that troubled Lang. Whatever else the doctor might be, he was a man.

On this day, they had no interruption from anyone. They had worked from the top of the house down, leaving the cellar to the last. It had been their major hope from the moment they gave up the room of Wilton as a possibility, and now they attacked it with the greatest care. There was a large wood room under the house, two big storage chambers for the stowage of supplies, and in the front of the house, where the slope of the land allowed windows to be placed, there were two empty rooms—for servants, no doubt—which never had been used. The windows were stuck shut by the strength of the first and last coat of paint that had been applied to them.

Through these chambers, and through the corridors connecting them, they went with methodical attention, searching, rummaging, tapping.

"You don't have to have a barrel to hide half a million dollars' worth of pearls," Pete Lang was never tired of cautioning his friend.

But when darkness came in the cellar and they had finished the wood room by dint of moving at least a cord of piled firewood, Pete Lang himself confessed that they were wrong. The pearls were not in the house.

It was a great blow to them. As Lang said, the logic all pointed to one conclusion. If the pearls were not in the house, then where were they? Certainly Wilton had not left his room to secure the supply that was in his pocket when he met Fennel.

"You remember," suggested Sherry, "the talk that Beatrice Wilton said she overheard in the woods between her uncle and a man whose voice sounded like Layman's? Wilton said that he hadn't *them*. He was excited and angry about it. What did he mean by *them* unless he meant the pearls?"

"You talk, kid, like a book," admitted the other. "Wilton lost 'em, then? All except a few that he had handy about him, sort of like keepsakes. Is that it?"

"That's the sense of it."

"And what would Layman know about them?"

"He's an old friend of the family."

"How old?"

"Some years at least. He was doctor for both the Wiltons."

"It may not have been Layman's voice at all," said Sherry at last. "If it had been, she wouldn't have merely guessed. She would have known. The things that we think we recognize are a long way from the reality. We never have any real doubt about the truth."

To this Lang agreed, and it was not hard to furnish another character to the man who had conversed with Wilton in the forest behind the house.

It seemed apparent, of course, that Wilton had in his possession—or had had until he lost them—a quantity of pearls or other things of price to which someone besides himself could lay claim. At least, he had not more than a partial interest in the treasure. The strange demeanor of Harry Capper, for instance, could be explained in this manner, as also the odd demands of Fennel, the drunkard and sham.

"If ever we could know the true story of what happened aboard the *Princess Marie*," said Lang, "then we'd be a lot nearer home. But the next thing for us to think about is how we're going to get funds. We can't very well beg them from Beatrice Wilton."

Sherry flushed at the mere thought. "We have the pearls that were meant for Fennel," he suggested.

"That's state property, by rights," objected Lang.

"We can take one of them. How many are there altogether?"

"Five good-size ones, eleven smaller ones, and eighteen little pearls," said Lang.

"You've counted them pretty well, Pete."

"I've spent some time looking at them, son. They're wortl

"I'll take one of the bigger ones," said Sherry, "and hoc' one of the pawnshops. D'you know what one of these tł worth?"

They selected a pearl together.

"I dunno," said Lang. "I sort of remember Sa' having a pearl that looked about that size in a scarf paid down a hundred and fifty dollars for it. I sup ought to get about a hundred, for this one."

"A hundred it is," answered Sherry. "It's ste' thing or someone . . . but not altogether fror goes."

With that, he went straight down to Clayrock and entered beneath the sign of the Three Moons that showed over the entrance of a shop on the main street. It was littered with the usual assortment of cheap watches and good ones, flashy, huge jewelry of paste, and smaller stones of price. Lumbermen and miners had left some of the gilt of their flooding boom days here in the dark shop. There were even jeweled revolvers, pawned at last by some hungry dandy of the frontier.

The place was run by a brisk, young man with an open, frank eye, and a fearless cheerful demeanor. He greeted Sherry with a broad smile.

"'Evening, Mister Sherry. Haven't been expecting you, but I never know when the big men of town may pay me a call. Are you buying or selling, Mister Sherry?"

Sherry looked at him in some hesitation. He was much inclined to find a pawnshop where his name was not so well known, but after a moment of thought he realized that his picture and his name had been spread so thoroughly through Clayrock that it would be impossible for him to remain in the dark.

"I've come to sell," he said, and laid the pearl on the counter.

"And the price?"

"Suppose I leave that to you?"

The pawnbroker took the jewel, passed it under a magnifying glass, and turned it quickly. Then he replaced the pearl gently on the counter. "Not a bad one," he said. "Suppose I say a hundred dollars?"

The price was exactly what Sherry had been led to expect he might get, and now the closeness of Lang's guess made him exclaim with a broad smile: "Well, I'm dashed!"

But the pawnbroker started. "Hold on," he said, growing a le red and hurried, "maybe there isn't such a flaw as I thought, . . ." He examined the pearl again. This time he carefully hed it on a slender scale. "Matter of fact," he said candidly, made a mistake. I can pay you two fifty, for that."

Sherry scowled. "I'll take not a cent under five hundred," he said.

The youth sighed, opened a cash drawer, and laid a bundle of bills before him. "Well," he said, "I can't drive sharp bargains with you, Mister Sherry."

XXIV

The largeness of this price still half stunned Sherry; the value of all the pearls in his pocket suddenly was enhanced; he was carrying about with him what would be a tidy little fortune to many a man. Moreover, the broker did not seem at all displeased with the bargain he had struck, but spread his hands upon the counter and beamed on Sherry as the latter stuffed the bills into his wallet.

"If I'd asked a thousand," said Sherry, "you'd have paid it just as willingly."

"There's pearls and pearls," answered the other. "Most of 'em that size wouldn't be worth five hundred, even. But this is a beauty. I'll send it East. And maybe the selling price of it even in the trade will scare a thousand dollars to death."

His frankness made Sherry smile, and the broker smiled back. He was an extraordinary young man, who seemed to make no attempt to cover his pride in his own shrewdness.

"You and Oliver Wilton keep the same sort of pearls in your pockets, I see," he said.

"Wilton?" exclaimed Sherry.

The pawnbroker narrowed his eyes ever so little. "Does that surprise you a lot?" he asked.

"Why," said Sherry, "I don't see why Wilton should want be selling pearls down here."

"Pawning, not selling. There's a pair of 'em." He to' a small tray, lined with blue velvet, and upon it were ʃ pearls of several sizes. Two big ones lay in the middle. "ʳ couple." He added: "Wilton knew their value, too."

"Wilton's not apt to redeem the tickets," said Sherry dryly.

And he went out into the blast of the sun's light and heat, still blinking and wondering. Why should Wilton have needed money? A good deal of money, at that. For the pair of pearls were both much larger, and fully as fine, it appeared, as the one that he had just sold.

With that in his mind, he hurried back to find Lang, and to him he confided the truth about the price of the pearl. It staggered the man of the range. Together, they laid out the pearls and examined them afresh. If one of them had been sold for $500 and was worth closer to $1,000, the whole of the little collection was now worth a greatly enhanced price.

"If there are many more of these, somewhere," said Lang, "it's a treasure, Tiny. Trouble has popped on account of them. Trouble is going to pop again. But where could Wilton have put the things . . . or lost 'em?"

They were wandering through the garden of the Wilton house as they talked, for the house was hot, and in the garden a breeze stirred beneath the trees.

"This stuff is worth too much to be carted around in a pocket," said Sherry. "I'll take it back to our room and stow it away. Be somewhere around here, and I'll come back."

Going back to their room, he chose a simple hiding place. A handkerchief made a pouch; he secured the loose edges with a bit of string, thrown over in a pair of half hitches, and he simply dropped the handkerchief into the pocket of an old raincoat that he used on cold, windy days, riding herd. If a search was made for any object of value, it would be a clever man indeed who thought of dipping his hand into the pocket of a dusty old coat. And even if a hand reached into that pocket, the handkerchief might not be examined.

Contented with his own cleverness, Sherry went out into the garden and hurried to find Lang again; he would make that keen fellow guess at the hiding place he had chosen and then enjoy some sort of a small triumph, for Lang was apt to smile with superior wisdom at the simplicity of his big friend. So, in his haste, Sherry cut straight for the point at which he had left Lang, and, leaving the path and its crunching gravel, he headed across a stretch of lawn and came in under the shadow of the trees in time to hear a voice growl: "Back him up against that tree, Jerry. Watch him. He's got his weather eye peeled on you. That's better."

Sherry slipped like a great cat among the big trunks of the pines, and so he came on a view of Pete Lang, backed against a large tree, his hands above his head, while one man covered him with a short-nosed revolver, and a second was in the act of reaching for Lang's gun.

"Drop your guns," said Sherry in his deep, booming voice. "And shove up your hands."

The two started violently. Half sheltered behind a tree, Sherry waited, ready with bullets if they were needed, but neither of the pair attempted to turn upon him.

"He's got the wind of us, Bud," said Jerry.

"He has," said Jerry. "It's the big boy, at that. We gotta strike our sails, Bud, to this squall." And, with that, he dropped his gun and raised his powerful arms unwillingly above his head.

Bud followed that good example, and Lang, relieved of pressure, instantly covered them with his own pair of weapons. Steadied and helpless beneath the noses of those big Colts, the strangers remained calmly enough while Sherry searched them. He took from each a dangerous-looking sheath knife, and from Bud another short-nosed gun, which was in a hip pocket.

"These are town guns, boys," said Sherry. "You shouldn't carry them out into the big open spaces. Back up there against that bank," he added. "You can put your hands down, if you want to. But mind you, we mean business. If you try to make a break, I'd have as little hesitation in dropping you as in shooti at a pair of tree stumps."

"Aw," said Bud, "we know you. Everybody knows you. I'm gonna make no break."

He was a little square-made man, with a bright, cheerful face and small eyes that were filled with life. His friend was in exact contrast—a chinless, lean fellow, with a kink in his neck, and an Adam's apple that worked prominently up and down. He allowed Bud to do the talking; indeed, his eyes were constantly seeking the face of his stubbier companion as though to win inspiration.

"We'll get on, then," agreed Sherry. "You two fellows were sent here by who?"

"By no one," said Bud.

"Bud," said Sherry, "are you going to try to pull the wool over our eyes?"

Lang broke in: "There's a mighty tight little jail here in Clayrock, and a sheriff that ain't partial to hold-up men. You may've heard of Sheriff Bert Moon? Try to pull one on us, and you hit the trail for jail and the pen afterward. Come clean, and we turn you off."

"Hold on," protested Sherry. "We have them now. We may wish like anything that we had them later."

"What do they matter?" asked Lang sternly. "They'll never bother either of us again, I have an idea. And we want to get at what sent them here. Bud, who sent you along?"

"We sent ourselves," declared Bud.

"That," said Lang bluntly, "is a lie. I never saw either of you before. You can't have anything against me."

"We got nothing against you," agreed Bud, "but you got something of ours on you."

"And what's that, Bud?"

"What did you leave down in the pawnshop?" asked Bud.

Lang stared at Sherry.

"You're a pair of 'em, are you?" he asked.

"From the *Princess Marie*? Sure we are," said Bud.

"This gets richer and richer," said Sherry. "You're off the *Princess Marie*, then?"

"We are."

"You sailed under Captain Wilton."

"Yes, he was the skipper."

"And no one sent you here?"

"Nobody. Who would? Lord knows we hunted far enough before we spotted the place where Wilton lived, and we come along too late to find him alive . . . the sneakin' low hound. That's what he was, a deadbeat and a hound."

That speech was from the heart; there was no doubt of that. And the face of Jerry, as he listened, wrinkled in savage disgust and sympathy.

"You sent yourselves here?" asked Lang, beginning to take charge of the conversation.

"We done just that. It took time. We was clean broke. Working a short job, here and there, picking up what coin we could, we've had a long beat to windward, but just when we'd weathered the point . . . here comes the big boy with his pair of gats and sticks us up on a reef again. It's tough, I say."

"It's tough," agreed Lang sadly. "You came for what's your own?"

"I came for that."

"And what goes to each of you?"

"Five of the big boys, like you pawned . . . eleven of the middle-size ones, and a bunch of the little fellers," said Bud with instant readiness.

Sherry glanced at Lang, and Lang returned the look with interest.

"What would that come to in cash?"

"About seven thousand iron men," said Bud. He sighed and rolled up his eyes at the thought of such a fortune.

"How many were aboard the *Princess Marie?*" asked Lang.

"Outside of the chief engineer and Capper . . . he was actin' first . . . and the skipper, there was seventeen of us."

"Seventeen times seven makes about a hundred and twenty thousand dollars."

"Or more, according to how good a market we could find," insisted Bud. "Look here, you and big boy. We got no grudge ag'in' you. You got the stuff. All right. Let it go at that. All we ask for is our right share. We done our work, didn't we? Look at me. It was me that was the last man aboard the boats. By rights, I'd ought to have somethin' extra. Well, I ain't yellin' for that. Only, we want our square cut. Nothin' more. Is that fair?"

"What made you think that we had the pearls?" asked Sherry.

"Would a pair of 'punchers off of the range be sporting pearls like that?" asked Bud bluntly.

"Sit down, old son," invited Lang. "We want to hear your yarn about the *Princess Marie*."

"Sure," said Bud willingly. "I'll tell you. Not as if you didn't know."

XXV

The account of Bud was straightforward enough, though filled with a good many inconsequential details such as a sailor cannot free his tongue of. He told how he and his companion, Jerry, had shipped on board the *Princess Marie* in San Francisco harbor.

"She was a fine-lookin' hooker," said Bud. "I never ask no better. A good fo'c's'le . . . roomy enough, and airy enough to keep your duds dry in wet weather, buckin' head winds. We never had no kick, to speak of. The skipper was a gent that kept aft and let the men keep forward. We wasn't undermanned. Overmanned, if anything. The chuck was prime. The watches was regular. Only Capper was a brute. He sailed second, but the first was sick most of the way and he died before the voyage was over. Then Capper, he got the run of the ship, pretty much."

At Hong Kong they discharged their cargo and ran down to Singapore looking for another. A week was wasted, sweltering at Singapore, before they went on to Colombo. Here and at Madras, they picked up a cargo and started for Kuching in Sarawak, Borneo, where they discharged part of it and took on some more.

And here it was, apparently, that the captain received his grand idea. Manila was given out as the next port of call, and they bucked up the north Borneo coast into the teeth of a heavy gale. Instead of holding on their course north of Palawan, and straight for Manila harbor, the *Princess Marie* now was turned through Balabac Strait and went humming south for the Sulu Islands.

That same day, a number of boxes, small but heavy, which had been taken aboard at Kuching, were brought up on the deck and opened. They proved to contain fine new rifles and two machine-guns.

Then Capper went forward and exposed the boxes and their contents to the whole assembled crew. He made a speech in which he pointed out that he had been for years about the Sulu Islands; he knew the people and he knew the pearl fisheries, and of one in particular he had heard that it was ripe for investigation. Great stacks of oysters were now in the sheds; the place was manned by not more than three or four whites, and the natives would never stand up to gunfire. For that matter, it was doubtful if there were more than half a dozen rifles at that station.

The proposal of Capper was simple and to the point. He suggested that they come up toward the fishery, anchor behind a masking point of land, and, under cover of the dark, go in with two of the boats and raid the place. They could capture it at the first rush, shooting into the air. After that, twenty-four hours of brisk work would place in their hands the cream of the spoils of the fishery.

The crew agreed readily. It was Capper himself who had selected the men in San Francisco, and he had taken aboard a choice gang of hardy fellows, who would stop at nothing. They were offered, now, one half of the total haul; the other half was to be split up among the officers, the share of Wilton, as skipper, being a quarter of the whole—not too large a portion, taking into account the fact that he was handling the ship and assuming the responsibility.

The first mate, still very ill, now gathered strength enough to come on deck, and there before the men he made a hot appeal to them all to pay no more attention to the captain and the second, so far as this raid was concerned, but to remember that these waters were alive with revenue cutters, and that there was a very small chance that they could ever get away with their loot in the face of wireless and telegraphs, which would soon give out the alarm.

However, the captain ordered the mate into his cabin, and none of the crew was shaken in their resolve. They looked upon this expedition more or less as the buccaneers looked in the old days upon an incursion into the Spanish Main. It was partly piracy, of course, but chiefly it was a grand old lark.

A note of seriousness was struck the very next morning, when it was discovered that the mate was no longer aboard. Capper stirred about among the men and pointed out that the mate had been sick for a long time, that his mind had been upset by the plan to raid the pearl fishery, and that he must have stepped to the rail and dived over during the night.

However, there was a dark feeling among the men that Capper must have taken the affair in hand and tapped the mate upon the head, and then passed him over the rail. There was no suspicion attached to the skipper on this occasion.

However, it was noticeable that Capper, from this day forward, had almost as much control over the ship as the skipper himself. He gave orders. He even argued with Wilton before the men, and the captain put up with it, as though perforce.

In the meantime, they were logging south in the most leisurely fashion, the engines barely turning over enough to give steerage way, and the ship rolling heavily and sluggishly while the crew hastily worked a coat of paint over her. Her color was completely altered, the bands upon the smokestack were changed, and the big letters of the name on the stern were painted out and replaced by *The Dove, of Bristol.*

This name, for a ship that was about to make such a predatory swoop, amused the men highly. At length, the painting was completed, and very late in the afternoon of the next day they ducked inside a coral reef and came to anchor in smooth water to the south of a jutting point of land.

With the darkness, the two boats put off. Only three men were left on board, under command of the boatswain. The rest, sixteen in number, with the captain in the sheets of the larger boat, rowed in around the point, with muffled oars. In the bow of each boat there was a machine-gun. Capper was handling one. Bud himself had the other. In case the station developed unexpected strength, the machine-guns were to cover a retreat.

The landing was perfectly simple. That night the sea was almost totally quiet, and with silent oars they pushed on until the prows quenched their speed in the white sand that gleamed faintly under the tropic stars.

They made straight to the station, unchallenged, and then charged in with devilish yells, shooting into the air, as Capper had suggested. Not a hand was raised to oppose them.

By midday of the following day, they had finished their work and were lugging at the oars on the way back to the ship that, having been flagged in the meantime, had worked up steam. And yet they made no great haste away from the island.

As they were tuning to come out through the gap between the reefs, a few riflemen came down to the shore and, hiding behind rocks, opened a desultory fire—not as though hoping to delay the ship, but simply in blind anger, to inflict some loss upon her. However, a few bursts of fire from the machine-guns quieted the marksmen ashore, and *The Dove, of Bristol* drew slowly away.

However, they had barely made offing from the island when smoke appeared on the horizon and came up toward them, hand over hand. At full speed, *The Dove, of Bristol* rushed north. The other vessel instantly changed course. There was no doubt that she was pursuing.

Full speed for the *Princess Marie* made little difference. The look-out presently descried a long, low hull beneath the smoke cloud of the other ship; it was a government cutter slicing the water like a knife and literally walking over them.

Capper, pale, and stern, and despairing, stood on the bridge and cursed with helpless rage. The captain retired to the chart house; everyone thought that he had funked the issue.

But presently he altered the course due east.

The pursuer was hull up, by this time. It was late afternoon. The sun hung not twice its own breadth above the horizon; and then a mutter ran through the crew that they were heading straight for a nest of reefs through which no ship in the world could possibly find a passage.

This murmur grew. The boatswain was made spokesman to go aft and complain to the skipper about the madness of the present course. At which Wilton came out and made a quiet speech. He pointed out that they were totally lost. They could not escape from the government boat by holding straight on their course. Darkness was about to drop over them, but shortly after, the searchlight of the pursuer would pick them out, and soon a shell would whistle over their heads and thus force them to heave to.

He proposed to head the ship straight on toward the reefs, and, as soon as the darkness came, he would open the cocks of the ship, and as she sank, steaming ahead, the boats would be manned. True, the reefs could not be passed by a large ship, but it would be child's play to get through them with the boats.

The crew, astonished by this bold suggestion, cheered their skipper. And all was done as he had conceived the scheme. Darkness dropped. The searchlight of the cutter began to fumble vaguely at

the blackness, the *Princess Marie* settled low in the water, and when
her decks were almost awash, the boats were shoved off and the
oars swept them away. They had not gone a hundred yards, when
the *Princess Marie* put her stern in the air and dived from view.

That same night a tremendous storm blew up; they landed
to escape the force of a hurricane out of the north. When it had
blown over the next morning, they pursued their way and finally
made a port, with a sad story of how the hurricane had overwhelmed the *Princess Marie* on a sunken reef, on which she had
broken up as the boats were taken off in the falling of the wind.

But now, while they waited for the coming of the ship that
would take them back to civilization, the captain, with the brown
satchel in which the pearls were stowed by him, suddenly disappeared from the town.

It was suggested that he might have headed for the far side
of the island. A searching party failed to bring him in, and so the
fruit of the pearl raid was gathered into his own hands.

The lips of the sailors were sealed. They could not very well
confess that they had been robbers before they were robbed, but
the prize that had been stolen from them was sufficiently large
to make every one of them desire to take vengeance into his own
hands. Others, no doubt, would follow the trail of Bud, and
Jerry, and Capper, to Clayrock, and trouble was bound to continue until the men had got their dues.

Such was the strange story of the sinking of the *Princess Marie.*

"Wilton's gone," said Bud in conclusion. "He had a brain,
but he was a crook. And finally he got his. And now, big boy, we
want to know where we come in?"

XXVI

It was necessary for the two confederates to stare at one another
again, as in consultation, after which Sherry said: "This fellow is
square, Lang."

"He's square," admitted Pete Lang, "but I don't see what difference that makes."

"I'm going to come clean to him," said Sherry. He said suddenly to the sailors: "You fellows can hear what I have to say. I don't think you'll believe me, but here goes. When Lang, here, found that Wilton lay dead in the grass, he discovered a handful of pearls in Wilton's pocket. There were five big pearls, and eleven of a middle size, and a number . . . seventeen, I think . . . of little ones. He took those pearls and didn't turn them in to the sheriff. For a good many reasons."

"You fool!" barked Lang at his friend. "Do you realize what you're saying?"

"I know what I'm saying," said Sherry. "But what's the use? Are we going to murder these fellows? I think not. And as long as they're alive they'll keep on troubling us . . . they and the rest of the crew behind them. Let me talk straight out."

"You see what you've got to say?" muttered Lang.

"I see, and I'll say it," retorted Sherry.

He continued to the two sailors, who now were as keen as lynxes.

"I'm not going into the thing any more in detail. I'm simply going to ask you to believe that we weren't stealing for ourselves. We were . . . "

"Hold on," said Lang. "I dunno that I shouldn't have my say about that. Why haven't we as good a right to the stuff as any other man?"

"Hey!" put in Jerry, his voice ringing with indignation. "Did you go to all the trouble of swipin' 'em? Did you have a ship sink under you? Did you have a typhoon blow up over your heads? Did you go wanderin' around broke for months, tryin' to locate the snake that had double-crossed you? And here you come up sayin' that you got an equal right to them pearls. Is that logic, partners?" He spread out his lank hands. Jerry was wounded to the heart.

"You swiped 'em," said Lang brutally. "I swipe 'em back. What you gotta say about that? Nobody owns 'em but the fishery. That's the straight of it. Where do you come in? If you steal a horse, does that make you have any claim to the horse . . . or to a rope to stretch your neck with? How's that for logic?"

It was such convincing logic that Jerry sat back and bit his lips nervously. His eyes worked this way and that, but, troubled though his soul might be, he could not find for it any relief in words.

Both the sailors sat bolt upright and stared at the pair—silenced but deeply hostile.

"Logic's not what we want here," said Sherry. "We want friendliness. And here's where I bid for it."

"If you didn't swipe the stuff," asked Bud angrily, "how come that you sold one of the pearls and shoved the money in your wallet?"

"Because we had to have something to live on while we're working on this case."

"And what call have you got to work on this here case?"

"To prove that Beatrice Wilton is not guilty," said Sherry with much earnestness.

"Say, Bud," said Jerry in some disgust, "ain't you heard nothin'? Don't you know nothin'?"

With this, he nodded at Sherry in a good deal of friendly sympathy, and the big man flushed darkly. His secret was known, then. Well, for that matter he had seen a thousand hints in the newspapers. He was "the knight of Beatrice Wilton," among other titles showered upon him.

"But we couldn't draw down pay for sitting still, could we?" asked Sherry. "You understand, boys, that we had to live if we were to help. So we soaked one of the pearls. I'll do more. I'll show you the rest of the ones that we have."

"Sure," said lean-and-lank Jerry.

"It ain't necessary," put in Bud with dignity. "I can tell when a gent is comin' clean with me. I'll take your word, big boy."

"I don't see where all of this rigmarole is heading for!" exclaimed Lang. "It beats me what you got in your head, Tiny."

"Of course it does," said Sherry with a superior air. "I'll let you in on it now. Do you believe that these fellows were a part of the crew of the *Princess Marie?*"

"Aw, I believe that, well enough."

"Then they'd know the rest of the crew?"

"I suppose so."

"Then they can tell us . . . and the sheriff . . . something about Fennel, can't they?"

"Ah, now I foller your drift. But I aim to say that Fennel never was a sailor at all."

"You're wrong, and you have to be wrong," insisted Sherry. "Fennel was one of the crew . . . he wanted his split of the pearls . . . he hated Wilton so badly that, when he was close to him, he didn't wait for the split, but murdered him."

"That would be nacheral enough," declared Bud. "But tell me about this Fennel. I've read something about him. Was there any Fennel in the crew, Jerry?"

"There was not, that I knowed of. But we went by front monikers, not the family names. How did he look?"

"Long and thin. A good, big head covered with ratty, ragged-looking hair. Unshaved most of the time. Very fond of his liquor. Clever, too. A sneaking sort of cleverness, I'd say."

The sailors looked gravely at one another, as though reading in books. "That's Davisson," said Jerry.

"Did he have a scar across his forehead?" asked Bud.

"No. Not a sign of a scar."

"It's not Davisson, then. And if it ain't Davisson, it's nobody from the *Princess Marie.*"

"And there you are," said Lang sourly. "You'll be helped on your way a long distance by this, Tiny Lew."

"Shut up!" answered Sherry angrily. "We've finally established one point . . . Fennel was *not* a member of the crew. If not, then he was an outside worker. Is that right?"

"And where does that lead you?"

"I don't know. But everything that we learn is something that we know," said Sherry with a rather childish stubbornness. "What I suggest is this. Get these boys on our side of the fence. If we don't, then when other members of the *Princess Marie* crew hit this town, as they're sure to do, they'll all be waiting for us in a mob, thinking that we have the loot."

"And how'll you get 'em on our side?" asked Lang, still skeptical.

"This way. Boys," he said to the sailors, "I'll offer you a bargain. It may not suit you, but here it is, the best that I can do. You know that the pair of us are doing what we can to help Miss Wilton out of jail, where she doesn't belong. But as sure as there's a heaven, what we do will be no good unless we find this fellow Fennel . . . or whatever his real name is . . . and prove that he committed the murder. Otherwise, there's nothing to do except smash open the jail, and you know that jail breaking isn't as easy as opening a can in a town where Sheriff Bert Moon keeps office hours. Are you following me?"

"Like a hound on the trail," said Bud.

"Then throw in with us. This trail goes to sea, where most landsmen can't follow it. I think that Fennel's trail goes to sea, also. Well, perhaps you could follow it where we can't. Suppose you throw in with us, and Beatrice Wilton is not found guilty . . . then we turn over to you these pearls. That means six or seven thousand dollars for the two of you. Not your full share, I know. But, otherwise, how do you get anything at all?"

Bud said instantly: "Big boy, I'm with you. I like your style fine. I'd sign with you any day. That goes for Jerry, too. Eh?"

"Sure," said Jerry rather vacantly.

"We being broke, though?" queried Bud.

Sherry drew out the wallet, and gave $250 into the hand of the sailor. "That's half the price of the pearl," he said.

Money possesses a peculiar eloquence and emphasis. Now, Bud held the bills in a firm grasp for a moment and stared at them. He had worked most of his life before the mast, and sailors' wages are not high. Then, with a knotted brow, he made exact division and handed half of the whole to Jerry, who was now plainly agape.

"We'll see you through this buster," said Bud quietly. "What do we do first?"

"Go down to Moon and say that you've been sailors. That you knew a man who looked like Fennel. The sheriff will let you see his stuff. Maybe that will tell you something. But right now you can perhaps give us an idea of how many of your other shipmates are apt to turn up here at Clayrock."

Said Jerry: "Three of the boys died in the Sulus before ever they sailed. Budge Sawyer fell from the end of the bridge and busted his back on the way home. Loomis and Cartwright was killed in a dynamite explosion in Frisco right after they landed on shore. Well, that's six out of twenty. The skipper's dead, and so is Capper . . . and good riddance! And here's me and Bud. Well, say there's ten more that might show up, but will they? I dunno. Some gents are pretty careless. It's a wild-goose chase, anyway. I never would've stayed on the road, except that Bud made me. I dunno. I don't think that many more of the crew will be showing up this way."

Bud said with his grave, bulldog manner. "Here's my hand, big boy. You, too." He shook with Sherry and Pete Lang. "We're hitting the grit right now. Whatever we find out, we'll let you know. So long!"

And, in a moment, they were off down the path.

Lang looked after them with a dubious eye. "Is there six thousand dollars' worth of brains in that outfit?" he asked. "Is there any chance of getting back what you offer to pay, old son?"

"I don't know," answered Sherry. "But if they're any help at all . . . great Scott, man, won't it be beyond all price in the world?"

But Pete Lang sighed and looked the other way, like a man dealing with a child.

XXVII

After that, Pete Lang remained at the house, but Sherry, growing nervous with inaction, started into the town to see what he could see, and almost at once encountered the tall form of Dr. Layman, coming along the street with his long, light stride, his trousers brushing together with a whish at the knees. He was white and thin-lipped with anger.

"The sheriff is as full of malice as a mad dog," declared the doctor. "By heaven, there's a flaw in the man's mind. He's unbalanced."

"He's a name for being a square-shooter," suggested Sherry, in doubt because of the violence of this accusation.

"Square-shooter? He's going to railroad Beatrice to the hangman's rope," declared Layman. "He's just refused to allow her to see anyone, or even to send out letters. A more high-handed outrage I never heard of."

"Not even see her lawyers?" asked Sherry.

"And precious lawyers she'll have," stormed Layman, "unless we can get at the funds of the estate. And how is that to be done unless she can execute a power of attorney and place it in my hands . . . or in any other hands. I've never heard of such illegal tyranny."

"It is," Sherry agreed. He thought a moment, and then added: "Some men naturally dislike women. Moon does."

"You're right, of course," acknowledged the doctor. "But there's this to be considered . . . he never had a chance, before, to put a woman in jail on a heavy charge. And now the tyrant in him is being shown . . . without precedent."

"Have you appealed to the judge?"

"What use is that? The judge is in Moon's pocket. Everything that Moon does is inspired, one would think. But, by Jupiter, I'm going to break his reputation to bits like bad wood." He went on without farewell, only to turn on his heel after a few strides and call back: "You know that Slade . . . the Phantom, or Fannie, or whatever they call him . . . is in town looking for you? Is there any bad blood between you two, or is he a friend? We've never crossed," added the doctor, and hurried on, like a man full of his own thoughts.

It was a double blow that Sherry had received. In the first place, the news that the sheriff had taken such a pronounced stand against Beatrice Wilton was a shock to him, not only because it was sure to make her way to freedom more difficult, but because it showed from the beginning that Herbert Moon was convinced of her guilt. And the reaction of Sherry was unlike that of Layman. The doctor, keen in the pursuit of the girl's freedom, seemed to have had no feeling except that injustice had been done, but Sherry, looking at the matter in another light, felt the weight of Moon's condemnation. For the sheriff was not a man to make up his mind lightly, and, before he would take such a vigorous attitude as that which he had adopted toward the girl, it was certain that he had searched the case thoroughly from beginning to end.

In a word, if Herbert Moon felt that Beatrice Wilton was guilty, guilty she undoubtedly was.

The chief work for Sherry, he resolved, as he marched on down the street, was not to prove her innocent, but to devise means of getting her out of the jail. And bitterly, now, he regretted the threats that he had poured upon the quiet little sheriff in the Wilton house, on the day of the coroner's examination. He had, in gambling parlance, tipped his hand, and the sheriff would be waiting for exactly such an attempt as Sherry now had in mind.

However, for the moment even the girl was thrust to the back of his mind. There was another point of greater importance, for the nonce. Slade! His name showed the manner in which he had graduated in the school of violence. Fannie Slade they called him now. But in his earlier days, before debauchery and a thousand crimes had lined his face and put iron in his heart, he had been known as Phantom Slade. Because like a ghost he stepped without sound, and his wild rides across country made his presence ubiquitous.

It was not likely that Slade had come to Clayrock for any friendly purpose. If he were asking for Sherry, it meant that he was intent on making trouble—his vocation in life.

It might well be that the fame of Sherry, so foolishly spread abroad by the pages of many newspapers—his fame as a gunfighter—had come to the ears of Slade and wakened the jealousy of the famous killer.

For such was Slade. It was said of him, as of some cut-throats of earlier days, that he killed men merely for the pleasure of seeing them fall. There was no chivalry in Fannie Slade. He would shoot from behind as readily as he would shoot from in front. He was a half-breed, and he had a half-breed's—or a tiger's—indifference to honorable methods of warfare. The tales that were told of him chilled the blood. Though still in the prime of life, he was old as a slayer. He had begun in his teens, said rumor. He was now over thirty. And he was said to have killed a man a year.

It was no wonder that Sherry grew cautious and his manner altered as he went down the street. All things had now a different meaning. There was as great a contrast as there is between day and night in the mind of a child—or in the minds of most grown men. All had been open and harmless the instant before, but now every alley mouth yawned at Sherry like a leveled gun, and every open window was a source of careful thought.

For so Slade acted. Like the rattler, he delivered his warning the instant he appeared. And, by so doing, he more or less established that he was to be the hunted as well as the hunter. The warned man would be sure to be upon his guard, might well be expected to deliver a counterattack. But Slade trusted to the superior secrecy and cunning of his own maneuvers to gain the upper hand.

However, it might all be another matter. Some mutual friend might have recommended Sherry to Slade. In hope of that, the big man went on. For he had no desire to risk his life in such an unequal battle. It was true that he had a gift of speed and surety with weapons, but he never had given to fighting for its own sake, the professional attention that Slade had devoted to the game. He had lived by labor; Slade had lived by his Colt.

Sherry went straight to the hotel and sat down on the verandah. It was an empty verandah when he arrived, but quickly it was filled. People turned in from the street in passing; others came out from the building. For everyone was anxious to be in the presence of this temporarily notorious character.

And then his next-door neighbor leaned a little toward him: "You're in for Slade, I guess?"

"Have you seen Slade?" asked Sherry.

"He's over in Ratner's Saloon."

"Did you see him there?"

"Yep. He lined up everybody and bought a drink."

"He wants me?"

"That's what he says."

"To talk or to shoot?" asked Sherry.

"I dunno. What does he usually want when he sends for a gent?"

Sherry was silent; the answer was too obvious.

"The best way is for you to sit tight," volunteered Sherry's neighbor. "You stay put where you are, with plenty of the boys around you. That way, Slade won't have a chance to get behind you."

"Will you do me a favor?"

"Proud an' happy to."

"Go over to Ratner's Saloon and ask Slade what he wants of me."

The other stiffened a little and changed color. But he was a man of courage. "I'll do it," he said. "Are you . . . are you gonna make a showdown of it, Sherry?"

"I'll hear his answer, first," said Sherry.

The other rose, and walked rapidly down the verandah steps. Once in the street, he paused, tightened his belt, jerked his hat on more firmly, and with all the air of a man going to undertake a really desperate commission, he started for Ratner's Saloon, the front door of which was visible across the street some distance down.

Through the swinging door went the messenger, and was gone a mortal minute. Then he appeared again, not walking, but literally hurled through the air. He landed in the street, rolled over and over in the dust, then picked himself up and came on the run back to the hotel.

When he arrived, a crowd gathered around him, but he fought his way through them to Sherry and stood before the latter, a battered, tattered specimen. One sleeve of his coat was missing and a great rent went up its back. His hat was gone. One eye was very red, and rapidly beginning to swell and turn purple.

"I done your dirty work for you, Sherry," he declared angrily. "And a fine reception they gave me. Slade has every ruffian in town around him. When I asked him your question, he said to me . . . 'Tell the low skunk that I'm here to get him, and that I'm comin' soon. Tell him to be ready. But what are you doin' down here, you sneakin' spy?'

"The rest of them took that up. They dived on me . . . half a dozen of 'em . . . beat me up, and turned me out. And you, Sherry, you . . . what're you gonna do about it?" He was a young fellow with plenty of fighting spirit, and now, with his fists clenched, he looked as though he were about to throw himself at Sherry's throat.

"Steady, steady," said Sherry. "Let me have a minute to think this thing over."

And think it over he did, and in dead silence. Caution told him to wait where he was or, better still, go home to the assured protection of Pete Lang, rather than trust to the motley crew here, where each man was only for himself. Then he looked at the half-obscured eye and the tattered coat of his emissary, and honest anger cleansed the heart of Lew Sherry.

Wait for Slade here? Even policy forbade that he wait in silence, his nerves wearing thin, while Slade took his ease, and came to strike when he was ready. He rose suddenly to his feet.

"What're you gonna do?" demanded the messenger again.

"I'm going to get you another coat," said Sherry, and went down the steps in one stride.

XXVIII

It was not far down the street to Ratner's place, but it seemed a great distance to Sherry, for he had clothed himself in his wrath as in a garment, and every step that he took increased his anger. For, after all, it was little short of murder that the great Fannie Slade now contemplated. He must know his own superiority over such a common cowpuncher from the range as Sherry was, but, eager to swell his own reputation by destroying that of this newly rising light, he had come to consume Sherry like a tiger on the trail.

And it maddened the big man to think of the gunman leaning at Ratner's bar, surrounded by his cronies, waiting for nerve to weaken in Sherry. And besides, what strange thoughts, what odd devices, were now rising in the imagination of the destroyer?

A brisk young man jogged a horse up the street and hailed Sherry. "I've come over from the sheriff's office," he said. "Sheriff

Moon knows that Slade is in town. He's heard that Slade is threatening you."

"And what is that to him?" asked Sherry, vexed.

"He sent me to tell you not to go near Slade. It's his business, as sheriff, to handle that man, and he wants no other person to interfere."

Sherry, truly amazed, looked in wonder at the boy.

The latter continued: "Sheriff Moon is waiting for Slade to come out of Ratner's Saloon. He's surrounded by his cronies and his hangers-on, in there, and any of them would as soon shoot a man in the back as look at him in the face. But when Slade comes out, the sheriff will tend to him. He expressly wanted me to tell you this."

"Young fellow," said Sherry, "this is darned kind of the sheriff. Tell him so from me. Who are you?"

"Sheriff Moon is my uncle. I am his sister's son," said the boy. "My name is Charles Crandall."

He was as clean a lad, with as straight an eye, as ever Sherry had seen.

"I didn't expect this from the sheriff," answered Sherry. "I've been rather rough on him. Now I thank him from the heart, but it's too late. I've got to go and get Slade." He strode on down the street.

But presently he was aware of a shadow following him. He jerked suddenly about and saw that the youth had dismounted and was coming from behind, quietly, and straight behind.

"And now what do you want?" asked Sherry.

"My uncle told me to prevent you from meeting Slade," said the boy.

"Will you prevent me by walking at my heels?" asked Sherry, half annoyed and half wondering.

"No, sir," answered Charles Crandall. "But at least I can help you when it comes to the pinch."

Sherry actually gasped. "Do you mean that?"

"Yes, Mister Sherry, of course."

"That you'd go into Ratner's place with me?"

"I'm under orders," said the boy.

"Look here!" exclaimed Sherry. "What are you doing in this town?"

"It's the school vacation," said Charles Crandall. "I came out to visit my uncle, you see."

"And now you're going to take a chance of breaking your neck for yourself? Crandall, I like you fine. You have as much nerve as any youngster I ever heard of, but now I order you to get away from behind me."

He stepped on, looking back over his shoulder; young Charles Crandall remained rooted where he was.

So Sherry went on again, turning many thoughts in his confused brain, and always harking back to the strangeness of this day, which had brought him a kindly word and a kindly hand from Herbert Moon.

Bitterly, bitterly he realized what all other men knew, that Herbert Moon was the soul of honor, of courtesy, of human gentleness, and therefore, the case of Beatrice Wilton seemed darker and darker.

And this sorrow, this inner gloom, went to color his anger and make it more savage, until he was cold with rage as he reached the door of Ratner's Saloon.

He paused for an instant and looked up the street, and down it. At either end the people were flooding from their houses and blocking the road with a solid mass of humanity, and still they poured out, like water from every crevice after the long wave has receded to the sea. He would have spectators for his death, at the least.

Then he struck the door with his fist and dashed it open, and, as he did so, he was conscious of a shadow just at his back. He glanced like lightning over his shoulder, and saw the handsome face of young Charles Crandall.

It was too late to turn back the gallant boy again. So Sherry stepped on into the saloon, and the first face that his eyes fell upon was that of Fannie Slade. He saw that man with a wonderful distinctness in a hundredth part of a second. And it was an unforgettable face, with bright silver tufts of hair at either temple, sunken eyes that flashed like metal out of the deep shadows beneath the brow, and lines of irony and pain and savagery marked on it deeply everywhere.

That face convulsed with anger at the sight of Sherry, but the eyes widened and grew blank, also. Plainly Fanny Slade was receiving the greatest surprise of his life, and he was not enjoying the shock.

But it is that way many a time—a reputation grows too great. The pedestal becomes so high that even the statue is afraid of falling. So Slade stared, unable to believe that any man dared to invade his lair.

"Are you ready, Slade?" called Sherry.

The great Fannie Slade leaned a little forward, his left hand extended along the edge of the bar, his right hand at his thigh, just hovering over the handles of his revolver, but he did not draw, and he did not speak.

"Keep back, all of you," said a quiet young voice behind Sherry. "I'll start shooting the first man who tries to interfere."

That was the sheriff's nephew. *A bit of real stuff,* thought Sherry.

The blankness was leaving the eyes of Slade, but still a ghost of it remained, and suddenly Sherry stepped forward. He dared not stand quietly, waiting for the gunman to make the first move.

"You sent for me, Slade, to tell me that you were coming," said Sherry. "I couldn't keep such a famous man waiting. Here I am." He stood close, looking down on the slayer.

And then the glance of Slade wavered in a flash to the side— and back again to Sherry. But it told Sherry enough. It was a blinding ray of light.

"Great guns," said Sherry. "I thought you were a man. I didn't expect to find merely a murdering sneak." And with his left hand, lightly he struck Slade upon the cheek. The gunfighter turned white as death, but that deadly and famous right hand remained frozen upon the handles of his gun.

Sherry turned his back and saw a line of sick faces along the bar. "This is a rotten show, boys," he said. "You'd better get your friend out of town, because I hear that the sheriff may want him."

And he walked out of the saloon, leaving deathly silence behind him. At his back stepped young Charles Crandall, his revolver still leveled, guarding the retreat of the big man. When they were outside, he sprang before Sherry and wrung his hand enthusiastically.

"That was a grand thing!" cried Charles Crandall. "That was the finest thing that I ever saw or heard of. Even Uncle Herbert never did a better thing in all his life!"

"You go back to your uncle," said Sherry, "and give him a message from me, word for word. Will you do that?"

"Yes, sir," said Crandall with an almost soldierly readiness.

"Tell him that he ought to keep you at home, because, if you wander around, one of these days you'll blow up."

"I don't know what you mean by that," protested the youngster.

"I don't suppose you do," Sherry said, nodding. "But *he* will. In the meantime, I want you to know that I'm your friend. I never would have come out of Ratner's alive without you at my back. You don't have to repeat that to the sheriff. I'll call on him and tell him that myself."

He left Charles Crandall with a face suffused with joy, and went slowly back up the street to the hotel. He did not arrive there first. Hurrying figures had left the saloon shortly after his departure, and they had given brief messages to the curious. So a murmur arose before Sherry and behind him as he went up to the youth of the tattered coat and black eye.

"Young fellow," said Sherry, "I thought that I could get a coat out of the crowd in Ratner's for you. But they didn't want to play. Come into the store with me, and I'll get you a new one."

A broad grin played over the battered face of the other. "Partner," he said with emotion, "I wouldn't change this here coat, now, for a broadcloth one . . . not with tails to it." He added, in a burst of enthusiasm: "It don't seem possible that you made Slade take water. Great guns. Fannie Slade. The killer. Now, every terrier in town will take after his scalp."

"They'll never catch up with him," suggested Sherry. "Slade has sloped, by this time, I think."

And, in fact, Slade had disappeared from Clayrock on a fast horse, and none of his escort of cronies rode with him. But as Sherry went down the street again, he saw that his own position in the town had altered considerably. Men and women had looked at him before with awe, to be sure, but also with dread, as one would admire a huge but savage dog. But now they regarded him with a more friendly air. Children suddenly darted out of gates and began to tag along behind him. A bold spirit ran past him and slapped at his great, ponderous, swinging hand. Sherry scooped him up as he fled and whirled him in the air, while the boy shrieked with fear—and found himself suddenly deposited upon a vast shoulder, then settled safely upon the ground again. So laughter arose and spilled back and forth riotously among the children, and they swarmed around the knees of the big man all the way to the sheriff's house.

It was the smallest dwelling in Clayrock; it was also the most poverty-stricken, but in front of it there was a garden of flowers that the sheriff kept going by much labor in the intervals between his manhunting expeditions. He was digging in that garden, now, on his knees, whistling cheerfully as he worked around the roots of an ancient rose bush.

"Hey!" shrilled a child in the crowd. "Look what we've brought home to you for lunch, Sheriff Moon!"

And they yelled with delight as Sherry strode triumphantly through the gate.

Sheriff Herbert Moon got up from his knees rather painfully, and with a slowness that made Sherry realize that time was stiffening the hero.

"Well, well, well," said Moon. "I'm glad to see you here. I was sorry to hear from Charles that you had taken such a foolish chance. But, of course, I'm glad that it turned out that way. I never would have dared to go into Ratner's for him, I'm sure. Come into the house and sit down, Sherry."

So spoke the sheriff, knowing that twenty youthful ears heard this tribute to Sherry at the speaker's own expense.

And then he led the giant into the little house, where Sherry had to bow his head to pass through the door, and where he hardly dared to stand erect even inside, because the rafters sloped down so low at the sides. Charles Crandall sprang up at the other end of the room.

"You run along," said the sheriff. "You're a little young to hear what we're going to say."

XXIX

The place looked like a Mexican hut, on the inside. That is to say, the floor was simply hard-packed earth, cool and comfortable in summer, soundless underfoot—but necessarily damp in the winter. There was only one room, but each of the four corners was used as a separate chamber. The stove, with pans and pots hanging behind it, filled one nook; a table, flanked by shelves of dishes and cups and saucers, took the next; the third contained a large roll-topped desk that looked absurdly out of place, but which, as everyone knew, probably contained more valuable information about criminals and criminal life than any depository in the Southwest.

The fourth corner was the sheriff's library, two or three hundred old, time-faded volumes being ranged along the shelves there. Near the desk was one couch, and in the "library" was a second, which supplied the sleeping accommodations. The rear door had been left open by Charles Crandall, and, therefore, Sherry was able to look out on the regular rows of a vegetable garden, behind which stood the barn. This was such a pretentious and solid structure that neighbors sometimes asked why the sheriff did not move his horses into his house, while he took up his residence in the stable. But he was apt to say in his good-humored way that his horses were worth much more than his skin.

It was not really a very uncomfortable dwelling, when one's ideas were finally accommodated to this scheme of things. In Mexican style, the floor and the couches and even the chairs were covered with goatskins; on the wall was ranged an armory of weapons, new and old shotguns of several makes and sizes, rifles, and a whole rack of revolvers, with boxes of ammunition beneath. Regularly, winter and summer, in heat or in cold, the patient sheriff stood in his rear yard and worked two hours with his guns. Neighbors peered over the fence and took note of these exhibitions, and what they saw prevented the world from considering that the sheriff had grown old.

"Will you tell me," said Sherry, "how you can go away on trips and leave all these things behind you? I don't think either of those doors would hold, even if they had locks and bolts and bars, which I don't see."

"This house is never locked," answered the sheriff.

"Then you've weeded all the thieves out of Clayrock?" said Sherry.

"One lifetime isn't long enough to do that." Herbert Moon smiled. "All that I'm able to do is to cut off the heads of the tallest weeds . . . keep them from choking out the wheat, so to speak. And I suppose that a good many fellows would like to have a look inside my desk, yonder, or put their hands on those guns."

"You hire someone to guard the place when you're away, then?"

"I can't afford that," said the sheriff. "Besides, who could I trust? But I have better guards than men ever could be. I'll show them to you."

He whistled softly, and instantly two sleek, white forms leaped into the doorway and came to their master—two powerfully made bull terriers with snaky heads, and little, dangerous eyes. They stood at attention like soldiers, their cropped ears pricking.

"This is the answer," said the sheriff. "When I'm away, the rear door is wedged open just enough for them to go in and out. They can't be poisoned, for they've been taught to take food from no hand except mine and that of my neighbor, Missus Miller. She looks after them while I'm gone, but even Missus Miller doesn't dare step into the yard. Once or twice there have been awkward situations when tramps came to beg at the door, but a tramp with a fast bull terrier at his heels can do wonderful jumping. Up to this time, they've always been able to clear the front fence in their stride; but I confess that I'm always relieved when I get home and find that Jack and Jill have hurt no one."

Sherry smiled. He could understand a great deal about this little man by the explanation he had given. For what could have been more effective than such an arrangement? And certainly even those accustomed to danger from men and guns would hesitate to face the teeth of these small white defenders. A wave of the sheriff's hand sent them slipping out of the house again.

Sherry said bluntly: "Sheriff, I've come to talk plain talk."

"I like that kind best," said Moon.

"You've had the name of a square-shooter, always. But now you have a girl in jail and you're bearing down on her."

"In what way, Sherry?"

"You've refused to let her see anyone . . . you've refused to let her send so much as a note out of her cell."

Herbert Moon did not attempt to deny the accusation, but he said with a nod: "One has to take a different line with nearly every prisoner."

"But what does the law say about this?"

"The law doesn't give me any such power," said Moon with amazing openness. "However, I often have to overstep the bounds of the law."

"Do you admit that?" gasped Sherry.

"In our country," replied the other, "the law is made entirely for the sake of the accused, to assure him of receiving justice. We're raised to believe that all men are free and equal, and according to the letter of the law an accused man, no matter what proofs are against him, is apt to be treated as though he were a little more free and equal than any other person in the land."

Sherry nodded. "I follow that," he said. "I don't want to make trouble about this. I'd rather stand behind you, Moon. But . . . tell me this. Are you sure that Beatrice Wilton killed her uncle?"

The sheriff made a little pause at this for, frank as his talk had been, this was a question that rather overstepped the bounds. At length he answered: "You want a free answer to that . . . an answer never to be repeated, of course?"

"Of course," agreed Sherry.

"Then I'm glad to tell you that my mind is entirely made up. It doesn't often happen that an officer of the law can throw himself into his work with surety. But I feel an absolute surety now."

Sherry sighed. "I hate to hear this," he admitted. "Is she as surely guilty as all this? Is there no way of throwing a little blame on Fennel?"

"My case is not entirely made up," answered the sheriff. "I'm frank to say that. But the truth is that this crime never in the world would have been committed if it had not been for Beatrice Wilton."

Sherry loosened his collar and took a great breath. "I think you're wrong," he said huskily. "But suppose that you get together enough evidence to convince a jury . . . what will they do with her?"

"Find her guilty of murder in the first degree, but, since she's pretty, they'll recommend a mild sentence, or some degree of mercy, I have no doubt."

"And then?"

"I know the judge, I think," replied the sheriff coldly.

"And you'll influence him to give her all that the law allows?"

"A good judge never can be influenced," answered Herbert Moon.

"Man, man," muttered Sherry. "She's young . . . a more beautiful woman was never made."

At this, Moon stood up from his chair. "A woman born with a pretty face is born with a curse," he said. "Her beauty becomes her end of living, her vocation. Her work is to let herself be seen. She doesn't need to be witty, or gentle, or kind. She's a tyrant. The world comes to her and bows down. If I were a married man, I'd pray that my daughters should be plain women. As for the beauties . . . heaven help them."

"And that's why you hate Beatrice Wilton?" asked Sherry gloomily.

Moon went to him and laid a hand on his shoulder. "My boy," he said, "I know that your heart is aching over this. I want to do something for you. If it will give you as much pleasure as pain, you are free to go to the jail and see the girl . . . and talk to her alone."

"Would you let me do that?"

"On one condition, that you take no written message for her from the jail. As many oral messages as you please. But not a syllable in writing."

"It's a good deal to offer me," admitted Sherry. "When may I go?"

"Now, if you wish. I'll send over word to the jailer. And you may see her again, as often as you wish, only promising that you'll never take a bit of writing from her."

"I'll give that promise."

"I'll take your hand on it, Sherry."

They shook hands, and Sherry, his mission performed, left the house in haste.

XXX

On the way to the jail, Sherry encountered Bud and Jerry, the two sailors ambling cheerfully along through the town. They hailed him with good-humored salutes, and he paused for talk.

"We seen the stuff of this here Fennel," said Jerry. "He was no sailor. He was a farmer. What sailor would have such a bunch of cheap junk? Besides, everything was new."

"You spotted that for sure?" said Sherry.

"Of course, we spotted it for sure. There's no doubt at all. And all that stuff come out of old Cap Wendell's in San Pedro. He carries that kind of junk. I tried to outfit there once myself," declared Bud Arthur.

It shocked Lew Sherry with surprise and with delight. "You could swear to that?"

"I seen one of Cap's labels sticking on an undershirt. Cotton and wool. Nineteen threads of cotton and one of wool. That's the kind of stuff that Cap uses."

"Boys," said Sherry, "will one of you go out to San Pedro for us?"

"We ship always together," said Jerry.

"Then go out together and talk to Cap Wendell. He might remember something about Fennel."

"And what good would that do? It's a long cruise out there and back," protested Bud.

"Of course it is," agreed Sherry. "But we've lost Fennel's trail here at Clayrock. Wherever he's gone, he's disappeared completely from under our eyes. But this Wendell might be able to tell you what ship Fennel landed from, and where he intended to ship again. And unless we can get him . . . a woman is going to hang for a murder that Fennel must have committed. Do you understand that, boys?"

They understood.

"We'll go," said Bud, the controlling spirit of the two. "If we ever can get to windward of Fennel, he'll never weather us, and we can promise you that. When does this here trial begin?"

"Tomorrow."

"A day out and a couple days back. We'll get the news if we can, but Cap Wendell ain't likely to remember any too much. He's a moldy old scoundrel, is Wendell."

They said good bye on the spot, and Sherry went on to the jail, where the sheriff's message already had been received. The jailer was a grim-looking fellow with a shock of red hair, very tousled, and a hard, white face.

"You play on the inside with Moon, do you?" he asked of Sherry. "Well, his orders go here. Come on into the office. I'll bring her in."

"Alone? Can I see her alone?" asked Sherry.

The jailer shook his head. "It ain't legal," he declared, "but Moon makes up his own laws around these here parts."

He was gone, and Sherry stood by the window, ill at ease, shifting from one foot to the other, feeling very much like a small boy late for school. He heard no steps disappear or approach— ample testimony to the soundness of the walls of the building— but suddenly the door opened, and Beatrice Wilton stood before him. The jailer loomed for an instant behind her, grinning strangely at Sherry, and then the door closed and they were alone.

She came hastily across to Sherry, with great relief in her face. "Eustace sent you!" she exclaimed. "Isn't that it? Eustace finally persuaded the sheriff?"

"No," said Sherry. "I went to Moon and talked to him. He said that I could come and talk to you here."

"You . . . and not Eustace Layman," she murmured, greatly amazed. "I don't understand that. But it doesn't matter. As long as I can send out a written message by you . . . you could be a witness to my signature, too. I . . . there's a pen and paper." She hurried to the desk, almost running, and sat down at it.

Then Sherry leaned over her. "I promised Moon that I wouldn't take out a message . . . a written message. Anything that you want to send by word of mouth. But nothing written."

She pushed the paper away from her and dropped the pen. She looked up at him quite wildly. Not since she had tried to take her own life when he and the sheriff were in the room had he seen her so completely unnerved. "You promised him?" she exclaimed.

"I had to, for otherwise he wouldn't have let me come here at all."

She clutched her hands together and her eyes flashed from side to side. "What can I do then," she muttered. Then, more confidently: "But you won't pay any attention to your promise? Of course you won't. He hasn't a right to treat me as he does. It will take me two minutes to write out the order to the bank. You will take it?"

"You don't understand," said Sherry patiently. "I gave him my word. I shook hands with him on it."

"What is a promise to a scoundrel?" asked the girl earnestly. "He keeps me here without a chance to talk to a lawyer . . . except at a distance, watched every minute. I haven't been able to raise a retaining fee. I'm helpless and hopeless. What am I to do? I never can win against Herbert Moon in this town and court without the finest lawyer in the country. And how can I bring in a great lawyer unless I have money? And my money in the bank I can't touch . . . I can't touch it because of the sheriff. So you see what he's doing?"

Anguish was depicted on the face of Sherry. But the voice of Herbert Moon was still, so to speak, sounding in his ear. He said: "It sounds pretty bad. But I think it will turn out better than you imagine. There never was a squarer man in the world than Moon."

"Ah," cried the girl, "you think that because you know how he's treated men. You don't know how he'd treat a woman. He's never had a woman before on a serious charge. And now he shows himself for the first time. No, no, not the first time. You can see it through his whole life. He hates women. He hates them!"

"I don't follow you there," confessed Sherry.

"Has he ever wasted his time on any woman or girl in his life? He's never married. Women don't exist for him . . . except to loathe them."

"That's happened before," said Sherry, "to men who were married to their guns and their work. Besides, he has such a beggarly poor salary, how could he ask a woman to share his life? Have you seen the house he lives in? A Mexican laborer lives in better style."

She stared at him with blank eyes. "You mean that you won't do it, then? You won't carry out a note for me?"

"I can't," said Sherry.

"But," she went on in a bare whisper, "you understand what it means? My life. My life . . . "

"I understand what you think," said Sherry huskily. "Heaven knows that I want to help you. But I've given him my hand on it . . . and my promise."

She drew herself up from the chair and seemed about to break into excited speech, but she suddenly collapsed and dropped her face on her arms, weeping heavily. Sherry drew back from her as though a gun were pointed at him. He looked at the door; he glanced behind him at the window; never in his life had his heart been so wrung.

He could only stammer: "I put my trust in Moon. You'll find that he'll give you a fair chance in the end. It's only now that we don't understand . . . "

That seemed to sting her back to some self-control and she threw up her head. "They begin tomorrow. They begin to hang me tomorrow. Oh, mark what I say. The sheriff has the judge in his hand. The weight of the sheriff has poisoned the mind of every man in the county, already. They couldn't pick a jury that wouldn't be ready to hang me. And tomorrow the trial begins. Who have I to defend me? No one but a foolish young lawyer. A man with no experience. And he's doing it on the chance of collecting his fees. I haven't been able to give him any promise in writing. I . . . I . . . they've tied my feet and hands and thrown me into a river to swim if I can. Don't you see it?"

He could only stare at her miserably, until at last her own expression of desperation altered to one of horror.

"You think with the sheriff," she breathed at last. "You think with Sheriff Moon . . . that I'm guilty."

He tried to answer, to disclaim, but truth tied his tongue, and forced him to be silent.

"You'd better go," she said in a trembling voice. "I don't think there's any good in your staying here longer. You'd better go . . . at once."

Sherry stumbled toward the door, but, with his hand on the cold metal of the knob, he managed to turn about and face her again. His brain was reeling.

"I came to ask how I could help," he said. "I shouldn't have come at all. But I want to tell you from my heart that the worst is never going to happen to you. They have thick walls here, but I don't think that they could keep me out."

"Is that what you came to say to me?" she asked. "That after I'm found guilty and judged to be worthy of hanging . . . then you'd come to break into the jail and take me away?"

He was silent, and saw her shaking her head.

"I never would go," she said. "Heaven knows that I've no desire to cheat the law."

Sherry jerked the door open without even a word of farewell and blundered out upon the street. It was blazing hot. The heat waves shimmered upward from the white, uneven dust, and from the white-washed wall the sun reflected as from a mirror, but it seemed to Sherry the coolest place in the world.

He mopped his brow and went on with the same uncertain step. He found that his lips were twitching, and his eyes, staring before him, continued to see a picture that he knew never would leave him—of Beatrice in the jail, looking on him with a despairing calmness, and denying that last, faint hope of escape.

XXXI

He was glad of the distance and the steep slope back to the Wilton house, for it gave him a chance of purging his mind, as it were, by the sheer exercise of physical effort, and he came to the house with a clear brain, at the least, to find, in their small cabin-like room, Peter Lang bent low over a piece of paper.

He looked up at his friend with a sidewise scowl of thought.

"What is it, Pete?" asked the big man with assumed lightness. "Key to a treasure?"

Lang looked back to his work and made no reply, while Sherry went on: "I've seen the sheriff."

At this Pete raised his head.

"He's straight, to my way of thinking. I never sat and talked to a finer man, Pete."

Lang yawned.

"He even gave me leave to go to the jail and talk to Beatrice Wilton."

At this, the cowpuncher started. "Gave you permission?"

"He did."

"It ain't possible. He wouldn't let Layman go near her."

"It's queer," said Sherry. "I know that it's queer. But up to the jail I went and had a talk to her."

"You say it like you'd been to a funeral."

"I'd promised the sheriff that I wouldn't take any message in writing from her to anyone. Of course, that was the one thing that she really wanted me to do."

"It upset her?"

"Of course. They've badgered her and tyrannized over her. I've never heard of any prisoner about to be tried for his life that has had such a rough deal as that girl."

Lang yawned again. "Leave me alone," he pleaded. "I'm busy."

"Finally," went on Sherry, "I told her that I'd never leave her to the law, if the decision went against her. What do you think she answered?"

"I don't know. I don't care," said Lang.

"That she wouldn't go a step with any man. That she didn't want anything from the law. Justice, I suppose she meant."

Here Lang favored his companion with a long and earnest stare. "Is that straight?" he asked.

"That's exactly what she said to me."

"I'm going out for a walk with you," said Lang. "Come along with me, will you?"

"I'm going to sleep. I need a nap. I'm tired."

"You're fresh as a baby compared with how tired I am. Shut up, and come along."

Sherry, grumbling, obeyed, and they went out to the garden. There in the tool shed, Lang took a strong shovel and handed Sherry a pick.

"Are you going to bury someone?" asked Sherry.

"Shut up," replied Lang. "Follow me."

He led the way straight back from the house into the woods behind it, and there he headed into the broken ground through which they had toiled with such difficulty on their first day at the Wilton house. Now, however, Lang moved in a weaving course that kept him going with comparative smoothness and speed.

"How much time have you spent out here solving the labyrinth?" asked Sherry.

But Lang did not answer. He kept to his work, setting a stiff pace, like a man whose brain is in a state of great anxiety. At length he came to a clearing. Into the middle of this he marched and faced toward the north, picking out a tree on that side. From the tree he paced several steps to the south, then turned sharply at right angles and marched in a new direction. He began over again at the southern side of the clearing and wherever his new course cut the old one, he marked the spots with a dig of his heel. Then, pausing, he considered the last three marks that he had made, stepped away from them, and drove his shovel into the ground with force.

"Try your pick here!" he commanded, and Sherry, now thoroughly in the spirit of the adventure, obeyed at once, burying the pick to the handle.

They began to tear up the ground, working very hard and fast for a half hour. In the course of that time, with pick and shovel, they had opened a deep hole, when Lang leaped out of the excavation and signed to Sherry to refill the hole.

Gloomily, irritated, Sherry obeyed, and, after they had piled the dirt back in and trampled it down as well as they could, Lang scattered pine needles carefully over the spot and tried to remove all signs that they had been digging there.

"I've missed . . . for today," he said.

"Suppose you tell me what crazy thing you're up to?"

"Well, this." He thrust a paper before Sherry. Upon it appeared a rudely sketched outline that might have served for the plan of the clearing in which they had been working, and inside the general sketch there was a checking of many figures.

"What the dickens does it mean?" asked Sherry.

"It means that I've been searching through old Wilton's room," answered Lang. "And finally I found this in his private desk."

"That desk is locked. How could you get into it?"

"How did somebody get in there before me?" asked Lang with a snap.

"Great guns, man, do you accuse me? What would I be doing in his desk? And how could I possibly get into it unless I knew the way to find the key of it?"

Lang said at last, after a glare of hostility: "You're right, old son. I'm wrong. I've almost had an idea that you were sort of working for yourself on the side, in this here case, but I'm wrong. I'm glad of it." He leaned a heavy hand upon Sherry's shoulder. "I'm about beat, Tiny," he declared. "It ought to be here."

"What?"

"The pearls, you doddering idiot!"

"Is that it? Is that what you've got there?"

"Well, I don't know," said Lang. "But that's my hunch. I think that I've put my hand on the key to the whole little mystery. I hope so, anyway."

"If we got them . . . then we could get what poor Beatrice Wilton needs . . . the finest lawyer in the country."

"Aye, and that's why he's hunting so hard for them, too."

"Who? For the pearls?"

"He's seen this paper," said the other with assurance. "He's seen it in the desk. I found this sheet on top of a pile. It wasn't on top of the pile yesterday. Somebody has been in Wilton's room looking the things over."

"Layman, then, by gravy!" cried Sherry.

"Layman?" echoed Lang, and laughed with excitement. "I tell you, me son, that the gent that looked at that paper and opened that desk is also the gent that murdered Wilton."

"The deuce! What brings you to that?"

"I don't know. I can't tell you all the steps."

"And, after all," cried Sherry suddenly, "why shouldn't Layman be the man? Why shouldn't Layman have murdered Wilton?"

"Him?" Lang frowned. "What would he have to gain by it?"

"Why . . . everything, if you'll stop to think of it. He was engaged to Beatrice Wilton, eh?"

"So they say."

"And if he married her, naturally he'd get his hands on her property."

"That's true. Yes. Go on."

"It stood to his interest to see that the year didn't elapse and Wilton come into guardianship over Beatrice Wilton. Great Lord, why haven't I thought of this before! The doctor, Lang. He's the man to think about. The doctor. I never even suspected him before. His interest to find the pearls, too, naturally . . . any-one's interest to find 'em. And who so apt to have access to this office as the doctor, too? I tell you, Pete, he's the killer. I wish to heaven that my brain were a little truer, and I'd prove it to you."

Lang regarded him dubiously, like a man more than half per-suaded, but at length he shook his head with decision.

"The doctor?" he said. "No, it's Fennel who did the job. Either Fennel and the girl, or Fennel alone."

"Fennel? I almost forget about him, since he disappeared."

"Of course you did. Fennel wanted to be forgotten. That's why he played such an open part at the first. He had a purpose in living at the hotel, d'you see? He had that all planned."

"Come, come!" exclaimed Sherry. "I won't admit that. That's a little deep for me."

"Fennel lived at the hotel, pretended to be a drunk, and talked a lot and very loud about how much he knew about Wilton, didn't he?"

"That's true."

"Then one day he walks up the hill, meets Wilton, and mur-ders him."

"I see that."

"Either he's a deep, smart gent, or else the girl supplies the brains and tells him what to do," suggested Lang.

"She? Pete, she had nothing to do with it."

"You don't believe what you say, yourself, so why try to tell me what you don't think, man?"

Sherry sighed. "She? Well, get back to Fennel. What do you think he was?"

"Faker, of course. You proved that, when you discovered the whiskey stains under the drain from the roof. You'll find that he was faked all the way through. Disguised, I mean. That's why he made such a public play and show of himself. He wanted to fix the wrong face in the eyes of the public. Then he'd just walk off and change, and be another man."

"That would take a deep schemer."

"And this is a deep job," declared Pete Lang, "because I'll tell you what . . . the girl has all the brains that anybody needs, and she'd play deep to have this job done according to the way she wants."

"She did it? She planned and hired it?" cried Sherry.

"Go away and don't bother me," pleaded Lang. "I gotta think."

XXXII

The trial opened the next day with a great crowd in Clayrock. The courtroom was filled. But Sherry, for one, did not care to be there. Instead, he preferred to walk about the streets of the town, talking here and there, for he remembered what Beatrice Wilton had told him the evening before—that prejudice was so strong against her in the county that no jury could be found that would not have adjudged her guilty before they foregathered in the jury box.

That statement of hers he wanted to prove, now. And it was hard for him to believe. Western men were not like that. He tried to fall into conversation on the subject half a dozen times until at last a man said to him bluntly: "Why d'you ask me what I think, Sherry? Everybody knows that you're for the girl. Well, what's the good of arguing about it?"

He had to wait until almost noon before he found an impartial listener, an oldish tough-looking mountaineer who regarded him with an unknowing eye, and with him Sherry, rejoiced, fell into talk.

"What'll happen to Beatrice Wilton?"

"I'll tell you what ought to happen," said the veteran.

"Well, tell me that."

"She had oughta hang!"

Sherry looked down to the ground and made a cigarette to cover his emotion. "I've heard others guess that," he said. "I don't see why."

"You don't? It looks pretty clear to me."

"Still I don't follow you. Why shouldn't it have been Fennel that did the killing?"

"That was the sailor drunk, eh? I tell you, if he had had anythin' to do with the case, the sheriff certainly would have had him a long time ago, wouldn't he?"

"I don't know that he would," said Sherry.

"And when did he ever miss?" asked the mountaineer aggressively.

Sherry was silent. There must have been failures, but he could not remember any. After all, the sheriff was apparently like a universal medicine, in the eyes of the men of his county. He could not fail to do what was right.

"I don't know," said Sherry at last. "But I suppose everybody makes mistakes now and then."

"Not Herb Moon," said the mountaineer. "He lives to do what's right, and he always does it. He don't live for nothin' else."

"But suppose he should be mistaken this one time . . . and the girl gets hanged?"

"Serve her right," said the other. "These rich folks, they're all crooked. Never knowed one that wasn't. What's she? Why's a woman to be favored over a man? Murder's murder, ain't it?"

"I suppose it is. That doesn't prove her guilty."

"Young feller," said the old man, flushing with anger, "don't set yourself up to be better and wiser than Herb Moon. There's others that have tried to do it, and they've always had a fall."

"I don't set myself up to be better and wiser. I say that the girl ought to have a fair chance."

"She'll get as fair a chance as she deserves. But look at the way that she's been carryin' on . . . hirin' a bully to run her enemies out of town. Makin' sure that nobody would be in the jury that would dare to vote ag'in' her!"

"Who do you mean?"

"I mean the great gunfighter, Sherry. If she'd hire a killer like that, what wouldn't she do? Murder? Murder ain't nothin' to rich people."

"I don't see that Sherry has been hired to run her enemies out of town."

"Ain't he for her?"

"I've heard that he is."

"Ain't he a gunfighter?"

"I don't think so."

"You don't think so! Young feller, your thinkin' is all crooked. Didn't Sherry take a showdown out of Fannie Slade and make him take water? Could anythin' less than a clever one have done that, I ask you?"

"And the girl's guilty because she has Sherry for a friend?" asked the big man bitterly.

"The sheriff's against her, isn't he?"

"Yes, I suppose he is. He's refused her the legal rights that belong to her."

"Legal be damned," declared the other with heat. "What's right in the eye of the sheriff is right enough to suit me. And who he thinks guilty, I'm willin' to think guilty. If he makes a mistake, I'll make one, too. There ain't a wiser or a finer man on earth than Herb Moon. That's what I'm here to state."

He had worked himself up into a fine frenzy, at this point, when a bystander took him by the arm and drew him away. What the newcomer said in a whisper could easily be guessed, for the old man, with a gasp, started off hastily down the street, glancing now and again back over his shoulder, as though he feared that Sherry, like some form out of a nightmare, might pursue him.

There was no such thought in Sherry's mind, however. He had proved amply that Beatrice Wilton was right, and that the attitude of the sheriff had so thoroughly poisoned all minds in the county that an impartial jury could not very well be picked. Beatrice Wilton was lost.

Sherry went back to lunch at the hotel and found himself regarded gloomily and askance. He could understand why he was considered to be the hired retainer of a losing cause, and the more formidable he was, the more unpopular. But he learned at the luncheon table that in one morning's work the jury had been selected, and that very afternoon testimony would begin to be taken.

He went toward the courtroom, down-headed, filled with thought. He had prepared his tools days before. He had prepared his scheme, also. Immediately adjoining the jail, so close to it that a man could hardly walk down the path that separated the two buildings, was an empty house, and if there were a cellar of any size in the place, he should be able to dig through and beneath the foundations of the jail, and cut a tunnel upward. That done, he still would have to force a way through the floor of the jail, and to do this in silence would probably be impossible.

He had determined on using blunt force. A charge of dynamite would open the floor. Once in the jail, another blast of dynamite would shatter the lock on the girl's cell. And, if she stubbornly refused to come with him, he could take her by force.

Lang would be waiting with three horses of the best in the rear of the vacant house. And once in the saddle, heaven send good luck to them and bad luck to Sheriff Herbert Moon.

Sherry by no means looked upon the task as a simple one. And he knew perfectly well that that grim-faced jailer would be the very man to fight to the death to retain the prisoners who were under his charge. Furthermore, the people of Clayrock were a hardy lot. Once embarked on his task, it would mean a pair of well-oiled Colts in action from the first, but Sherry, gloomily adding up the result, determined on the work.

He diverged from the straight course toward the court in order to pass the jail and, doing so, to see again the vacant house. There it was, weather-beaten, dilapidated, with the To Rent shingle projecting from its front. But as Sherry came by, he saw a man seated in the wide-open doorway with a rifle leaning against the doorjamb beside him.

"Hello," said Sherry. "House rented at last?"

"Not rented. Occupied," said the rifleman. And he patted his gun with a fond hand, and grinned at Sherry with a great deal of meaning.

The big man went on with a slower step. It was, somehow, the most signal proof he had run across of the omniscient brain of the sheriff. For he had no doubt that Herbert Moon had taken possession of the house for the very purpose of securing the last approach to the jail itself. And, going on past the wall of the jail, he noted its solidity, its depth, as signified by the frowning depths of the dark windows. It looked like a veritable fortress of the law. And he, single-handed, would have a wretched task in storming it.

He knew that Lang would follow him far, but he also knew that the cowpuncher never would commit himself to such a desperate act for the sake of a woman who he already believed to be deeply implicated in the murder. Whatever was to be done, must be done by Sherry in person.

So, marching slowly past the front of the jail, he regarded the door itself. It was ponderous, iron-clasped, and iron-bolted within, as he had observed on the preceding day. Yet a powerful charge of powder would doubtless smash it in, and once inside . . . Well, it seemed more desperate than the plan of attack from beneath the building, but, after all, the most desperate measures sometimes meet with the greatest success.

Little Herbert Moon came down the steps of the jail at that moment and nodded cheerfully at Sherry. "You had your interview?" he asked.

"I did," said Sherry sadly.

"There's spirit in that girl," declared the sheriff. "A confounded lot of spirit, of course. And I admire her for it. But, at the same time, the law has to take its way. At the worst, it won't be the rope, Sherry, and ten or fifteen years of model conduct in the prison ought to give her a fair chance of a pardon from the governor. Western men are fair enough to women, you know."

"Except you, Moon!" exclaimed Sherry in wrath. "Except you, man. You hate her as if she were a fiend. Will you tell me that I'm wrong?"

"If she murdered Wilton," said the sheriff, "does she deserve anything but hate?" Then he added smoothly: "If you want to see me again, one of these days, you'll always find me down here at the jail."

"Nearly living here?"

"Living here in fact . . . day and night. When I have a prisoner as beautiful as Beatrice Wilton . . . why, of course I have to take the best and most special care of her. You'll understand that, my lad."

And Sherry turned away toward the court with despair. The last hope had been stripped from his mind. For he knew that he never could force his way into the jail while the sheriff remained there on guard.

XXXIII

To Sherry all that passed in the next few days had the unreality and the horror of a nightmare, for he saw Beatrice Wilton being pressed irresistibly toward condemnation by judge and jury. And in the meantime it appeared to Sherry as though the entire country were licking its lips with horrid pleasure. Clayrock literally was filled with the clicking of cameras, and in the hot, stuffy courtroom, day by day, scores of eyes stared in morbid interest at the prisoner.

She bore herself very well in one respect and very badly in another. She was as calm and cool as stone. On the stand, her voice had no tremors. She looked at the other witnesses for and against her without a frown or a smile, and she never appeared perturbed by anything that was put forward in evidence. This bearing of hers gave a good deal of dignity and importance to her case, but it practically destroyed her.

Two young lawyers worked out her side of the argument, and against them was the hard-headed district attorney. He had ways of violence, almost instinctively, because he was accustomed to deal with male criminals of the worst sort. To the bludgeoning of his rough assaults, the counsel of Beatrice Wilton begged her to oppose a feminine delicacy. If she would only be overcome, or appear to be overcome, by the brutality of the opposition, it might well be that she could win the sympathy of the jury. But she refused to make concessions of any kind. She remained erect in her chair, unflinching, calm, while the district attorney heaped upon her all the abuse of implication that declared her to be a cold-minded murderess, relentless, cruel, stern as a man. And, while he made these points in cross-examination, he seemed to be pointing to her, again and again, as though saying to the jury: "Notice this. She never flinches. The woman is a perfect monster."

As for the defense, there was only one hope, and that was to establish Fennel as a sinister figure, a man who obviously intended to work some harm to Wilton from the moment he came to Clayrock, and who eventually succeeded in murdering his man.

To do that, they called upon Sherry and worked up his testimony as brightly as possible. It appeared through him that Fennel was an obvious sham. That his pretended drunkenness had been assumed for some ulterior purpose. That he was probably not a sailor at all. And certainly this man with the sinister intention had come to Wilton, had been walking with him at the moment of the murder. What folly, then, to imagine that such a woman as Beatrice Wilton deserved any share of the guilt when Fennel was not as yet detected or trailed? Why should the law seize upon the lamb instead of the wolf, simply because the lamb was nearest at hand?

But the cross-examination of the district attorney was terribly damaging. If Sherry was the star witness for the defense, he also turned out to be the star witness for the prosecution. He had to relate in detail how he had run in pursuit, had found Beatrice cowering, had been forced to carry her back to the place of the crime. And all this evidence had to be wrung from a most manifestly reluctant witness, who stood with his great fists balled, and a glare in his eyes, and perspiration streaking down his face.

"Look!" said the district attorney, with inexcusable brutality. "The man sees what his words are doing. He cannot help but understand that he is destroying the case of the woman he would give his life to assist. There, gentlemen of the jury, is a picture of misery and of . . . "

Here the judge stopped the peroration but it had had its effect. Sherry stood down from the witness stand, at last, perfectly confident that he had beaten to the ground the last hope of Beatrice Wilton, and he fixed upon her an eye of agony as he went out.

She, for her part, turned in her chair and nodded and smiled toward him with such sweetness that it stopped him like a blow. He went on unsteadily.

He heard voices on either side of him, muttering. He could not help but hear one woman say: "Poor fellow. He loves her, you see. I'm sorry for him, but not for that cold-blooded little minx."

Sherry went out into the open air; Dr. Eustace Layman came out and stood beside him. The doctor was always present at every moment of the trial. He had a chair comparatively close to the two young lawyers who were defending Beatrice, and from time to time, as thoughts for the conduct of the case occurred to him, he scribbled notes and passed them across to the legal hands.

As the trial continued, Sherry's respect for the doctor increased enormously. For one thing, there was no pretense or sham about him. He never paraded his feelings. He never obtruded upon anyone the knowledge that this girl was his betrothed. But, keeping as cool and as quiet as Beatrice Wilton herself, he gave his whole energy of mind to helping where he could.

"I think I've sent her to prison for life," said Sherry bluntly.

And suddenly the other astonished him by saying: "And suppose the sheriff is right, after all, and you and I are wrong, Sherry?"

The big man turned to him in bewilderment.

"You and I are the only people in the entire world who think she's innocent," added the doctor. And then he concluded: "But it never makes any real difference to a man. He believes what he wants to believe, and that's true of you and of me, eh?"

Sherry went off up the street; the doctor went the other way. The court had adjourned, and Sherry relieved his feelings by taking his horse and riding furiously off into the country, never turning back for the Wilton house until his animal was wet with sweat. Then, with creaking saddle leather, he climbed the clay rock and put up his mustang in the stable.

When he came to the front of the house, he stopped, shocked. Up the steps to Wilton's entrance went a thin streak of crimson. Before the door, it widened to a little pool.

Blood!

He went in hurriedly, and followed that same trail, with growing horror, to his own room. He found the door locked, and, in answer to the wrangling of his hand upon the knob, a voice that he barely recognized as that of Lang called to him: "Sherry?"

"Yes," he answered.

Then: "Wait . . . I'll unlock the door."

There was a faint sound of fumbling, then the lock turned, and Sherry pushed into the chamber. Lang had collapsed upon a bunk. He was stripped to the waist, and a great bandage made of a sheet was wound around his middle. It was much stained with blood, as was everything in the room.

"Great Scott!" cried Sherry. "What's happened, man?"

"Fennel," said Lang faintly. "I'm cooked, and Fennel did it." He lay flat on the bunk, breathing with difficulty. The sheet had been drawn so tight that his chest heaved with every inspiration.

"Let me have a look at that . . . he shot you!" exclaimed Sherry.

"There's no good looking," said Lang faintly. "I'm about done, old man. I think I always had an idea that I'd get my finish in this dirty work. You wanted it . . . Sherry."

The big man groaned.

"Let me talk," said Lang. "You know the drawing that I found in the room of Wilton? I guessed that it was the plan for the hiding place where he'd put the pearls. I missed it when I went out with you. Today I looked it over again and finally I had my inspiration. I went out to the same clearing, and worked everything by reverse. The very first whack of the pick, it clinked on metal. I dragged up a little copper box. Opened it up. It was filled to the brim with pearls, man. And while I was looking, I got this through the back." He paused, breathing again with difficulty. "I fell on my face," he went on, "but I pulled my gun as I was going down. I managed to twist around, and I had a glimpse of Fennel getting ready to shoot again . . . and his face looked like . . . like a man that had been living like a beast out here in the woods. Why, he's been hiding in these here bad lands all the time."

"Waiting for someone to begin a hunt for the stuff that he couldn't find?" suggested Sherry.

"That's it. I'm getting wobbly in the head. Like a new-born calf, old son. Listen hard. I swung my gun around on Fennel, and, instead of risking another shot, he slipped away through the trees. Then I took the box and started back for home. I had to crawl most of the way. Once I fainted. Thank heaven, he didn't follow me close enough to find me then. I got here. Since then, I've been waiting for you, praying for you . . . and dying like a dog, old man."

"You've talked enough," declared Sherry. "Keep the rest of your wind. I'm going to have you out of this, Pete. I dragged you into it. You never liked the business. And now . . . "

"Steady, steady," said Pete Lang. "I'm not going to last many more minutes. I wanted to last long enough to tell you who Fennel most likely is. It'll give even you a shock. This here gent that played a drunken sailor and all the rest is nobody but . . . "

He had raised himself a little upon one elbow, in his excitement, and now he interrupted himself with a faint gasp, and his staring eyes went past Sherry to the open doorway. There was a puffing, hissing sound, and then a heavy spat of a bullet piercing bone. Pete Lang sank back on the bunk, dead.

Sherry had whirled the instant he heard the sound, and, whirling, he had both guns in his hands.

In the distance, close to the front door of the house, he had a glimpse of that never-to-be-forgotten face of Fennel, shrouded almost to the eyes with matted hair.

The front door was jerked open. Sherry fired as Fennel sprang through. Then, as he leaped in pursuit, he heard the lock turn. He threw his whole weight against the door. It was perfectly solid and threw him back, half stunned.

A light, quick step struck the steps and then crunched on the gravel of the path, and he knew that Fennel was gone once more from his ken.

He went back slowly, sick at heart, to the death room, and there he leaned gloomily above the body of his dead friend.

Who was Fennel? That question could not be answered by the calmly smiling lips of Pete Lang, who lay with a certain air of triumph, as it seemed to Sherry, one hand spread out over the copper box beside him, for which he had given his life.

XXXIV

Pete Lang was gone, and the last testimony of the work he had done lay under the dead man's hand. Sherry took up the box and opened it with a sense of loathing. But that loathing disappeared at the first glance. The little box was filled to the brim with creamy light. He sifted it through his fingers, and it showered back in a beautiful rain into the box. Was it not for the sake of this box that three men already had died—Wilton, Capper, Pete Lang?

Perhaps he himself would be the fourth. A sort of superstitious horror possessed Sherry. Whatever he did, he would not keep that treasure in his possession. He took the box under his arm, settled his hat on his head, and, leaving by the back door, started straight down the hill.

Coming out of the garden to the street below, he encountered Dr. Eustace Layman, coming up with his usual brisk, light stride. He nodded cheerfully at Sherry.

"This hill is put here for our sins," said the doctor.

"How is Miss Wilton?" asked Sherry.

"She? As well as can be expected, as they say. She knows, now."

"That the case will go against her?"

"Yes."

"After I'd testified. Of course it was what I said that turned the trick."

"And what difference did it make?" asked Layman. "The sheriff already knew what you had to say. They could have had it out of him on the stand, if they'd wished. By Jove, you've cut your hand, Sherry."

Sherry looked down and saw the crimson on his fingers. "My hand isn't cut," he said.

"And what in the world has happened, Sherry?"

"Lang has been murdered by Fennel . . . after he found the pearls."

"Good heavens! Lang murdered! Fennel? Fennel, did you say? Do you mean that, Sherry?"

"I saw his cursed face," said Sherry bitterly.

The doctor grew greatly excited. "I want to follow this clearly. Lang killed by Fennel. You saw the brute do it? Lang . . . after he'd found the pearls. And Fennel murdered him and stole the jewels and . . . "

"He didn't steal them. They're under my arm in this box, just now."

"The pearls?"

"Yes."

"My head spins, Sherry. Lang dead . . . Fennel . . . poor Lang. There was a brave, honest fellow. A little sour, but brave as they come. But do you see what this horrible affair means for Beatrice?"

"For her?" asked Sherry dully.

"It means that she'll get off scot-free. Don't you understand? It's like a stroke of luck. This second murder practically proves that Fennel committed the first one. Isn't that clear as day?"

"Ah," sighed the big man. "I hadn't thought of that." And suddenly he lifted his fallen head. "The life of poor Pete to save her," he groaned.

"But even if that weren't the case, you have a fortune under your arm there, man!" cried Layman. "With a hundredth part of it, you can save her. You can bring in a great lawyer who will soon tangle up this affair so completely that the district attorney and that prejudiced judge won't know where they're standing."

"Use part of this?" asked Sherry. "I couldn't touch it. It goes to the sheriff, now. It's nothing of mine."

The doctor stepped a little back from him, angry and surprised. "I don't understand," he said with some bitterness. "I thought that you really wanted her to win out."

"Did you?" murmured Sherry. "And am I to steal to do it? Lang has died for her. I think that's enough. His blood against hers. I'm going on, Layman."

He turned and strode past the doctor, and went hurrying down into the hot streets of the city. He went to the jail, and there he found the sheriff. He was not easily admitted. As he went in to interview Herbert Moon, two armed men stood in the doorway behind him. Sherry looked upon them with a vague smile.

"I'm not dangerous," he said to the sheriff. "My teeth have been pulled for today, Moon. Will you send those fellows away?"

The sheriff, instead of answering, looked steadily at the stained hands of the giant.

"It's the blood of Pete Lang," said Sherry. "Fennel killed him today."

The sheriff leaped from his chair. "Fennel again? He wouldn't dare again!" exclaimed Herbert Moon.

"Fennel has killed Pete Lang. I saw him with my own eyes. And this is why Pete was shot in the first place." He lifted the lid of the box of pearls.

The sheriff dipped his hand into them, and let a rain of them fall back. Then he waved the two guards from the doorway.

"I brought it in to you," said Sherry, "because I think that this ought to be enough to free Beatrice Wilton."

The sheriff opened a small safe that stood in a corner of the office and into it he thrust the box and its treasure.

"This goes a little beyond me," he murmured. "I expected almost anything, but not quite this." He was pale with emotion.

"And she's cleared?" insisted Sherry.

"Beatrice Wilton?"

"Yes."

"In what way?" asked the sheriff, frowning.

"I'm not an expert in these affairs. But when the jury knows that Fennel has been seen to commit another murder, won't they be apt to put the burden of the first one on him?"

"Do you think so?"

"I do."

"You're wrong," answered the sheriff. "After today in the courtroom, I don't think there's a chance to defend her. Perhaps I haven't a right to say that, but I've always wanted to be frank with you, Sherry."

Sherry flushed darkly. "You know law," he admitted, "but I have an idea that we don't pay and get nothing in the world. Lang died for that girl, Moon. And, by George, you'll see that he didn't die in vain for her."

"Do you know the story of these pearls?" asked the sheriff suddenly.

"I've heard it. You'll hear it yourself, before very long."

"From whom?"

"Two sailors . . . "

"The ones who asked to see Fennel's outfit?"

"That's right."

"The coroner again," said the sheriff to himself. "The third time in the same house. Both the Wiltons. Now this cowpuncher. Sherry, will you ride up the hill with me? If I can't bring justice home in this case, I've reached the end of my rope and I'll leave my office. I'm an old man, Sherry, and my brain is weakening."

"You?" exclaimed Sherry. "There's no other man in the world who thinks so."

"*Bah!*" snarled Herbert Moon savagely. "Do you hear me? If I'd acted quicker, done as I felt I should have done long ago, your friend Pete Lang would be alive at this moment." He went to the wall, picked his hat from a peg, and jammed it down upon his head.

Sherry was still staring after this last statement. "What did you know? What should you have done?" he asked earnestly.

The sheriff hesitated. "You've seen this case from the beginning!" he said at last.

"I didn't see the death of Everett Wilton," said Sherry.

"That's true, that's true. But even without that, haven't you been able to guess?"

"That Beatrice Wilton is the cause of all this?"

"The cause? I never called her the cause. A tool is not a cause, man. An instrument is not a cause of a murder." He took Sherry suddenly by the arm.

"Let's get away from this building. I hate walls. I loathe brick and stone set up in courses. Sometimes I think that what we speak inside a room remains there like a thought floating in the air, and the next person who comes in will be able to read it. Heaven forgive if my thought should be read. It would be ruin to a great cause, young man."

It occurred to Sherry that, after all, there might be something in what the sheriff had said about advancing years. Certainly he had been talking in a very odd manner.

They went out onto the street together.

"You have friends in Clayrock," said the sheriff.

"I? Not a one."

"Ah, but you have. You have more friends here than you think. They admire Lew Sherry. They admire his size and his strength, and his straight shooting. They admire the man who broke down Fannie Slade, at the last. You have plenty of friends, though they hold off for a time, while you're mixed up in this murder mystery. But today or tomorrow you might meet some friendly spirits here in Clayrock, Sherry. Do you understand what I mean?"

"I don't," he admitted frankly. "What you've been saying to me sounds a little bit queerer than anything any man ever has said to me before."

"I suppose it does," said Moon. "But I'll be franker. I want to tell you that, if a syllable of what I've said to you in the last few moments gets abroad, it will undo a great work for me."

"The conviction of Beatrice Wilton," scowled Sherry.

The sheriff turned upon him impatiently. "I give you my word that she's not even in my mind at this moment. I'm thinking of bigger quarry."

"And what do you want me to do?"

"Give me a solemn promise that you'll keep your mouth shut about what I've said to you."

"I will," said Sherry, "because I don't understand a word that you've spoken."

XXXV

The trial lasted four days. The case went to the jury at noon of that day, and thirty minutes later the jury filed back into the box to give its verdict.

All of Clayrock was there, or as much of Clayrock as could be squeezed into the room. Every window was blocked with heads. The door was beset by a solidly wedged mob of at least a hundred persons, and in the midst of a tense silence, the foreman pronounced—"Guilty!"—and a long, shuddering sigh went through the audience.

Sherry had been expecting the blow with such perfect certainty that he had armed himself against the shock, and now he turned his gloomy gaze upon his companions in the court. He noted, particularly, the gleaming eyes that the women fixed upon Beatrice Wilton, and the proud head of Beatrice herself, sustaining this burden that had been dropped upon her spirit. He saw familiar heads, here and there—the bartender from the hotel, agape, his brutal face vaguely smiling as he drank in the sensation, the sheriff on one of the front benches, at the side, strangely, of Dr. Eustace Layman.

And, above all, he noted that one of the young lawyers who had fought out the case for Beatrice, now turned and murmured something to his associate, and they both chuckled together. A piece of callousness that made the blood of Sherry run cold.

Voices mumbled. He saw Beatrice Wilton led out and standing before the judge, a man guarding her upon either side. He heard the judge demanding if she had anything to say why sentence should not be pronounced upon her, and then there began a sharp scuffling at the rear of the courtroom, and voices clamoring in high tones. The judge rapped angrily for order. His most solemn moment in many years of law was being spoiled.

Then one of Beatrice Wilton's lawyers—Craven was his name—started a little forward from his chair.

"Your Honor," he said, "there is nothing that my client can say except that she is innocent. We have been waiting for several days, however, in the hope of something more. That hope is now fulfilled. Your Honor, the disturbance from the back of the room comes from two witnesses who have just arrived from a long journey. Their testimony will prove that Beatrice Wilton is totally innocent, and it will place the whole burden of the crime definitely upon the shoulders of Fennel, the slayer of Peter Lang. Will you reopen the case and let me put them on the stand?"

Had the judge been the most formal official in the world, he could not have resisted the vast stir of excitement that troubled the courtroom.

Way was made. Up the courtroom aisle came two swaggering individuals, walking as though to the sway of a deck—one tall and one short—Bud Arthur and his bunkie, Jerry.

Sherry looked upon them with a vague hope of he knew not what. They were brought to the witness bench. Bud Arthur was sworn in. The jury sat tense in its jury box. The judge himself was tingling with excitement, and ghostly whispers passed through the crowd.

Young Craven, like a skipper who loves a storm wind, stood in the court and smiled from side to side. "Your Honor," he said, "we intend to liberate Miss Wilton. In her place we shall put the real criminal. He is now in this courtroom."

Even the spectacular entrance of Jerry and Bud was as nothing compared with the sensation that followed at this point.

"We have had one member of this pair ready since last night," went on the lawyer. "But we have been waiting for the arrival of the second man, who . . . "

Here the district attorney sprang up with an impassioned objection. The judge, like one tired of the formalities of the law, simply raised his hand.

"Sit down, Charlie," he said. "We've had a good many days condemning this young woman . . . and now if there's anything to be said in her defense, I'm going to hear it, no matter how it's put before us."

At this, the crowd roared with applause. The jury grinned and grunted with agreement. The suspicion and dislike that had surrounded Beatrice Wilton these many days was dissolved at a stroke.

"Mister Arthur," said the young Mr. Craven, "what is your employment?"

"Sailor."

"And what brought you to Clayrock?"

"To get what was coming to me."

"From what? Coming to you from what?"

"My share of the pearls that Captain Oliver Wilton had swiped down in the Sulus."

The shock of this statement fairly stunned the crowd. Beatrice Wilton looked keenly across at her lawyer, and he nodded to her.

As much as to say that he was sorry that he had had to keep her so long in the dark, but soon he would make all things clear.

"We will follow you after that. You came to Clayrock to see Mister Wilton?"

"Yes."

"Did you see him?"

"Not quite. He was dead."

"What did you do?"

"Hung around the pawn shops. We figgered that if Wilton was dead, somebody else would have the stuff. They'd likely pawn some of it for ready money. That's what happened. Lew Sherry, he pawned a pearl."

There was a deep rumbling at this. People next to Sherry shrank away from him. Someone called out loudly: "If Sherry's the murderer, he ought to be taken in hand. That man's dangerous!"

"My dear friends," said the lawyer, addressing the crowd with a total lack of court etiquette, "Lew Sherry had nothing whatever to do with the murders, as you'll shortly understand. But there is another man in this courtroom who is now trembling in his boots, though he puts a brave face upon it. Mister Arthur, you saw a pearl pawned?"

"Yes, I seen Sherry pawn it. I was watching that shop for three days. I trailed him. I'd heard about him before. Me and my partner, Jerry, come up to the Wilton garden, and there we cornered Pete Lang all alone. We figured that, if Sherry knew where the stuff was, Lang would know. We cornered Lang. We had him with his hands up, when Sherry took us from behind and turned the tables complete. He got us helpless. A pair of guns in Sherry's hands is dog-gone discouragin'."

At this the crowd laughed, and the judge himself did not call for silence. Even the clerk, writing swiftly, paused to chuckle. Vast good humor possessed everyone. They were about to witness a kill, and they were content to see the race from the beginning.

"Sherry put us right," said Bud Arthur. He stood up in his place. "Do I get you in wrong if I tell everything, Sherry?" he asked.

And the deeply booming voice of Sherry made answer: "Tell everything from the beginning, and tell it straight."

There was another gasp of delight from the throng.

"Sherry let us know that when Wilton was found dead, Lang had got out of his pocket a handful of jewels and a piece of paper. That paper was a letter from Fennel, askin' to see Wilton and asking for his split of the loot. Lang and Sherry had held back that stuff, because the idea was that it showed that Fennel had gone to ask for pearls, and Wilton had taken out the share of Fennel to give to him. Lang and Sherry, they were plumb anxious not to get Miss Wilton into any trouble."

This naïve statement brought a cheer from everyone except the judge, who beat upon his desk, but smiled even as he tried to frown.

"Sherry told me," went on Arthur, "that he had pawned one of those pearls, not for the sake of makin' money to blow, but to have enough funds to keep him and Lang goin' on the job, because he still hoped that he could do somethin' for the girl. He showed us the rest of the pearls that they had, and he offered to split them with me and Jerry if we could help in the work. I didn't know how we could help, but Sherry said we should look over the stuff that Fennel had left behind him. We went down and done that."

"And what did you learn?" coached Craven, the lawyer.

"We seen that it come out of Cap Wendell's shop in San Pedro. It was just poor enough to suit him. It didn't look like a sailor's outfit, either. It was just faked up. There was two sizes of socks, for instance. One size would've fitted Miss Wilton. The other was big enough for Lew Sherry."

"Will you keep your witness to the point?" asked the judge good-naturedly, waving the district attorney back into his chair as that gentleman leaped up to make another legal assault.

"I'll do my best." Craven smiled. "And then what happened, Mister Arthur?"

"We seen Sherry. He says . . . 'Go out to San Pedro and find out if Wendell remembers anythin' about the gent that bought the layout.'

"We done that as fast as the train would snake us along. We got to San Pedro and we walked into Cap Wendell's shop. ''Mornin', boys,' says he. 'A bit of a blow they have been havin' off the coast, ain't they?'"

"Answer the questions that I put to you." commanded Craven.

"Yes, sir."

"Well, then, you asked Wendell about the buyer of the sea chest and its contents. You were able to identify them?"

"Sure," said Bud Arthur. "It ain't often that a seaman wants to buy a whole new outfit. Mostly he's just fillin' in holes, here and there, where the swabs have cleaned him out on board ship. Wendell remembered this gent pretty well. He'd come in in ragged-lookin' clothes. He had a broad-brimmed hat pulled down over his face. Looked like he'd seen better days."

"What was his face like?"

"Wendell, he couldn't see it very clear at first. He got the gent to take off his hat, after a while though. Then he seen that he had a sizable, fine big bump of a forehead that made the rest of his face look small. And he had a kind of a bald head . . . balder than it should've been for his age, and his face was pretty pale and thin. And this here gent was pretty tall, and made sort of light and active, like he'd make a good hand for goin' aloft."

"Your Honor," said Craven to the judge, "may I take this witness off the stand and put on another, at this point?" He added: "I want to ask Doctor Eustace Layman what he was doing in San Pedro buying a sailor's outfit, under the name of Fennel."

XXXVI

So the blow had fallen. And, to a man, the people of the court-room arose.

They saw Sheriff Herbert Moon rising at the side of Eustace Layman, and they saw that in the hand of the sheriff there was a man-size revolver that was pressed into the ribs of the doctor.

"Layman? Layman?" exclaimed the judge, bewildered. And then, with a vast effort, he re-gathered the official dignity and calm—which, of course, never can be disturbed.

Dr. Layman was entirely calm. "Do I understand that I am invited to take the witness stand?" he asked.

"That's what you can understand," said the sheriff. "With your permission, Your Honor, I'll search this gentleman, first."

"By what right do you presume to search me?" said the doctor as calmly as before.

"By the right of arrest," answered the sheriff, his manner equally polite, but firm.

"And for what crime am I arrested?" asked Layman.

"For the murders of Oliver Wilton and Peter Lang," said the sheriff.

And then, out of the throat of Sherry, tormented with wonder, burst the cry: "Fennel! *That* is Fennel!"

For now he saw as with an inspired vision that the strangely shaped head of Fennel might well be the doctor's, that towering forehead masked with a wig of matted hair. He saw that vision. To attempt to understand how the doctor could have played the double role was beyond him. He waited, tense and wondering.

The sheriff was fanning Layman, and producing a stub-nosed revolver from a hip pocket, and from beneath his left armpit a long, slender gun with a peculiar attachment at the end of the muzzle—the veritable type of the .22-caliber revolver with the silencer that had destroyed Oliver Wilton and poor Peter Lang. There was a gasping intake of breath around the courtroom as this detail was noted. Even the judge sat rigid in his chair, and Eustace Layman grew pale and set of face.

Bud Arthur was taken from the stand. Layman replaced him.

The district attorney made a quick turn up and down the space before his chair and slumped heavily down into it. Plainly he was taken totally aback.

The preliminaries of identification were quickly ended.

"Mister Layman," said Craven, "fifteen days ago, did you or did you not go to the store of Wendell in San Pedro and buy the outfit that afterward appeared in the possession of the so-called Fennel in this town?"

The doctor gathered himself, hesitated. "I cannot answer," he said, "without advice of counsel."

"Did you or did you not," roared Craven, apparently suddenly furious, "several months ago, talk with the Chinese cook when you met him one evening in the woods back of the Wilton house, and did he tell you at that time that he had seen Oliver Wilton thrust his brother, Everett Wilton, over the edge of the cliff to fall down into the rush of the water below?"

"I believe," said the doctor as cool as ever, "that you are trying to put a statement into my mouth. I decline to answer."

"Is it not true," said the eager young lawyer, "that you used this knowledge to blackmail Oliver Wilton, forcing him to admit you into his house, to place you constantly with his niece, and to encourage her engagement to you?"

Layman said not a word.

Everyone in the courtroom was leaning forward except Beatrice Wilton, who sat stunned and helpless with the shock of these strange new charges.

"Your Honor," said Craven, "we are going to attempt to demonstrate these charges. From the first, Sheriff Moon has suspected the truth about this case, but he has done all that he could to give no sign of his suspicions, for fear lest the bird fly from the cage. He has waited to the last moment, collecting proofs. And the last proof has been furnished by the arrival of Arthur and his friend from San Pedro.

"I hope that we have already offered sufficient testimony to make it necessary to reopen this case. After that, I shall demonstrate that the sheriff's suspicions were absolutely correct. I am going to show by witnesses and by every reasonable inference that Doctor Eustace Layman is an adventurer. I am going to show you that there are other crimes in his past, though none as heinous as these. I am going to prove to you that he first forced himself upon Miss Wilton and made himself useful to her after the death of her father, until she permitted herself to be engaged to him. That he was contented with the arrangement only so long as he thought it would make him heir to the fortune of Everett Wilton . . . that when he learned that the control of this fortune was about to pass into the hands of Oliver Wilton, he determined to do away with that man, and succeeded. That when Sherry and Lang, two brave and devoted men . . . "

A rushing murmur, like the sound of a storm, swept through the court, and then a loud roar of applause deafened Sherry. He looked about him, bewildered. Shining eyes were turned toward him. Hands smote his broad back. Words of approval and cheer greeted him.

Craven took more heart. The judge, as stunned as any witness in the case, could only stare and let the torrent of words flow on. Even the district attorney was helpless.

"When these two heroic men," went on Craven, "enlisted themselves in the service of Miss Wilton after the murder of her uncle, at first Doctor Layman was pleased enough to have their assistance. But then he discovered that Mister Sherry was pushing close to a discovery of the true identity of the supposed Fennel. When he began to fear this, he determined to do away with Mister Sherry. We are going to prove through the testimony of the notorious Fannie Slade, now in the hands of Sheriff Moon and held until this proper moment for testimony, that that man was hired by Layman to come to Clayrock and, together with his attendant bullies, hunt down and murder Sherry. We all know how that plot was foiled by the extraordinary daring of Mister Sherry himself . . . "

Applause again. A thunderclap of rejoicing!

"Throughout, you will see that Mister Sherry, always, was the block upon which the well-devised schemes of the doctor were wrecked. The sheriff was the first to realize this, dimly in the beginning. He continued to throw forward all possible evidence against Miss Wilton . . . it was the bait that kept in Clayrock this detestable murderer."

Craven paused. Dead silence followed his last words. Baleful eyes glared at the doctor, and he, his pale face unmoved, looked grimly back at everyone without flinching.

"Then came the time," said Craven, "when Lang himself discovered that Fennel and the doctor were one. At last, he guessed it very strongly. He consulted the sheriff. The sheriff begged him to say nothing . . . to wait for a more opportune time. And in that manner, to the great grief of the sheriff and of all honest men, poor Lang became a martyr to the cause to which he and his friend had given themselves so freely. What are we to say, Your Honor, of men like these two, who fought for the sake of justice to a helpless girl?"

Now Beatrice Wilton had borne up against all the assaults of her apparent enemies, but at this public touch of sympathy, she melted into tears.

The judge himself was moved.

"Still," went on Craven, "it appeared that the doctor was going to have a fair chance of winning. He could not know the mind of the sheriff. He could not know of the trip that the two sailors had taken to San Pedro. He could not know that Wendell himself, responding to a telegram, has actually started from San Pedro, and will be in this courtroom at any moment to identify Eustace Layman as the false Fennel. This masquerader, this murderer with silent guns, this detestable scoundrel, to defend himself in case of need, actually suggested to Miss Wilton that she use the weapon and train herself with it as for her own defense at the time when the murder of her father enabled him to persuade her that her own life probably stood in great danger.

"That was his plan, and that was the plan that would have succeeded if it had not been for the combined efforts of our sheriff, and of Lewis Sherry. The woman Eustace Layman was engaged to marry was, in case the law came down too hard upon his heels, to bear the danger of the charge. He did not want to lose her. But better that her life should be ruined than that his precious neck should be stretched! And then, having murdered Lang before that man could tell Sherry of his suspicions as to the real identity of the murderer, he attempted again, in the person of his proper self, to persuade Sherry to keep the pearls . . . of which you are to hear more later and in greater detail . . . and use them in hiring more efficient lawyers for the defense of Miss Wilton.

"Because he began to see, now, that it was unlikely that he could get his hands upon the Wilton fortune. The sheriff had blocked him there. From the very first, with apparent tyranny, he had managed to prevent Miss Wilton from seeing the doctor, or from conveying to the outside a single scrap of writing by means of which she could bestow upon him the right to draw checks on the bank in her name. Had that power been so conferred, you need have no doubt that the admirable doctor would soon have gathered in the entire estate, and then departed for other lands."

He paused for breath, and then added: "That, Your Honor, is the case which we will now attempt to prove. As for the clumsy defense which I have hitherto made for Miss Wilton, I ask her pardon and yours. My hands were tied. The terrible strain she has passed through has been the price that she had to pay for the sake of attempting to bring justice home to this double villain. A strain so terrible that she has been tempted to destroy herself, being in total despair. No amends can be made to her, really. But the first short step will be, of course, to ask the jury to reconsider their verdict, and to declare her blameless, as she has been in every way from the first. And then justice on this cold-faced and secret murderer!

"I am going to tell to you, also, the story of an unfortunate man, Oliver Wilton . . . a good man who committed one crime, that spectacular raid upon the pearl fishery in the far-off Sulus. And because of that he was driven from evil to evil. He was forced to take the life of his brother, who was beginning to learn the truth about the loss of the *Princess Marie*. He was forced to make for himself a steel-lined room, because he knew that danger was on his heels. But one wise step he took, and that was to employ the man who could not save his own forfeited life, but who could bring justice down upon the arch criminal of all."

XXXVII

How many typewriters purred furiously, writing down pages of copy; how many telegraphers clicked out the long columns of news; how many cameras snapped every detail over again—the courthouse, the courtroom, the judge, the jury—smiling broadly, all twelve, the young lawyer, the cold face of Eustace Layman, ever calmly self-contained, the furious excitement of the crowd, Beatrice Wilton's wide eyes as she listened to the words that spelled her safety, the portrait of brave Peter Lang, murdered, repeated with a black border, and views of how the strong men of Clayrock rose in their might and seized upon Lewis Sherry, and heaved him upon their shoulders in all his unwieldy bulk, and bore him protesting and struggling from the courtroom, and paraded him through the streets of Clayrock, and elected him with a universal acclaim to that small brotherhood of honest men and heroes who can fight for a lost cause without hope of a reward.

But Sherry himself, a lonely man, sat at last in a room in the hotel, and gazed moodily out the window. He felt that he had been drenched in death and tragedy. Capper, Everett Wilton, Oliver Wilton, Peter Lang, had all been destroyed. And now, perhaps, the doctor's life would pay the final forfeit. And yet not the sense of gloomy tragedy alone was sufficient to give him this feeling of an empty heart.

A tap came at the door. The sheriff stood before him. They clasped hands and looked long and gravely upon one another.

"I came to tell you that the last step has been taken," said the sheriff.

"Has he confessed?"

"By implication. Layman is dead."

"He killed himself?"

"He had resolution. You'll find a peculiar contempt for life among some doctors. This fellow found a long splinter of stone in his cell in the jail. He drove it into his temple and died instantly. The best way, I have no doubt. And yet, rather a foolish thing. There was only one really important clue, one fact against him . . . that he had bought the clothes in San Pedro that afterward appeared in the sea chest of Fennel."

Sherry sank again into thought. Now that the tangle is cleared away," he said finally, "I want to ask you why it is that you never attempted to arrest me for the killing of Capper?"

"Because I knew that you were not guilty."

"You knew that?"

"I'll show you the proof."

He took Sherry down to the room where, on that first memorable evening that had finally involved the cowpuncher in all this train of drama, he and Capper had been dragged, senseless. In the baseboard that ran around the room, he pointed out a deep hole.

"If you had shot Capper in a struggle, and the bullet had driven on through his head, it would have entered the wall at the height of a man. But, as a matter of fact, the bullet entered this baseboard."

"That is what Wilton told me, that I deliberately murdered the man in his sleep."

"Did he tell you that? Of course, to get you under his thumb. You were the sort of a man he needed. Very well, but see the angle of this hole." He placed a pencil in it. "To what does it point?"

"Toward the window."

"From the window came that shot. Mark the cunning of Wilton. He had stolen your revolver. He waited there outside the window for a time when you were rapidly regaining consciousness, because your bulk enabled you to throw off more quickly the effects of the drug that he, Wilton, had placed in your drink. As you rose to your knees, he fired through the window and killed Capper, and then he threw the revolver so that it landed at your own feet."

Sherry stared. "And then, Sheriff, why didn't you arrest Wilton?"

"Because if I had, it would have ended my chance of dipping a good deal deeper into an important mystery. I could guess that Wilton wanted to get rid of Capper. Then it appeared that he needed a bodyguard against other dangers. What were those dangers? What had Wilton done? I was fumbling in the dark. And lives have been lost on account of my delay, I know. But there is only one that I regret . . . Lang. The memory of that man will never be out of my head. As for the others . . . Everett Wilton was killed before I so much as suspected the murderer. Oliver Wilton, Layman-Fennel, Capper, were all rascals, of course. I'd like to use a gentler name for Oliver Wilton. But, after all, he was a murderer. And as for Lang, I have one consolation . . . that he died doing his duty, like a brave man. We don't sorrow a great deal for men who die on battlefields for their country, Sherry. Why should we feel differently about the heroes of peace, who haven't brass bands to urge them on and medals to reward them?"

"You've done a great thing in this case," said Sherry.

"I was a man standing in the dark, waiting for a light," replied the sheriff. "You brought me the light, old man, when you sent that pair of sailors to San Pedro. Miss Wilton has given them so much money that they won't be sober the rest of their lives . . . and, when they've spent it, they know that they can come back to her for more. What a woman, Sherry! What a heart, and what a soul."

"Is she steadier?" asked Sherry.

"As steady as a rock. She wants to see you."

"I'm starting back for the range," said Sherry hastily.

"Why?"

"Where I can find enough fresh air to blow this trouble out of my brain."

"Are you starting at once?"

"Yes."

"Without even seeing her, man.?"

"I'll send her a note," said Sherry.

"You won't have to do that."

"No?"

"Because," said the sheriff, "I had an idea that you would be exactly such a fool as this. And I suggested that she'd better come down here to the hotel to find you."

Sherry started up. "The dickens you did," he said.

And here came a light, light tap at the door.

The sheriff opened it. He said: "I was right. The young fool was about to run away. Perhaps you can talk him into better sense. I'm going down to get a drink. I think I need one."

"But . . . wait one instant . . . Sheriff . . ." stammered Beatrice Wilton.

"I'll be back before you know it," said the sheriff, and resolutely closed the door behind him. And then they heard the lock click.

Sherry strode to it and shook the knob. "Confound him," he hissed. "He's locked the door."

She hurried to the window and looked anxiously down, almost as though she were contemplating an escape in that direction.

Then they turned and slowly faced one another.

"You were leaving Clayrock?" she asked with a sort of cold politeness.

"I was," answered Sherry bluntly.

"Without giving me a chance to see you?"

"I know," said Sherry. "You wanted to thank me, of course. But . . . to tell you the truth, I didn't want thanks." He let a ring of emotion get into a part of that sentence, and bit his lip afterward, ashamed of it.

"There's the business side of it, then," said the girl.

"Yes?"

"I mean to say, that my uncle had offered you a thousand dollars a day. For ten days. And now there's no reason under the sun why you shouldn't take the money."

"Money?" said Sherry, half choked. "Money? For me?" Then, as she looked at him, half frightened, he added: "There's Lang. He has an invalid brother somewhere. You could pay that money to him."

"I shall do it. And take care of the poor man, besides. Poor Peter Lang . . . " Then she added: "Is there simply nothing that you'll let me do for you?"

"For me? There's nothing that I need. There's nothing that I want," answered Sherry. "I'm going back to the range right away. That's the place for me . . . I never was meant for a life in a town, you see."

She looked at him with a sort of despair. "I think it's hardly fair and kind to me," she said. "You go away and leave me in terrible debt to you."

"I don't want to bother you. You see, there's nothing that I need."

"Nothing?"

"No."

She looked down at the floor, and then forced her eyes to meet his "There's nothing you could ask of me that I wouldn't give," she said.

"Nothing?" he cried.

"No," she said.

Suddenly he was standing over her with twitching hands. "I pray to heaven that I don't misunderstand," he said.

"I pray that you don't," she said.

So, a long time later—it seemed only an instant—the sheriff returned and tapped discreetly on the door. "It's taken me an hour to get that drink," he announced. "May I come in?"

"An hour!" cried the girl.

The door was unlocked. The sheriff stood, with his faint smile, in the doorway.

"A whole hour since he went away?" exclaimed Sherry, and stared at the girl.

But suddenly she smiled, and touched his arm. "It isn't so very long," she said. "One hour out of a whole life."

THE END

About the Author

Max Brand is the best-known pen name of Frederick Faust, creator of Dr. Kildare, Destry, and many other fictional characters popular with readers and viewers worldwide. Faust wrote for a variety of audiences in many genres. His enormous output, totaling approximately thirty million words or the equivalent of five hundred thirty ordinary books, covered nearly every field: crime, fantasy, historical romance, espionage, Westerns, science fiction, adventure, animal stories, love, war, and fashionable society, big business and big medicine. Eighty motion pictures have been based on his work along with many radio and television programs. For good measure he also published four volumes of poetry. Perhaps no other author has reached more people in more different ways.

Born in Seattle in 1892, orphaned early, Faust grew up in the rural San Joaquin Valley of California. At Berkeley he became a student rebel and one-man literary movement, contributing prodigiously to all campus publications. Denied a degree because of unconventional conduct, he embarked on a series of adventures culminating in New York City where, after a period of near starvation, he received simultaneous recognition as a serious poet and successful author of fiction. Later, he traveled widely, making his home in New York, then in Florence, and finally in Los Angeles.

Once the United States entered the Second World War, Faust abandoned his lucrative writing career and his work as a screenwriter to serve as a war correspondent with the infantry in Italy, despite his fifty-one years and a bad heart. He was killed during a night attack on a hilltop village held by the German army. New books based on magazine serials or unpublished manuscripts or restored versions continue to appear so that, alive or dead, he has averaged a new book every four months for seventy-five years. Beyond this, some work by him is newly reprinted every week of every year in one or another format somewhere in the world. A great deal more about this author and his work can be found in *The Max Brand Companion* (Greenwood Press, 1997) edited by Jon Tuska and Vicki Piekarski. His website is http://www.max-brandonline.com/.